MORE PRECIOUS
THAN GOLD

HEARTS OF GOLD SERIES BOOK 2

RENEE YANCY

OTHER TITLES BY RENEE YANCY

Dedicated to:
My beautiful daughter, Sarah,
my green-eyed girl,
light of my eyes and heart of my heart,
I think I put a little of you in every character I write,

and

To the student nurses of Bellevue Hospital in 1918,
none of whom left their posts but bravely stayed to care for
the victims of the pandemic flu, some of whom lost their own
lives in doing so,

and

To my fellow nurses today around the world,
who are still caring for victims of the COVID pandemic, God
bless you all.

The law of the LORD is perfect,
refreshing the soul.
The statutes of the LORD are trustworthy,
making wise the simple.
The precepts of the LORD are right,
giving joy to the heart.
The commands of the LORD are radiant,
giving light to the eyes.
The fear of the LORD is pure,
enduring forever.
The decrees of the LORD are firm,
and all of them are righteous.
They are more precious than gold,
than much pure gold;
They are sweeter than honey,
than honey from the honeycomb.

Psalm 19:7-10

ONE

From a Greek vase to a New York debutante is a far cry echoing through the centuries, but a fashion artist can bridge it with a few strokes of the brush.

The New York Tribune, February 1917

FEBRUARY 4, 1917
Upper East Side, Manhattan, New York

ALL SHE NEEDED WAS a drop of Dragon's Blood.

Kitty Winthrop feathered the crimson paint onto the sketch of the ball gown. Done! Trying to ignore the muted conversation going on in the bedroom above her, she scribbled her initials with a flourish at the bottom.

For two days her parents had been discussing the arrival of a mysterious letter, but they quieted whenever Kitty walked into the room. It left her wondering what in the world was going on.

"What are you up to, Kitty?" Her mother slid open the pocket doors to the disordered dining room, where Kitty's painting supplies and the New York Tribune lay sprawled over the mahogany table.

"Working on my portfolio, Mama." She turned the easel so her mother could see the sketch. "I'm sorry I've made such a mess, but this room has the best light in the house."

Mama glanced at the newspaper and frowned at the photos of the most recent balls in New York City that filled the Society Pages. "I don't understand why you persist in reading that garbage."

Kitty bristled. "It's not garbage. I read the descriptions for inspiration."

Mama's eyes narrowed. "I think it's more than that."

Kitty turned away from her mother's searching glance. She didn't know Kitty had a daydream of dancing at a high society ball. But Mama needn't worry because there was no imminent danger of it happening any time soon.

"That world is a façade, Kitty," Mama said sternly, "artificial and superficial. It would never fit you."

And how could her mother know that? Kitty bit back the sharp retort at the tip of her tongue. She would never purposely hurt her mother.

Mama glanced at the front-page section of the paper and sighed.

"What is it?"

Mama pointed to the Tribune headline.

Wilson Breaks With Germany
War Imminent

. . .

"I SAW THAT EARLIER," Kitty said. "It's getting serious, isn't it?"

Her mother nodded; her blue eyes clouded like the sea on a stormy day. "We're closer than ever to getting involved in the war in Europe."

Then she turned the easel to study the sketch. "It's beautiful," she said, in a more cheerful tone. Her eyes widened as she took in Kitty's apparel. "Mercy me, what are you wearing?"

Kitty smoothed the wide sash at her waist and held out her arms, revealing the wide kimono sleeves and the exotic pattern of Japanese lanterns she'd painted on her former white cotton dressing gown. "Do you like it? Anything Oriental is all the rage right now. I altered it a bit, Mama, to suit myself. I took the material from the bottom."

"I can see that." Her gaze traveled from Kitty's knees to her head. "And what have you done to your hair—are those my knitting needles?"

Kitty laughed. "I was experimenting, and I couldn't find anything else to use. Here."

She pulled the steel skewers out of her topknot and let the mass of wavy curls fall to her waist.

Mama smiled faintly. "If I didn't know better, I'd think you were the daughter of a gypsy." But the smile didn't reach her eyes, and she had twisted her handkerchief into a wrinkled mess.

"Or some Bohemian." Papa walked in behind Mama. "You've got paint on your nose, Kitty."

He had an amused glint in his eyes behind the wire-rimmed spectacles, and Kitty grinned back at him. But the line etched between her mother's brows sobered her.

"Mama, what's wrong? You've been walking around with a black cloud over you the past two days."

Her mother cleared her throat. "I have something to tell you. Come into the parlor."

Kitty's heart danced a mad polka at the urgency in Mama's voice. It must be bad news.

She followed her parents into the cozy sitting room that appeared more like a library than a parlor, with its dark polished furniture, simple draperies, and books. Hundreds of books in glass-fronted mahogany cabinets that reached from floor to ceiling.

"I've been worried." Kitty curled up on the sofa and tucked her feet underneath her. "I wondered when you'd tell me what's going on. Is everything all right?"

"It's about my family." Her mother's fair complexion paled even further. "I know this will be a shock. That's why I couldn't decide whether to tell you or not. My mother—she's alive."

Kitty blinked. "Alive? *Alive?*"

"Yes."

"I thought all your family was dead." How had her parents hidden this all these years? "Is that what the letter was about?"

"Yes." Her mother hesitated. "I never told you about her because…we've been estranged for many years."

Kitty frowned. She'd always wondered why Mama never spoke about her parents and had no photos of her family around the brownstone like Papa did.

"Where is she?"

"Here in New York."

Kitty digested this piece of information. "Why were you estranged?"

Mama clasped her hands together. "I did something to displease her, and she wouldn't forgive me."

"You?" Kitty snorted. That was even more surprising than the announcement of a living grandmother. "You're the sweetest and gentlest person I've ever known, Mama." She couldn't imagine her mother doing anything terrible enough to warrant being disowned.

Papa put his arm around her mother's shoulders and nuzzled her cheek. Kitty rolled her eyes heavenward. Even though they'd been married for almost twenty years, her parents still acted like newlyweds.

"Your mother is a sweetheart," Papa said.

Kitty scrutinized them. "So why tell me now? What's changed?"

Mama retrieved a piece of paper from her pocket. "After all these years, I've had a letter from her. She wants to meet her only grandchild."

So, Kitty had a grandmother now. With both her parents having been only children, she had no aunts or uncles or cousins in her childhood, unlike most of her friends at school. And Papa's parents had died before she was born. It was like getting a Christmas present in July.

"That's wonderful. When?"

Mama handed her the letter. "Next Sunday."

Kitty unfolded the jasmine-scented sheet of paper and read the elegant copperplate handwriting.

DEAREST EVANGELINE:

I'll come right to the point, dear. I'm getting older, my health is failing, and I don't how many years are left to me. In these recent weeks, a sincere desire to meet my only grand-

*daughter has overtaken me. I hope you will forgive your dear
old mother and let bygones be bygones.*

*I will be at home Sunday, February 11, if you find it in
your heart to come and see me. I will have no other callers.
Please come at three p.m. for tea and bring Katharine.*

Until then, dearest.

Vera Katharine Kohl Lindenmayer

KITTY READ THE NOTE AGAIN. "So, you named me
for her." She paused. "But I thought your maiden name was
Lind."

"I chose to disassociate myself from my family name
after I married your father. No one in my new circle needed
to know my history."

Kitty blinked. "You don't mean...not *the* Lindenmayers.
The Fifth Avenue Lindenmayers?"

Her mother stiffened and gripped the edge of the sofa.
"Yes."

Kitty shook her head. "You're a Lindenmayer? Oh, my
goodness!" She frowned, thinking. "I've heard stories
about them. Didn't they have a daughter who—" She
paused and stared at her mother. "Oh! It can't be! You're
her? The heiress who left the Duke of Hampshire at the
altar?"

"Guilty, I'm afraid." Mama's voice was resigned.

Kitty shrieked and sprang to her feet as a shock went
through her with the same force of the rogue wave that
knocked her into the sea last summer.

"Well, dizzy me! This is too much. I can't breathe."
Then another thought occurred to her. "That means *I'm* a
Lindenmayer."

Like the rich girls who sat at the front of the church in

their French finery by Charles Worth and Madame Vionnet.

"Calm down," Papa said. He gave a sideways glance at Mama. "It's much ado about nothing."

Kitty collapsed onto the sofa and fanned herself with a copy of Harper's Monthly. "But this is exciting! All this time I never knew."

Mama sighed and reached for Papa's hand. "There was no reason for you to know, sweetheart. I left that life at the altar with the duke."

"Why? Why didn't you marry him?"

Mama smiled, a genuine smile this time that softened her face and lit her beautiful eyes from within. She gave Papa a tender look. "Because I was in love with your father."

"Why didn't your mother like Papa?"

"Because he was a lowly seminary student. She had other plans for me."

"And that's why your mother never forgave you?"

"Cut me off completely, yes."

"But how could she do that to her own daughter? No matter how angry she was, it seems very cruel."

Her mother nodded. "It was difficult. My only consolation was that I had your father." She squeezed Papa's hand. "And that made up for everything else."

Kitty pondered this. "Do you think she's really changed?"

Her mother hesitated. "I think...I must believe it to be true. And give her the chance to know you."

Kitty stood up, her thoughts revolving like the Ferris wheel at Coney Island. "May I be excused?"

Mama nodded. "Of course."

Kitty skipped up the stairs to her bedroom at the back of

the brownstone and stood at the tall casement window that overlooked Mama's garden.

Although patches of snow dotted the dead grass and the flower beds lay brown and broken, a sudden expectation peeked out of her heart like the spring rain coaxes the snowdrops to raise their fragile heads.

She and her parents had discussed the possibility of attending the New York School of Design in the fall, now that she was eighteen.

Just last Sunday, she'd been distracted from Papa's sermon by the ravishing hat perched on Adelaide Langdon's hair three rows ahead. Purple velvet in elegant tucks around the crown with a gorgeous spray of pink osprey feathers at the side.

Kitty had rearranged the hat in her mind to suit herself, replacing the feather with an emerald green one, and shortening it a bit, as it was at least a foot tall, and Kitty had to lean sideways to see her father on the podium.

Her mother had given her a warning nudge, but only a moment later Kitty's thoughts had returned like a boomerang to the lavish photos splashed across the Society Pages in the Tribune that morning of the spectacular ball given in honor of Elizabeth Carnegie.

Kitty had perused all of them and then, taking sketchbook and pencil in hand, designed her own gowns with an elegant drape here and a beaded hemline there, inspired by the descriptions.

And yet, when she read the society pages and saw the daughters of the rich in church with their expensive French wardrobes, as exciting as it was to design beautiful ball gowns, in her heart she secretly wished to *be* one of them and wear the gorgeous gowns.

How thrilling it would be to dance with dashing young

men vying for your attention. Heaven knows, in her middle-class social set she didn't have much chance to wear designer gowns or meet any debonair beaus.

She turned and bowed, held her arms out to an imaginary partner, and waltzed about the bedroom until she sank onto her bed and hugged a pillow, her thoughts doing a pirouette with the possibilities.

Perhaps she might dance at a ball in a glittering gown and meet her own prince if her grandmother proved to be her fairy godmother.

"Dizzy me," she whispered, "I'm a Lindenmayer."

TWO

I am giddy, expectation whirls me round. The imaginary relish is so sweet that it enchants my senses.

William Shakespeare

FEBRUARY 11, 1917

THE ONE WEEK wait to meet her grandmother crawled like a snail. Even the cascade of streaming rain this afternoon couldn't quell the excitement that had steadily built inside her until she was ready to pop like a Christmas cracker.

The carriage pulled away from the curb on East 70th Street and turned onto Park Avenue. Mama had remained unnaturally quiet all morning and had taken extra pains dressing this rainy morning, too, finally choosing a toile lavender dress with a matching parasol.

Now her gloved fingers tapped a restless cadence on the carriage seat.

Kitty put her hand over her mother's. "Don't be nervous."

Her mother bit her lip. "I don't know what to expect. I haven't seen her for nineteen years."

"That *is* an awfully long time."

"Oh, you." Mama smacked Kitty's arm playfully. "I suppose to you it is. An eon, at least."

When the carriage turned onto Fifth Avenue, her lady-like mother, who always prided herself on staying 'cool, calm, and collected,' fidgeted like she'd landed on an ant's nest.

"Kitty." Mama sat forward. "Let's turn around. This is a mistake. We can send our regrets."

Kitty resisted the urge to roll her eyes. "Are you serious? I want to meet her! And she wants to meet me."

"I know..." Mama said slowly, "that's exactly it. I can't help wondering why."

Kitty threw up her hands. "She said why in the letter. She wants to make amends."

"I think it's more than that." Mama hesitated. "You've never known her, Kitty. She won't be what you think of as a traditional grandmother. She can be manipulative. And cruel. Although, doubtlessly, she will be on her best behavior with you."

"Honestly, you make her sound like a gorgon, if not worse." The carriage stopped before the gleaming white limestone walls of 660 Fifth Avenue. "And now that you've brought me all the way here, you want to run away?"

A faint sheen of perspiration broke out on her mother's forehead. "I was wrong, Kitty. We're going home."

She flung open the trap door on the carriage wall to

speak to the driver. "Turn around, please, we've decided not to stop here."

Kitty opened the door on her side, stepped out into the rain, and opened her umbrella. "I'll understand if you want to go home. But I'm going to meet my grandmother Lindenmayer."

"No, Kitty." Mama reached to grab her, but Kitty took a step back.

"I'm doing this, Mama. With you, or without you."

Her mother glanced toward the mansion, shuddered, and shook her head. "I can't do it."

What on earth? "Mama, you go home. It's all right."

Mama leaned out of the carriage. "Kitty, come back. Please!"

"Come with me." She waited, as rain streamed off her umbrella and splattered on the pavement.

Her mother turned away and closed the carriage door. Was she really going to let her meet Grandmother Lindenmayer alone?

When there was no further movement from the carriage, Kitty climbed the short stone staircase.

The door opened before she could lift the lion's-head knocker, and a uniformed butler with silver hair and a neat mustache bowed and ushered her into a magnificent two-story entrance hall decorated with crystal chandeliers, silver mirrors, and palm trees in gilded pots. White roses and lilies scented the air.

"Miss Katharine Winthrop, please, here to see Mrs. Lindenmayer."

He nodded. "Yes, miss, you're expected."

Instead of taking her coat, he stared long and searchingly at her face. Moisture welled up in his eyes. "You look so much like her, Miss."

"My mother?"

"Yes, Miss. I watched her grow up in this house. She was always such a sweet and kind child."

"She still is."

"She did not come with you? I had hoped to see her."

Kitty hesitated. "She wasn't sure she was quite up to it."

The butler nodded; his face downcast. "I understand. Please tell her Percy sends his best regards. I think of her often."

"I will do that, Percy. Thank you."

Percy bowed. "And now allow me to take your coat."

She nodded, and he helped her out of her black wool overcoat and took her umbrella.

"This way, please."

She followed Percy up the grand marble staircase to the second floor, trying to subdue her rapid breathing and act as if she was a girl used to arriving at magnificent mansions like this one.

The butler opened a gilded glass door and bowed. "Please go in, Miss Winthrop."

A plump figure rose from a chaise lounge near the French doors.

A petite woman, stuffed into a mauve silk tea gown adorned with cobwebby lace, walked toward her. Fleshy folds of fat encircled her eyes, and her midnight black hair, obviously dyed, was piled on top of her head, a strange contrast to her pale skin.

She extended her hand, glittering with diamond rings nearly lost in the flesh of her pudgy fingers.

"Katharine?"

Her grandmother's gaze lit on her like a ray of white-hot light, and Kitty's stomach turned cartwheels. This must be what the insects stuck on pins in the school science lab felt like.

"Yes." She shook her grandmother's hand, not sure if that was the thing to do or not.

"Vera Lindenmayer. I'm so pleased you were able to come. Won't you sit down?" She gestured toward the French windows at a table set for tea with delicate porcelain and silver.

"Am I to presume your mother did not accompany you?"

"I...that is, we..." Kitty stammered.

The door opened, and Mama walked in, pale and stiff as a piece of laundry frozen on the clothesline. "I'm here, Mother," she said.

Gladness washed over Kitty like a warm wave, and her shoulders relaxed. But as the two women came face to face, Kitty's breath caught in her throat.

A muscle clenched in Mama's cheek, her profile as stark and unyielding as the marble statues in the reception hall below. Some ominous, palpable sense of warning flowed coldly from her mother's still figure toward Vera Lindenmayer.

Their gazes locked, and Kitty shivered. She'd never seen that look on her mother's face before.

Then Grandmother threw her arms around Kitty's mother, and the unsettling moment was gone, lost in her grandmother's silvery laughter.

"You look beautiful, darling! That color suits you. How wonderful to see you. What a fool I've been all these years."

She waved a hand at the other vacant chair. "Please do sit down."

She rang a silver bell, and a moment later, a maid

entered with a wicker tea cart filled with covered silver dishes and a tray of petit fours.

"I'll pour," her grandmother said. The maid bobbed a curtsy and quit the room.

Kitty beamed at Mama as she took the seat next to her. "Thank you," she whispered.

She squeezed her mother's hand under the table before turning her attention to her grandmother. "What a fascinating house. Mama said you designed it yourself."

Her grandmother nodded, causing her coiffure to shift and reveal she was wearing a wig. "I did. Worked right along with the architects. In the trenches, you could say, right there with them."

"But how did you conceive such a huge undertaking?"

"Trips abroad to France, England, and Italy. They know a thing or two about architecture in those countries."

"Fascinating. So, you came home, full of ideas, and set to work."

Kitty glanced at her mother, who sipped her tea, her face a perfect blank.

She was the consummate lady sitting there in the lavender dress that made her eyes bluer than violets. Grandmother would never suspect that she'd wanted to turn back.

"Exactly." Grandmother took a bite of pastry. "But I want to know about you, Katharine. Do you have any hobbies? Have you been to school? Do you have plans for the future?"

Kitty set her cup down. "I do. I love to draw and design. I finished at Henredon's School for Young Ladies last December. I'm thinking about going to college in the fall. Perhaps for design, or possibly nursing."

Grandmother's eyes flicked toward Mama at the word 'college.'

Mama smiled. "Kitty's had a penchant since she was small for finding injured animals, and nursing them back to health," Mama said. "At one time, we had two robins, an abandoned puppy with a broken leg, and an orphaned squirrel in the nursery."

Her grandmother raised a slim, penciled eyebrow. "My word. And your parents had no objection to you bringing these creatures home?"

"Oh, no, not at all." She laughed. "Mama has her own ministry for lost and abandoned babies. I call them her wharflings."

"*Wharflings*? What on earth?"

"The abandoned children who live on the docks. Mama takes them in and finds homes for them. She teaches the older ones to read and write and helps them find jobs through the church congregation. So, you see, I've had a good example."

"Ah," her grandmother said, "I've no doubt of that."

Some disdainful undercurrents in her grandmother's voice grated on Kitty, and she wanted to protect her mother. "Mama, now that I think about it, how *did* you find them? I've no idea." Apparently, Vera had had no part in it.

Her mother's smile faded. "Mother and I were leaving New York to sail for England. For the season there."

Grandmother shifted in her seat and fiddled with a button on her dress.

"It was unusually foggy that morning, and the chauffeur got lost looking for Pier 54. Somehow, we ended up in an old section of deserted docks, and James went to find someone to ask directions."

"I sacked him soon after," her grandmother muttered.

Mama smiled faintly. "The fog began to lift. And I saw something."

"What?"

"I wasn't sure. So, I got out of the carriage." She smiled. "Mother wasn't too happy about that. As I crept closer, I saw three small boys sleeping tangled together on a pile of newspapers. Barefoot and threadbare, their little faces pinched with cold."

Grandmother crossed her arms and glanced at the clock.

"A rugged old sailor had come back with James to direct us. I asked him what those children were doing there. Why weren't they home with their parents?" Mama's lips twisted. "He laughed at my naiveté. That was my first introduction into how the other half lived."

Kitty frowned. "What do you mean?"

"They were all orphans and abandoned children. 'Wharf rats,' he called them. They had no one. I emptied my purse and asked the sailor to buy them food and shoes if there was enough left over."

"A fool's errand," Grandmother said, under her breath.

"Oh, so that's where the name came from. But what did you mean about the 'other half'?"

Mama sat forward, her blue eyes intent. "That while I, and others in my social class, lived in luxury, there were people, children, babies with nothing. One of my ball gowns could have fed ten families for a year." She paused. "I can still see them in my mind, Kitty, heaped together for warmth, dirty, malnourished, and dressed in rags."

Grandmother pinched the bridge of her nose and sighed. "Always so melodramatic, Evangeline. There are people who help with that sort of thing nowadays. Charities, and aid societies, and such."

"But someone has to actually go and do it, Mother."

There was a steely grit in Mama's voice Kitty had never heard before.

Grandmother's lips thinned, and she set her teacup down. "Isn't that enough of your sad story for now?"

She glared at her daughter, and Mama returned her gaze calmly, a slight smile hovering at the corners of her mouth.

Then Grandmother tossed her head and forced a smile. "Let's not argue, Evangeline, after all these years." She dabbed her lips with a napkin and stood up. "Why don't you show Katharine the house now?" She turned to Kitty. "That is, if you'd like to see it."

"Very much so." Kitty stood up too, anxious to leave the tense moment behind. "And Grandmother, would you please call me Kitty?"

"Is that your name?"

"Katharine is my given name, but everyone calls me Kitty."

Her grandmother sniffed. "I don't particularly like nicknames, never did. You have a beautiful name. You should be proud of it since it's also my own. So, I will call you Katharine."

She smiled imperiously, like a queen awarding a favor to a subject. "And you must call me Oma. That's German for grandmother."

She rose and smoothed the lace of her tea gown. "I will meet you back here in three-quarters of an hour. That should be sufficient to show Katharine around the house."

After Oma left the room, Kitty gave her mother a wry smile. "Dizzy me, Mama, you certainly got under her skin."

Her mother grinned. "I did. One for me."

"Has she always been like that?"

Mama nodded as she walked toward the door. "If she doesn't get her way. Remember that, sweetheart."

Kitty smiled wryly. "Now I understand why she calls you Evangeline."

"She was the only one who did so." Mama smiled faintly. "Even my father called me Lindy."

They descended the marble staircase to the main floor, and Mama showed her through the formal rooms on the main level, the drawing room, the dining room, and the breakfast room with its stained-glass window portraying the martyrdom of St. Sebastian.

The guest bedrooms on the second floor were each furnished and upholstered in a different color. At the end of another hallway, her mother opened a door. "This was my room."

Kitty studied the pale green watered-silk draperies at the casement windows, the green velvet window seat. "It's quite different from the rest of the house. But it suits you somehow. I can see you here."

Kitty wandered to the windows overlooking Fifth Avenue and her mother followed. But instead of admiring the view, her mother closely examined the woodwork.

"What are you looking at?"

"Oh, nothing." Mama ran her fingers over the paint, stopping at what looked like nail holes. "Remembering, that's all."

Kitty went to the wardrobe room door, standing ajar.

"Is there anything in there?" her mother asked.

"One gown." A silk gown in a silvery blue-green.

Mama walked over and put her fingers to her mouth. "Oh, my."

"Is it yours?"

"It was."

Kitty took the dress and held it up to her mother. "It's the perfect color for you."

Her mother smiled. "*L'eau de mer*. This is the only gown I chose for myself in Paris that spring. Against my mother's wishes."

"It's beautiful. I can only imagine how gorgeous you must have looked." She checked the label. "Charles Worth!"

Mama nodded.

"What happened to the rest of your wardrobe, Mama?"

"I've no idea." She returned the gown to the wardrobe. "Let's keep going."

"What's this one?" Kitty pointed to a door set at the end of a secluded hall.

"That was my father's study." Mama turned away.

"Are you going to show it to me?"

Her mother hesitated. "If you wish."

Simpler and more masculine than the rest of the house, the oak-paneled study had a coffered ceiling and a black onyx fireplace.

A faint scent of pipe tobacco lingered in the room. Two walls held books, which on closer inspection proved to be mainly on the subject of business and horses. The fanciest thing in the room, beside the Tiffany lamp on the desk, was an elaborate cuckoo clock on the wall with carved wooden figures of musicians and a duck pond.

Mama switched the lamp on, and Kitty pounced on the silver-framed photograph it revealed on the desktop.

"Oh, my goodness, Mama, it's you, isn't it? In the dress!"

It was taken in profile, from the back. Her mother rested one elegant hand on an upholstered bench and gazed into the distance. The photograph revealed the lissome line of her slender frame and accentuated the long pure curve of her throat and neck.

"I knew you were devastatingly beautiful."

Her mother didn't answer, and Kitty turned to find tears running silently down her mother's face.

"What's wrong?"

Mama shook her head and pulled a handkerchief from her pocket. She dabbed at her eyes, laughed, and then blew her nose. "It's his pipe tobacco."

She fluttered her hand in the air. "And here's the imprint of his head at the back of his chair." Gently she touched it. "I can almost hear his voice." She swallowed. "I never knew he kept this photograph on his desk. I miss him so much."

Kitty winced. "I'm sorry. I didn't realize coming in here would affect you so."

"Of course, you didn't. You couldn't have. But he was a dear, dear man."

"When did he die?"

Mama's lips hardened. "Two years after I abandoned the duke."

"Where is he buried?"

Her mother shook her head. "I don't know."

Kitty blinked. How could she not know? Every spring, she and her parents visited the graves of Papa's parents. They tended the rosebushes and enjoyed a walk through the verdant gardens of Forest Hill.

Mama studied her. "My mother didn't tell me when my father died, you see. Your father saw it in the paper." Then she smiled. "Close your mouth, dear."

Kitty snapped her mouth shut. "Mama, that...I can't even imagine how terrible that must have been for you."

How could a woman treat her own daughter so cruelly?

She nodded. "I attended the funeral alone, swathed in black veiling. I wouldn't let your father come with me. I didn't want to be recognized. Later, I found out Papa had been ill for some time."

More tears slipped down her pale cheeks, and Kitty put her arm around her and leaned in close, her heart breaking for her mother's pain.

Mama wiped the tears away with her fingers. "Nothing would have stopped me from coming if I had known, even if I had to sneak in through the servant's entrance. Poor Papa. She never gave me the chance to say goodbye." She wiped her eyes.

"That's why I'm warning you, dearest. I'm not so sure she's changed. Be careful."

The cuckoo sprang out from its tiny wooden door and chirped four o'clock. The wooden musicians, with an accordion, a bass drum, a horn, and a tuba, swayed side to side as the duck pond revolved and the music box played a familiar tune.

"How cunning," Kitty said, moving closer. "What is that song?"

"*Der Fröhliche Wanderer*. The Happy Wanderer."

Mama hummed along. "Val-der-ree, val-der-ra. Val-der-eee, Val-der-aha-ha-ha-ha-ha-ha."

She smiled. "My father's people came from the Black Forest in Germany where these clocks are made, and it fascinated me when I was a little girl. But we've only fifteen minutes left, and you haven't seen the ballroom."

Kitty hung back a moment and quickly slipped the photograph of her mother out of the frame and into her pocket before catching up with her mother down the hall.

The gold ballroom on the second floor took Kitty's breath away.

Like the reception hall, it soared two stories high. Even

without the candles lit in the massive gilt and crystal chandeliers, the room glittered.

She ran her fingers over the gilded paneling. "Your mother certainly favors gold." She walked into the empty pit of a colossal green agate fireplace that could hold twenty people standing up. "And she does everything big, doesn't she?"

Mama chuckled. "You're catching on quickly."

"I can just imagine myself dancing at a ball," Kitty said dreamily, "with a beautiful gown." She stopped. "So, you must have danced here, then, Mama? Was it wonderful?"

"It was a long time ago, Kitty. I barely remember." She glanced at her wristwatch. "But we need to hurry. My mother doesn't tolerate tardiness. I've left my favorite room for last."

Mama opened a heavy carved oak door at the end of another hallway lined with Oriental carpet.

"The library?" Kitty nodded. "That makes sense. We have more books in our home than any of my other schoolmates."

Her mother ran her fingers lightly over the back of a worn leather Chesterfield sofa, and a dreamy smile curled her lips.

"You're smiling." Kitty gave her a curious look. "Why?"

"My happiest times in this house were spent in this room. This is where I met your father."

"In the library? What was he doing here?"

"My father offered him the use of it." She smiled, remembering. "Neither my mother nor my father realized how much time I spent in here." Then she giggled. "And I didn't tell them."

Kitty got an entrancing glimpse of her mother as a young girl. No wonder Papa had fallen in love with her.

But for Kitty, the gold ballroom was the most exciting room in the mansion. If they had more time, she would have liked to have seen it again.

When they arrived back at the salon, Vera was ensconced on the chaise lounge. "Come sit by me, Katharine." She held out her hand and moved over to make room. Kitty perched on the edge of the lounge and smiled.

"My goodness, child, you've such a lovely smile. You've raised a beautiful daughter, Evangeline. I'm sorry that I missed the years of her childhood by being so stubborn. I hope you will allow me to make amends."

She smiled and drew out a robin's-egg blue box tied with a white silk ribbon. "I took the liberty of having this made for you, Katharine, to celebrate this special day, and I hope your mother will allow you to keep it."

Kitty turned to her mother. "May I open it, Mama?"

The glacial stiffness had returned to her mother's face, but she gave a tiny nod.

Kitty untied the ribbon and opened the Tiffany box. The black velvet ring case inside revealed a glowing amethyst circled by diamonds and set in gold.

"Ohhh." Her stomach did another cartwheel, happy this time. "It's enchanting."

"Your birthstone, Katharine. February, I believe?"

"Yes."

"Look inside the band, dear."

"From Oma, with love." Kitty turned to her mother. "Please say I may keep it, Mama!"

"Of course, sweetheart," Mama said too quickly.

The line had returned between her brows, but Kitty didn't stop to consider why.

The ring fit perfectly on the fourth finger of her right hand, and she held it up to the light. "Thank you, Oma. It's exquisite." She leaned over and kissed her grandmother's pudgy cheek.

"You're very welcome, Katharine. It looks well on her, doesn't it, Evangeline?"

Mama nodded.

"I'm so pleased you came to visit today." Oma stood. "I hope this will be the first of many more pleasant times to come."

Percy met them in the marble foyer, and to Kitty's great surprise, Mama embraced the butler and kissed his wrinkled cheek.

"Dearest Percy, it's so lovely to see you after all these years."

He bowed. "The old promise still holds, Miss Lindy."

Mama laughed delightedly. "I shall hold you to it if the time ever comes."

Once settled in the carriage, Kitty turned to her mother. "What was Percy talking about? The promise?"

Mama smiled. "To come into service for me should I ever have need."

"He was very touched to see you."

Her mother's smile faded. "He was my only friend in that house. Aside from Papa, of course, and my maid Claudine and my governess, dear old Miss Kendall."

Kitty held her hand up to admire the glittering diamonds in her ring. "What a perfectly wonderful time. And to think you didn't want to go. She seemed happy to see you."

Her mother nodded. "She did."

"Are you glad you went?"

"I don't know yet." She shrugged her slender shoulders. "Time will tell."

"So, you did all those things I read about in the society pages, didn't you? Balls, and luncheons, and dinner parties."

"I did, Kitty, but I never enjoyed them. Young women were more restricted then, as to what they could do, where they could go. I doubt you would have enjoyed it either, free spirit that you are." Her mother smiled and patted her hand.

"But I would like to have had the chance to try."

"Kitty." Mama turned to face her, frowning. "There's so much going on now, and that old life means nothing to me. Do you understand? We might be going to war with Germany."

"I know. Because of the Housatonic."

Even though she rarely read the front pages there had been no escaping that headline. A few hours after President Wilson severed relations with Germany, the American freighter had been attacked and sunk by a U-boat without warning. Twenty-five Americans had perished.

"Yes."

"But that hasn't happened yet, and President Wilson is appealing to the other neutral nations. At least, that's what the paper said."

Her mother arched an eyebrow. "At least you're reading something other than the society pages."

Kitty still had so many questions. "Do you have any of your ball gowns?"

Her mother drew a frustrated breath. "I already told you no."

"And you went abroad with your mother?"

"I did," her mother said tightly.

"And bought your dresses in Paris?"

"She chose them, Kitty. I never had any say in the matter. Except for the one gown you saw hanging in the closet."

"How could you give up that life?"

"It was simple." Her mother's words were sharp and clipped. "I detested the life my mother had planned for me. To fulfill her ambition for a royal title in the family she tried to force me to marry a man I didn't love!"

Kitty gasped. Her mother rarely lost her temper or expressed displeasure, even when Papa had accidentally thrown away her favorite hat. And she never ever shouted.

"I... I'm sorry, Mama," she said, crestfallen. "Please forgive me. I didn't mean to make you angry."

Her mother took a deep breath. "I didn't mean to bark at you either, darling. But do you remember your English Literature classes in school?" She smiled faintly. "In the words of William Shakespeare, 'all that glitters is not gold.' You'll have to trust me that it's true."

She leaned back and closed her eyes. "And now I don't wish to discuss it any further."

Kitty wilted into her seat.

Clearly, this visit to her childhood home had disturbed something within Mama. The memories of her father. But oh, what a glorious, splendid mansion her grandmother possessed. She could never have dreamed that her grandmother was Vera Lindenmayer. Maybe she would extend an invitation to actually stay with her. Would Mama allow that?

And her mother had left a famous duke at the altar, creating a scandal in New York society that was still spoken of today. Kitty stole a glance at her mother.

What a secret she'd hidden all these years.

THREE

Put even the plainest woman into a beautiful dress and unconsciously she will try to live up to it.

Lady Lucile Duff-Gordon

FEBRUARY 19, 1917

KITTY JIGGLED on the leather seat in the back of Oma's Pierce-Arrow limousine, impatient to get home with her news.

Oma had called that morning and invited her and Mama to tea. However, Mama was at the church with her wharflings, and Papa had consented to let her go alone to the mansion on Fifth Avenue.

Oma allowed Kitty to examine the elegant silk, satin, and velvet ball gowns and dresses in her wardrobe, all made in Paris. Kitty had marveled at their superb construction, tried on some of Oma's hats, and admired herself in the huge silver triptych mirror.

Then they'd had a sumptuous tea with more delicacies than she'd ever sampled before at tea time—curried chicken cream puffs, tiny heart-shaped cakes with sugared violets and rose petals, lemon tarts, French macarons. *C'est magnifique!*

The final treat was the luxurious ride home in Oma's shining limousine. She couldn't help but be aware of the admiring and envious stares of people as the automobile passed by.

And now this amazing news.

Barrett dropped her off in front of the brownstone, and she pelted up the steps and opened the heavy front door with a crash that startled their elderly maid Jenny, passing through the hallway with a basket of laundry.

"Oh, my! Kitty!" She collapsed onto the stairs and clapped a hand to her heart. "Are ye tryin' to kill me then, ye wee eejit?"

Jenny was more like an elderly doting aunt than a servant, having been with the Winthrop family since Papa was a small boy. The red hair Kitty had known as a child had turned a glowing silver.

"I'm so sorry." Kitty took the basket from Jenny. "Let me whisk this upstairs while you recover."

"Och, get on wi' ye." She aimed a pretend whack at Kitty's backside when she passed her.

Kitty found her parents in the parlor when she came back down, Papa reading and Mama watering her pink begonias on the windowsill.

"You'll never guess!"

Both her parents turned at her words.

"Oma wants me to make my debut!"

Her mother nearly dropped her watering can and plopped down abruptly on the sofa. Her father lowered the newspaper and glanced at Mama, whose expression had turned blank.

"Mama, did you hear me? Oma says I can make my debut, and she wants to have a ball in my honor!"

Mama pressed her lips together. "I heard you, darling. Come and sit with me."

Kitty did as she asked.

"That is very generous of your grandmother. However," Mama hesitated, "this comes out of nowhere, Kitty. It's all so sudden. What about your plans for college?"

"I do want to go to college, Mama. What if I can find a way to do both?"

Her father rubbed his chin. "That might be managed. But I agree with your mother. You haven't been raised in that world, and I'm afraid it's nothing like you imagine."

Oh, why was Papa being such an ogre? Kitty tried to remain calm. "But I'd like to try." Her mother stayed silent. "Can't you see it's an opportunity for me? Oma says there's nothing to stop me. I'm a Lindenmayer, by blood, and I have every right to be introduced to society." She hesitated. "Wouldn't that be wonderful?"

Her mother closed her eyes, her face deadly pale.

Her father frowned. "We raised you differently, sweetheart. Our values and beliefs are different from many of those in high society." He glanced at her mother. "Your mother could tell you stories—"

"I want to make my own story, Papa! Can't you understand?"

She went to her mother, knelt at her feet, and took her hands. "Mama, please. I know you didn't want that life. But I want the chance to try. You rejected it. But what if it suits me?"

Her mother frowned and shook her head. "It won't, Kitty."

"Please be reasonable, Mama. I want this. Didn't you ever want something so badly that you could taste it?"

A glimmer of a smile came over her mother's face. "Yes."

She smiled at Papa with a look of love so sweet it pierced Kitty's heart.

Then Mama sighed. "Your father and I will discuss it, Kitty. That's all I will promise for the moment."

"Yippee!" She sprang to her feet and danced around the room.

"Kitty," her mother said, "we haven't consented yet."

"Yes, Mama." She dropped a kiss on the top of her mother's hair. "Thank you, Papa." Then she danced out of the parlor and up to her bedroom, where she threw herself on her bed and let out a whoop.

TWO DAYS LATER, after Papa and Mama had given their reluctant permission, Oma's Pierce-Arrow pulled up in front of the old brownstone, and Kitty ran out to meet her grandmother.

The chauffeur opened the rear door and Kitty bounced inside.

"Sedately, please," Oma said. "You must always remember you are a high-born young lady."

"I can't help it, I'm excited! My very first ball gown!"

"There, there." Oma's tone turned indulgent. "The first of many."

"Really?"

"Of course, darling. You're going to need an entire wardrobe. If this ridiculous war in Europe didn't prevent me, I'd take you to Paris for your gowns."

The limousine pulled up in front of 19 East 54th Street. *Maison Lucile* was emblazoned above the shop door, and Kitty's heart did a little jig.

"Lady Duff-Gordon?" Kitty tried to keep her voice at a normal modulation, mindful of her grandmother's earlier criticism. "I've read about her in the papers. She has an amazing sense of design."

"She does indeed," Oma said approvingly, "and I'm not a little impressed that you know who she is."

"I've read the society pages for as long as I remember."

"Oh? Then I daresay you will be acquainted with many of the people you will be meeting in these upcoming weeks."

The chauffeur opened the limousine door and helped Oma out, then came around to her. An elegant young man in a morning frock opened the salon door and ushered them in.

"Vera, how nice to see you again." A petite woman with pearls around her neck and copper curls covered with a paisley bandeau kissed Oma on both cheeks.

Then she turned and held a diamond-studded lorgnette up to her eyes. "So, this is your granddaughter? *Charmante, très charmant.*"

Lady Duff-Gordon examined her from every angle. "It will be my pleasure to design for you." She had Kitty step up to a small wooden platform to take her measurements, calling out the numbers to an assistant.

"I have aspirations to become a designer myself," Kitty said timidly. She hoped her grandmother wouldn't consider it bad taste to make such a statement.

Lady Duff-Gordon stopped and peered up at Kitty. "Indeed?"

"Yes, I've been working on my portfolio for the New York School of Design."

"Bah!" Lady Duff-Gordon said. "You don't need that. Bring your portfolio next time, and I will examine it and tell you if you have the talent."

"Thank you."

Four hours later, Kitty's debut gown had been sketched out, a frothy concoction of white Chantilly lace adorned with white silk ribbon rosettes. Lady Duff-Gordon had asked her opinion on materials and details and allowed Kitty to design a tea gown. After that came the day dresses, the walking suits, the opera capes, and all the other sundry items a well-dressed young woman needed in high society, according to her grandmother.

Then they had a lovely tea, with Lady Duff-Gordon holding an embossed silver cigarette holder in one hand and petting her Pekingese with the other.

It was supper time when they left with swatches of material from the dresses and tea gowns to match the materials for hats, slippers, and fans.

"Tomorrow morning, we'll visit the milliner." Oma rearranged her skirts on the luxurious leather seats in the Pierce-Arrow. "And then I've arranged lessons for you at the Galliano Dance School in the afternoon for the next two weeks. You'll have to practice very hard to be ready, Katharine."

"I will. When I set my mind to something I'm very determined." She leaned over and kissed her grandmother's wrinkled cheek. "Thank you for all of this, Oma. How can I ever repay you?"

Her grandmother smiled and patted her hand. "Perhaps you'll make a brilliant marriage, Katharine. I would be satisfied with that."

FOUR

GERMANY SEEKS ALLIANCE AGAINST US
ASKS JAPAN AND MEXICO TO JOIN HER
FULL TEXT OF PROPOSAL MADE PUBLIC

The New York Times, Thursday, March 1, 1917

Kitty yawned and followed the scent of cinnamon to the kitchen where their cook, Mrs. MacKinnon, had taken a pan of cinnamon rolls out of the oven.

Her parents sat in the breakfast nook, their heads together over the morning newspapers.

"Good morning," she said. Mrs. Mac nodded to her but there was no response from her parents.

"Good morning," Kitty said, louder this time.

They looked up, startled. "Good morning, sweetheart," her father said, dapper even in his dressing robe and his hair mussed.

"Sleep well?" Mama asked. Her long dark hair hung in a loose braid over her shoulder.

Actually, Kitty hadn't slept much at all. Even in her dreams, she found herself feverishly practicing the complicated steps of the waltz and the quadrilles for the coming debut ball—something she'd rather not share with her parents.

"Like a log." She suppressed another yawn.

Then she realized her mother hadn't smiled and her father's face looked drawn and tight.

"What's wrong?"

Papa turned the paper so she could read it.

Germany Asks Mexico to Seek Alliance with Japan for War on U.S.

KITTY BEGAN to read the article then sank into a chair as the import of it left her knees weak. Suddenly the war far away "over there" in Europe loomed closer.

"It means war, then? With Germany?"

Papa shrugged. "Probably. President Wilson won't be able to ignore this, I'm afraid. So much for keeping America neutral."

"Texas, New Mexico, and Arizona promised as a reward." Mama read from the sub-headline and shook her head. "That's most of the southwest United States."

"Kitty." Papa exchanged a glance with her mother. "We're entering a dark and uncertain time. I don't think a debut ball right now is a good idea."

Kitty pressed her lips together. "But Papa, it's all arranged."

Her father sighed. "I'm sorry, sweetheart."

Papa was probably correct. But, oh, how she hated to give up the idea. And all those dancing lessons.

But if America was on the brink of war...she nodded slowly. "Very well, Papa. I will tell Oma this afternoon. I have a fitting at Madame Lucile's."

"I can speak to her," Mama said, "if that would be easier."

"No, it's all right. I'll tell her."

LIGHT SNOW FELL as Kitty waited outside the brownstone with her portfolio tucked under her arm.

How would her grandmother take the news of no debut ball? She'd already made several scathing comments about the war being "ridiculous." And now this.

The Pierce-Arrow pulled up at the curb, and Barrett jumped out.

"Good afternoon, Miss." He opened the rear door for her.

Oma waited, in a black mink hat and a coat that included the unfortunate mink's head and feet on opposite ends of the collar.

Her gaze immediately fell on the portfolio. "May I see it?"

Kitty passed it to her, hiding a shudder at the mink's black glass eyes which stared straight at her.

As the Pierce-Arrow traversed the snowy streets toward Madame Lucile's, Oma carefully studied each page, pausing now and then to peer closer at a detail. Then she snapped the portfolio closed.

"I'm no expert, but I think you have some talent for this,

Katharine. Now I suppose we'll see what the real expert thinks."

"Oma." Kitty steeled herself. "I have something to tell you."

"Oh?" She fastened her sharp gaze on Kitty. "And what might that be?"

"Did you by any chance read the newspaper this morning?"

Oma laughed heartily, her double chin quivering. "Heavens, no. Bad news always spoils my day, and that's all the papers report lately." Then her eyes narrowed. "Why?"

"Something's happened that may bring us into war with Germany."

"Oh, for goodness' sake, not the *war* again. I'm so sick of hearing about it." She tossed her head like a recalcitrant five-year-old.

"But this is serious, Oma."

Her grandmother shrugged and waved a languid hand in the air. "It's no real concern of mine."

"Let them eat cake," Kitty muttered under her breath.

A dart of irritation went through her at her grandmother's childish behavior.

"What was that?"

"I said, it's serious enough to prevent my debut ball."

"W-what?" Oma's head swung back so fast her mink hat fell over one eye. "What did you say?" She pushed the hat off her forehead and glared at Kitty.

"Germany has promised to give Mexico the southwestern United States if they join Germany. That's what was in the papers this morning."

Oma snorted. "What's that got to do with your debut ball? Mexico is a long way from here."

Kitty opened and closed her mouth several times, flummoxed by her grandmother's obtuseness. "America may be going to war. It's not an appropriate time for that sort of social occasion."

"Was this your mother's idea?" For a moment Oma's lip curled, but she quickly replaced the scornful expression on her face with a bland one.

"Actually, it was Papa's."

Oma's lips tightened. She turned her face forward and sat in silence, her hand stroking the mink's head, and moving her head this way and that in silent conversation with herself, occasionally uttering a word or two.

When the Pierce-Arrow pulled up at the curb outside Madame Lucile's, Oma leaned sideways, her eyes shining, and grasped Kitty's arm. "I've got it! This could be a blessing in disguise, Katharine. What's a debut ball for anyway? To introduce you to society."

She laughed shortly. "But who is truly important in that society? Just me and a few old ladies." She patted Kitty's arm. "We don't need a debut ball. I'll give a luncheon for you instead. And then..."

She paused and sat back. "I'll throw you a ball at the Met. We'll say it's to raise funds for the military, or the war effort, or some such thing." She clapped her hands. "No one, not even your parents, could condemn a ball with such good intentions."

FIVE

There is but one season of the year when salmon should be served hot at a choice repast; that is in the spring and early summer, and even then, it is too satisfying, not sufficiently delicate.

The man who gives salmon during the winter, I care not what sauce he serves with it, does an injury to himself and his guests.

Ward McAllister, self-appointed arbiter of New York society from the 1860s to the early 1890s.

MARCH 16, 1917

After a whirlwind fortnight of etiquette lessons and dance classes at Galliano's, the day of the luncheon arrived, along with a vicious cold.

Kitty's head felt like a soaked sponge, so filled with fluid that she imagined it must be leaking out her eyes and ears.

"Can you muddle through, Katharine?" Her grandmother examined her with a critical eye. "I'd cancel the luncheon except I've already booked the Met for the ball, and this would push it back another week."

She glanced at Kitty's dress. "Even with a red nose, you look quite nice."

Kitty had chosen a pale lavender crepe with a tiered skirt that revealed the latest in hemlines, ending above her ankles.

She had twisted her hair into a chignon and wore a simple pearl necklace and her grandmother's ring as her only adornments. In the pocket of the dress, she had stashed several handkerchiefs, hoping she wouldn't need them.

Kitty nodded. "I think so—" She broke off to sneeze and groped for a handkerchief. Then in rapid succession, she sneezed five more times. "Dizzy me, this is-is-ah-ah-ah-choooo!"

Oma snapped her fingers. "My word, why didn't I think of it sooner?" She took Kitty's arm. "Come with me, Katharine."

She hustled Kitty up the marble staircase and down the carpeted hallway to her bedroom.

Kitty had seen Oma's bedroom once before, but today the plethora of pink silk draperies, lacy ruffles, and fat cupids overhung with Oma's heavy jasmine perfume was overwhelming, and she sneezed again.

Oma rang for her maid. "Fetch the vaporizer lamp, please," she said when Fleurette appeared.

The maid nodded and hurried away.

"Come sit down." Oma rummaged in a drawer at the dressing table. "I'm looking for the medicine."

Fleurette returned with the vaporizer, which looked like a miniature kerosene lamp, and set it on the table.

Oma held up a green glass bottle. "Found it." She

glanced at the tiny French clock on the dressing table. "And we've no time to waste."

Oma handed the bottle to Fleurette, who lit the tiny lamp and turned up the flame, then poured a small amount of the medication into the tin pan above the burner.

Kitty picked the bottle up to read the label.

Vapor-Ol Treatment No. 6. Contains 45 percent alcohol, and Opium, three grains to each fluid ounce. For asthma and other spasmodic affections.

"Wait a minute," Kitty said. "I don't have asthma. Are you sure about this?"

Oma peered into the mirror. "It's a miracle worker, Katharine, I assure you." She gave a little tug at her wig and smiled at her reflection. "I wouldn't be without it when I have a cold or influenza. Now, lean over and breathe it in. Quickly now."

Fleurette swung the tiny pan over the flame and the liquid began to vaporize. The fumes had a heavy sweetish odor, almost like the maple syrup Papa liked to put on his pancakes, and Kitty hesitated.

"Get a good snootful, Katharine. We haven't much time." Oma urged her with a wave of her hand.

Reluctantly Kitty breathed in the vapor.

"Again," Oma said.

Kitty obeyed.

"One more," Oma said.

Kitty leaned back, her head woozy. "I think that's enough." Lassitude seeped through her veins like warm water.

"Why don't you go to your room and rest a bit. I'll send for you when it's time."

Kitty nodded and got to her feet. Instead of feeling like a soaked sponge, her head now felt weightless and almost disconnected from her body. She imagined reaching up to fetch it back and giggled.

Oma frowned. "Are you quite yourself, Katharine?"

"Oh, yes. Fine." She giggled again.

Oma glanced at Fleurette. "Help her to her bedroom."

Fleurette took Kitty's arm to guide her. She couldn't quite feel her feet, as if she was walking on clouds. But she hadn't sneezed once since the medicine, the Vapor-Ol or whatever it was.

They arrived at her bedroom and Kitty went in. She was sleepy suddenly, and the chaise lounge beckoned invitingly, all plump pillows with a fuzzy wool throw.

A moment later, a loud knock sounded at her door. "It's time," a voice called.

Kitty sat up and blinked rapidly. It was one o'clock already? But a minute ago it had been noon. She didn't remember actually lying down on the chaise or Fleurette leaving.

She stumbled downstairs and met her grandmother in the foyer.

"Feeling better, dear?"

Kitty nodded. Strangely enough, she did. She smoothed her skirts and straightened her posture as she waited next to her grandmother to meet the lions. Or if not lions, what? Inquisitors? At any rate, she hoped to pass inspection.

The ladies arrived together by private limousine. One by one, Percy bowed and took their wraps. They turned toward their hostess, but their sharp collective gaze lit on Kitty like a lightning bolt striking the ground.

"So pleased you could come, dear ladies." Oma's voice sounded as smooth as butter. "Allow me to present my granddaughter, Miss Katharine Winthrop."

Kitty stepped forward, back erect, and curtsied to each

lady as they were introduced. The anxiety that had stalked her all morning had disappeared. Behind the ladies, Percy gave her an encouraging nod.

"Mrs. Alva Vanderbilt Belmont."

This doyenne of high society was all roundness and plump cheeks, with a tiny cupid's bow mouth. Her unsmiling deep brown gaze raked Kitty from chignon to shoes.

"So nice to meet you," Kitty said.

"Mrs. Pierre Cabot."

A martinet if there ever was one. Lips so thin as to be almost non-existent, a long, hooked nose and deep lines from nose to mouth added to her forbidding demeanor. But then she smiled, transforming her elderly face completely.

"So nice to meet you, dear," she said, with a friendly nod.

"Mrs. Tessie Oehlrichs."

Mrs. Oehlrichs had a pleasant smile and a tip-tilted nose, with abundant black hair piled under her hat.

"And Mrs. Prudence Vanderfelder."

Mrs. Vanderfelder was the shortest of the four, massively obese, with tiny bird-like wrists and ankles in startling contrast. A true butterball. Her triple chins and heavy forehead squished her eyes, nose, and lips, into the center of her face. She gazed up at Kitty like a basilisk and nodded stiffly.

"Shall we proceed to the dining room?" Oma led the way through the marble hallways to the smaller informal dining room.

She had fussed for days over the flowers, china, and silverware pattern to use, finally settling on pink roses and ranunculus with baby's breath for the centerpiece, and plain French porcelain and silver.

Kitty waited until the ladies had taken their seats to seat herself to the right of her grandmother.

Oma's nod to Percy launched the luncheon. The ladies took their napkins up, all the while examining Kitty and watching her movements. Utensils to the right and left of the plate were placed in order of use, from the outside in.

The soup was brought in a silver tureen, and served by one of the footmen, under Percy's supervision.

Hearing Oma's voice in her head, Kitty took up her soup spoon, aware that all three ladies were covertly observing her, even as they chatted away with Oma.

Spoon away from yourself, and never, ever slurp. And for heaven's sake, don't click your spoon against the bowl, whatever you do. Or your teeth, either.

She'd only managed three slow spoonfuls of the lobster bisque when Oma signaled Percy for the next course.

The soup bowls and tureen were removed and the salad brought in. This proved to be even more difficult than the soup as the salad had a vinaigrette dressing.

One must wait until no further dressing drips off the bite on your fork, lest it fall into your lap.

The salad must be eaten with a knife and fork, and again Kitty was so mindful of all the directions Oma had given her, she barely tasted it.

Broiled salmon with minted spring peas comprised the main course. She took the fish knife and fork and carefully started on the salmon.

Never put too much food in your mouth.

Never mash or mix food on your plate.

Never blow on hot food or drink.

As she tried to remember all the rules, she stopped in the middle of a chew. A tiny fishbone had lodged between her teeth. Surreptitiously, she raised her napkin to her lips and, under cover of the cloth, attempted to remove the offending bone. After wiggling it back and forth, she managed to dislodge it and carefully place it on the rim of her plate.

Sitting and moving so stiffly had strained the back of her neck and uncomfortable perspiration broke out under her armpits.

Across the table, Mrs. Vanderfelder's eyes narrowed. Had she read Kitty's discomfort somehow? This luncheon couldn't be over soon enough.

Now for the peas.

Peas are the ultimate test of true breeding, being eaten with a fork.

Hopefully, they wouldn't be her social demise.

Kitty didn't dare take more than three peas on her fork, praying they would make it to her mouth without tumbling off the tines.

Next to her, Oma held her breath. The three guests stared as Kitty raised the utensil to her lips, their converged gazes rising with the fork.

A sudden prickly tingle zinged underneath her nose. "Ah—ah—ah-chooo!"

The force of her colossal sneeze shot the bright green peas off the fork and her free hand flew up to catch them before they could hit the Inquisitors across the table.

Everyone froze.

"Please excuse me," Kitty said faintly.

She took her napkin and walked out of the dining room, close to tears, pausing in the hall to wipe the smashed peas off her fingers. Now she'd done it.

Percy appeared behind her, a new napkin in his hand.

"I've ruined everything, Percy."

He shook his silver head emphatically. "No, miss. It's

what you do now that's important." He drew her further down the hall. "It happens, miss. Everyone makes mistakes. Now you go back in there and act like nothing's happened."

He took the soiled napkin and handed her the fresh one. "Smile, be charming, and it will pass."

Slowly, Kitty walked toward the dining room. When she turned at the door, Percy still stood in the hall, nodding and gesturing for her to go in.

She straightened her shoulders, took a deep breath, and turned the knob.

The ladies sat in silence as she seated herself and spread the fresh napkin across her lap.

Gathering her courage, she smiled at the ladies, meeting their gaze one by one. "Thank you for waiting."

The Italian clock on the sideboard ticked sharply, the only sound amid the smothering silence that hung in the room like the heavy calm before a thunderstorm.

She picked up her knife and fork and delicately ate a morsel of salmon. The Inquisitors had given up any vestige of attempting to finish their own meal, their gazes fixed on Kitty.

This was it. Do or die.

She picked up two peas on her fork and placed them successfully into her mouth. Then she laid her fork and knife properly on the rim of the plate at the 12 o'clock to 3 o'clock position to indicate she had finished.

A silent sigh of relief seemed to work its way around the table. Kitty let out the breath she'd been holding. Only dessert was left.

It arrived at Oma's nod to Percy. Individual Baked Alaska. Difficult again, as the ice cream had a tendency to separate from the cake and fall off the utensil.

Mrs. Vanderbilt Belmont paused to watch Kitty as she

cut a tiny bite, willing it to stay together. Slowly she put it to her lips and was rewarded by a tiny approving nod from the formidable woman.

But a spoon would make so much more sense.

Kitty stifled a sigh. She'd never imagined all the rules and practices of "good etiquette" could be so dull. Or tricky.

Finally, the dessert plates were taken away, and tea and coffee served, which Kitty declined, not willing to take any more risks.

"So, Miss Winthrop." Mrs. Vanderfelder's three chins waggled as she spoke. "What accomplishments do you possess?"

Mrs. Belmont and Mrs. Cabot turned toward her at the question.

Here it came. The Inquisition.

Kitty lowered her voice and took her time answering. "I can sketch and paint, Mrs. Vanderfelder."

Mrs. Cabot smiled at her. "Any musical instruments?"

"Unfortunately, I possess no skill in that area, Mrs. Cabot."

"Needlework?" Mrs. Vanderfelder asked.

Kitty hesitated. "Not precious needlework. I do sew and sew very well. I have also done some dress design."

Mrs. Vanderfelder ever so slightly shrugged her plump shoulders.

Next to her, Oma stilled. Had Kitty committed a faux pas by mentioning dress designing?

"Oh, for heaven's sakes, Prudence." Mrs. Vanderbilt Belmont gave an exasperated sigh. "No one is doing needlework anymore."

Mrs. Vanderfelder gave an injured sniff.

"I'd much rather know a girl is doing something useful

with her life these days," Mrs. Belmont said. "Using the brain God gave her."

She paused. "I could use someone like you, Miss Winthrop, for my Political Equality Association."

"Oh, no, you don't, Alva." Oma shook her finger at Mrs. Belmont. "I won't have my granddaughter protesting in front of the White House for women's suffrage."

Mrs. Belmont appeared unfazed. "You wouldn't like to cast a vote for the presidential candidate of your choice, Vera?"

The two women glared at each other. Then Oma shrugged. "You know I agree with your views, Alva. But let me get her introduced to society first."

Mrs. Belmont laughed, a big booming laugh that took Kitty unaware and made her smile involuntarily, thinking there was nothing soft and feminine about it in the least.

Oma stood then, the signal that the luncheon was over. Kitty followed her grandmother back to the front foyer along with their guests.

Mrs. Cabot pulled her aside. "You're going to be just fine, dear," she said with the sweet smile that softened her craggy features. "Just don't forget who you are."

Something to ponder.

When the great gilded and bronze doors had shut after their guests, Kitty sagged against the marble banister.

Oma turned to her, beaming. "You did splendidly. Especially after the matter of the peas. Couldn't have done it better myself."

Kitty perked up. "I passed the test?"

Did these ruling ladies of elite society now see her as a refined young lady, with impeccable manners, perfect posture, elegantly dressed, with a cultured attitude and a well-modulated voice?

"Yes," her grandmother said.

Kitty hoped so. All she wanted was a chance to dance at a ball. If this was what she had to do to achieve it, then so be it.

"I'm starving," she said to Oma.

SIX

A Magnificent Collection of Paris Gowns from the Leading Couturiers of the French Capitol is now Displayed in the Imported and Special Costumes on the Third Floor.

B. Altman & Co ad,
The New York Sun, March 17, 1917

KITTY TELEPHONED her mother the next morning to tell her about the luncheon.

"Mama," she said when her mother answered. "I'd like to stay a few days longer with Oma if you wouldn't mind? We have an appointment with Madame Lucile for a fitting tomorrow morning, and then I'm invited to a luncheon with Oma tomorrow afternoon. Oh, and I forgot, there's a party two nights from tonight Oma wants me to attend. You don't mind, do you?"

There was no answer from the other end of the line. "Mama? Are you there?"

"I'm here." Another long pause. "Kitty—"

"Oh, please don't say no. I don't want to disappoint Oma. She's gone to great trouble to plan all this for me."

Silence. *Why was she being like this?* "Mama, it would mean the world to me. I'll come home at the end of the week. I promise."

"Very well."

"Thank you, thank you! I must go now. My breakfast is ready. Love you!"

She hung up the phone.

A FEW DAYS LATER, the delivery from *Maison Lucile* arrived at 660 Fifth Avenue, all addressed to Miss Katharine Winthrop.

Boxes of dresses, hats, shoes, and gloves buried the carpet in Kitty's bedroom. Oma sat in an upholstered chair with her feet on a stool, watching as Kitty opened one box, then another. Fleurette, her grandmother's maid, took each item after it had been exclaimed over and hung it in the closet.

A knock sounded at the bedroom door, and Mama walked in.

"Mama, hello! You're just in time. My wardrobe from Miss Lucile has arrived. Come and see."

"Good afternoon, Evangeline." Oma smiled.

"Hello, Mother."

Quietly, Mama entered and took a seat on the window bench. "What's happened to my old bedroom? I don't recognize it."

"Oma had it redone just for me. Isn't it beautiful?"

A French decorator had been hired and the room

refashioned in pale peach and coral, Kitty's favorite colors, accented with gold.

An antique tester bed with flowing draperies dominated one end of the room, a dressing table with an antique Venetian mirror occupied the other, and sheer silk draperies hung at the windows.

"It's very nice." There was a queer undertone in her mother's voice, but she had pasted that odd blank look on her face, the one she wore when she was displeased about something but didn't want anyone to know.

Kitty turned away to finish opening the boxes, wondering what her mother was upset about.

When all the boxes were emptied, her mother stood. "Kitty, do you remember what day it is?"

Kitty frowned. "Thursday? Or is it Friday?"

"It's Saturday. You were to be home yesterday."

Kitty clapped a hand to her mouth. "Oh, I am so sorry. I completely forgot." She glanced sideways at her grandmother. "We've been so busy between appointments and calling hours, and dress fittings."

"I'm sure she didn't mean to overlook the time, Evangeline."

Her mother ignored Oma. "Please come home with me now, Kitty."

Kitty frowned. When her mother put her stern face on, she couldn't be dissuaded. "Very well, Mama."

She collected her things and packed them in a new leather valise, another gift from Oma.

"Wait," her grandmother said. "If you would indulge me a moment longer, Evangeline, I have two more surprises for Katharine."

Mama's lips tightened, but she didn't reply.

Oma rose and pulled out a large cardboard box tied

with ribbon from underneath the bed and marked *Maison Lucile*. She placed it on the counterpane and beckoned Kitty over.

Conscious of her mother watching, Kitty untied the ribbon and parted the layers of tissue paper to reveal a shimmering ball gown, watered-silk in a luscious peach with a gold-beaded bodice.

The underskirt was gold illusion netting, and the effect of the peach silk over the gold was transcendently beautiful.

Kitty dashed to the mirror with the gown and held it up to her. It played up her creamy skin and made her eyes appear greener.

"Oh, Oma, it's beautiful. I've never seen anything so lovely in my life!"

"For the ball in your honor next week, my dear. You'll be the most beautiful girl there."

Mama crossed her arms over her chest, her face a wooden mask.

"And one last surprise." Oma handed her a red leather Cartier box. An emerald and diamond necklace with matching earrings glittered on the black velvet.

Mama stepped between them with her fists clenched. "Mother, this is too much."

Kitty shrank back as her mother and grandmother faced each other, Mama grim and threatening, Oma's face carefully placid.

Then Oma took a step back and waved Mama away. "I know you disapprove, Evangeline, but you don't understand. I'm helping the jewelers, the milliners, and the designers by giving them my business. Not to mention the grocers, the florists, and the musicians. Surely you wouldn't begrudge them the opportunity to do business?"

A muscle clenched in her mother's cheek, and she took

a deep breath. "You know perfectly well what I mean. You've gone too far."

"At least I have a granddaughter who appreciates what I'm trying to do for her." Oma's words cracked through the air in the room, her eyes hard.

Kitty's breath caught in her chest, and Oma immediately put a hand to her forehead and moaned. "I'm so sorry, Evangeline," she said, her voice as smooth as the silk of Kitty's ball gown. "I've had a massive headache all day and it's gotten the best of me. I didn't mean to speak so sharply. I apologize, Evangeline." She gestured to Kitty. "Do run along, now, Katharine, with your mother. I'm going to rest."

Mama refused Oma's offer of a limousine ride and had Percy call a carriage instead. The silence on the way home hung as heavy as fog at midnight. Kitty longed to ask her mother what exactly had happened in the bedroom, but her mother's bleak face stopped her.

But Kitty couldn't bear to have her mother upset. "Mama, I...Oma only wants what's best for me."

Her mother turned on the seat and put her hand over Kitty's. "As do I, dearest. Even more so than your grandmother, who has only known you for a few weeks. You are the heart of my heart."

"I don't wish to displease you, Mama. I know you were against me making my debut."

"Not against *you*, dearest," she said quickly, "never against you. I left that world for a reason, Kitty. It can be manipulative and shallow. More than anything I wanted to be useful, to do something meaningful with my life. Not just be the girl in the gilded cage."

"And you have, Mama. How many wharflings have you placed in homes over the years? Hundreds?"

Her mother smiled, and it was like the sun breaking out

of the clouds, lighting up her beautiful eyes from within. "I never counted. But there were always more. More children who needed to be rescued from the awful places they found themselves in. Abandoned and unloved, cold, hungry, and preyed upon."

She laughed. "I remember people in the congregation thought I was mad when I brought the first two into our home. You were just a baby then. What a kerfuffle I caused. But of course, your father was my greatest supporter, and, in time, it all worked out. And now some of my wharflings are married and have babies of their own."

She paused. "There's another reason I wanted you to come home. If you're thinking about the New York College of Design, we need to submit your application soon."

Kitty shook her head. "I do want to go to college, Mama, but I can always go later. Right now, Oma has offered me the opportunity to do some of the things I've always dreamed of."

Mama's lips tightened. "Where did you get those ideas, I wonder? I certainly didn't plant them in your head." Then she smiled wistfully. "Are you sure you're my daughter and not some cuckoo in the nest?"

Kitty patted her mother's hand. "All I have to do is look in the mirror to know that."

Mama's eyes clouded, and the tiny line between her brows deepened. "I don't want you to get hurt, dearest." Her mother's lips trembled. "I've tried to tell you what that world is like. You're a smart girl, Kitty, an intelligent young woman. It would be a waste of your talents and abilities."

"It's only temporary, Mama. Just a few months." She squeezed her mother's hand. "I don't want to disappoint you, but you must let me try. After all, in the end, you made your own choice, didn't you? It could have been a mistake. And you weren't any older than I am now."

Her mother sighed. "I can't deny that."

Kitty leaned forward and took her mother's hands. "Mama, please. Have a little faith in me. And allow me the same opportunity to make my own mistakes."

"I have great faith in you. It's that shallow world I don't trust. But..." She paused and searched Kitty's face, then smiled. "Go ahead and try your wings, dearest. I'll always be here if you need me."

SEVEN

There is no scene in which pleasure reigns more triumphantly than in the ballroom. The assemblage of fashion, of beauty, of elegance, and taste.

The music rising with its voluptuous swell, the elegant attitudes and airy evolutions of graceful forms, the mirth in every step, unite to give to the spirits a buoyancy, to the heart a gayety, and to the passions a warmth, unequaled by any other species of amusement.

The Complete Ballroom Handbook, 1887

APRIL 2, 1917

For the Red Cross Ball, Oma had the Metropolitan Opera House transformed into a summer fairyland with ferns and greenery, grottos with draping bougainvillea, mossy rocks, and a sparkling waterfall that splashed into a stream with live goldfish darting under the surface.

Next to her grandmother, as the guest of honor, Kitty

stood in her splendid peach and gold ball gown to greet the guests. Although she made a good faith attempt to associate each face with a name, after the first hundred, it quickly became a blur.

Her gold filigree dance card, another gift from her grandmother, filled quickly after the introductions were over, and when the orchestra struck the opening notes of the quadrille, her first partner claimed her.

"Miss Winthrop, how ravishing you look tonight. Certainly, the loveliest girl here."

"How you do go on, Mr. Singer."

They clasped hands and turned. "It's true. You remind me of Eos, goddess of the dawn, in that color."

They whirled and their palms met. "Thank you, sir. You pay me too many compliments, I fear."

"They are deserved. Have you any openings on your card for me later?"

The quadrille ended, and they bowed to one another. "I'm afraid not, sir."

A waltz began, and her next partner, William Koehler III, popped up behind Mr. Singer. "Good evening, Miss Winthrop." He held out his hand. "Shall we?"

He whirled her into the flowing steps of the waltz, and she moved with him fairly well. Thank goodness for the dancing lessons.

"May I say that you are a vision tonight, Miss Winthrop? You look—"

"Oh, please don't tell me I look like a goddess."

Oh, my, how ungracious of her. *Where had that come from?*

"Er, um..." He fumbled for something to say.

"Oh, dear, I'm so sorry. I take it you were indeed about to say something of the sort?"

To make up for her rudeness, she smiled up at him, which only seem to disconcert him further. His step faltered, but he quickly recovered and swung her back into the rhythm of the dance.

"Aphrodite," he muttered. "But I see that you don't enjoy remarks about your beauty, Miss Winthrop. Please accept my apologies if I have offended you in any way."

"Of course, you haven't."

My goodness. Oma had told her that conversations between unmarried women and single men had to be conventional, but this was plain idiotic.

Mr. Koehler didn't speak to her again, bowed at the end of the dance, and hurried off. If she didn't know better, she'd think his pants were on fire.

Her next partner, dapper Colin McConnell, son and heir of the McConnell Steel Company, claimed her for the mazurka.

"My compliments, Miss Winthrop, on your beauty tonight. I couldn't keep my eyes off you during that last dance."

Kitty had an almost irresistible urge to roll her eyes.

'There was a reason why I left that world, Kitty. It can be manipulative and shallow.'

Her mother's words came back to her as Mr. McConnell took her hand, placed his other hand on her waist, and moved them into the complicated steps of the dance.

Perhaps these conversations didn't need to be vacuous. "How does your father's steel company fare these days, Mr. McConnell?"

McConnell blinked. "My father's company? What a strange question."

"Is it? I merely wished to have a conversation."

"About business?" He threw back his head and laughed, giving her a good view of his tonsils. "Young ladies don't discuss these sorts of things, Miss Winthrop. Hasn't your grandmother explained these things to you?"

Kitty stiffened at his disdainful tone, and he smiled.

"Perhaps you get it from your mother, Miss Winthrop? I've heard she became quite outspoken at the altar."

Kitty gasped and wrenched away from him. The other dancers whirled around them, casting curious glances their way. A tiny smile lurked at the edges of Mr. McConnell's lips as he shrugged his elegant shoulders.

Abruptly, Kitty whirled and marched away, barely able to see. Insufferable wretch. Insulting her mother. How dare he?

She blundered her way to one of the ladies' lounges, fortunately empty except for the attendant maid, and barricaded herself in the furthest water closet.

It was cooler and quieter in here. She leaned her forehead against the cold tile as her breathing calmed. Some of the sparkle in the beautiful evening ebbed away.

The lounge door opened, and several ladies entered, voices chattering all at once.

"My word, isn't Sophia Eggleston an absolute vision tonight?"

Kitty held her skirts away from the door and peered through the crack. It was Mrs. Oehlrichs who had spoken, clustered with Mrs. Vanderfelder and Mrs. Belmont around the mirror, a rainbow of colorful silks, satins, and graying hair.

"And Ellen Tarleton," Mrs. Vanderfelder said, stuffed like a Thanksgiving turkey into tight blue velvet, "amazing what a Worth gown will do for a girl with such unfortunate looks."

There were sniggers of laughter.

"Lovely tonight, though, isn't it?" Mrs. Oehlrichs said. "The decorations?"

"You think so? I find them rather overblown actually." Mrs. Vanderfelder laughed. "Rather like the hostess."

More jeering laughter.

"And did you notice all the roses match her dress?" Mrs. Belmont observed her reflection in the mirror and adjusted a curl. "The granddaughter? What's her name again, Winthrop?"

"Yes. Katharine Winthrop. The interloper. Who does she think she is, anyway?" The derisive voice of Mrs. Oehlrichs cut Kitty to the quick. "After all this time and all the scandal, Vera now presents her granddaughter? Tasteless."

"And where is the mother? The famous Evangeline Lindenmayer?" Mrs. Belmont sniffed. "That's what I'm dying to know."

"Oh, she daren't show her face, after what she did." Mrs. Vanderfelder shook her head, causing the pearls on her tiara to bob alarmingly. "Perhaps Vera hopes to achieve with this girl what she couldn't accomplish with her own daughter."

"Hope springs eternal." Mrs. Belmont sneered, and the other ladies joined in.

"But the old girl does throw a good party, you must admit," Mrs. Vanderfelder said. "No expense spared for this new granddaughter of hers."

"I'll say." Mrs. Oehlrichs peered closer at her reflection in the mirror and rubbed at a spot on her chin. "She certainly appeared out of nowhere. Queening it over all of us."

More giggles.

"I've heard Howard Singer is mad for her!" Mrs. Oehlrichs shook her head. "Absolutely giddy."

"Oh, I'd wager a bet old lady Lindenmayer will be holding out for someone grander."

Mrs. Vandefelder laughed. "I'm sure of it."

Mrs. Oehlrichs gave one final pat to her coiffure. "Ready, girls?"

The lounge door opened and closed again. Slowly, Kitty straightened, let her skirts go, and left the water closet. So, the old adage was true. Eavesdroppers seldom heard anything good of themselves.

Numbly, she washed her hands and accepted a towel from the maid hovering nearby. Behind her, another water closet door opened and a pert blonde girl in a spectacular fuchsia ball gown strode out. Her blonde curls were artfully arranged within a diamond tiara. Bracelets of sapphires and diamonds circled her wrist, and she had a sapphire in her necklace as large as Papa's pocket watch. She washed her hands and turned to Kitty.

"Hello." She extended her bare hand. "I'm Mary Alice Mulhaney. Miss Winthrop, correct?"

Kitty nodded. "Guilty, I'm afraid." And she gave a little laugh, remembering that her mother spoke the same words to her a few weeks ago.

"Oh, I'm so pleased to see that you can laugh, considering what those brats said a few moments ago. They're simply jealous, my dear. Of your face, your lineage, and your fortune."

"Thank you. That's very kind. But I have no fortune."

"Oh, but you will, I'm sure. Who else is your grandmother going to leave her money to?"

"I'm sure I never thought about it."

Mary Alice laughed and patted Kitty's arm. "How delightfully provincial of you."

She put her gloves on and pulled Kitty's arm through hers. "Now, let's go give them something to talk about, shall we? I have someone I'd like you to meet."

They entered the ballroom together and immediately heads turned in their direction.

"All the old biddies will be simply mad to see us together," Miss Mulhaney whispered.

"Why is that? You must know, as everyone else seems to, that I'm ignorant about these things."

"Surely, you've noticed that none of the ladies, either young or old, have been especially welcoming?"

"I did."

"As those dreadful urchins in the lounge said, you're an interloper. The unknown quantity. They think you don't belong here."

"Perhaps I don't, after all."

"Rubbish!" Miss Mulhaney shook her finger at Kitty. "You can't let them get to you. It's what I mentioned before. You're the most beautiful girl here, by far, with the largest fortune. Their greatest fear has materialized in you."

She pulled out her fan, a delicate confection of antique lace and blue silk rosebuds.

"And what might that be?"

"Why, darling, it's that you'll snatch the most eligible man here."

Kitty smiled then. "I confess that never occurred to me. I've been too busy trying to remember all my grandmother's rules. Not to mention that I have absolutely no idea who the most eligible bachelor here is."

Miss Mulhaney shut her fan with a snap. "I'm about to introduce you to him."

"You are not interested in him yourself, Miss Mulhaney?"

"Oh, please, call me Mary Alice. And no." She ran a delicate hand over her coiffure. "I'm already engaged. To Viscount Tarnley."

Discreetly she indicated a bougainvillea-covered pillar a short distance away, where a rangy blond man with a ruddy complexion stood in conversation with another man in white tie and tails. "I'll be a countess eventually."

She rubbed her hands together and gave Kitty a devilish smile. "Now this is going to be fabulous. Their faces will turn green, I'm sure."

"The brats?"

"And their interfering mamas."

Mary Alice linked arms with Kitty and walked toward her fiancé. The two men turned at their approach.

"Miss Winthrop, may I present my fiancé, Viscount Tarnley, son and heir to the Earl of Tarnley and Balthazar Fitzwilliam Bennett, Earl of Eavenlea, son and heir to the Duke of Eavenlea."

Both men bowed. Kitty hoped she could keep their titles straight. The Earl of Eavenlea possessed middling height, with brown hair the color of walnuts and pale green eyes. A closely shaved beard and mustache revealed the most beautiful pair of lips Kitty had ever seen on a man.

"Very pleased to meet you, Miss Winthrop," he said, in a clipped English accent.

"Please forgive me, gentlemen," Kitty said. "I apologize if it's incorrect for me to ask, but what am I to call you?"

Viscount Tarnley laughed. "Call me Bobby. I love the informality you Americans have."

"Lord Eavenlea, please," the earl said, "I'm not quite as comfortable with American customs as Tarnley is."

For such a beautiful man, he had an unprepossessing manner, ducking his head as he spoke. There was a pause, and Miss Mulhaney ever so slightly raised an eyebrow at the earl.

"Uh, yes, Miss Winthrop, would you, I mean, might you have an opening on your dance card for me?" He ducked his head again and took a step back.

A wistfulness lingered about him. Her dance card had been filled hours ago but she pulled it up by the gold silk ribbon and perused it anyway. Howard Singer was penciled in for the next dance, a waltz.

"Actually, I do have an opening, Lord Eavenlea, for the very next dance."

His luminous gray-green eyes lit up. "Splendid, Miss Winthrop." He held out his hand. "Shall we?"

He was an excellent dancer, much better than she. But of course, he'd been doing this all his life. He expertly covered her missteps and seemed reluctant to release her hand when the dance finished.

"Would you like to sit and chat for a while?" A hopeful look replaced the wistfulness.

Kitty nodded, and he led her to an upholstered bench in a nook of potted palm trees.

Heads turned as they passed, and comments were whispered behind gloved fingers. Kitty tossed her head, and a stubborn determination to enjoy the evening rose within her. She favored the earl with a brilliant smile as he sat down, and he gulped noticeably.

"Have you been in New York very long, Lord Eavenlea?"

"Since last spring," the earl said.

"My goodness, you haven't been home for a year?"

"Can't be helped." He shrugged. "The war in Europe is

keeping me here. My father refuses to let me come home since Germany announced its plan to wage unrestricted submarine warfare. I am his only heir, you see."

"Oh, yes, the 'Zimmerman telegram,' they're calling it now."

He nodded. "I'm not sure when I'll be able to return."

"Papa thought it was a hoax at first."

Lord Eavenlea nodded. "Many people did. Until Zimmerman himself confirmed it. And now all of Europe is waiting to see if America enters the war."

Then he shook his head. "But forgive me for being so morose. Young ladies don't need to concern themselves with such things."

"It's understandable. You're concerned for your country." Perhaps now would be a good time to change the subject. "I didn't see you in the receiving line earlier, Lord Eavenlea."

He colored slightly. "No. I prefer to slip in quietly." He gave a nervous laugh. "Generally, I stay away from social gatherings like this."

"Why is that?"

"I'm not very good at small talk. Or charming the ladies."

"You're doing fine right now."

"At the small talk?'

She laughed then, and his smile turned shy as his face reddened. "At the charming," she said, "I find you very endearing."

His eyes widened. "In that case, Miss Winthrop, may I be so audacious as to ask for another dance?"

"You may." She extended her hand.

He whirled her onto the ballroom floor to the poignant notes of the violin in The Merry Widow waltz. Amid the swirling gowns in every color of the rainbow, it felt like dancing on a cloud.

And the way he gazed down at her, his eyes alight. She sighed at the tender pressure of his hand on her waist as the throbbing liquid notes of the violin disappeared in the crescendo of strings at the finale.

This is what she had dreamed of. Dancing as light as a feather in the arms of a handsome prince. Or in this case, the heir to a dukedom.

The strings cut off suddenly as a man walked to center stage and grimly clapped his hands for silence. The hum of conversation ebbed away as music and laughter came to a halt.

"Ladies and gentlemen, please forgive me for interrupting your evening." The stillness in the ballroom grew acute as smiles disappeared, men stood straighter, and women gripped their husbands' arms as they moved closer to the stage.

"The White House has just announced news of great import." He paused and glanced at the paper in his hands. "A few moments ago, President Wilson asked Congress to declare war on Germany."

EIGHT

Volunteers First, Roosevelt's Idea, Troops to France in Two Months

The New York Times, Monday, April 16, 1917

THE ANNOUNCEMENT that America was going to war didn't seem to stop the social calendar of New York's high society.

Most of the young men Kitty spoke with at parties and danced with at the balls seemed to think the tide of war would turn once the United States arrived in France. A few had even enlisted.

This morning her mother had called Oma's home and asked Kitty to come home for a few days, and she gladly agreed.

The cozy parlor of her parents' home with its dark polished furniture and walls of books would be a nice change after the miles of marble hallways at Oma's "chateau."

She smiled when she found her parents in the parlor sitting close together on the sofa. Her parents were different from every other married couple she knew. They still held hands, and often her father would whisper something in her mother's ear that turned her pretty face bright pink.

But now her mother clutched a handkerchief in her fist, and there were tears on her cheeks. Papa's ever-present grin was nowhere to be seen.

"Come in, sweetheart," he said, his dear handsome face serious. "I've made a decision."

A sense of dread clamped around her heart like a vise.

"Kitty, after much thought and prayer, I've enlisted with the Army as a chaplain."

A shudder went through her mother. Kitty shook her head as if to clear it. Had she heard him correctly? "But Papa, aren't you too old?"

He laughed then, and even her mother smiled. "Kitty, even though to you forty-two is ancient, I assure you it's not." The smile dropped away from his face. "Our soldiers will need all the encouragement, support, and prayer that we can give them."

Kitty couldn't begin to imagine life without her father. He had always been here, any time she needed him. "But Papa...I don't know what we'll do without you."

Papa tightened his arm around her mother. "It will be difficult for me to be away from you both. But you have each other."

"But why do *you* have to go, Papa? Isn't there someone else, other younger ministers who can do this?"

"I can only speak for myself, Kitty. And I believe this is the right thing to do."

"How long will you be gone?"

At this, her mother choked and dabbed at her eyes.

"There's no way to know, sweetheart. Perhaps with America entering the war, the conflict in Europe will be resolved sooner and I'll be home before you know it."

Kitty choked back the hard lump that rose in her throat. "When...when do you go?"

At this, her mother turned and buried her face in Papa's shirt front. He put his arms around her shaking body. "I leave for Paris in two months."

WEDNESDAY, June 13, 1917

Papa's two months at home rushed by.

The summer sky twilight had deepened to rose and gold, and a sweet breeze laden with the scent of Mama's roses rustled the lace curtains at the parlor windows.

Mama's eyes were puffy, but she bravely pasted a tremulous smile on her face as Papa walked into the parlor, tall, straight-backed, and clean-shaven in his Army uniform, his officer's cap on his head with its patent leather brim, and a wide leather belt around his waist. A cross at each shoulder and on his cap attested to his office of chaplain.

He saluted them smartly. "Major John Winthrop, 2nd Battalion, 16th Infantry Regiment, reporting for duty."

"Oh, Jack." Mama went into his arms. "How will I bear it? I can't, I can't." She buried her face in his neck, her slender shoulders shaking.

"You must, darling." He looked over her head at Kitty. "We all must."

"And why must you leave tonight?" Kitty asked. "Why can't we accompany you?"

"It's being kept quiet at the moment. I don't know why. But it's better here in the comfort of our own home. It would be a madhouse on the wharf, and I've no wish for you to see that."

"A madhouse, Papa? Why?"

Her father gave her a grave look. "Much weeping and gnashing of teeth, sweetheart, to use a Bible phrase."

Kitty frowned. "At the Red Cross ball, everyone cheered when the declaration of war was announced. The boys, especially. Some of them left immediately to sign up. They were excited to do so."

"The innocence of youth." Her father smiled sadly. "I'm afraid they don't know what awaits them in France."

"Glory and advancement, according to them," Kitty said.

Her mother turned, frowning. "Kitty, surely you understand that some of them won't be coming back?"

Kitty sat down abruptly. "Won't be coming back? I...I hadn't actually thought about it. Oma has kept me so busy with the social calendar that I..." She closed her mouth, hearing the shallowness of her own words.

Her mother walked to the parlor table and picked up the newspaper lying there. Wordlessly, she handed it to her.

Kitty took the paper and unfolded the front page. The headline jumped out at her.

41 Killed, 121 Injured In Air-Raid of Eastern London
Big Attack In Clouds Follows

THE STORY CONTINUED, in smaller print below the headline.

60 Children Among Victims of German Raiders

"PEOPLE ARE DYING, KITTY," her father said softly. He gave a sideways glance at Mama.

Kitty stood, frozen to the spot, as a cold shiver trickled down her spine. How could she have been so blind and stupid? No wonder Mama had been crying. She couldn't know if she'd ever see Papa again.

Kitty choked and took a step toward him. Right here, right now, she would have to say goodbye to her beloved father, not knowing if he would return.

"Oh, Papa!" She flung herself into his arms. "I don't know where my mind has been these last few weeks. It never seemed real until now that you...you—"

"Don't say it, sweetheart," her father whispered. "We must pray and hope for the best. I need you to be strong for your mother."

He straightened, held one arm out to Mama, and gathered both of them to his chest. "The Lord will keep us in the shelter of His wings, as He always has. We must remember that. And now, let me pray for you both."

He cleared his throat and pulled them closer. "May the Lord bless you and keep you, may the Lord make His face to shine on you and be gracious to you, may the Lord turn His face toward you and give you peace."

He kissed Kitty's forehead. "I love you with all my heart, Kitty."

Jenny came into the parlor, her wrinkled cheeks wet

with tears and her apron twisted in her hands. "I dinna ken what we'll do without ye, Jack."

"Now, Jenny," Papa said, "you'll do as you've always done, rule the roost with an iron fist. And take care of my girls."

He put his arms around her as Mrs. Mac, the cook, hovered at the doorway.

"Oh, Mr. Winthrop, sir, I'll be praying for you every day, I will."

Papa released Jenny and shook Mrs. Mac's hand. "Thank you for that. And I hope you'll send me some of your shortbread and molasses jumbles. I'll be the envy of every soldier in my regiment if you do."

"To be sure, Mr. Winthrop. Oh, God bless and keep you." She engulfed him in a hug then ran out of the room, her handkerchief to her eyes, followed by Jenny.

Papa smiled at Kitty and drew her close one last time. "I love you, sweetheart."

She didn't want to let him go and hugged him fiercely. "Take care, Papa. I will miss you so."

He kissed her forehead, released her, and held his hand out to her mother. Together they left the house for a private goodbye outside before the carriage arrived to take him to the Lower New York Bay and the ship that would transport him to the battlefields of France.

Kitty buried her face in her hands. Tears dripped through her fingers. Her poor mother. She and Papa had never spent a night apart in the twenty years of their marriage. How painful to say goodbye, not knowing whether she would ever see him again.

Presently, a soft touch came upon her hair, and her mother sank onto the sofa next to her. "We'll get through this together, dearest." She rocked Kitty gently as she wept.

In bed that night, Kitty put a pillow over her head to blot out the sound of her mother's weeping in the bedroom next door.

For the first time in her life, her father wasn't here, as he had always been, but headed down a long dark road to an unknown future. The deep abyss that had opened inside her felt bottomless now.

———

KITTY ROSE before her mother and made a pot of coffee. Mama had given Mrs. Mac and Jenny the day off, perhaps anticipating that she'd be in no condition to face them.

It was almost nine o'clock before her mother came down, haggard and heavy-eyed after a sleepless night.

"Good morning, Mama." She served her mother a cup and sat down across from her.

"We'll manage, Kitty." Mama's voice, while unsteady, sounded resolute. "I don't know how, but we will."

"Of course, we will. We have each other."

They sipped their coffee in silence, Kitty's heart torn at the sight of her mother's ravaged face even as the morning sunlight slanted through the window curtains and the robins sang outside.

It seemed like every other normal morning except nothing was normal now.

The telephone in the hallway rang, and Kitty went to answer it.

"Hello."

"Katharine?"

"Yes, Oma."

"How are you and your mother holding up?"

"About as well as can be expected."

Oma hesitated. "I know how difficult this must be for your mother. I know...how much they love each other."

She cleared her throat. "I'm calling now because I wanted to invite you and your mother to spend some time with me at Seaside, my summer cottage in Newport. Don't say anything until you hear me out," her grandmother added quickly. "It would do you both good, with Jack away now, to get out of the city. A change of scenery might be just the thing. You wouldn't have to worry about anything."

"That's kind of you, Oma. I will speak with her and let you know."

Kitty hung up the telephone and went back to the kitchen.

"My mother?"

"Yes." Kitty sat down and poured a fresh cup of coffee. "She's invited us to spend some time at her summer cottage in Newport."

"Seaside." Mama wrinkled her nose. "She calls it a cottage, because it only has fifty rooms, compared to her chateau on Fifth Avenue."

Then she smiled. "I did enjoy Seaside when I was little. Finding beach glass and shells in the sand, picnics, and swimming. Almost as much as I enjoyed spending summers with dear old Uncle Henry at Mahicantuck in Hyde Park."

"It sounds wonderful, Mama. I'd love to go. But I'm not leaving you. I'll only go if you go, too."

Mama shook her head. "She'll be hosting balls and luncheons on the lawn. There will be people I'd rather not run into."

"But you needn't see them. Oma can't host a party every night. There are sure to be lots of quiet days we can spend together taking walks on the beach and exploring

Newport." She grinned. "And you could keep an eye on me."

Mama tipped her head to one side, considering. "Well... it might be nice to get away for a few weeks. I'll have to make some arrangements for my wharflings."

"Is that a yes, Mama?"

Her mother nodded. "I suppose it is."

"Dizzy me." Kitty stood and put her cup in the sink. "We'd better start packing."

JULY 1, 1917

Two weeks later, Kitty and her mother sat at breakfast on the terrace of Oma's summer "cottage," overlooking the Atlantic.

It was an impressive mansion built, according to Oma, with over five thousand pounds of specially imported Italian marble.

Kitty was cutting into her poached egg when Percy came through the French doors and brought Mama a letter on a silver tray.

"It's from Papa." Her slender fingers shook as she slit the envelope with a hairpin.

Mama read through the letter and smiled. "Dear Jack," she whispered, "always making the best of things." She handed the letter to Kitty.

JUNE 28, 1917

Dearest Lindy,

The 26th Battalion arrived safely in France on the 26th. Our transport was a former fruit ship, renamed the USAT

Tenadores, and for protection, our convoy was surrounded by the Navy cruisers Seattle and DeKalb, and the destroyers Wilkes, Terry, and Roe. But we never saw any evidence of submarine activity. While underway, we were kept very busy on the ship, reveille at 0600 and then training on deck until we fell into our bunks after retreat.

Upon arrival at St. Nazaire, we were allowed a day of rest, and then it was on to training with the French Army. Soon we will head for Paris.

I pray that our dear Lord keep you in His love until we see each other again. Give my love to Kitty. I will try to write again very soon.

Always, your loving,
Jack

"HE SOUNDS WELL." Kitty handed the letter back to her mother, and her mother nodded, reading the letter again.

Oma bustled out and handed Kitty a bundle of letters. "Invitations, Katharine. Look through them and see if any appeal to you."

She deposited her considerable weight onto a chair and allowed Percy to pour her tea. "There'll be no lack of things to do while you're here."

Kitty leafed through the stack of heavy cream-colored envelopes. Beach parties, teas, summer balls, formal dinners. A wax seal on one envelope, with a coat of arms in the upper corner, caught her eye.

"That one is from the Earl of Eavenlea." Oma pursed her lips and nodded approvingly. "Apparently you made quite an impression on him at the Met Ball."

Mama took the newspaper and buried her face in it, but

not quickly enough to hide the frown that creased her forehead.

Kitty held the invitation out for her grandmother to read. "It's for a luncheon party on his yacht. I think I'd like to accept this one, Oma."

"Excellent choice, Katharine."

JULY 15, 1917

"HURRY, Katharine, or we'll be late."

Kitty started down the staircase. "I'm ready."

Her grandmother observed her descent and nodded approvingly. "You look quite smart."

The sailor-style dress was constructed of white linen, with a loose, comfortable cut, navy blue collar and cuffs on elbow-length sleeves and embroidered white stars on the collar. Rubber-soled flats with squared bows completed the look with a straw boater hat.

"It's quite comfortable." Kitty turned so Oma could see the back of the skirt, which reached to mid-calf. "And no corset! That's the best thing of all. You should try it, Oma."

Her grandmother was tightly corseted as usual, in a two-piece summer suit in navy blue with long sleeves, and her face was already flushed.

"Humph." Oma eyed the hem of Kitty's dress. "I'm not sure I approve of the direction of fashion these days. All these young hussies shingling their hair and raising their skirts."

"It's the war, Oma. Many of those young hussies are working in factories and mill yards for the war effort. They have to wear something more suitable for that kind of work."

"I suppose so." Her grandmother sniffed. "But why do they have to cut their hair?"

"Freedom, I would guess. Less to do in the morning before you go to work?"

They walked outside to the Pierce-Arrow for the short ride to Newport Harbor.

"This is exciting, Oma. I've never been on a yacht before."

Her grandmother shrugged. "I usually prefer to keep my feet on land."

Kitty giggled. "A landlubber."

"A what?"

"That's what they call someone who hates the water."

Her grandmother waved her hand. "I've been on many yachts over the years, but I never wanted one for myself. I didn't see the need for the expense."

"It's a first for me, Oma. So many firsts in my life this past spring and summer, all due to you." She leaned over and kissed her grandmother on the cheek. "Thank you."

"Happy to do it, Katharine."

It was a lovely day for sailing, and Newport Harbor on Narragansett Bay was full of people with the same idea. The carriage dropped them off at the Yacht Club, where Lord Eavenlea greeted them at the door dressed in crisp white trousers and a double-breasted navy coat with brass buttons. He wore a captain's hat with gold cording and a patent leather brim, set at a jaunty angle on his head.

"Good afternoon, dear ladies." He bowed. "I'm so glad you could come. I believe you know my other guests, Miss Mulhaney, and her fiancé, Viscount Tarnley."

The Viscount turned to Oma and bowed. "Mrs.

Lindenmayer, always a pleasure to see you. You're looking very well."

Her grandmother preened at the compliment. "Thank you, Viscount."

The group strolled down to the docks where a small launch waited. Lord Eavenlea assisted them in and nodded at the crew member, who rowed them out into the harbor where Lord Eavenlea's yacht was moored.

FORTITUDE was painted in black letters along the long and lean white hull. It had two masts sailing gaily-colored pennants and a row of portholes close to the water line.

"No sails," Kitty said, as they drew closer.

"Steam powered, so no," Lord Eavenlea said. "But now diesel engines are replacing steam."

A stairway unfolded down the side, and they made their way to the polished deck where the crew waited to greet them.

"This is Captain McQuade," Lord Eavenlea said, "and the rest of the crew, Turner and Jackson."

"Three years ago, this harbor was filled with yachts like this one." Oma gazed at the harbor behind the ship.

"What happened to all of them?" Kitty tried to imagine a bigger yacht than this one and failed.

"Donated to the government for the dratted war." Oma heaved a huge sigh. "We'd be enjoying the Riviera and the Mediterranean Sea right now, Katharine, if this stupid war hadn't ruined all my plans."

Kitty winced. Didn't Oma remember that Papa was serving at the front? Behind her grandmother, Mary Alice shook her head and mouthed "Never mind" at Kitty.

"That sounds lovely, Mrs. Lindenmayer," Mary Alice

said, "but right now I think it's wonderful to be here on Narragansett Bay on this amazing yacht."

Lord Eavenlea beamed. "Let me give you the tour."

They followed him down the wood deck, which had insets of clear glass inserted in the floor. He steered them toward a dark wood staircase that led down to the slatted door in the open shape of a moon.

"This is the main saloon." He pushed the doors open.

Instead of the European décor so prized by her grandmother, embellished with gold curlicues and filigree, heavy draperies and portieres, this room was simply paneled in a light wood. Sunshine poured in from the skylights set into the decks above, and Japanese lanterns provided additional light.

"This is beautiful." Kitty walked closer to examine a trifold screen painted with wisteria on a golden background.

"It's an antique Japanese shoji screen. Do you like it?"

"I do. It's soothing, somehow. Serene and elegant."

"Exactly." Lord Eavenlea nodded, and behind him, Oma shrugged.

Her grandmother no doubt preferred the *Petit Trianon* over anything as newfangled as this.

Kitty squelched a smile and ran her fingers over the chrysanthemum pattern of pale silver and blue silk woven into the fabric of the sofa. A carved wooden screen stood behind a pair of chairs in the same silk, and even the fireplace was deceptively simple, low, and tiled in pale green.

"You have a wonderful decorator, Lord Eavenlea."

"Actually, I designed this interior myself."

"Then I'm even more impressed. You have a wonderful eye."

He bowed slightly and smiled. "Thank you."

Mary Alice walked to the fireplace and peered at the tile. "Is this jade, Lord Eavenlea?"

"Very good, Miss Mulhaney, it is indeed."

"Have you been to Japan?"

He shook his head. "Not yet. But I've always thought I'd like to travel there on my honeymoon." He looked straight at Kitty when he said this, and behind Lord Eavenlea, Mary Alice widened her eyes at Kitty and sent her a wicked smile.

"I believe we're about ready to cast off," he said. "Please come upstairs."

Soon Fortitude was underway. At the prow of the ship, there were comfortable chairs to recline in as they sailed out of the harbor. Seagulls wheeled overhead, and the salty breeze was exhilarating.

Lord Eavenlea walked to the prow, and then crooked a finger at Kitty. She leaned over the gunwale, and there, in the water, sleek porpoises dove and jumped ahead of the frothing water at the bowline.

"Oh, how lovely." She laughed in delight and turned to find Lord Eavenlea, his elbow propped on the gunwale, gazing at her.

"I've heard you have some talent for designing too, Miss Winthrop."

"Oh? Now, where did you hear that?"

"Your grandmother mentioned it. I would love to see some of your work."

"It's mostly women's clothing."

"I'd still be interested to see it." He glanced back to the rest of their group. "It's time for cocktails on the poop deck, Miss Winthrop. Shall we?"

The yacht cruised back to Newport harbor during dinner and dropped anchor in the bay.

Mary Alice and Lord Tarnley took their leave early and

went back to shore in the dinghy to attend another engagement.

Oma decided to return to the poop deck to "allow my dinner time to digest," and Kitty repressed a smile, sure that her grandmother wanted to loosen that tight belt in private.

Kitty thought she had seen Oma wink at Lord Eavenlea, but she couldn't be sure. He turned to her. "Would you accompany me on a promenade of the ship?"

After a turn around the decks, they stopped at the stern of the yacht, lined with built-in upholstered benches.

Whorled clouds had gathered in the west, tinted in opalescent shades of peach and lavender, contrasting with the darker purple waters of the bay below.

"Tell me about your home, Lord Eavenlea, you've mentioned it before, Windymere?"

"Windermere." He nodded. "In southwestern England. A lovely place."

"And your parents live there now?"

He hesitated. "The duke, my father, does. My mother lives in London."

"Oh." She paused. "Is that...usual?"

His lips tightened. "It happens. They're happier apart, have been for decades."

"That must have been difficult for you."

Lord Eavenlea shrugged. "I was away at boarding school, and rarely saw my parents to begin with."

Kitty blinked, struggling to imagine such a childhood. "How old were you?"

"When I went to school? Six."

Kitty tried to envision what it must be like to say good-bye to your small son at the tender age of six and send him off to be raised by strangers.

"I can see that you're horrified, Miss Winthrop. I assure

you, it's perfectly normal in England." He smiled. "Even at home, children don't spend much time with their parents."

"Indeed?"

He shook his head. "They're in the nursery in their own wing of the house, with their nursemaid, most of the time. And then when they're old enough, they have a governess until they go to school."

"So, what does the mother do then, with all her time, if she's not raising the children?"

"She plans the menus with the cook, arranges flowers, supervises the staff. Perhaps some charitable work for the families who work on the estate."

"Sounds perfectly dreadful." Oops, she hadn't meant to be that outspoken. "Dizzy me, I'm so sorry." She groped for something additional to say. "I'm afraid I've insulted you."

Lord Eavenlea leaned closer and searched her face. "Not at all. But am I to think you ask these questions because you're trying to see if it would fit you? The life of a duchess?"

Kitty sprang to her feet. Better not encourage him. "No, not at all."

He barred her way with his arm. "Wait, Miss Winthrop, I didn't mean to offend you." He let his arm drop to the side. "I confess that I hope it's so." He smiled wistfully. "You must realize by now that I am completely captivated by you."

Oh, dear. "Thank you for a lovely evening." She avoided his eyes and set off toward the poop deck, ready to go home.

The staircase had narrow, open steps, and the crewman, Turner, went down first. Then her grandmother stopped a few steps down. "Drat, I've caught my heel."

She reached down but her tight corset and abdominal

girth prevented her from getting anywhere near her foot. "Humph." She panted, trying to stretch further.

"Hang on, ma'am." Turner climbed back toward her.

In the next instant, Oma leaned over too far and dropped like a cannonball headfirst into the water, taking the unfortunate crewman with her. She came up choking and sputtering, her wig gone, and grabbed hold of Turner, pushing him underwater in her panic.

He surfaced, gasped for air, and treaded water. "Don't struggle, ma'am, I'll help y—" Oma latched onto his neck and clutched him tightly, forcing him underwater again.

Lord Eavenlea ran down the deck and grabbed a lifebuoy ring. He tossed it toward her grandmother but only managed to hit her in the head with it. She screamed and let go of Turner, who lunged after the lifebuoy.

"Go after her," Kitty yelled to Lord Eavenlea. "She's floundering."

Lord Eavenlea retreated from her furious face and raised his hands. "I don't know how to swim."

"Is there anyone on this boat who does?"

"It's a ship, Miss Winthrop, not a boat," Lord Eavenlea said with an injured sniff. "I'll get someone."

"Unbelievable!"

Kitty wrenched off her shoes and dove over the side. In three strokes, she got one arm around her grandmother's waist. "You're fine," she said. Oma tried to climb up her body. "Let go now." When Oma didn't respond, Kitty shook her hard. "Oma, let go. I've got you."

Oma choked and nodded, going limp, her few remaining wisps of hair plastered to her skull. Turner swam over with the ring, and Oma grasped hold of it.

Together he and Kitty towed her toward the dinghy. He climbed aboard and pulled Kitty in. They each took one of

Oma's arms and somehow managed to haul all two hundred and seventy-five pounds of her into the dinghy, where she flopped like a beached whale on the floor of the boat.

"Like rolling a hippopotamus," Turner muttered under his breath.

Kitty was too exhausted to object.

"Come back up, Miss Winthrop," Lord Eavenlea called. "We need to get you dry."

"Throw me some blankets."

When the blankets had been tossed down, Kitty turned to the crewman. "Back to the dock, Turner, as quickly as you can."

He shifted his oars to row.

"Hold a minute." Kitty reached over the gunwale and grabbed something out of the water. "Here, Oma." She wrung the water out of the dripping mass of artificial hair. "Your wig." Oma barely nodded, her teeth chattering.

"Go," Kitty said. She set Oma's wig on her nearly bald head as the dinghy rowed away, and Kitty didn't look back.

WHEN THEY ARRIVED at the wharf, Kitty had the crewman call Seaside to send Oma's carriage. Once home, Fleurette took over care of Oma from Kitty, hustling her off to a hot bath. Kitty headed to her bedroom for the same thing. After a hot shower and a clean nightgown, she got into bed.

What a crazy night. The earl had been completely useless as Oma nearly drowned. As Kitty thought back over the evening, she realized the entire evening had been rather aimless. Polite conversation and not much else. Boring, actually.

But what else did she want? Or expect?

"Dizzy me," she said aloud. "Maybe Mama was right, and I'm not meant for this sort of life after all."

She sat up at the side of the bed and opened the drawer of the bedside table to retrieve the large manila envelope tucked inside.

She withdrew the application form, filled it out, placed it in the return envelope, and stamped it. In her dressing gown, she crept downstairs to the pantry and stuck it in the middle of the outgoing mail pile.

OMA CAME DOWN with a vicious cold the next morning, leaving Kitty on her own with Mama for several days.

Together they picnicked on the beach, dangled their feet off the stone pier into the ocean, searched for sea glass, and took long walks up the coast.

Today Mama drowsed under an umbrella on the sandy beach with Papa's latest letter clutched in her hand. Kitty raked the sand with the edge of a clamshell.

A ferocious rain had blown up yesterday and the day after a storm was the best time to search for sea glass. Kitty had collected quite a nice assortment in the last few weeks, but she still hadn't found a piece of the rare and elusive rose-colored glass.

"Ooh." She plucked a pale blue frosted piece of glass from the sand. "Here's a nice one."

Mama opened one eye to glance at it. "It is." She settled back on her chair. "But I declare, Kitty, you need to wear a hat," her mother said sleepily, "all your freckles are coming out."

Mama never went out on the beach without a large hat to shade her complexion.

Kitty wrinkled her nose. "Too late now. And anyway, I rather like them."

Mama smiled slyly from under the brim of her hat. "I'm sure my mother won't approve."

Kitty snorted. "Are you kidding? After she nearly drowned the other night, she thinks I walk on water."

She added the pale blue glass to the small pile of greens and browns in front of her. "And anyway, in a few more weeks, my freckles may not matter."

"What?" Mama sat up on her chair. "What does that mean?"

"Oh, just that I might have a surprise for you one of these days."

"I'm not sure I like surprises."

Kitty laughed. "You'll like this one."

"Tell me then."

"Nope." Kitty smiled at her mother. "You'll have to wait."

Then she gasped and got to her feet. A few steps away she squatted down and dug out the glass. "Look! I found one at last."

She walked to the water's edge to rinse it off. Oh, my. The rose glass had a tiny flower embossed on it, perhaps from a perfume bottle lost years ago at sea.

"Dizzy me." She handed it to her mother. "I think it's a good omen."

NINE

Things do not change; we change.

Henry David Thoreau

JULY 30, 1917

HER MOTHER'S step and attitude were light this morning, and she hummed as she entered the sunny breakfast room at Seaside. Kitty guessed the envelope in her hand had something to do with it.

"I've had another letter from your father." Mama seated herself and handed the envelope to Kitty.

The stained and battered envelope, postmarked "June 1917 Army Postal Service," had a round purple stamp on the front stating "AEF Passed and Censored."

A lump rose in her throat at the sight of her father's handwriting.

. . .

JULY 4, 1917

Darling:

Today our battalion assembled at Les Invalides, the burial place of Napoleon and a site sacred to the French people. From there, we marched through the cobblestoned streets of Paris to encourage the war-weary French.

We are the first American soldiers the people of Paris have seen. How they cheered as our regimental color guard passed by with the red, white, and blue of 'Old Glory,' mirroring the colors of their own beloved flag.

We stopped at the tomb of the Marquis de Lafayette, our own Revolutionary War hero who did so much to aid America in her fight for independence from tyranny. How wonderful to be able to do something now for the French people who aided us in our time of need.

When we arrived at the tomb, one of General Pershing's aides, Lt. Colonel Charles Stanton, spoke some moving words.

"America has joined forces with the Allied Powers, and what we have of blood and treasure are yours. Therefore, it is that with loving pride we drape the colors in tribute of respect to this citizen of your great republic. And here and now, in the presence of the illustrious dead, we pledge our hearts and our honor in carrying this war to a successful issue. Nous voilà, Lafayette! We are here!"

Oh, the cheers that went skyward from the Parisians! Vive l'Amérique! I felt privileged to be part of it today and will not soon forget the thrill of pride that went through me.

Tomorrow we begin training with a French division called Les Chasseurs Alpins, nicknamed les Diables Bleus, the Blue Devils. I hope that in person they are not quite as fearsome as their name!

I will write again as soon as I can.

All my love, always,

JACK

KITTY SWALLOWED hard and handed the letter back. "He sounds well."

"Yes, he does." Mama nodded at the pile of letters and invitations on the table. "Anything interesting?"

Kitty handed Mama the letter that had arrived from New York City yesterday. "This one looks wonderful."

Her mother pulled the slim case out of her pocket that held the half-spectacles she had taken to wearing lately. When she glanced at the return address, her eyes widened. After a quick, shocked smile at Kitty, she unfolded the letter.

Kitty waited. First, her mother's eyebrows lifted, then she gasped as astonishment stole over her fine features. "Oh, darling, how wonderful. Congratulations!"

She stood up and hugged Kitty tightly. "I'm so proud of you."

Kitty took a breath. "I still have to pass a medical examination and a dental exam. But if all's well, I'll be entering the nursing class that begins on the first of September."

"What's happening on September first?" Oma swept into the room, her Japanese morning kimono trailing behind her, and her wig askew on her head. "Anything special?"

Kitty smiled at her grandmother. "Yes, indeed, very

special." She cleared her throat. "I've been accepted into the nursing program at Bellevue Hospital."

Oma's eyes bulged, showing white all around, and her hand flew to her throat. "Is this a joke, Katharine?" She staggered back a step. "It's in very poor taste."

"It's not a joke, Oma." Kitty kept her voice gentle, aware of her grandmother's sure disappointment. "I've decided to become a nurse."

Oma frowned and grasped the back of a chair to support herself. "Where did you get such an outrageous idea?" Her daggered gaze went to Mama.

Her mother lifted her hands in the air. "I had absolutely nothing to do with it. This is all Kitty." Mama smiled. "It's completely her own idea. And I'm very proud of her."

Oma's lips tightened, and she glared at Kitty. "And you didn't think to discuss it with me first?" She pulled out a chair and sagged into it.

Kitty sat next to her grandmother. "I didn't discuss it with anyone, Oma," she said gently, "I had to make the decision alone."

"But what about all my plans for the upcoming season?" Oma wailed and wrung her hands. "Everything I've done this past spring and summer to set you up for a marvelous autumn season?"

"I'm sorry, Oma. I hate to disappoint you, and I'm ever so thankful for all you have done for me. But this is the right step for me at this time."

Her grandmother got to her feet, her face flushed and her breathing irregular. A pulse throbbed at her temple as she glared at Mama, who had quietly resumed her seat.

Oma's lips twisted in an ugly scowl. "Are you sure you haven't tried to persuade her, Evangeline?"

Kitty tried to interject. "She didn't—"

Oma raised her hand and cut Kitty off. "I'm not speaking to you, Katharine."

Her mother shook her head. "I've already told you I had nothing to do with it, Mother."

Oma stiffened, her nostrils pinched and the cords on her wrinkled neck standing out with the effort to control herself. Her lips worked furiously as she sputtered, at a loss for words.

"Well!" She drew herself up rigidly. "If you must, you must. I'm grieved and very disappointed that you didn't consult me, at least, after all I've done for you. I—" She broke off. "I'm sure you'll want to return home immediately in order to prepare. Come and say goodbye when you leave."

She hurried out, her back stiff and her chin held high.

Kitty turned to her mother. "Did she just tell us to leave?"

Her mother smiled. "She did.

TEN

A great charity carnival will be held at Coney Island, beginning next Saturday, for the benefit of the Red Cross and other war relief organizations. The affair will be staged in the Sea Beach Palace on Surf Avenue.

The New York Times, Sunday, July 22, 1917

KITTY CAREFULLY FOLDED the student nurse uniforms laid out on the bed and tucked them into the suitcase.

She had five blue and white pinstriped cotton dresses, with long full sleeves and detachable white cuffs and collars. A full-length bibbed white apron went over this, and of these, she had ten because the handbook suggested that frequent changes of apron might be required.

Jenny came into the bedroom, out of breath after climbing the stairs with the basket of Kitty's freshly washed and dried unmentionables. "I dinna ken what we're going to do without ye around the house, Kitty."

Kitty tucked the last apron into her valise. "You'll keep Mama company, for one thing. It's been so difficult for her without Papa."

"Aye, it has." Jenny set the basket down and unloaded the contents. "The dear boy. I pray for him every night. Does he know about ye goin' to school now?"

"I've written to him about it but...we haven't had a letter in a while."

She knew Mama lived in fear of something happening to Papa, but she staunchly refused to search the newspaper's daily listing of those missing in action or killed in battle in France.

Kitty sighed and packed her underwear. "I hope we hear from him soon. For Mama's sake."

"Och, he'll be so proud of ye. As I am."

"Thank you, Jenny. I'll miss you, too."

Mama entered then, with her hands full of assorted oddments. "I've some stationery for you and stamps. A little sewing kit. A new can of tooth powder." She laid them on the desk. "And some sachets I made with lavender from the garden."

Kitty lifted one of the gauze bags to her nose and inhaled the spicy floral scent. "Mmm. Thank you, Mama. To remind me of home."

"Yes." Her mother smiled. "And tomorrow's your last day home. I'm free of all my church duties to spend it with you. Although, I have a fair idea of what you'd like to do." She smiled at Kitty. "Coney Island?"

"Coney Island!"

They said it at the same time and burst out laughing.

Ever since she'd been a small child, that famous amusement park had been her favorite place.

They usually went at least twice every summer to see the new rides and attractions because Coney Island changed constantly, and you never knew what you'd find when you returned.

"It's settled then," her mother said. "Coney Island it is."

THE NEXT MORNING dawned clear and balmy, and they took the Sea Beach subway train express to Coney Island from the 59th Street station.

When they walked onto Surf Avenue, Kitty stood still and let the wave that was Coney Island roll over her. The shrill cries of seagulls overhead, the screams of people on the thrilling rides, the rumble of the wooden roller coasters, the piping organ music of the carousels.

And over all that, the delicious smell of hot dogs, grilled clams, and buttered popcorn mingling with the scent of burnt sugar and salt-tinged air.

Mama had an amused smile on her pretty face, shaded as usual by a large picture hat. "What would you like to do first?"

"The babies, Mama. I don't know why, but I always have to see the babies first."

The baby exhibit was off Surf Avenue, not far from the train terminal. The billboard over the door proclaimed:

Infant Incubators with Living Infants!

BELOW that an even larger sign announced:

All the World Loves a Baby!

It certainly seemed true. The lengthy line of eager customers waiting for entrance included schoolgirls with their hair in pigtails, elderly matrons, well-dressed married couples, and workmen in canvas pants. But the line moved quickly, and they soon paid their twenty-five cents admission fee to enter.

The spacious and airy, white-painted room was scrupulously clean. The incubators, glass and steel boxes on metal legs and mounted to the wall, lined the perimeter.

An iron guardrail separated the babies from the public, but many visitors leaned over this to get a closer look at the tiny infants.

A pipe connected to each box sent cleaned and warmed air into the incubators. Small cards above held the baby's initials, date of birth, and other information.

The infants were swaddled, but here and there a tiny face or fingers peeped out. The babies were attended by nurses in starched uniforms and white caps.

Mama nodded at the nurses, who moved quietly and confidently about their duties. "Just think, Kitty, that could be you in a few years."

"Yes. It's exciting to think about it. Look, the nurse is taking one out." Kitty crowded close to the rail.

The nurse smiled and opened the glass door to retrieve a tiny bundle with black hair. She wrapped another blanket around the baby and sat down in a rocker with a small glass bottle of milk for her feeding.

When the nurse finished, she held the baby up so they

could see the tiny sleeping face and eyelashes that lay like stars against the baby's cheeks. "This is Betsy," the nurse said.

"She looks perfect." Kitty marveled at how small the infant was. "Look at her tiny ears and nose."

"I could fit her into the palm of my hand," a natty gentleman next to Mama said. He lifted his hand and spread his fingers. "Amazing work Dr. Couney does here. There he is now."

A tall, distinguished man in a suit and white doctor's coat entered the room. He had a shock of black hair, a walrus mustache, and horn-rimmed glasses on his long nose. He smiled at the room of visitors.

"Good morning to you all." He nodded at the incubators. "Come to see my babies, have you? Does anyone have a question?"

Kitty raised her hand. "What's the smallest baby you've taken care of, Doctor?"

He smiled. "Excellent question. One pound, ten ounces."

The crowd gasped.

He shook his head. "Unfortunately, that baby did not survive. But we gave him a chance, and every day, we're learning new things about taking care of these little ones."

"Why do you have the babies here at Coney Island?" the gent next to Mama asked.

Dr. Couney smiled faintly. "Because no other hospital at this time is willing to try to save these infants. By charging you good folks a small fee, I'm able to provide superior medical care gratis. The parents don't have to pay a penny."

Heads nodded in approval.

"Where do you get your nurses from, Dr. Couney?" Kitty noted that all the nurses wore a different white cap.

"From right here in New York and accredited schools all over the country. They have extensive specialized training to care for these babies. We have very strict criteria for their treatment."

A pug-nosed schoolgirl standing with her mother waved her hand back and forth.

"Yes?" Dr. Couney smiled at her.

"Where do you get the eggs for the incubators?"

There were a few snorts of laughter and then a smiling silence while everyone waited for Dr. Couney to answer.

"Ahem," the doctor said. He winked at the girl and lifted an eyebrow at her mother. "I believe that's a question for your mother to answer later, my dear."

He glanced at the people waiting their turn at the entrance. "And now, good people," he said, "I must ask you to move along so that our other visitors may come through."

Once outside in the sunshine, Kitty linked arms with her mother as they strolled further down Surf Avenue, the main thoroughfare, crowded with people, concessions, food vendors, and barkers trying to lure people to their booth or show.

"Three balls for a dime. Just one thin dime! Step right up, ladies and gents, take a toss!"

"Right this way, sirs and ladies, next show starts in three minutes! See the Snake Lady, the Lizard man, and Ajax, the Arabian sword swallower. And here he is, here he is, c'mon out, Ajax, and give 'em a taste!"

A hulking oriental man in baggy silk trousers and a scarlet turban stepped out and bowed deeply.

"C'mon, folks, get closer so you don't miss a thing!"

Ajax brandished a wicked-looking sword and waved it

around his head, giving the crowd a good view of his brawny chest and impressive bicep muscles. Then he touched it to a small open brazier, and the blade burst into flame.

With one smooth movement, he tipped his head back and swallowed the sword to the hilt as the crowd gasped. Then he swiftly removed the still flaming weapon, blew it out, and disappeared behind the flap.

"It's all in here, folks, just ten cents, show's about to start, let's go!"

They continued down the avenue, passing the Ring the Cane game, a shooting gallery, and a fortune-teller.

Kitty stopped in front of Feltman's. "Let's get a hot dog and ride the carousel, Mama."

They got their ten-cent hot dogs, piled them high with mustard and onions, and entered the pavilion to eat them and watch the riders.

The three-story pavilion that housed the carousel allowed sunlight to pour through its high arched windows and illuminate the triple rows of magnificently carved wooden horses with flowing manes and flaring nostrils. Gold and silver leaf accented the jeweled tones of sapphire, emerald, and ruby paint that adorned them.

Wreaths of carved and painted roses circled the necks of some, while others had "jewels" set into their bridles and trappings.

Hundreds of colored lights ran along the concentric circles of the roof supports, the perimeter of the canopy, the support poles, and the rounding board, and reflected in the multiple mirrors set amid the gaily painted scenes set in roundels that adorned the inside frieze. And over all this, rang out the gay calliope music, of which Feltman's was the loudest in all of Coney.

They paid their fare and found their horses, a wild

prancer for Kitty on the outside row and next to her, a more sedate mare for Mama. Soon all the horses had been claimed and the carousel began to turn. The organ launched into a familiar tune, *Flying Trapeze*.

One of the carousel workers swung the long bodkin loaded with steel rings into place for the riders on the outside row to try to grab. Somewhere inside the bodkin, the elusive brass ring lay hidden.

Kitty launched into the chorus, and Mama joined in, laughing.

Everyone who knew the words sang along. As the carousel rotated and the calliope played on, Kitty stretched as tall as she could with all her might each time they passed the bodkin.

"Be careful, Kitty. You're going to fall."

"I have to try, Mama. You never know, I might get it."

The calliope went into the final verse of the song. She had one last chance. As the platform rotated one last time past the bodkin, she stood on her tiptoes, feeling the joints in her shoulders protest, and reached as far as she could. And she did it! She plucked a ring off the bodkin. When the carousel stopped, Kitty held up the steel ring for Mama to see.

"Alas, not a brass one."

Mama smiled. "But precious just the same."

Kitty tucked it into her pocket. "I'm going to keep it as a souvenir."

Arm in arm, they continued down Surf Avenue until Kitty stopped before a portrait studio. "Let's get our picture taken, Mama, for a souvenir of today."

They made their way into the studio to choose between dozens of backdrops and prop settings, including an antique sleigh with a pennant of Coney Island across the front, a motor car, a background with stars and a huge crescent moon with a cheery face to sit on, a boat with ocean waves as a backdrop, a canoe with fishing poles, and so many more.

They settled for one that featured a gaily striped hot air balloon with Kitty and Mama in the wicker basket holding fast to the ropes.

Then they went on to have dinner at Stauch's with all Kitty's favorites: grilled clams, corn on the cob, and root beer.

"I'm stuffed, Kitty." Mama covered her mouth to burp and giggled. "My goodness. What next?"

"I thought about the Steeplechase but..."

Mama shook her finger at Kitty. "Oh, no, you don't. I'm not going through that."

Kitty laughed. She had been eleven the last time she and Papa had gone on the Steeplechase Race.

Patrons entered through the Barrel of Fun, which tossed them every which way. Once they regained their feet, she and Papa boarded their mechanical horse, Kitty riding behind, and joined the race around the huge pavilion through the fast dips and turns of the mechanical track, across a miniature lake, and through a tunnel to the finish line.

But the most fun came as they exited the ride through the Pavilion of Fun's Insanitarium and Blowhole theatre, greeted by midgets dressed as clowns and armed with slap-sticks to prod them on their way out.

Then, when distracted by the clowns, a blast of air from a concealed blowhole had knocked Papa's hat off and sent Kitty's skirts flying above her head.

All this had been observed and wildly cheered by the

audience below, themselves recent victims of the same shenanigans.

And Mama had seen it all. "You'll never get me on that stage."

"Of course, you're correct, Mama. Now that I'm a young lady, I don't care to have my dress blasted above my head, either."

They strolled down the long wharf that stretched out into Lower New York Bay. The sky behind the New York skyline had turned gold and flaming orange as the sun said good night, and they sat on a bench to take it in.

Kitty sighed. "I couldn't have asked for a more wonderful day, Mama." She leaned over and kissed her mother's cheek. "Thank you."

Mama smiled. "I've enjoyed it immensely, too."

A fish jumped and snapped at an insect before falling back into the sea. They watched the rings of its reentry widen then disappear.

From the Steeplechase ballroom, the faint music, horns, and drums, of *Over There* swept over the water. They listened silently to the popular tune.

JOHNNIE GET YOUR GUN, *get your gun, get your gun,*
　　Take it on the run, on the run, on the run;
　　Hear them calling you and me;
　　Every son of liberty.
　　Hurry right away, no delay, go today,
　　Make your daddy glad, to have had such a lad,
　　Tell your sweetheart not to pine,
　　To be proud her boy's in line
　　Then Kitty softly sang the chorus:
　　Over there, over there,

Send the word, send the word over there,
That the Yanks are coming, the Yanks are coming,
The drums rum-tumming everywhere.
So prepare, say a prayer,
Send the word, send the word to beware,
We'll be over, we're coming over,
And we won't come back till it's over over there.
Johnnie get your gun, get your gun, get your gun,
Johnnie show the Hun, you're a son-of-a-gun,
Hoist the flag and let her fly,
Yankee Doodle do or die.
Pack your little kit, show your grit, do your bit,
Soldiers to the ranks from the towns and the tanks,
Make your mother proud of you,
And to liberty be true.

MAMA GAZED out over the water. "I wish it were over now."

"I know." Kitty laid her hand over her mother's and gave it a gentle squeeze.

Mama sighed. "It's all I think about, from the moment I wake up until I go to bed.

Wondering what he's doing. Hoping he's all right."

Kitty nodded.

"And every time I hear or read about a battle and Americans dying, my heart spasms so painfully." She put a hand to her chest. "I never knew how much it would hurt to have him gone like this. I'm only half a person without him."

Kitty put her arm around her mother and leaned close, cheek to cheek. "I'm sure he thinks of you constantly. As a matter of fact, I know he can't help but think of you." She sat up. "I have a confession to make."

"Oh?"

"Remember the first time we went to your mother's house?"

Mama nodded.

"And the photograph of you in the celadon gown?"

She nodded again; her head tipped to one side with a wry smile.

"After you left the room, I slipped it out of the frame and put it in my pocket."

"Really?"

"Yes. I wanted it. And you said your mother never went in the study, so I didn't think she'd miss it. And then, when Papa left that night in June, I slipped it to him upstairs."

Kitty swallowed, remembering. "He kissed it and put it in his cap. He said every time he took it off, there you'd be, waiting for him."

"Oh, Kitty, that was so sweet. I'm glad he has it." Her voice took on a faraway tone. "I wore that gown the night he sneaked into the Patriarchs Ball to find me. My mother couldn't be there that evening. But she had my maid Claudine lay out the gown I was to wear, a horrid yellow silk with big tassels on the skirt." She wrinkled her nose.

"Was it a Charles Worth gown?"

"Yes."

"I didn't think Worth could make an ugly gown."

"Well, this one was. And the color. Ugh." Her mother shivered. "Canary yellow."

"So, you didn't wear it."

Mama smiled. "No. For the first time in my life, I defied my mother and wore the celadon silk. And your father came to the ball in white tie and tails. Oh, he was so handsome I could hardly breathe. Heads turned." She smiled crookedly at Kitty.

"Please go on." This peek into her mother's past had Kitty charmed and beguiled.

"He told me that I'd never looked so beautiful." Her mother's eyes shone at the memory. "And then we danced. Just one glorious dance, because my mother showed up then."

"And what happened?"

"I couldn't let her see us together. We separated, and he slipped away." Then she smiled. "That was the night I knew I was in love with him."

They sat in the warm silence as waves lapped gently at the pier.

Mama turned toward her. "Kitty, you've never said why you changed your mind about the social scene. Will you tell me now?"

Kitty faced her mother in the waning sunlight. "There isn't much to tell. You were absolutely right. It's a shallow, artificial world."

She sighed. "It was fun at first. Oma indulged me in every way possible. But after a while, it all seemed pointless. The same niceties over and over, the same boring conversations."

She winced as Mrs. Oehlrichs' and Mrs. Vanderfelder's callous comments came to mind. "Sometimes people were cruel."

"I'm sorry you had to experience that, dear." Mama touched Kitty's cheek.

Kitty nestled against her mother and leaned her head on Mama's shoulder. "Why is it that young people can't take advice? I should have listened to you."

Mama laughed. "I do think you must find out for yourself. Julius Caesar said 'most people learn more by doing something than reading about it. Experience is the best teacher.' But someday you'll learn how difficult it is to allow your children to experience those experiences."

"I'm sorry I caused you grief. But I mean to make you proud. Wait and see."

Mama stroked Kitty's cheek. "I'm already proud of you, Kitty, now and always. Always remember that."

ELEVEN

To acquire not only the practical, but also the theoretical groundwork of her profession, a woman must devote three of the best years of her life to special preparation and to obtaining a thorough understanding of the principles of nursing.

Nursing Ethics, Isabel Hampton Robb, 1917

AUGUST 31, 1917

KITTY STEPPED out of the hansom cab before the wrought iron gates of Bellevue Hospital.

Her mother leaned out of the cab window. "Are you sure you don't want me to come in with you?" She gazed up at the imposing brick building.

"I'm sure, Mama. I must do it on my own."

"Let it be so then." Her mother smiled at her. "I'm very proud of you, sweetheart."

"But I haven't accomplished anything yet, Mama. I have three months of probation before it's even determined whether I'm deemed able to enter the nursing program."

"I'm proud of you just the same. And I have no doubt that you will be accepted into the program." She smiled. "Be off now. Write when you can."

Kitty leaned into the carriage window and kissed her mother's soft cheek. "I will."

Her mother fluttered her handkerchief from the window until the cab rounded a corner and disappeared.

Kitty picked up her valise and stepped off the curb behind another young woman with blazing red hair who hurried several steps in front of her.

A dark-haired young man with eyes black as raisins sped by the redheaded girl on a bicycle. "*Buongiorno, testarossa!*" He gave her hair a swipe as he passed.

The girl dropped her bag and picked up a stone. "And good morning to you, ye wee eejit!"

Swift as light she threw the stone and knocked the boy's hat off. An impassioned spew of liquid syllables issued from the boy's mouth as he stopped and circled back to retrieve his hat.

The girl picked up another stone, bigger this time.

"Off with ye now, ye maggot!" She raised her fist and the angry expression slid off his face, replaced by downcast eyes.

"*Mi diaspiace, signorina.*" He bowed low. "*Sei troppo bella!*" Then he jumped back on his bicycle, flashed a cheeky grin full of white teeth, and sped off.

Kitty laughed out loud, delighted, and the girl turned.

She was lovely, with eyes like silvery blue ice, and a sprinkling of freckles across her nose.

"My, you certainly took care of him," Kitty said. She held out her free hand. "I'm Kitty Winthrop."

"Top o' the morning to ye, Kitty. I'm Annabelle Boyle." Her grip was firm, her fingers strong.

"What was that he said to you? *Testarossa?*"

Annabelle tossed her head. "Redhead. Trying to insult me." She shrugged. "I've heard everything you can imagine. Matchhead. Ginger knob. Carrot top. I'm used to it. As ye must be." Annabelle's gaze went to Kitty's hair.

Kitty chuckled. "A boy in my class called me lava head once. I hope you're here to register as a nursing student, Annabelle, because I'd certainly like to know you better."

Annabelle cracked a smile that stretched her cheeks wide. "Aye, we redheads have to stick together, don't we?"

She linked her free arm through Kitty's, and together they walked through the iron gates to the main entrance of Bellevue.

An hour later, she and Annabelle had registered with ninety-eight other probationers and been assigned rooms in Osborn Hall, the six-story nurses' residence on East 26th Street that occupied an entire city block.

A modest portal admitted them into a spacious foyer, divided by square oak pillars into two sections. A golden-hued wallpaper of satiny texture covered the walls and gave an impression of luminous light.

Wide doors of glass topped with glass fanlights formed the entire left wall, and through this a staircase led up to the immense dining room, paneled in oak wainscoting.

According to the little Guide to Osborn Hall that the students had been given, the frieze above the paneling had been done by Maxfield Parrish, with groups of poplar trees, winding rivers, and grassy hillocks.

On this same floor stood a large ballroom, with waxed floors ready for the next special occasion.

Through tall French doors, a wide balcony extended from the ballroom, large enough for tea tables. It overlooked an enclosed courtyard rose garden, and the heady perfume of its red, pink, and white blooms reached them where they stood.

The halls of each floor widened at intervals to form cozy sitting nooks and window seats that invited chats and confidences.

A "kitchenette" on each floor enabled one to make a cup of tea or iron a dress, and the living rooms were bright and airy with white woodwork and chintz upholstery and draperies.

Kitty's room on the fifth floor had a fine view of Brooklyn across the East River when she lifted the roller shade.

The narrow cubicle held a white enameled bed, a dresser with mirror, a corner writing desk, and a chair.

The radiator stood underneath the single window, and there were hooks for pictures on the walls which were covered in a pretty chintz pattern of roses and violets that matched the draperies at the window.

A knock sounded at the door. "Hey, *Testarossa!*" Annabelle's red head peered around the door.

"Come in," Kitty said, "but you're *Testarossa*, not me."

Annabelle flopped onto Kitty's bed and propped her feet on the footboard. "I'll be T1, and you'll be T2. How about that?" She sat up. "You did notice that we are the only two redheads in the class?"

"I didn't, actually. I was too busy listening to Miss Trent reading us the rules and telling us what they expect of us."

She plucked the sheaf of papers off the writing desk. "Ethics, Household Economics, Food Selection, Cookery." She wrinkled her nose. "That should be enlightening. I only know how to boil an egg and make coffee."

She read on. "Chemistry, Hygiene, Anatomy and Physiology, *Materia Medica*—Drugs and Solutions, Nursing Practice and Theory."

She heaved a great sigh. "Dizzy me, we'll have to keep our noses to the grindstone to get through all of this. And I declare, you don't seem the least bit worried, T_1."

"I'm not. That's why we're here, aye?" She jumped up. "And we don't have to start until tomorrow. Isn't this a gorgeous place to live? They've thought of everything, and I've heard there's even a garden on the roof. Let's go look."

Probationers of all shapes and sizes milled about the building. Most were going downstairs to investigate the libraries, dining hall, and reception rooms that had been provided for them, but Annabelle took the stairs up instead with Kitty behind.

"Oh!" They gasped in unison as they stepped out onto the roof, for it didn't resemble a roof in the least. Cedar pergolas as large as a dining room were stationed in different areas, covered with a profusion of clematis and wisteria vines, with lattice screens that created leafy bowers to sit and relax in.

Tubs of evergreens ran along the roofline against a decorative wrought iron railing, and there were pots of cheerful pansies, snapdragons, and ivy everywhere.

Benches were tucked here and there among the greenery and over all the clear blue September sky stretched to the horizon.

"How lovely," Kitty said. "I never expected anything like this."

The roof door opened behind them, and a tall blonde raw-boned young woman stepped out. "Ahh." She closed her eyes and took a deep lungful of air. "Peace and quiet."

Then she opened her eyes. "Pardon me, but all the commotion downstairs was getting the best of me. I'm Maisie McCloud." Then she grinned and Kitty liked her instantly. "But you can call me Moose."

She strode over and gave each of them a firm handshake, her hands as big as a man's.

"My goodness, that's an apt nickname, Moose." Annabelle looked Moose up and down. "You must be six feet tall."

"Six and one." She grinned again. "But you should see my two brothers. They're all of six and a half."

The three wandered over the garden, examined the flowers, and settled in one of the pergolas.

"So where are you two from?" Moose folded her tall frame into a wicker chair. "I hail from Millbrook, New York. My father's a dairy farmer, and I've got two brothers and three sisters."

"I can top that," Annabelle said. "I've got seven brothers and sisters, and one of them is my identical twin."

Kitty laughed. "You both top me. I'm an only child. From Brooklyn."

"I'm Brooklyn, too." Annabelle smiled. "So, we're neighbors."

Other probationers had found their way to the roof garden, and more students introduced themselves.

Maria Tonelli, a pretty brunette with big dark eyes, was from Queens. Florence Emminger, a fast-talking blonde from Tonawanda, New York. And Ruth Horton, a petite black-haired girl with an unexpectedly booming laugh, from Poughkeepsie.

"So," Florence said, "are we ready to be probationers?"

They all nodded.

"We only have to survive three months of classes and learn to take orders," Ruth said. "My older sister graduated last year, and she said the hardest part was waiting to see if she'd be admitted to the nursing program."

"We have to prove our worth, I suppose," Kitty said. "And according to the rule book, 'adhere to a strict code of decorum.'"

Florence stood and withdrew a slim volume from her pocket. "Nurses are to be unfailingly kind and patient in caring for the sick and helpless, willing to perform all duties conducive to their welfare and comfort."

A wicked smile crept over her face. "The nurse is reminded that while a relaxation from the formality of hospital etiquette is desirable for rest and recreation, nevertheless levity and boisterousness will not be tolerated."

The girls broke into laughter at the stern expression on Florence's face. She shook her finger at them and went on. "She must be prompt and regular in attendance at class. At least one hour per day must be spent in study."

"That shouldn't be too difficult," Maria said. "Have you seen the library in the residence? It's beautiful."

"Ahem." Florence fixed each of them with a steely eye. "Gentlemen whom the nurse's family considers acceptable acquaintances for her may call at the Residence during ordinary visiting hours. Under no circumstances are male visitors allowed in the nurse's rooms. Immediate expulsion from school will result from behavior of this type."

"No worries there." Annabelle rolled her eyes. "We're going to be too busy to do anything but class and work."

Kitty checked her watch. "It's nearly six. Now we'll find out what the food is like."

THE FOLLOWING twelve weeks were the busiest of Kitty's life. Up at five, breakfast at six, class from seven until eleven, lunch, then five hours on the wards, dusting, mopping, sweeping, and washing dishes. And doing anything the head nurse or physicians asked them to do without question.

By the time they met at six for dinner, it was all she could to spend the requisite hour in study before falling into bed and waking up to do it all over again.

But it was worth it on the evening of Friday, November 30, when the probationers assembled on the stage in Bellevue's small auditorium.

The group of students had shrunk to sixty-three, but Kitty's group of friends remained the same with the exception of Maria Tonelli, who had decided, in her own words, that she'd rather "marry and raise a brood of *bambinos*."

The audience rustled with anticipation. Kitty found her mother in the crowd and waved. Miss Henrietta Hayes, the Superintendent of Nurses, came to the podium, and the capping ceremony began.

The students, in a dignified line, one by one approached Miss Hayes, who pinned the Bellevue nurse's cap, affectionately known as the "Bellevue Fluff," over their hair.

It was made of pleated white organdy with a tiny ruffle at the bottom, and every student nurse wore a broad smile as they returned to their places. Upon successful completion of their studies, a black velvet ribbon would be added above the frill to signify the student had graduated and was now recognized as a trained nurse.

The students picked up the candles under each seat and waited as a candle passed down to light it. Then, holding the lighted candles, the students solemnly together recited the Florence Nightingale Pledge.

I solemnly pledge myself before God and in the presence of this assembly to pass my life in purity and to practice my profession faithfully.

I shall abstain from whatever is deleterious and mischievous, and shall not take or knowingly administer any harmful drug.

I shall do all in my power to maintain and elevate the standard of my profession and will hold in confidence all personal matters committed to my keeping and all family affairs coming to my knowledge in the practice of my calling.

With loyalty will I endeavor to aid the physician in his work, and devote myself to the welfare of those committed to my care.

"CONGRATULATIONS TO YOU ALL," Miss Hayes announced. "Light refreshments will now be served in the dining room."

A round of applause went up for the students, and then they were free to find their families.

"Kitty, darling." Mama hurried towards her with arms wide open. "Oh, how proud I am of you."

They embraced, and Kitty let out a long breath in the shelter of her mother's arms. "Thank you. I've made it through the first part, at least."

"I have no doubt you will complete the course you've

set for yourself." Mama kissed Kitty's cheek. "Papa would be so proud."

TWELVE

The face should be trained never to show a trace of anxiety or alarm, no matter how grave the occasion; no surprise should be expressed even by so much as the lifting of an eyebrow.

Nursing Ethics, Isabel Hampton Robb, 1917

NOW CLASSES ON ANTISEPTICS, bacteriology, and instruction on bandaging and dressings alternated with twelve-hour shifts on the various wards, beginning with the medical floor. The first two weeks had gone well.

Kitty had adapted to the new schedule and found she enjoyed taking care of the older patients.

On the first day of the third week, they had been on duty a quarter of an hour when cries of distress emanated from a low iron bed in a corner of the ward.

Elderly Mr. Johnson sat up and scrabbled through his mussed bedclothes. "Oh dear, oh dear, I've lost it." He raked his hands through his hair, setting his white curls on end. "It must have fallen under the bed. Oh, dear, oh, dear!"

"Can I help you, Mr. Johnson?" Kitty laid a gentle hand on his scrawny shoulder, feeling the thinness of his frame under the cotton pajamas. "What have you lost, sir? Perhaps I can assist you."

"Oh, oh, oh." He wrung his hands. "It must be under the bed. I have to find it."

Kitty untied her pinafore, unpinned her nurse's cap, and set them on the patient's bedside stand. Then she got down on her hands and knees.

It had taken nearly an hour to starch and iron her uniform and white pinafore before reporting for duty this evening, and already the shift had taken its toll on her uniform.

She sighed and poked her head under the bed. "What am I looking for, Mr. Johnson?"

The bedsprings above her head creaked with the patient's frantic movements and a bare foot with horny toenails dropped down next to her.

"Stay in bed, sir. I'll find it. But what am I looking for?"

The foot disappeared but there was still no answer, only Mr. Johnson's repeated exclamations of distress. Kitty grimaced and flattened her body to slide her upper torso into the dim recesses under the bed.

Aside from a few dust balls, nothing else emerged from the darkness. Someone on the day shift hadn't done a thorough job of dusting. Gingerly, she felt around with both her hands.

"I don't see anything under here, Mr. Johnson." She sneezed violently twice.

"I know it's under there." His voice quavered. "It must have rolled into the corner."

Kitty groaned. There was no help for it. She reached her hand to the bed leg and pulled herself the rest of the way under the bed, holding her breath. She patted her hand around the floor again and came up empty.

"It would help if I knew what I was looking for, Mr. Johnson."

She tried to keep the irritation out of her voice as her hand touched something round and hard and cold. She picked it up, turned it over, then recoiled and let out a muffled shriek. The back of her head hit the mattress boards so hard she saw stars.

A glass eye glared back at her in the gloom, the blue iris surrounded completely by bright white. She nearly dropped it again but managed to wriggle herself out backward from underneath the bed.

She pushed herself to her feet and brushed dust and cobwebs off her uniform. "Well, dizzy me," she said. She gave several vociferous sneezes. "Is this what you were looking for?"

Mr. Johnson snatched the artificial eye from her palm. "That's it!" He rubbed the eye on his nightclothes, gave it a lick, and popped it in. "Thank you, nurse."

Kitty gagged and turned away as Annabelle paused by the bed. "And what mischief have you got yourself into now, Kitty?"

She peered closer and plucked a cobweb off Kitty's uniform. "For sure and you look like you've been diggin' in the garden."

"You don't want to know." Kitty shuddered. That glass eye was sure to appear in her dreams tonight. "And what about you?"

Annabelle wrinkled her nose. "Moose asked me to help get one of her patients on the commode. But she forgot to put the pot back in after the last patient, and I didn't notice it until it was too late."

"Oh, no." Maisie "Moose" McCloud had a heart of gold but lacked a certain something in the common-sense department.

"Aye." Annabelle nodded. "Poop and pee be goin' every which way." She tapped the bucket she carried, stuffed with stained rags. "What a kerfuffle. Moose shrieked and froze on the spot. Good thing Miss Trent was nowhere nearby. For sure and Moose would've been dismissed."

"Miss Winthrop, Miss Boyle!" A stern voice barked behind them.

The aforementioned Miss Trent loomed up beside them, her steel spectacles balanced precariously on her long nose. "What are you doing here, lollygagging?" Her eyes widened as she took in the sorry state of Kitty's blue and white striped uniform. "You should be ashamed of yourself, Miss Winthrop, to appear on the ward in such a state. And where are your cap and apron?"

Mr. Johnson spoke up. "She was helping me, nurse. I couldn't find my glass eye."

He tapped it, and Kitty shuddered.

"It rolled under the bed."

"I had to crawl under it, Miss Trent. I will go and change at once."

"See that you do."

Behind Miss Trent's back, Annabelle rolled her eyes, and Kitty suppressed a giggle.

At the end of the long line of beds, a doctor bent over the foot of a patient. He regarded her as she walked the length of the ward, a tiny smile at the edges of his mouth.

She hadn't seen him on the ward before and my, he was quite handsome. The tiny smile widened into a grin, and she abruptly focused her gaze on the windows at the end of the room, marching with a determined air.

He stood as she passed and held out his hand. "Samuel Hayden." He gave a slight bow.

Kitty blinked. Doctors didn't usually speak with student nurses unless there was an order to be given. And they certainly didn't introduce themselves, occupying some rarefied region high above the students' heads.

"Um, Katharine Winthrop."

He smiled down at her in a friendly fashion. He had a classically handsome face, with a strong square chin, a straight nose, and pale skin that set off his blue eyes. But a thin jagged scar ran underneath his left eye, down along the line of his jaw, and curved up to meet his lower lip.

"Buggy whip." He shrugged.

Heat surged into Kitty's face. "Pardon me." She averted her face. Hopefully, Miss Trent wasn't observing this. Kitty turned slightly to check.

"Oh, she's gone. You're safe, for now." His blue eyes held a twinkle in them.

"I must go." She hurried away as quickly as she could.

"Hsssst."

Kitty turned as Annabelle caught up with her. "Sure, and what was that, missy?" She gave Kitty an impish smile. "Speaking with the doctors now?"

"He stopped me, not the other way around."

"But he's handsome, isn't he?" Annabelle fell into step with her. "Better not let Miss Trent catch you."

"Better not let Miss Trent catch *you* out here with me, T1."

Kitty opened the door and couldn't resist sneaking a quick look over her shoulder at Dr. Hayden. He stood where she had left him, smiling back at her.

THE NEXT AFTERNOON Kitty waited somberly with the other fifteen students in her group outside the door marked "Morgue."

The basement level of Bellevue always felt chill and clammy and several of the girls clasped their arms around themselves tightly.

"I hope I can do this." A frown marred Annabelle's pretty face.

"It's no worse than seeing a cow butchered," Moose said cheerfully.

"I've never seen a cow butchered. Or anything else, for that matter." Annabelle sighed. "I wish we could get this over."

"Nancy Thornton fainted dead away when her group watched it." Florence nodded her head. "She withdrew right after. And Nora Parks threw up on Miss Trent's feet."

The girls giggled at this.

"Maybe that's why they have us watch one," Moose said, "to see how strong our stomachs are. What do you think, Kitty?"

"I think my stomach is growling because I didn't eat breakfast. Didn't want to take a chance on getting sick like Nora."

"Oh, dear." Florence gulped and turned pale. "I did eat. Pancakes, eggs, and sausage."

"You'll be fine, Flo." Moose clapped a large hand on Florence's shoulder. "Think about what we've been learning in anatomy."

Miss Trent came around the corner then, the heels of her shoes clicking briskly on the tile floor. "Ah, you're all here. Good."

The students parted to let her through, and she turned at the door. "Hold your noses if you must. But I sincerely hope everyone's behavior and attention today will be exemplary."

With that, she opened the steel door, led them through a small office, and on into a large room, tiled all in white from ceiling to floor. Many small doors stacked on top of each other in rows filled one wall. A long table, tilted up at one end and topped with a marble slab, stood in the center of the room.

On the table lay an obese male body, its face covered with a small cloth. Curly brown hair fell away at the sides of it.

Several of the girls gulped and averted their eyes from the man's private parts. Kitty pressed her lips together. Although she'd never seen a naked man, she knew from Anatomy class what to expect, so she merely redirected her attention to the short plump man with a pencil mustache and a tiny, forked beard who stood at the end of the table and greeted them, scalpel in hand.

"Good morning, mademoiselles," he said, in French-accented English. "I am Dr. Bonnaire."

He took his place on the far side of the corpse, while the group of students stood backed against the wall, as far as possible from the table.

Dr. Bonnaire waved his scalpel. "Come closer, s'il vous plait."

Reluctantly, Kitty and the other girls shuffled closer, looking grim.

"Don't be afraid." He grinned. "He can't hurt you. He's dead."

There were a few nervous giggles, and Miss Trent frowned.

"You must ask any questions you have. This is how we learn, *n'est-ce pas?*"

Some of the girls nodded their heads.

"First, we examine the body. This is a fifty-six-year-old male, admitted for a hemorrhage from the esophagus, who died twelve hours ago. We autopsy to learn what caused his death."

He pointed the scalpel to a round, lumpy scar at the side of the neck. "This is an old, healed burn. This patient sustained many injuries over the course of his life. See these scars?" He indicated several on the hands and arms. "He worked hard with his hands."

No one answered, their eyes fixated on the shining blade. Behind Kitty, someone cleared their throat, and several of the girls were breathing rapidly.

"Now we begin," Dr. Bonnaire said.

He made a swift Y-shaped incision across the top of the chest and repeated it across the lower abdomen. Behind Kitty, someone gasped. Then the scalpel flashed again and cut a long incision joining the first two. He put the scalpel down, and peeled back the two edges of the incision, using the scalpel to dissect away the muscles, exposing the ribs.

Next to her, Florence choked and fled the room.

There was a two-inch-thick layer of yellow fat below the skin. Funny, Kitty had always thought the fat on a person would be white. This was yellow, like chicken fat.

There was very little blood. Probably related to the hemorrhage the patient had sustained. Then it occurred to her that without a beating heart, there wouldn't be much blood at all.

Dr. Bonnaire next took an instrument like a small pair of pruning shears. Kitty knew from her time in Surgical Sterilization that it was a rib cutter.

"Before we can examine the organs, we must remove the rib cage."

He leaned over the body and carefully cut through the ribs on one side of the chest, each cut emitting a crunching noise as the sharp curved blades went through the bone. Then he repeated the same action on the other side. Carefully, he lifted off the rib cage and sternum in one piece and laid it on the table.

Annabelle gulped and breathed heavily through her nose. Kitty found her hand and squeezed it. "Hang on," she whispered under her breath.

Dr. Bonnaire peeled back a whitish film covering the organs like a lacy curtain. "The omentum," he said.

Now the viscera were exposed.

One by one, he pointed each organ out and then removed it. With quick cuts of the scalpel, he removed the esophagus and trachea. Then he severed the stomach, laid it on the table, and opened it to examine its contents.

A vile odor rose from the half-digested contents, and Annabelle gagged, dropped Kitty's hand, and ran out of the room, followed by Moose, who had her hand to her mouth.

Dr. Bonnaire chuckled. "Now the lungs and heart."

In class, each organ had been studied in detail, and in her mind, she had thought of them individually and separate, as pictured in her anatomy text. Now she realized they were packed compactly into the body, all touching one another.

Dr. Bonnaire opened the heart with his scalpel to show them the four cavities and their valves within. "This heart is too big," he said. "It's been working hard for many years. But I see no clots, no infarction, nothing to indicate any other heart disease."

He reached into the body cavity again. "Now the liver." He lifted it out with two hands. "Ah! Here we are."

He laid the organ on the table, pointing out the right and left lobes. Instead of the smooth reddish-purple surface they had been taught about in class, this liver appeared knobby and dark.

"You see this diffuse nodularity of the surface, induced by underlying fibrous scarring?" He shook his head. "Cirrhosis caused the patient's death."

He turned the liver over to show them where the gallbladder nestled inside, then removed it and held up the greenish bag leaking yellow fluid. "Filled with stones."

Methodically he went on, removing the pancreas and the spleen, the kidneys, and adrenals, and finally the mass of small and large intestines. Now the body cavity was completely empty.

Dr. Bonnaire went on speaking but Kitty no longer heard him. Her attention focused on the remains of the body on the table. The torso looked like a canoe, completely hollowed except for the long line of bloody spinal vertebrae that jutted into the body cavity like an intricate sculpture.

She swallowed. The morgue tag tied to his big toe stated "Murphy, A."

This was all that was left of a human being.

Someone who had once been a child, and a vigorous young man. And now it was all gone. But *where* had it gone, all the things that made a person? His thoughts and dreams, his personality, his creativity and imagination, those elemental and yet ethereal things that made up a human being?

With sudden comprehension, the connection between body and spirit revealed itself. Somehow, deep inside, she understood that this wasn't the end.

The sure and sudden awareness that there was more to life than this pile of organs and dead flesh flowed through her like an epiphany.

Ecclesiastes 12:7 drifted into her consciousness.

Then shall the dust return to the earth as it was, and the spirit shall return unto God who gave it.

"Miss Winthrop."

Kitty came out of her reverie and blinked to find she was the only student left in the room. Every last one of them had fled.

"I congratulate you, Miss Winthrop." Miss Trent beamed at her. "You alone of your group managed to stay until the end."

"Thank you." She turned to the pathologist. "It was a privilege, Doctor Bonnaire," she said.

THIRTEEN

Boys and girls, here's the fastest sled on the hill! You'll be the winner in every race with the new Flexible Flyer, the famous steering sled with non-skid runners.

Flexible Flyer ad, Christmas, 1917

DECEMBER 11, 1917

KITTY ROSE EARLY. Miracle of miracles, she was off duty today and so were Annabelle and Moose. They had all agreed that this was as rare as snow in July, and therefore they must spend the day together. They planned to take the streetcar to Macy's, do some Christmas shopping, and have supper somewhere.

They checked for mail on the way down to breakfast, and Kitty had a letter from her father. "You girls go on, and I'll be there in a minute."

She pulled a hairpin from her hair and slit the envelope.

NOVEMBER 4, *1917*
Somewhere in France

DEAREST KITTY:

How are you, my darling girl? How I miss your face and your funny observations on life. I trust all is going well with your schoolwork. Let me say once more how proud I am of you. But then I always knew that you would excel at anything you put your mind to.

Our regiment suffered its first casualties yesterday when the 16th Infantry repelled a German night raid. We were in the trenches.

I was able to minister to all three dying men. Such bravery and resolution these young men have, such fortitude and generosity of character as they breathed their last in the bottom of a muddy and bloody trench. It is my privilege to be here, to give them what comfort and encouragement I can, in the name of our dear Lord.

The "boys" frequently ask me to pray for their wives, sweethearts, and children back home in America. Such a prayer list I have! But I am happy to do it.

I must stop now and try to sleep. Have no fear for me, Kitty. I have the Lord's protection and calling. I know I am exactly where I am supposed to be, and that is in the hands of God our Father.

EVER YOUR LOVING,

. . .

PAPA

KITTY SIGHED as she pocketed the letter. *Please keep him safe, dear Lord.* Thousands of other women were praying the same thing for their sons and husbands and fathers.

She found Moose and Annabelle finishing their breakfast in the dining room.

"I'm ready when you are," Kitty said. "I'm not hungry this morning." Papa's letter had scared her appetite away.

"Shall we take the trolley or walk?"

"How far is it? I've never been to any of the department stores in the city," Moose said.

"Then you're in for a treat." Kitty linked arms with both girls. "Let's walk. All the shops decorate their windows for Christmas. Just wait 'til you see Macy's!"

Annabelle took a deep breath of the frosty air. "Sure, and it's only a good spit from here. We haven't been outside in weeks."

That was certainly true. Twelve-hour shifts and classroom studies on top of that left very little time for anything else besides laundry and sleep.

Snow fell as they set off, slow lazy flakes drifting down like feathers. A wagon piled high with freshly cut Christmas trees passed and left behind the spicy scent of balsam and pine.

Soon, the bright red banner storefront of Woolworth's came into view. Shoppers, vendors, and children with their noses pressed up against the glass windows filled the sidewalk. Dolls of every size and shape in boxes with white tissue paper filled one display. In another, an army of tin soldiers marched in formation.

Eager shoppers thronged the aisles inside, and Christmas carols were being broadcast through the store. Silver garlands were strung between the rows of glass-fronted cabinets, with glittered stars nestled among them.

"My goodness." Moose stared about, wide-eyed. "This is nothing like the general store back home. I don't know where to start."

"Let's go to Toyland first," Kitty said. "You mentioned presents for your little brothers and sisters." She spied the sign overhead that pointed to the North Pole. "This way."

A smiling, full-size Santa welcomed them. They passed through the evergreen-hung doorway into a wonderland of toys, dolls, games, tin trucks, bicycles, and noisemakers.

There were drums and building blocks and stuffed animals galore. Red felt Christmas stockings stuffed with tiny toys and gewgaws were suspended from the ceiling, ready to purchase for some lucky child. There were toy guns and holsters and miniature Western boots and toy watches.

One entire table held nothing but tiny pots and pans, toy silverware, doll dishes, and tea sets. There were harmonicas, guitars, play cash registers, and trucks.

Moose chose dolls for her two little sisters and a toy rifle for her little brother. Next, they headed to the kitchenware department where Annabelle chose a pudding pan for her mother and bought her father a new pipe in the tobacco department.

Then it was on to the gift wrap area, for pretty paper and foil to wrap the gifts. So many pretty Christmas baubles from ornaments to wreaths and garlands.

They continued up 34th Street to Macy's Department Store.

"I know it's a splurge, but I want to get my mother

something special," Kitty said. "It's been so hard on her with Papa away in France and me away at school."

Delicious scents assailed their noses once inside the store which had been gaily decorated for Christmas with greenery on every post. A red carpet ran down the main aisle and all the shades on the counter lamps had been changed to red. Even the chandeliers overhead had been strung with pine garlands and glittering red and green glass beads.

Ahead of them was the perfume counter, and they made their way around the beautiful displays for Quelques Fleurs by Houbigant and L'Heure Bleue by Guerlain until they came to the Coty counter. Papa had given her mother Coty's L'Origan several years ago.

Kitty stopped before a display of pale golden-green perfume in crystal bottles. The placard next to it held a poster of the perfume with a gold foil label that read Chypre by Coty.

A tall languid blonde dressed all in black held up the tester. "It's brand new from Coty. Would you like to try it?"

Kitty nodded and held out her wrist.

"This is their newest fragrance fresh from Paris." She pronounced it "Par-ee."

She sprayed a tiny amount on Kitty's wrist. "Reminiscent of the sunbaked isle of Cyprus, with notes of jasmine, honey, and moss."

"Mmm. That is nice." It reminded Kitty of sunny days outside with a fresh grassy yet floral rose scent.

"The base notes are oakwood and sandalwood. Anyone else?" She waved the tester bottle at Annabelle and Moose who both shook their heads at once.

The saleswoman raised an eyebrow at Kitty. "What do you think?"

"I'll take it, please." She was sure Mama would love it.

Then they took the elevator to the sixth floor to see the latest fashions.

"Oh, my, skirts are certainly getting shorter," Annabelle said.

They glanced at their own costumes with skirts nearly touching the floor.

"I wonder if the superintendent of nurses will allow us to shorten our uniform skirts," Kitty said. "It would allow us some freedom."

"I wouldn't bet on it." Annabelle fingered a dress made of navy peau-de-soie with a handkerchief hemline. "These would show our ankles."

"Can you imagine Miss Trent's face? I'm famished. Let's go find some supper."

They passed the lingerie department on their way to the elevator.

"My word." Annabelle stopped before a display of silk underwear.

Moose held up a pair of silk bloomers. "Look how thin the material is."

"It's the war." A saleswoman dressed in tailored gray wool approached them. "There's a shortage of high-quality linen and cotton from France, so American manufacturers have turned to using silk. Pretty, aren't they?"

Moose snorted and held up a pair of drawers made of transparent mousseline de soie. "Can you imagine if Miss Trent caught us wearing these?"

The girls giggled.

"Much prettier if you ask me." Kitty ran a finger over a row of tiny ribbon flowers on a chemise.

Moose glanced at the watch pinned on her shirtwaist. "It's almost six. Let's find some supper."

They headed for the elevator.

"I'm so hungry I could eat a horse," Kitty said, as the elevator doors opened.

In front of them stood Dr. Hayden in an overcoat and fedora hat. He bowed politely and moved back as the girls stepped onto the elevator.

How utterly embarrassing. If Dr. Hayden had heard her hoydenish comment, he hadn't indicated it.

"Good afternoon, ladies," he said politely.

They nodded and murmured a greeting. Kitty faced forward, her face burning, and studied the intricate wrought-iron grilles of the elevator door. Stiff silence prevailed as the car completed its downward trip and discharged them to the first floor.

Kitty walked as quickly as she could to the exit door and went out. "Oh my." Across the street, an enormous American flag stretched over the entire 5th Avenue façade of the B. Altman Department Store. A kiosk on the curb was selling war bonds and stamps.

"BUY A SHARE OF VICTORY!" blared the sign across the top of the booth. "MAKE EVERY DAY BOND DAY!" decorated the poster on the base.

Moose and Annabelle caught up with her with Dr. Hayden close behind.

"Doing their patriotic duty," Dr. Hayden said. "That's got to be the biggest flag in all of Manhattan."

"Kitty's father, I...I mean, Miss Winthrop's father is serving in France." Moose blushed.

"Oh? My younger brother Jimmy is there, as well." His eyes twinkled at Kitty. "I believe I heard one of you remark that she was hungry. May I take you ladies to tea?"

"Oh, we couldn't poss—" Kitty began to refuse as the other girls nodded yes.

"But...I don't think," Kitty stammered, "the school rules...we aren't...allowed."

Standing slightly behind Dr. Hayden, Annabelle smirked at Kitty.

"I won't tell if you won't," Dr. Hayden said. "Have you been to the Charleston Garden restaurant?"

All three shook their heads.

"Come then. My treat."

He offered his arm to Kitty, and she took it after a moment, wondering if this was real and hoping they wouldn't run into any of the instructors and administrators from Bellevue.

Charleston Garden was on the eighth floor of B. Altman's. All three girls exclaimed at once when they stepped out of the elevator. In front of them stood the two-story façade of a Southern-style mansion with white columns complete with hanging lanterns.

Murals depicting lush flowers had been painted on the other three walls, and the effect was that you had stepped into an airy flower garden. Glass-topped tables with delicate wrought-iron chairs completed the space.

"It's supposed to look like a mansion straight out of Charleston, South Carolina." Dr. Hayden led them to a table for four. "Hence the name."

A waitress brought menus, they ordered, and soon a merry conversation ensued.

Dr. Hayden proved to be nothing like the other physicians Kitty was accustomed to dealing with. Was it perhaps because he was young? Every time he turned to speak to her, Kitty's face felt warm.

"So, your father is also serving with the Army, Miss Winthrop?" He took a bite of his baked ham. "My brother Jimmy is with the 16th Infantry, 2nd Battalion. Where is your father?"

Oh, no. That was Papa's exact regiment and his letter this morning had mentioned that the first deaths had occurred. Jimmy could be among them.

"Um, he is with the...dizzy me..." She pushed her macaroni salad around her plate. "I'm sorry, I can't quite remember. He is serving as a chaplain."

"That's wonderful. I'm sure he is gravely needed."

His blue gaze rested on her a bit longer than necessary, and from the corner of her eye, she saw Moose nudge Annabelle. Perhaps Dr. Hayden noticed as well because he leaned back and regaled them with tales from his internship.

He took his leave from them on the sidewalk in front of Altman's.

Annabelle and Moose watched his tall figure move into the crowd. "He's got it bad, T2," Annabelle said.

"Annabelle." Kitty put her hands on her hips. "I'll thank you to stop this kind of talk. He's not interested in me."

"Well, then, why are you turning red? Ye wee maggot, you've got it just as bad for him."

"Annabelle!" Kitty checked over her shoulder to make sure Dr. Hayden was nowhere nearby.

"I rest my case," Annabelle said. Moose grinned.

FOURTEEN

Rigor mortis begins in the upper part of the body, usually in the maxillary muscles, and spreads gradually from above downward. The time it sets in after death varies from ten minutes to twelve or even twenty-four hours after death.

Bacteriology & Surgical Technique for Nurses, Emily M. Stoney

JANUARY 3, 1918

THE REST of the season passed quickly, and after a few days at home with Mama to celebrate a quiet Christmas, Kitty was back at Bellevue in early January to finish her medical rotation.

Things had gone well for those two weeks as Kitty, Annabelle, and Moose completed their clinicals on Ward B, the women's medical floor.

The day before their last shift Moose approached Kitty. "I've got to do post-mortem care, and then would you help me wheel the stretcher to the morgue?"

The greenish pallor of Moose's complexion reminded Kitty how much Moose hated this particular task.

The students were no longer strangers to death, and post-mortem care was the last nursing service they could give their patients.

Moose had a fear of touching dead bodies, however, even though she'd been raised on a farm and had been familiar with the cycle of life and death long before she came to Bellevue.

But regardless of personal feeling, post-mortem care was a part of nursing and had to be done. It was the last act of nursing care one did for their patient.

Kitty smiled. "Want some help?"

"Oh, would you? I'd be ever so grateful." Moose's shoulders relaxed. "It's Mrs. Baldacci."

Kitty followed Moose down the aisle to a bed with screens around it. "Do you have everything you need?"

"Yes."

"All right then."

The two girls washed Mrs. Baldacci's body, brushed her hair, and readied the shroud. Kitty tied the chin strap on.

"Wait. I forgot her teeth." Moose hurried around the screen to fetch them. Kitty untied the strap and Moose pulled Mrs. Baldacci's jaw down with some difficulty.

"Hmph," Moose said. "Rigor mortis setting in already?"

Kitty helped apply some pressure, and they got the lips open and the jaw pushed down.

"My stars, this is difficult."

Moose finally got the upper and lower plate in and closed the patient's mouth. Kitty retied the chin strap while

Moose attached the identifying toe tag. Together they placed the deceased woman in the shroud and tied it up.

Quietly, they left the ward, rolled the stretcher to the morgue, delivered it to the attendant, and signed off the papers. It was time to go home when they returned to the ward. They reported off to the oncoming shift and walked home to the nurses' dormitory.

BRIGHT AND EARLY THE next morning they were back on the ward, preparing to serve breakfast.

Moose put a tray in front of Mrs. Heaney, a frail elderly Irishwoman who had been admitted with pneumonia. "I need me teeth, nurse."

"Right." Moose bounded back, opened the bedside table, retrieved the dentures, and handed them to the patient.

Mrs. Heaney frowned. "Those ain't right. Mine are over here." She dropped the dentures on the bed and pointed to the stand on the other side.

Two beds away, Kitty heard a strangled gasp from Moose, who clutched her throat and went rigid.

Kitty hurried over. "What's wrong?"

"I need me teeth, that's what's wrong. Get 'em for me." Mrs. Heaney pointed to the other bedside stand. Kitty went to look, but there were no dentures in the drawer. "I don't see them, ma'am." Quickly she searched the compartment below. "They're not here either."

"Oh, dear Lord in heaven." Moose's eyes showed white all around.

Mrs. Heaney picked up a fork and speared a piece of bacon. "They've got to be there. I just used 'em last night."

She waved her fork around. "Hurry up. I'm hungry. Can't eat without me teeth."

Moose went white and grabbed the edge of the bed frame as a horrible thought occurred to Kitty. "Oh, no. Moose. You didn't."

Moose moaned. "I did. Oh," she wailed, "what am I going to do?"

Kitty cast a quick look about the ward. Florence and Annabelle were serving breakfast on the other side. The charge nurse sat writing reports at the desk. Miss Trent was nowhere to be seen.

Kitty hurried over to Annabelle. "Can you and Flo cover for me and Moose a minute? We've got to make an emergency trip to the morgue."

"Sure." Annabelle frowned. "But there aren't any emergencies in the *morgue*."

"There is now. Thanks a million. I'll explain later."

She rushed back to Mrs. Heaney's bed, threw the dentures into the pocket of her apron, and hurried to Moose, who hadn't moved.

Kitty gripped her arm. "Come on."

She marched Moose out of the ward and down the hallway to the next wing where the morgue was located.

Down the stairs they went to the basement, where long dim hallways traveled underneath the hospital buildings.

"Oh, oh, oh. I feel sick." Moose moaned. "I'm going to be expelled, I know it."

"Not if I can help it. Keep going. Speed it up."

Obediently, Moose matched her pace, then stopped suddenly and looked around the hallway.

"Wait. Where are we going?"

"Where do you think?"

If the situation hadn't been so serious, Kitty would have laughed at the horrified look on Moose's face.

"Oh, no!" Moose glanced about for an escape, her eyes wild.

"Oh, *yes.*" Kitty grabbed Moose's arm and started to drag her down the hallway.

"I can't," Moose wailed.

"You must."

Moose was hyperventilating by the time they reached the morgue.

Kitty paused before the door. "Get hold of yourself. We can do this. We've got to do it, or you're going home. Is that what you want?"

Moose shook her head.

"So then. Calm yourself. We'll get it done, and no one will be the wiser. All right?"

Moose gulped, then nodded. "All right." She took a deep breath. "I'm ready."

Kitty rang the bell, and the white-coated attendant, a lanky young man with a shock of blond hair, answered the door.

Kitty smiled prettily at him. "Is the body of Mrs. Baldacci still here?" *Please, God.*

The attendant pulled a clipboard off the wall and consulted it. "Yup. Sure is."

"Um, we need a minute with the body, please."

The attendant shrugged and opened the door. "Sure. Number 57."

He waved them past the morgue office to the large, tiled room beyond where the autopsies took place, seated himself at the office desk, and picked up the mortuary management book he'd been reading.

Kitty and Moose hurried to the wall of numbered doors.

"Here it is," Kitty said. She pulled on the door handle and the stretcher inside rolled out easily. Fortunately, the opened door hid them from the attendant's sight.

Moose groaned. "Oh, dear, oh dear, oh dear."

"You sound like the white rabbit from Alice in Wonderland."

Moose giggled and put her hand to her mouth to stifle it, casting a backward look at the morgue attendant. "Don't make me laugh. This is awful."

"Then stop saying 'oh, dear.' Come on."

Kitty untied the cord around the neck of the body, got it loose, and opened the shroud to expose the waxy white face and staring blue eyes of Mrs. Baldacci.

"Her eyes are open." Moose gasped, recoiling. "Oh, ohhhh—" Her face paled, and she gripped the steel edge of the stretcher, swaying on her feet. "I feel sick."

"If you faint on me, I'll kill you." Kitty glared at Moose. "I mean it."

Moose giggled again and then groaned. "Why do her eyes have to be open?" She darted a glance at Mrs. Baldacci and quickly looked away. "It's so creepy."

"Don't look then. You know that can happen."

Moose gagged. "I'm going to throw up."

"Don't you dare. Now *go*," Kitty said.

With trembling hands, Moose reached for Mrs. Baldacci's lower jaw and gingerly attempted to push it down. When it didn't budge, Kitty wedged a finger between the corpse's stiff lips and tried to force it down on the opposite side.

"Dizzy me, I thought this was hard yesterday." She looked at Moose. "Push your finger through the lips. Maybe if we can each get a finger between the gums, we can get it open."

"Hey, what's going on in here?" The morgue attendant stood frowning in the doorway, book in hand, looking back and forth at the two of them.

"We're almost done, thanks, we're fine." Kitty tried again, to no avail. "Come on," she whispered to Moose, "try again."

The attendant walked over to stand behind them. "Just what are you girls trying to do here, anyway?"

"What's your name?" Kitty asked.

"Justin. Justin Van Hooft."

"Well, Mr. Van Hooft, we have a problem."

"Oh?"

"You see, Mrs. Baldacci had the wrong dentures put in during post-mortem care."

"Oh, yeah? What idiot did that?"

Moose winced. "It was a mistake."

"So, it was you, huh?" He grinned at Moose.

Moose nodded.

"Justin, we've just got to get those dentures out and the right ones in." Kitty plucked the dentures from her pocket and held them up.

"Well, why didn't you just say so?" Van Hooft went over to the glass-fronted instrument cabinet and rooted around in a drawer. "Happens all the time. Here we go." He held up a small metal bar that narrowed at one end. "Stand back, ladies."

He inserted the narrow end carefully between Mrs. Baldacci's gums and cranked the jaw open. He wrestled the dentures out and handed them to Moose, who choked and gagged at the same time.

Van Hooft slipped the correct dentures in and removed the bar. At that moment there was a large rumble of air from the nether regions of Mrs. Baldacci's body. Moose screamed and jumped back.

"Relax." Van Hooft laughed. "Happens all the time, don't worry. It's normal for bodies to make sounds like that. Boy, I could tell you stories that would make your hair—"

"Perhaps another time, Mr. Van Hooft," Kitty said. Moose's face had turned that greenish color again. "We really must return to our patients as soon as possible."

Kitty retied the chin strap and closed the shroud while Van Hooft found a towel to wrap the dentures in and gave it to Moose.

"Thank you so much." Kitty smiled at Van Hooft as she steered Moose to the door. "You've been a big help."

They left the morgue, Moose holding the towel-wrapped dentures stiffly in front of her.

Kitty smiled grimly at Moose. "You'd better pray Mrs. Heaney doesn't ask where they were."

They rushed back to Ward C. Thank goodness, Miss Trent hadn't arrived yet and Annabelle and Flo had managed to serve all the breakfast trays.

Moose ran to wash the dentures and rushed back to Mrs. Heaney's bedside.

"It's about time. Me breakfast's cold," Mrs. Heaney said.

"I'll order you a fresh one." Moose handed her the dentures. "Here you go."

Mrs. Heaney cast a critical eye on the denture plates. "Aye, that's them, all right." She dunked them in her water glass and put them in.

"Dizzy me, Moose." Kitty sighed. "Don't you ever do that to me again."

"I don't intend to." Moose looked ready to cry. "From now on, I'm going to double check *everything*."

FIFTEEN

A wise sympathy, tempered by judgment, is expected of every good nurse, but has no connection with the maudlin, too impulsive variety, which is an evidence of weakness.

She will show her sympathy by thoughtful little deeds and acts far better than by many words, holding hands, or worse than all, shedding tears.

Nursing Ethics, Isabel Hampton Robb, 1917

THE WARD for children was much the same as the adult medical and surgical units, with a polished wood floor and tall windows equipped with roller shades and a transom at the top that could be opened for air.

Eighteen low, white-painted iron beds lined each side of the room, with a clipboard affixed to the foot with the patient's chart.

A square table in the center of the room served as the nurse's desk. The only difference was the toys scattered here and there.

Kitty pulled one of the portable dressing screens around

the bed of Fayvel Orenstein and laid the bowl and instruments on his bedside table.

Her first assignment this morning was to assist the doctor in removing packing from the patient's nose. She took the chart from the end of his bed. Nine-year-old male with platelet disorder. Admitted for severe nosebleed.

She returned the chart to its place and examined the boy.

Pale skin. Small for his age, more like a six-year-old. Tiny and frail with shiny brown hair in a bowl cut. Big luminous brown eyes peeked at her over the blanket he held tight under his chin.

"Good morning." She smiled at him. "Can you tell me how to pronounce your name correctly?"

His brown eyes widened, and he dropped the blanket and sat up. "You know this number?" He held up his hand and wiggled his fingers and thumb.

"Five?"

He nodded. "Five. And then the 'L' at the end. Five-l." He smiled. "It means little fish."

"I'm happy to meet you, little fish. I'm here to assist your doctor this morning when he removes your packing."

"That is good." Fayvel pointed at the ends of stained gauze protruding from his nostrils. "I cannot smell anything."

Dr. Hayden peeked around the screen. "Ah, Fayvel. Ready for me, I see."

Was it her imagination or had his eyes lit up when he saw her? She didn't know, but unfortunately, she blushed, and there was no way to hide it.

Dr. Hayden glanced at Kitty. "Ready, nurse?"

She nodded and drew the bedside table closer, trying to recover her poise.

"First, though, I must draw a little blood."

Fayvel's face blanched, and he snatched the blanket to his chin again.

"It will only take a moment, Fayvel," Kitty said, in a soothing voice. "Would it help if I held your hand?"

Fayvel nodded. Kitty sat on the edge of the bed and took his small hand in hers. "Now then."

From his pocket, Dr. Hayden removed a glass syringe and screwed the needle into it. He quickly applied a rubber tourniquet and flicked a finger against the vein in the boy's arm. "Here we go."

Fayvel closed his eyes and squeezed Kitty's hand tightly while Dr. Hayden inserted the needle and drew blood into the syringe. He held a pad of lint over the needle as he withdrew it. He held it there for a moment and then removed the pad. Blood oozed from the venipuncture site.

Dr. Hayden nodded at it. "His lack of platelets causes that, Miss Winthrop. Here." He handed her a fresh pad. "Hold this while I take the blood to the laboratory."

"I have no plates?" Fayvel looked back and forth between Kitty and the doctor, his eyes wide with fear. "Why do I need plates? My bubbe has some at home she can bring."

"Platelets, Fayvel. Part of your blood that helps it to clot. You—" Kitty paused.

How did one explain to a child that the lack of platelets in his blood was a serious problem?

"Nu." He shrugged his shoulders. "This is life. Don't worry for me."

Kitty removed the lint pad and threw it in the pail near the bed. How did a child so young get such an old view of life? She didn't know what to say to him.

"Oy, boychick, keeping the nurses busy, I see."

A short woman, most of her dark hair covered by a white headcloth, bustled to the bedside, a covered bowl in her hands. "I have chicken soup for you with *knaydelach.*" She uncovered the bowl and pulled a spoon from her pocket.

Kitty took an appreciative sniff of the steam rising from the golden soup studded with dumplings. "It smells wonderful. The doctor will be removing his packing as soon as he returns. After that's out, Fayvel will be able to enjoy it so much more."

Mrs. Orenstein shrugged her shoulders, much like Fayvel had a moment earlier. "So ve wait then." She recovered the bowl.

"Here we are," Dr. Hayden said. "We'll get you fixed up now, Fayvel."

Kitty pushed the tray with the bowl and instruments closer to the bed. The doctor picked up a tweezer and carefully snared one of the strings hanging from the end of the gauze.

Slowly he pulled gauze from the boy's nostril, crusted with mucus and dried blood. He nodded at Kitty, who used a scissors to snip the end off and drop it into the steel bowl.

Again, the tweezer was used to drag another long length of stained gauze from the boy's nose, and then still another.

"All right?" he asked Fayvel, who nodded. "Now for the other side." The procedure was repeated until bloodied gauze heaped the bowl.

Fayvel gagged as the last piece of gauze was slowly pulled out, and then he grinned. "My head no longer feels like a pumpkin," he said. "Now I can have my *knaydelach,* Muter."

Dr. Hayden laughed. "As much as you can hold."

Mrs. Orenstein beamed.

"I'd like to keep him a few more days, to build him up before he can go home."

Mrs. Orenstein nodded, busy uncovering the soup.

Kitty bundled the bowl, the gauze, and the instruments together and left to dispose of them, following Dr. Hayden down the long space between the double row of beds.

"Dr. Hayden," she called.

He turned, raising an eyebrow, as she caught up with him.

"What sort of prognosis does Fayvel have?"

He searched her face before he answered, his eyes grim. "Not particularly positive. Unless his body starts producing more platelets." He sighed. "There isn't much else to be done. Bleeding of any kind could be fatal, I'm afraid. Good day, Miss Winthrop."

He strode off. Kitty continued her walk to the soiled utility room. Once discharged home, any active boy would daily encounter bumps and bruises as he played and worked. His mother would have to keep him quiet. How difficult, especially if he had to go out to work, as many of her young patients did, in the mills and factories of New York City.

─────────

FAYVEL CONTINUED TO IMPROVE, and a week later, Dr. Hayden pronounced him well enough to go home.

Kitty was with Fayvel when Mr. Orenstein arrived. His ragged coat was missing a button and the flapping sole of one shoe had been strapped with string, but his haggard face broke into a joyous smile when he saw Fayvel.

"Tatti!" Fayvel jumped off his bed into his father's arms

and kissed his weathered cheek. "But where is Muter?" He looked past his father.

Some of the happiness in Mr. Orenstein's face faded. "She could not come. Too much still to be done."

"Nu." Fayvel nodded. "I will be glad to go home and help."

Kitty had already bundled up Fayvel's things, including a sketch pad and three new pencils Dr. Hayden had given him as a parting gift.

Kitty had purchased some charcoal sticks and watercolors, and Fayvel's thin face had lit up like the chandelier in her grandmother's foyer when he saw the new art supplies.

Kitty gave discharge instructions to Mr. Orenstein and then stooped to kiss Fayvel goodbye.

She wasn't sure if kissing a patient was allowed, but Miss Trent was nowhere near, and Kitty was going to miss this little boy very much.

Fayvel laid his cheek against hers. "Thank you, miss," he whispered.

He took his father's hand, and they had taken a few steps toward the door when Fayvel turned and ran back to Kitty.

"Oh, miss." He wrapped his arms around her, and his thin little body shook. "I'm going to miss you."

A pang went through Kitty's heart. "And I will miss you, too, my little fish. So much."

Fayvel turned to his father. "Can I invite her to visit, Tatti?"

Mr. Orenstein hesitated, twisting his cap in his hands.

"I'm sure your parents are much too busy for that, Fayvel," Kitty said quickly.

"Tatti?" Fayvel hunched his shoulders, imploring his father with his expressive brown eyes. "Please?"

Mr. Orenstein chuckled. "So, *boychick*, that make you happy, eh?" He looked at Kitty. "What day is good for you?"

"Well, my next day off is...next Wednesday."

Mr. Orenstein nodded. "Then we expect you that day. For tea. One ninety-seven Pitt Street off Delancey. Four o'clock?"

"Certainly. Thank you."

Fayvel took his father's hand. "So, we don't have to say goodbye, miss. Instead, I say, 'see ya soon,' just like the Americans. Okay?" He pulled his cap over his forehead and gave her a cheeky grin as he left with his father.

"My, Kitty." Moose walked over from the bed she was making in the next aisle. "You've had quite an effect on that boy. I think he's a little in love with you."

Kitty laughed. "I'm a little in love with him. He's the sweetest boy."

Miss Trent appeared then. "What's amiss? Why are you standing here talking? There's work to be done."

"Yes, Miss Trent," they answered at the same time.

SIXTEEN

Baby dead, Mother ill; No food or fuel. Police find Hall Family in Sad Straits in Keap St. Head of family out of job.

The Brooklyn Daily Eagle,
Wednesday, January 30, 1918

WEDNESDAY MORNING, it occurred to Kitty that perhaps she should have checked the rule book to see if visiting a former patient at home was allowed before she consented to visit Fayvel.

She didn't find anything forbidding it, though, when she skimmed through it. Her gaze caught the rule about having no men in the dormitory, and the face of Dr. Hayden popped into her head. Immediately, her face grew hot.

She had seen a lot of him lately. Moose and Annabelle teased her constantly about him, and she lived in fear that he would overhear them one of these days.

But she couldn't deny that her heart beat faster when he

was near. She would look up to find him watching her from across the ward and instead of embarrassment at being caught, the corners of his lips would curl in a certain knowing smile. *She* would be the one to look away. So far, Miss Trent hadn't noticed.

But there was sure to be trouble if she did.

KITTY TOOK the streetcar to Delancey Street on the Lower East Side and entered a teeming world foreign to her.

Five- and six-story buildings of brick and stone lined the pavement, many with balconies flying laundry off the rails. Peddlers' carts lined the street, selling everything from cabbages to suspenders to brooms.

Horse-drawn carts squeezed their way through the throng. Bearded men in caps and fedoras and women in headscarves with baskets over their arms crowded the street.

Children ran bareheaded in the cold, running and ducking between wagon wheels. Dogs barked, children shouted, babies cried, horses' hooves clip-clopped on the cobbled stones, and over all this, the fierce haggling and negotiating of peddlers competing against each other for business in a language Kitty didn't recognize.

Kitty stopped at one of the carts to purchase apples for Fayvel and his family. Pitt Street was a short block from Delancey but much narrower.

No trees grew in front of these stone buildings with their plain facades, nor were there any flower gardens anywhere, only packed dirt and stones showing through the piles of dirty snow.

She walked along, searching above the lintels for the

street numbers, and caught sight of Fayvel sitting on an iron stairway, watching a game of marbles.

Fayvel spotted her and jumped down to meet her, his face lighting up.

"I've waited for you, Miss." He took her hand and gazed up at her. "I'm so happy you came." His thin cheeks stretched wide with his smile.

Kitty showed him the paper bag of apples. "For you and your family."

Fayvel peeked inside and beamed. "My muter will be happy for these."

Kitty followed him up the crumbling staircase and through the door into a dark foyer, dimly lit by a dirty skylight in the roof five floors above.

The air smelled of ammoniac urine and boiled cabbage overlaid with ancient dirt, and it was so cold she could see her breath.

"We are fifth floor, Miss."

She followed him up the stairs, past paint peeling off walls, trying not to notice the dirt and mouse droppings piled up in the step corners.

Different odors assailed her senses as they climbed higher in the building, depending, she supposed, on what the inhabitants of those apartments had cooked for breakfast and lunch.

By the time they had climbed to the fifth floor, Kitty was out of breath.

The Orensteins' apartment was toward the back of the building. Fayvel reached out and touched a tiny cylindrical case mounted on the doorpost, and then kissed his hand.

"What is that, Fayvel?"

"It's a mezuzah, miss. It holds part of the Torah."

Then he opened the door into a cramped room no bigger than Kitty's tiny bedroom in the nurses' dormitory.

It wasn't much warmer inside. A single window faced the dirty brick walls of the next tenement building a few feet away. Mrs. Orenstein sat at a sewing machine in one corner and rose to greet Kitty.

"Shalom. Welcome to our home."

Two girls stood up from the scarred wood table holding piles of safety pins, elastic strips, buckles, and other items she didn't recognize.

Mrs. Orenstein indicated the taller girl. "This is Tirzah, my oldest. And this is Miriam."

Tirzah looked about sixteen, and Miriam perhaps eight. Both girls had dark hair wound about their head in plaits and possessed the same warm brown eyes as Fayvel.

They smiled shyly at Kitty as they said, "Shalom."

"And this is my muter." Mrs. Orenstein stepped aside, and there on the floor lay a wizened elderly lady on a pallet, her head covered by a scarf. She nodded at Kitty and smiled, revealing toothless gums.

"I'm happy to meet you all. This is for you." She handed the bag of apples to Mrs. Orenstein. "But it seems I've interrupted your work."

Mrs. Orenstein shrugged. "Nu. This is what we do each day, all day. But today is special because we have a guest." She pulled out a chair. "Please. Sit. The tea is almost ready."

Tirzah and Miriam went to help their mother.

At one end of the main room, a narrow iron bedstead stood against the wall. The other wall had a window into the kitchen, where pots hung on wall hooks, and a wooden shelf held bottles and tins. Small items of laundry hung from a line stretched across it.

Fayvel noticed her looking. "Come. I show you." He took her hand and led her into the kitchen where a coal stove stood, and next to it, a narrow bed. "My tatti and muter sleep there." He pointed to the bed.

"And where do you sleep, Fayvel?"

He pointed through the window to the iron bedstead. "There. With my sisters." He lowered his voice. "Miriam kicks." He shook his head. "*Oy vey*, does she kick."

Three people in that one small bed?

Fayvel opened a short door in the kitchen wall and gestured for her to look inside the cubbyhole. "This is for my bubbe."

A chamber pot stood in one corner and a small chest of drawers in the other. There was no window. Fayvel pointed to the space left on the floor. "Bubbe can't walk so my tatti must carry her here every night."

"Come," Mrs. Orenstein called. "Tea is ready."

Favel and Kitty went back to the main room. On a wooden shelf stood an item Kitty had never seen before. A gleaming copper urn with steam curling from the top and a spigot below, from which Mrs. Orenstein drew the fresh tea.

"What is that?" she asked Fayvel. "I've never seen one before."

"This is samovar." Mrs. Orenstein smiled proudly. "Very old." She touched the spigot, beautifully engraved with scrolls and vines. "Belong to my grandmother in Russia. I bring when we come to America."

"It's beautiful."

Mrs. Orenstein pulled out a vacant chair. "Please. Sit."

Tirzah served Kitty first. Kitty wrapped her fingers around the hot teacup, letting its heat warm her fingers.

Tirzah finished serving her little sister, brother, and grand-mother before serving herself.

Mrs. Orenstein went into the kitchen and returned with a metal tin, which opened to release a mouth-watering scent.

"*Rugelach.*" She held out the tin to Kitty. "I make special for you."

The confection had flaky layers of golden-brown pastry with a sticky filling inside.

She took a bite. "Oh, my, Mrs. Orenstein, this is delicious. What's in it?" The tender pastry with a fruit and nut filling melted in her mouth.

"*Der Aprikos,*" She looked at Fayvel and shrugged helplessly.

"Apricots, miss." He took a bite. "Oh, Muter, so good!" He licked his lips, and Mrs. Orenstein chuckled.

They were on their second serving of tea and pastry when the apartment door opened and Mr. Orenstein entered, carrying a heavy cloth bag on his shoulders almost as big as he was. With a grunt, he slung it off his shoulders onto the floor.

"Tatti!" Fayvel ran to him, and Mr. Orenstein picked him up, raising him high into the air before wrapping him in a bear hug.

"Shalom." Mr. Orenstein nodded to Kitty as he let Fayvel down.

"Hello."

"Come, Motek." Mrs. Orenstein patted the back of an empty chair. "Have some tea and *rugelach.*"

She bustled about getting a cup of tea and filling a plate with pastries to set before her husband.

Kitty glanced at the big cloth bag on the floor, wondering what was in it.

"It's parts, miss," Fayvel said, around a mouthful of *rugelach*.

"Can you read my mind, Fayvel?" She laughed. "I think you know what I'm thinking before I do."

Fayvel left the table and opened the bag to show her what was inside. "Parts. To make hose supporters. Garters."

From the corner of her eye, Kitty noticed Mr. Orenstein glance at a clock on the wall and the bag of 'parts.'"

"Can you show me?" Perhaps she could stay and help. She had been there over an hour, taking time away from their labors.

Fayvel dashed about the small room, gathering the various items that had been put aside. "See? Like this."

With deft fingers, he attached an elastic strip to a buckle and used a safety pin to keep it together. "Then Muter sews it on her machine."

"Could I help you for a few hours? To make up for the time you've lost?"

Mrs. Orenstein looked at her husband, who nodded. "That would be very good. Maybe we finish early."

Kitty helped clear the table, and then Tirzah and Miriam heaped the materials on it and took their places.

"You sit with me, I help you," Fayvel said.

Soon they were all engrossed in making the garters and drinking the seemingly endless supply of tea from the samovar.

Kitty got the hang of it quickly, and soon she was assembling the garters as fast as Fayvel and the girls. "Mr. Orenstein, how long have you been in America?"

Mr. Orenstein took a sip of his tea and placed it carefully on the table before answering. "We come from Russia in 1905. From Odessa. You know Odessa?"

Kitty had a vague memory of Odessa in geography class. "Near the Black Sea?"

"Yes." He shook his head. "Was very bad then, very bad." He sighed. "We live in a *shtetl*, you know *shtetl*?"

Kitty shook her head, and Mr. Orenstein looked at Fayvel.

"It's a village, miss, a village for Jews. Jews only."

"Yes." Mr. Orenstein nodded. "For Jews only. Because we are hated there. Many pogroms taking place there. You know this word, pogrom?"

Again, Kitty had to say no.

"It's massacre. You understand? Exter—extermi—"

"Extermination?"

"Yes, yes. Extermination. Start in city of Odessa and spread to countryside. My brother and his family all killed. I was sheepherder. My family was with me in the fields when they burn the village. We saw the smoke. We knew what it was. We stayed in the fields for two days and nights before we dare to return. All dead. Even the children. The animals." His face crumpled. "All dead."

Mrs. Orenstein rose and went to her husband. "Sh-h-h. Never mind, Motek, never mind. We are here." She touched his cheek tenderly. "We are in America now."

Mr. Orenstein covered his wife's hand where it rested on his cheek. "Yes. Yes. It is good."

Kitty's hands stilled on the scrap of elastic in her hands. She'd had no idea of the persecution they'd faced in Russia and wished she hadn't asked. "I'm so sorry. I didn't know. How awful for you."

Mr. Orenstein shrugged. "Nu. It is good we are here." He took a breath and straightened his shoulders. "Now in greatest city in the world. Where we have hospital, when Fayvel needs, *nu*? So, we rejoice."

Quiet fell over the room as they worked on the garters. Kitty's back soon ached from sitting so still and hunched over, and she'd only been doing it for an hour.

"What are you paid for your work?"

Mr. Orenstein replied without looking up. "A penny for each one. We work six days a week."

Kitty looked at the pile of completed garters sitting on the cloth bag and did some quick calculations in her head.

Two hundred garters at a penny apiece. That would be two dollars a day, twelve dollars a week. "And what is your rent here? If you don't mind my asking," she said.

"Eight dollars a month."

Eight dollars a month. That left forty for everything else. Food. Coal. Clothes. Medicine. Now she understood the reason for Mr. Orenstein's battered shoes and threadbare coat.

When the dim light through the sole window in the apartment disappeared, Mrs. Orenstein lit a lamp.

There were still many more garters to assemble, and it was nearly eight o'clock when they finished. Mrs. Orenstein got up from her sewing machine, stretched her arms, and went into the tiny kitchen.

"I must be going." Kitty stood and repressed a groan. Her back was as stiff as the board holding the samovar.

"I will go down with you. For cab." Mr. Orenstein nodded at Kitty. "Safer at nighttime."

"Of course."

There was no bathroom in the apartment. She should have realized this sooner before she had drunk all that tea. But her bladder was protesting, and she wouldn't make it back to Bellevue without answering nature's call.

"Fayvel," she whispered, "where is the water closet?"

"I show you." He went into the kitchen and retrieved a key from a hook on the wall and they left the apartment.

Kitty followed Fayvel to the far end of the hall, wincing as the stench of urine and feces grew stronger with every step.

He stopped before a narrow door with a slit cut into the top and unlocked it.

"How many families use this toilet, Fayvel?"

"Mine and our neighbors, the Liebermans."

"How many people are in that family?"

Fayvel's eye widened. "So many!" He counted on his fingers. "Schlomo, Rivkah, Saul, Benny..." He went on, at last holding up all ten fingers. "Including their muter and tatti. Ten."

With Fayvel's family added that made sixteen people. One toilet for sixteen people.

Fayvel handed her the key. "I wait for you in apartment."

Kitty opened the door and choked at the fetid air that wafted out. The wood closet stood three feet square and had a window over the toilet that opened into an air shaft. For ventilation, she supposed, although it didn't seem to help very much except to freeze the air as cold as it was outside.

Filth covered the floor and the inside of the bowl. Torn sheets of newspaper hung from a rusty nail. Kitty shuddered, comparing it to the bathrooms in the nurses' dormitory at Bellevue.

She decided she could wait.

The ride home in the hansom cab didn't take long but her bladder felt every bump and jolt in the road. Although running in the dormitory wasn't allowed, she took the stairs two at a time to the fifth floor and burst into the bathroom barely in time.

Definitely, no tea for her if she ever visited Fayvel and his family again.

SEVENTEEN

*Red Cross Issues Call to Nurses for War Service; Between
30,000 and 40,000 will be needed.*

The Ithaca Journal, Tuesday, February 12, 1918

THE PEDIATRIC WARD and all the other wards and
pavilions at Bellevue were running short of nurses.

A unit to establish a possible base hospital had been
formed in 1916, and this month the unit had been called
up. Soon a contingent of sixty-five Bellevue graduate nurses
would be leaving for France with Chief Nurse Beatrice
Bramber.

Many other experienced Bellevue physicians and
nurses had answered the call to serve their countrymen in
Europe. The remaining doctors, staff nurses, nursing
students, and probationers would have to take up the slack.

The war was intensifying in Europe.

Papa hadn't said so in his letters, but Kitty read the

New York Tribune every day with the same eagerness she used to peruse the Society pages, hoping to read that the war would soon be over, and Papa could come home.

Instead, this morning she'd read the report of the ship SS Tuscania torpedoed and sunk by a German U-boat. Among the dead were one hundred and forty-seven American soldiers. She prayed that the young nurses soon to travel to the battlefields of France would arrive safely.

She pulled Papa's most recent letter, battered and travel-stained, from her pocket to read his dear words again.

JANUARY 31, *1918*

DEAREST KITTY:

I HAVE ONLY *a few moments with which to write you a few words. I have been very busy attending to the wounded and the dead. It is a great privilege to serve these brave young men, and I am daily impressed with their courage and endurance in exceedingly difficult times.*

You should know that I am a jack of all trades here. Besides praying, conducting services, and writing letters home for the boys, I have also been pressed into service building barricades and installing barbed-wire obstacles. I believe you will be impressed with my muscles when I return home!

Every night I gaze at the lovely photograph of your mother you so thoughtfully provided me with before I left for France. I kiss her face and dream of the time I can return home to my two girls.

Ever your loving

PAPA

KITTY SIGHED, kissed the letter, and tucked it back into her pocket. It was time to start her twelve-hour shift.

Later that morning, Fayvel was readmitted. Kitty was bathing a toddler when orderlies carried Fayvel into the ward, his nostrils and sinuses once again packed with gauze.

The moment she finished with her patient she hurried to his bedside.

"You couldn't stay away, little fish?" Kitty took his hand, resisting the urge to press his cold fingers to her lips. *How much blood had he lost this time?*

He smiled up at her and shook his head weakly. "I missed you..."

"Save your strength. I'll be here when you need me. Try to sleep now."

She pulled the blankets over him and tucked his cold hand under the bedclothes. She stood and gazed at his pale, pinched face and offered up a silent prayer for this little boy who had stolen her heart. Then she went to the clean utility room and retrieved an extra blanket for him.

Dr. Hayden caught her at the nurse's desk later. "So, your little friend has returned, Miss Winthrop. He's in a bad way."

She nodded, her heart heavy and, for once, unaffected by Dr. Hayden's presence.

"I know." She looked away and dashed at the tears welling in her eyes. If she talked about Fayvel, she would cry.

She sensed that Dr. Hayden understood. "Keep praying for him," he said gently.

A few days later, Dr. Hayden removed Fayvel's gauze, buoying Kitty's hope that the boy had improved enough to go home.

When she asked Dr. Hayden, his reply was guarded. "We'll see. Perhaps in a few days."

But those few days for Fayvel turned into three weeks. He continued to have mild hemorrhages from his nose, and Dr. Hayden was reluctant to discharge him.

During those weeks, Kitty found herself lingering at Fayvel's bedside when she wasn't on duty.

FEBRUARY 24, 1918

After returning from church services, Kitty sat down to study in the beautifully appointed library at the nurses' residence, Osborn Hall.

She had a few hours before the start of the evening shift, but she couldn't keep her mind on the text. The image of Fayvel's wan little face kept popping up.

She stood and searched the bookshelves. Reference books had been provided for the students, but she could find no texts on diseases of the blood. Perhaps the medical library at the hospital would have something.

She bundled up and crossed East 26th Street, pulling up her collar against the glacial wind blowing across the East River.

The medical library was tucked away in a corner on the second floor. Pale winter sunshine streamed through the tall windows in the book-lined walls. Additional free-standing bookcases crammed with texts, papers, and medical journals filled the space, along with long oak tables lit by stained-glass lamps.

Dust motes shimmered in the light and over everything hung the earthy ancient scent of old books, and she breathed it in like perfume.

A young woman was busy working in an immense card catalog file next to a desk in the middle of the room A desk sign stated her name as Miss Griswold, Librarian.

"Good evening, Miss Griswold," Kitty said.

The librarian turned and looked at Kitty over her half-glasses. "How may I help you?"

"I'm looking for some texts or books on blood diseases."

"I see. Anything in particular?"

"Yes. Aplastic anemia."

"Just a moment." Miss Griswold returned to the card catalog. Humming to herself, she looked through several different cases before pulling a handful of cards. "Right this way."

Kitty followed the librarian as she pulled two textbooks and a medical journal from the shelves. "There you go." She handed the books to Kitty. "Sit anywhere you like."

Several men studied at different tables. She recognized some as physicians from the floors and others were interns and medical residents.

Though most remained focused on studying, several gazed at her curiously, likely because she was the only woman in the room.

She headed to a vacant table near the back wall, away from everyone else, and started reading. The disease involved the failure of the bone marrow to produce red blood cells, white blood cells, and platelets which were necessary for blood clotting.

So Fayvel was susceptible to infection as well with his

low white blood cell count. She had worked her way through the textbooks and had started on the medical journal when she felt a light tap on her shoulder.

"Well, well, well." Dr. Hayden slid into the chair next to her and smiled. "I don't believe I've ever seen a nursing student in here. You must be the first. And it appears that you've caught some interest." He glanced around the library. "There are three young men already in love with you, I fear."

"Don't do that." Kitty's back stiffened. She wasn't in the mood for banter, and it didn't become him.

"Do what? Call attention to your beauty?"

"You know exactly what I mean. Play with me like that."

Dr. Hayden frowned, and the joviality left his face. "You're right. I apologize. I...I supposed you must be accustomed to that sort of thing. Every young lady of my own acquaintance seems to expect it."

"Perhaps you are keeping company with the wrong sort of lady, then, Dr. Hayden."

He mimicked catching an arrow and thrusting it into his chest. "*Touché*. I must remember in the future not to engage in verbal jousting with you. You are far too quick for me."

She doubted that. But what did he mean in the future?

"Let us return to a safer subject. What are you studying?" He glanced at the journal article. "Ah, I see."

"I want to understand the disease Fayvel has."

Dr. Hayden nodded. "Of course. There is much we don't know about it. And no cure has been discovered yet, so it's more a matter of supportive treatment."

He sat back and fixed her with a bemused look. "You constantly surprise me, Miss Winthrop."

"And why is that?"

He didn't answer immediately, instead studying her face pensively. She felt exposed under his gaze, and her face grew warm.

"You're quite the pupil. You have a sharp mind."

"Thank you."

"I'd like to take you to dinner."

Kitty's breath caught in her throat at the abrupt switch in the conversation. "Is that allowed? A student nurse and a physician?"

"I don't see why not. My intentions are honorable."

At this, Kitty blushed even more fiercely. "I...I didn't mean to suggest—"

"Of course, you didn't. So then, let's arrange a date."

"Um, I'm not really sure that's a good idea."

She was having a difficult time maintaining eye contact with him. His nearness set her heart beating like a trapped bird, and it didn't seem likely to slow down any time soon.

"Whyever not?" Then he frowned. "Is it that you don't like me, Miss Winthrop?" He glanced away and a stiff smile hovered at the corners of his mouth. "I had thought differently, but perhaps I was wrong?"

Kitty laughed. "I do like you. I don't know what my nursing instructors will think. If it's allowed. I will have to check my rule book."

Dr. Hayden's features relaxed, and he threw his head back and laughed out loud, drawing annoyed looks and whispers of "Shushhh!" from those studying at nearby tables.

"You're going to get me in trouble, Miss Winthrop," he whispered.

She was already in trouble. His blue eyes and dangerously attractive smile had her close to cardiac failure.

"When is your next day off?"

"Friday."

"Then let's meet at seven o'clock. At the corner of 25th and 1st Avenue, far enough from the hospital so we don't get caught." He smiled at her with a mischievous gleam in his eye. "There's a wonderful little restaurant in Little Italy I'd love to take you to."

He stood. "I've got to make rounds. I'll see you on the wards."

Kitty stared down at the journal but no longer saw the words. She returned the materials to the librarian and then walked home in a daze.

"Dizzy me," she said. "A date with the doctor."

Over the next few days, she struggled to focus on her studies as she agonized over what to wear on her date with Dr. Hayden. Should she ask Annabelle? She possessed excellent taste in clothes.

Kitty discarded that thought out of hand. Her red-headed compatriot would tease her unmercifully if she learned about Kitty's coming date with Samuel Hayden.

Friday afternoon, she had pulled most of her dresses out of the closet and was standing in her unmentionables considering them when Moose and Annabelle poked their heads around her door.

Kitty repressed a groan. Being in the same rotation group of students meant that they had the same days off.

"What's going on, T2? Housecleaning?" Annabelle's sharp blue gaze darted about the room.

"We were thinking of going to the Rivoli Theatre tonight." Moose pushed a dress aside and folded her lanky body onto the bed. "Tarzan of the Apes is playing. Want to go?"

Any other time, Kitty would have snatched at the invitation. They didn't get many chances to go to the movies.

"Um...I don't think so."

"Why not?" Annabelle narrowed her eyes at Kitty and tipped her head to one side. "What are you up to, Kitty?"

"Uh, I have something else planned."

Annabelle pounced on her. "Tell all! Is it the doctor?"

"Oh, you're incorrigible, Annabelle." Kitty rolled her eyes. "I should have known I can't keep anything from you."

Moose laughed. "It's no secret, Kitty. We all see the way he looks at you when you're busy with a patient, don't we, Annabelle?"

"Aye. Like a lovesick calf, he is." She imitated Dr. Hayden, widening her eyes and letting her tongue loll out of her mouth.

"Stop it." Kitty put her hands on her hips and glared at her friends. "Just quit it."

"Aye." Annabelle laughed. "He's got it bad."

Kitty let out a breath of frustration.

"Don't get your knickers in a twist." Annabelle smiled at Kitty. "We'll keep your secret." She glanced at the dresses. "So, I'm supposin' you're trying to decide what to wear?"

Kitty nodded. Annabelle pursed her lips and studied the garments. "This one." She held up a dark purple gabardine skirt and jacket. "Would look amazin' with your hair."

"That's it then. Now you two scoot, so I can finish getting ready."

Moose stood. "Come find us later. We want all the details."

SNOWFLAKES SWIRLED in the frigid breeze off the East River as Kitty hurried to the corner of 25th and 1st, hoping the restaurant wasn't too far away.

This was the coldest winter in New York she could remember, and she had her hat pulled down and a thick wool muffler wrapped around her face to the eyes.

Dr. Hayden stood on the corner, bundled in a fur overcoat, his fedora replaced by a hat with fur earflaps that made her laugh out loud when he turned around to meet her.

"Laughing at my headgear, are you? It's cold out here."

"Don't I know it? I can't feel my cheeks."

"Come along before you freeze." He helped her into the closed carriage waiting at the curb and climbed in after her, taking the seat facing her. "It's much too cold to walk tonight as I had originally planned."

The cab turned south on 2nd Ave.

"No regrets I hope, Miss Winthrop?"

"None."

"That's excellent. I'm taking you to one of my favorite restaurants. Angelo's on Mulberry in Little Italy. The best Italian food in New York."

"Mmm. Sounds good. I've never had real Italian food."

"You're in for a treat."

The buildings on Mulberry Street looked much like Fayvel's neighborhood with the street signs in Italian instead of Hebrew.

Meat shops with salamis and pepperonis hanging in the windows, bakeries, signs for olive oil, and cheese. Peddlers on the street wheeled their carts home after a long day.

Angelo's on Mulberry turned out to be a family restaurant with white-jacketed waiters in a rustic setting with frescoed walls.

Kitty glanced through the huge menu and placed it on the table.

"Since you're the expert, I'm going to let you order for me."

"I'd be happy to. Do you like seafood?"

"I do."

Their waiter approached. Dr. Hayden gave their order, pronouncing the Italian names as the waiter nodded and swiftly wrote on his pad.

"Very good, signor." Smiling, the waiter nodded and hurried off.

"That was impressive. Do you speak Italian?" Kitty realized there was so much she didn't know about Samuel Hayden.

"A little. I grew up not far from here."

"Really."

"My mother was Italian." He grinned. "I make a mean meatball."

"A man who can cook? How rare. And your father? Is Hayden English?"

"Irish. Years back it was O'Hayden, and some ancestor dropped the O."

The waiter brought their first course, an appetizer that smelled heavenly.

"Here we have the *Mozzarella di Bufala Affumicata all Griglia*. Fancy Italian for smoked mozzarella with wild mushrooms and dried tomatoes."

It tasted as delicious as it smelled. After that came their main course, *Linguini alla Vongole*, fresh tender clams served in their shells in a white wine garlic sauce on a bed of perfectly cooked pasta. At least, Dr. Hayden said it was perfectly cooked. She wouldn't know as she had never tasted pasta in her life.

"My, this is so good. I love clams, but I've never had them like this. I usually get mine at Coney Island."

Dr. Hayden's eyes lit up. "I love Coney Island! But I haven't been there in a few years. Too busy with my studies."

"What was your favorite thing to do?"

"Eat." He laughed. "Seriously, I love carnival food. But as far as rides? It would have to be the Steeplechase."

"I love that ride. And the incubator babies."

Dr. Hayden swallowed a mouthful of pasta. "We should go. As soon as spring arrives. What do you say?"

"Dr. Hayden, I..."

"Please call me Samuel. And may I call you Kitty?"

His blue eyes looked so earnest. She'd almost forgotten that he was a physician and far above her on the totem pole of authority at Bellevue. He spoke to her as an equal.

And she had to admit it was quite attractive to be treated as if she had a brain.

She nodded. "It might take me a bit to get used to it, Samuel."

"I hope you're having as much fun as I am tonight?"

"Yes. Very much so."

Dinner ended with cannoli, another Italian specialty she had never tasted, and the cream-filled pastries were the perfect end to the meal.

As the cab pulled up in front of Osborn Hall, Samuel laid his hand over hers. "This has been such a special night I can hardly believe it's actually happened."

He drew closer, and the woodsy scent of his cologne tickled her nose. "I hope it's the first of many more to come." He touched her cheek and drew her face towards his to press a tender kiss on her lips. "Good night, dearest Kitty."

Moments later, she drifted into the dormitory in a nebulous cloud. Was she in love? It certainly felt like it. She broke out of her daze and ran up the stairs to tell Annabelle and Moose about her evening.

EIGHTEEN

FRENCH AND BRITISH PUSH GERMANS BACK, PRISONERS TAKEN AND VILLAGES REGAINED, AMERICAN ARMY STARTS FOR BATTLE FRONT

The New York Times Monday, April 1, 1918

Kitty hadn't been home since Christmas, and when Miss Trent gave Kitty an unexpected half-day off, Kitty called Mama and headed there.

What a wonderful feeling to walk down East 70th Street with the sun on her face, the daffodils and tulips coming up, and the grass greening in the sunshine.

Even more wonderful was to sprint up the stairs into the brownstone, smell cookies baking, and walk straight into her mother's arms.

"What a delightful surprise, darling." Mama stood back

and examined Kitty. "You look well. Your studies are progressing?"

"Oh, yes."

Jenny walked into the room, carrying a basket of fresh laundry. "I thought I heard your voice." She dropped the basket and held out her arms. "It's verra fine to see ye, my wee bairn."

Kitty gave Jenny a big hug as Mrs. Mac came out of the kitchen with flour on her apron.

"You're just in time, Kitty," Mrs. Mac said. "I'm making a boatload of my molasses jumbles for your father, and I'll send some home with you."

"Mmm. The girls and I will love that."

"Shall I bring you some coffee in the parlor, Miss Lindy?"

"That would be lovely, Mrs. Mac. Thank you."

Jenny picked up her basket and trudged upstairs while Mrs. Mac disappeared into the kitchen.

Mama put her arm around Kitty. "Now come sit down and tell me about everything."

Kitty sank onto the overstuffed sofa, glanced around the room, and let out a deep sigh. "Oh, it's so good to be home." She sighed. "I didn't realize just how much until now."

"I'm glad," Mama said.

Kitty filled Mama in with the recent happenings at school and then gave her a mischievous smile. "Now you know almost everything, Mama."

Mama chuckled. "So, there's more?"

"Yes." Kitty sat up. "There's a man. A doctor at Bellevue."

"Indeed?" Mama smiled. "And you care for him?"

"I do."

"Tell me about him."

"His name is Samuel Hayden. He's a medical doctor. And there was an attraction right from the first. Usually, physicians never notice the student nurses or speak to them. But he stopped me on the ward one day to introduce himself." Kitty remembered the way she had blushed when she realized she'd been staring at his scar. "But he's not stuffy at all, like most of the other doctors."

"How old is he?"

"I think he's about twenty-eight. He's been out of school a few years."

"And..." Mama paused and raised an eyebrow. "What does he look like?"

"So handsome. But he doesn't act like he is. He does have a facial scar, a long thin one from a buggy whip accident in his childhood. But it only makes him more attractive to me."

Mrs. Mac bustled in with the tray of coffee and cookies then and set it on the hassock.

Kitty picked up one of the warm molasses cookies sprinkled with sugar and took a big bite. "Yumm." She took another bite. "Oh, my goodness, so good, Mrs. Mac."

The cook beamed. "Thank you, Kitty. I've got plenty to send with you for the girls." She turned and walked from the room, smiling.

Kitty held up a coffee cup. "I've even missed this china, Mama. I never realized how much a part of home it is."

Mama laughed. "It's Spode, called 'Tobacco Leaf.' It's been in the family for a long time."

She ran her finger over the blue leaves and pink flowers. "It belonged to your father's mother, and I loved it from the start. I never thought of getting anything else." She poured coffee for them both. "Take a cup back with you if you like. To remind you of home."

The corner of today's New York Times peeked out from underneath the coffee tray. Kitty had read it that morning in the dining room of Osborne Hall.

"You've read the paper today?"

Mama nodded. "Yes."

They sat in silence for a minute.

"They're heading for the front." Kitty hated to say it out loud. Now worry and anxiety over Papa would increase exponentially for them both.

"I already knew it was coming." She pulled a letter from the pocket of her skirt. "I received this a few days ago."

Kitty unfolded the letter.

MARCH 21, *1918*

DEAREST LINDY,

THIS MAY BE *the last letter I can write for a while. We haven't received our marching orders yet, but rumors are circulating that we will soon be headed for the front.*

Training has gone well, and I have many opportunities to minister to the men, share an encouraging word or prayer, and help some of our injured by writing letters home for them.

And the training has revealed some muscles I never knew I had! You will be surprised to see me when I come home. I have regained my once-youthful manly figure.

We are being well-fed and during our recreation time, some of the men sing songs from home, and in our midst, we also have an opera singer, of all things. He keeps us enter-

tained by singing arias from The Marriage of Figaro and The Barber of Seville.

So, you see we are not at a loss for culture here, even though we are living in tents.

Please try not to worry about me. I know I am exactly where I am supposed to be—in the middle of our Lord's will. I pray for you and Kitty daily, as I know you do for me.

Be well, my sweetest love, and we will be reunited soon.

All my love,

YOUR JACK

KITTY'S THROAT THICKENED. "He always sounds so positive, doesn't he?

Mama nodded. "He's always been like that, too, as long as I've known him. Always sure of the goodness of God."

"When you fell in love with him, how did you know he was the one?" Kitty tucked her feet underneath her and turned to face her mother. "How will I know?"

Mama smiled. "I can only speak for myself. I didn't have many close friends. My mother wouldn't allow it."

"You said it was at the Patriarchs Ball when you realized it. How long had you known him before that?"

"Not long. Months. Looking back now, I think I fell in love with him almost immediately, but it took some time for me to realize it."

"What was it like? How did you feel?"

"It felt right," Mama said. "It was simple and easy being with him. He treated me as someone with their own thoughts and opinions. We had discussions on all sorts of things."

That seemed the same as she and Samuel, and Kitty laughed.

"What?"

"That sounds like Samuel and me. Two medical people discussing brain tumors while we're eating a plateful of pasta." Kitty grinned. "He has an Italian mother and an Irish father."

"He sounds like a wonderful man, Kitty. I hope I'm able to meet him soon."

"I would love that. Perhaps you could come some evening and go to dinner with us?"

"Certainly. I will look forward to it. It's a date, then."

Mama smiled her beautiful smile, and Kitty was overcome with love for her.

She moved closer and hugged her mother. "You're the best. How do I deserve you?" She kissed her mother's cheek and sat back.

"I'm not a saint, darling. I do have my quirks and bad habits."

"Chocolate isn't a bad habit, it's a necessary part of life."

"Oh, you."

You never know when you'll need a piece of chocolate to set the day right, Mama would say.

Papa and Kitty had shared a lifelong laugh at the way Mama stashed chocolate in different spots in the house.

Kitty poured another cup of coffee as the grandfather clock in the hall struck three o'clock. "I'll have to be getting back soon."

"Can you stay for supper? Mrs. Mac is making beef stroganoff."

Kitty groaned. "My favorite! I would if I didn't have a big exam tomorrow on anatomy and physiology of the nervous system. I probably should have used this afternoon to study, but I couldn't turn down the opportunity to come home for a few hours."

A short while later, Mama called a cab for her. Mrs. Mac presented her with a large paper sack of molasses jumbles that must have weighed all of five pounds.

"I double-wrapped it for safety," Mrs. Mac said.

"They won't last very long once I get back to Osborn Hall." Kitty smiled. "The smell alone will ensure I have a line outside my door that goes down the hall. Thanks, Mrs. Mac."

Jenny came to hug Kitty tight. "Study hard," she whispered into Kitty's ear. "We're all so proud of you."

Mama walked outside with her when the cab beeped its horn. "Goodbye, darling." She hugged Kitty tight. "Call me soon."

"I will. Love you." Kitty got into the back seat of the cab.

"Love you more." Her mother said and shut the door.

NINETEEN

When the circus left its home at Madison Square Garden yesterday afternoon to give its annual show at Bellevue Hospital, Dr. George O. Hanlon, the Superintendent of the hospital, thought he had only 1,400 patients.

But when somebody stepped on the safety valve of the calliope just as the procession of monkeys and elephants started through the gates, an epidemic of disease suddenly affected every child within sound of the jazzy music.

The New York Times, Thursday, April 18, 1918

FAYVEL WAS in and out of the pediatric ward many times during February and March, and with each admission, he grew weaker.

Now as spring arrived with April sunshine, leaving behind one of the coldest winters recorded in New York City, he had been admitted yet again with a severe hemorrhage and had gone to surgery for the nasal packing.

But the pediatric ward hummed with excitement today because the circus was coming to town. The Ringling Brothers Circus' annual visit to Bellevue occurred every spring and no one was more excited about it than Fayvel.

"Do you think there will be elephants, miss?" He bounced up and down on the bed, causing the strings hanging from his nostrils to wave wildly. "Today I do not care that my head feels as stuffed as one of Muter's *kishke*."

Kitty laughed. "And what is a *kishke*, my little fish? Would I like it?"

"Everyone likes *kishke*." Fayvel nodded solemnly. "What's not to like? It's onions, celery, carrots, grain, and *schmaltz*, all stuffed into a casing. It simmers in a stew all day, and then, for supper—" Fayvel rubbed his stomach. "*Nu*, so good."

"And what is *schmaltz*?"

"Chicken fat." He smiled. "You come soon for supper. I ask Muter to make *kishke* for you, okay?"

After lunch, the nurses wrapped the children in warm robes, pink striped for the girls and gray for the boys.

Down to the courtyard they went on crutches, in wheelchairs, and on stretchers. A temporary grandstand had been erected in the courtyard, and here the children gathered, covered with blankets and scarves to protect them from the breezes that blew across the East River.

More patients, children and adults alike, crowded the windows and perched on the wrought-iron balconies that stretched across the facades of the three walls that enclosed the grassy courtyard.

Kitty sat with Fayvel and the other children from the pediatric ward at the very front, their small figures vibrating with repressed excitement, straining to look down the avenue where the circus would appear.

The faint whistling notes of a calliope reached the waiting children and cries of excitement ran through them. Those who could walk leaped to their feet and peered down the road. One tiny tot with a big pink bow in her curls waved her arms back and forth.

Soon the clip-clop of horses' hooves mingled with the calliope notes, growing ever louder and gayer, and then it was here! Dee deet deetle leetle deet deety dee deet! Dee deet deetle leetle deet deety dee deet!

Pulled by two white horses with golden bridles and scarlet plumes, the calliope in the shiny red wagon with 'Ringling Brothers' painted in large letters on the side drove into the ring. A clown with orange hair and a black derby was at the keys.

Clowns on stilts dressed in stars and stripes entered the ring, throwing out candy to the excited children.

More clowns rolled and danced and tumbled through the crowd, handing out boxes of Cracker Jack, and others danced in front of the children, holding monkeys dressed in striped and wildly patterned outfits that matched their own.

A line of camels came next, and a zebra, and then the elephants, each with a blue and gold beaded headdress. One, two, three, four, and five massive elephants ambled into the circle, holding each other's tails.

On their trainer's command whistle, they stood on their hind legs and raised their front feet in the air.

Another command and the biggest elephant lay down on the ground and the other four each put a foot on him. Then a whistle and the elephants paraded out and the clowns bounced back in.

A silver cannon rolled into the ring, and more clowns and midgets dressed in plaid and polka dots with white-painted faces, big red lips, and floppy oversized shoes cavorted around it.

One clown jumped and dropped inside the cannon, another clown set fire to it and with a huge vroom! the clown shot out, his pants on fire, and frantically ran around the ring, chased by the other clown who threw a bucket of water on the fire to put it out.

Prancing horses came next, high-stepping around the ring to show their skills. Then a bare-chested Indian chief with a full feathered war bonnet appeared, accompanied by two beautiful Indian girls in buckskin skirts and long black braids.

A large wooden circle like a tabletop was rolled out and the two girls went to stand in front, smiling at the crowd. Then, lo and behold, in rapid succession the Indian chief threw tomahawks at the girls and the target, so lightning fast you only heard the whirr of the blade as they thudded in a straight line into the wood between the girls.

A clown bounced over and handed Fayvel a peanut, and a trainer in a uniform with bright brass buttons walked an elephant over.

"This here is Blondie," he said. "She's a very sweet girl. Hold up that peanut, and I'll show you," he said to Fayvel.

Fayvel held up the peanut and then the elephant's long gray trunk stretched out and hovered above the peanut.

Both Kitty and Fayvel had a good view of the wrinkled skin and appendage as the nostrils twitched delicately and then plucked the peanut from Fayvel's hand.

The child beamed, his thin face alight with excitement. "Can I do it again?"

The trainer nodded and threw him another nut. Fayvel stood and cautiously advanced toward the elephant. But this time, instead of taking the peanut, the elephant's nose danced around Fayvel's hair, sniffing.

"She's kissing me." Fayvel giggled, scrunching his shoulders. "It tickles." He held up the peanut once again, and Blondie took it.

Fayvel turned toward Kitty as the trainer and Blondie moved on. "Did you see that?"

"I did. I think Blondie liked you, little fish."

"This is the best day of my life. I wish Muter could have been here to see Blondie." Then he grinned. "But you're my next favorite, miss."

The afternoon went on under a cloudless spring sky with dancing acrobats, jugglers, and midgets riding unicycles.

It was a tired little boy that Kitty tucked into bed later that evening, clutching his Cracker Jack prize, a colorful tin lithograph horse. Soon all their small charges in the ward were fast asleep.

"They'll be dreaming about elephants and clowns tonight." Annabelle stopped by the desk where Kitty was finishing her report. "Sure, and it was grand for the wee ones today."

Kitty nodded. "And the adults too, T1."

TWENTY

Your eyes have seen my unformed substance, and in Your book were all written the days that were ordained for me, when as yet there was not one of them.

Psalm 139:16

APRIL 18, 1918

WHEN KITTY ARRIVED on the pediatric ward the next morning, Fayvel's bed was empty.

Fresh blood stained his pillow and bedclothes, a lot of blood, and her heart clenched painfully. Had the circus the day before been too much for him? Should she have kept him quiet inside? *Oh, please, dear Lord—*

Florence Emminger hurried over. She had been the student nurse in charge during the night. "Oh, Kitty, he had a severe hemorrhage early this morning. They rushed him to surgery."

"Even with the packing?" Kitty could hardly believe it. The packing had always stopped the hemorrhage before.

"It was bad." Florence's face was strained. "He had blood gushing from his mouth. It soaked through and—"

Kitty held up her hand, feeling ill. "I...I get the picture, Flo."

"I'm so sorry. I know how attached you are to him."

Kitty nodded, automatically stripped the bed, dragged the mattress to the dirty utility room, and called to order another mattress all the while praying fervently for Fayvel.

An hour later, the surgery orderlies brought him back to his bed. Kitty had moved it next to the nurse's desk.

His poor nose was distended with the fresh gauze bandages used to stop the bleeding, and he was deathly pale, almost as white as his sheets.

A glass bottle of blood hung from a pole near his head, infusing slowly through the rubber tubing and needle in the crook of his arm.

The orderly handed her the patient clipboard. "He's still a bit sleepy, but he should come around soon."

Kitty checked Fayvel's pulse, took his temperature, checked the blood line, and IV site. She brushed a wisp of hair off his pale forehead, wondering again if all the excitement yesterday had caused the bleed.

With a heavy heart, Kitty went about her duties as the shift went on. There were beds to make, medicine to administer, children to bathe and feed.

But every few moments, Kitty glanced toward Fayvel, who, despite what the orderly said, slept for many more hours before finally stirring.

Kitty hurried to his bedside. Fayvel's brown eyes fixed

on her, and he weakly raised his hand. She took it, trying to warm his cold fingers. "Don't speak, my little fish. You must save your strength."

His eyelids flickered, and he sank back into sleep.

Over the next few days, despite receiving more blood and excellent care, Fayvel didn't rally. Kitty hoped that when the surgeon removed the packing Fayvel would feel better, but that didn't help either.

Fayvel grew weaker and his face began to swell. He was taken back to surgery so his nasal passages could be examined under anesthesia.

Fayvel's parents were waiting when he was brought back. The surgeon, Dr. Greer, came with Fayvel and requested privacy to speak to Mr. and Mrs. Orenstein.

Kitty made Fayvel comfortable and left the bedside to wait at the nurse's desk. As Dr. Greer spoke with Fayvel's parents, Mrs. Orenstein broke into tears. Mr. Orenstein shook his head and held up his hand as if to ward off any further words from the surgeon. Then he, too, wept.

Dr. Greer took his leave of them and brought Fayvel's chart to the desk.

"What is it, Doctor?" The students never directly addressed a physician unless they had been asked a question. But Kitty had to know.

Dr. Greer's lips twisted, and he shook his head. "It was a sponge."

"Excuse me?"

"A sponge. One damn sponge left in the sinus when we took out the packing the last time."

He shook his head again and glanced back at the Orensteins, who now sat at Fayvel's bedside, holding his hands. "One of his sinus cavities is badly infected. We removed the sponge and washed out the nasal passages with antiseptic. Now, all we can do is pray and hope for the best."

Kitty felt ill.

It was the duty of the nurse assisting the surgeon during an operation to count the sponges before and after, several times, in order to have the correct count. Someone had miscounted. And one sponge left in there to fester was all it took to cause a massive infection.

Fayvel grew weaker over the next few days. He couldn't eat, although Kitty tried to tempt him with puddings and sweets. At the end of the week, Fayvel's bed was moved into a corner, and screens were set up around it for privacy.

Kitty spent as much time with Fayvel as she could, staying after her shift and coming in on her infrequent day off. One evening she peeked around the screen to say good night.

"Would you stay with me until I fall asleep, miss?" he said in a tiny voice. He looked so small and forlorn in the hospital bed. "My muter could not come." His lower lip wobbled.

Kitty's throat tightened. "Of course, I will, my little fish." She sat down on the bed and brought his cold fingers to her lips and kissed them.

One corner of his mouth lifted slightly in a smile.

"Would you like me to read to you?"

He shook his head. "I want to talk."

She pulled a chair close to the bed, and Fayvel moved over so he could lean against her, and she put her arm around him.

His fingers found hers again, and he leaned his head against her arm. "You know what I want to do when I grow up?"

Pain lanced through her chest. "And what is that, little one?"

"I want to be an artist and paint pictures."

"And what will you paint?"

"Animals. Ships. Maybe the circus."

Kitty laughed quietly. "Or maybe you will paint people. Famous people."

"You have to make a drawing first," he said, "a sketch."

"Is that right?"

"That's what Michelangelo did."

"Indeed? And how do you know about him?"

"My teacher at school." He nestled closer and looked up at her, the pupils of his brown eyes large and limpid in the dimness. "It seems such a long time since I went to school now, I hardly remember what it was like."

"I hope you will be able to go back, Fayvel. I hope it very much."

Oh, please, little fish, please, please don't ask me.

He gave her a long look and then sighed. "I made something for you."

"You did?"

He nodded. "Look in the cabinet. In the top."

Kitty turned to reach into the drawer of the bedside table and found a small bundle of papers tied with string.

She handed it to him and placed an extra pillow behind him so he could sit up. He untied the packet with feeble fingers, and her heart twisted inside her chest.

He handed her one. "That's my cat."

It was a pencil drawing of a plump tabby curled up on a window sill.

"It's very good."

"And this is my muter."

The sketch had caught his mother exactly, as she stood at the coal stove in an apron, holding a long wooden spoon.

"Fayvel, that's impressive."

He beamed at her praise. "This is my neighborhood."

The familiar tall tenement buildings lined both sides of the street to the top of the page, allowing only filtered sunlight to penetrate the gloom.

Lines of laundry stretched across the small space between the buildings, further blotting the light. Ragged children played around the stoops, and one tall man in a bowler hat and cane had posed jauntily for Fayvel.

The flags paving the alley were wet, and barrels of garbage lined one ell. A white-haired woman peered out of a window toward Fayvel, her care-worn and wrinkled face delineated with such skill that Kitty could feel her pain.

And then, in the center of the sketch, one lone window sill held a potted red geranium, the only color in the sketch, reaching up in the dim sunlight.

She didn't know what to say. This dying child had an incredible gift, one that would never be realized. A lump rose in her throat.

"Fayvel, this is so well done, I'm speechless."

"This for you."

Kitty turned the sketch over and gave a little gasp. Fayvel smiled. Staring back at her was the handsome face of Dr. Hayden, with the strong proud lines of forehead and cheek, and the thin scar that rimmed his jawline and only accentuated his male beauty.

"Fayvel," she said sternly.

Fayvel giggled, and the sound of it broke Kitty's heart. "That how he looks at you. All the time I see when you not look at him."

He ruffled through the pages and pulled out another. "This is for you, too."

The lump in her throat swelled bigger as she took the sketch. He had drawn her in profile, in her uniform and cap, leaning over a child in a white iron crib. The edges of the sketch were dark but around her head, he had drawn a nimbus of light.

Kitty swallowed, not trusting herself to speak. She squeezed his fingers and blinked back tears. "Is that really how you see me, Fayvel?" she whispered.

He searched her face, then raised a weak hand and brushed a tear off her cheek. "Always." Then he closed his eyes, gave a little sigh, and went to sleep.

The next day Kitty started on the pediatric night shift rotation. A gangrenous spot developed in the skin below Fayvel's nose.

Slowly, the black area grew and invaded the tissues until it encompassed his nose and mouth. He lapsed into semi-consciousness.

The lower part of his face collapsed and fell inward, leaving a gaping open wound that exposed his teeth and gangrenous sinuses, and Fayvel became unresponsive.

His parents sat silently by his bedside, tears running down their faces.

Kitty looked in frequently as she went about her duties. The small figure under the white bedclothes seemed to dwindle with each struggling breath during that long night.

When dawn broke the next morning, Kitty gave report to Annabelle, the oncoming day nurse, and pulled a chair to sit outside the screen and out of view of the rest of the ward.

She waited, listening to the shallow breaths that grew farther and farther apart until they ceased and Fayvel died quietly about noon.

Kitty informed Annabelle, who called the house super-visor to come and pronounce death and record the time for the death certificate.

Fayvel's parents sat at his bedside for the remainder of the day and into the evening until sunset because it was Shabbat, and no burial could take place until after sundown.

Kitty waited outside, her throat dry and her heart heavy. When darkness had fallen, they emerged from behind the screen.

"Mr. and Mrs. Orenstein, I am so very sorry."

"Thank you for taking good care of our *boychick*." Mrs. Orenstein crumpled against her husband, and he put his arm around her. He nodded as tears ran into his beard.

Slowly, holding each other, they turned and left the ward.

Kitty performed Fayvel's post-mortem care. She brought warm water and tenderly washed his wasted body and tied the identification tag onto his toe.

She wrapped him in his shroud, and before she covered his face, she brushed a wisp of his hair off his forehead and kissed the smooth skin of his forehead.

Then she pulled up the shroud and tucked the tin litho horse next to him. Alone, Kitty slowly wheeled the stretcher with his small body to the morgue. The desolation in her heart deepened with each step that echoed off the cold tile in the hallways.

She reached the morgue and rang the bell for admittance. Justin Van Hooft answered and started to say a cheery hello when he must have noticed her face, for he cut himself off in the middle of "Hello." Silently, he took the stretcher from her.

Kitty leaned over and kissed Fayvel through the shroud

one last time. "Go with God, my precious little fish," she whispered.

In a daze, she returned to her room in the dormitory to sleep for an hour before she had to report back for the night shift.

But she couldn't sleep.

Why, God? Why did such a precious little boy have to die such an awful death?

An hour later she was still awake.

And no answer had come.

TWENTY-ONE

Only a nurse of long experience knows what profound control is sometimes required to keep one's true feelings from coming to the surface.

Nursing Ethics, Isabel Hampton Robb, 1917

APRIL 25, 1918

WHILE KITTY MOURNED FAYVEL, the spring influenza struck the city of New York.

The student nurses were pressed into taking extra shifts to help the overburdened nurses. Scores of patients with respiratory symptoms, chills, fever, and fatigue poured into Bellevue. While most recovered, the mortality rate was higher than usual and seemed to disproportionately affect young adults.

For several weeks, the students worked alongside the doctors and nurses of Bellevue.

The days became an endless stream of dirty linen needing to be washed and boiled and patients to be attended to. About the time the number of new cases began to decrease, Moose caught influenza and had to be taken off her duties.

Two days after Moose fell ill, Kitty stood in the clean utility room, sorting linens. She'd worked for fourteen hours straight, so she wasn't surprised that her back ached and her feet hurt.

In another hour, she could go to bed, and she was looking forward to taking off her corset and putting her feet up.

Annabelle hurried into the room, her face pale and drawn.

Kitty dropped the sheet she was folding. "What's wrong?"

Annabelle started to sob, and Kitty's heart turned over. She put her hand on Annabelle's shoulder. "Is it my father? Is he dead?"

Annabelle wiped the tears from her face and cleared her throat. "No, no." She shook her head. "It's Moose. She's dying."

"What?" Kitty stared at Annabelle. "How is that possible? We just saw her yesterday and she was getting better."

ANNABELLE AND KITTY rushed to Medical Ward C, where the few nurses and doctors that had been diagnosed with influenza were being treated.

Moose lay in a bed damp with her sweat. Her hoarse

breathing rasped throughout the room, and her lips were blue.

Moose, the big, strong country girl. How had this happened? How could she have gotten this sick this fast?

The charge nurse came over. "We've called her family to come," she whispered.

Kitty choked back a sob and looked at Annabelle. "Let's bathe her and change the bed."

Annabelle nodded, and together they worked to make their friend more comfortable.

Moose woke as they pulled a clean nightdress over her head. Kitty stifled a gasp at how Moose's body had wasted over the past few days.

"Hey." Moose's voice sounded unsteady.

"Hey, yourself. How dare you get the flu when we need you on the floor?" Tears welled in Kitty's eyes.

A faint smile crept across Moose's pale face. "I didn't pick...a good time...did I?"

Annabelle and Kitty pulled chairs close to Moose's bedside and reached out for her hands.

Moose squeezed back weakly. "So good...to see you." She let go and turned to the side as a coughing spasm overcame her. Kitty and Annabelle looked on helplessly as Moose wiped her mouth and sank back on her pillows.

"In my desk, Kitty. My book of Shakespeare's sonnets. I want you...to have it."

"Don't do that, Moose. You're not going to die." Kitty clenched her fists so hard the nails bit into her palms. "Don't even think it."

Beside her, Annabelle dissolved into tears. Moose reached out and touched her head. "Annabelle...take my... Bible...to remember me by."

At this, Annabelle sobbed harder. Kitty shook her head back and forth, as tears burned, and words wouldn't come.

"It's...going to be fine, girls...I know where I'm going... and to whom." Moose closed her eyes. "I want you...to know...I appreciate all you did...to help me."

"Oh, Moose."

At that moment, Miss Trent appeared and stood at the foot of the bed. She laid her hand gently on Annabelle's shoulder. "Come along, dear. You need to rest. And you, too, Miss Winthrop. You're both exhausted. I know how hard you've been working." She glanced at Moose's still form. "Let her sleep, too."

In a daze, Kitty and Annabelle kissed Moose good night. Miss Trent walked them into the hall.

"I will stay with her until her family comes." Miss Trent straightened her collar. "She won't be alone."

Kitty nodded dumbly. She and Annabelle returned to the nurses' dormitory and went to bed. Moose died later that night, surrounded by her family.

And the iron band that had locked around Kitty's heart like a vise after the death of Fayvel cinched even tighter.

KITTY SAT IN THE NURSES' lounge with a copy of the Brooklyn Daily Eagle. Though she tried not to, she couldn't help but search the casualty lists for news of the Expeditionary Force Papa was part of.

The daily reports weren't good. So many killed or wounded. Fighting was fierce across the Aisne front. *Where Papa is.* She lifted a quick prayer for his strength and safety.

Another article on the front page caught her eye.

DISEASE LIKE GRIPPE IS EPIDEMIC IN SPAIN
KING ALFONSO SICK

THE FLU HAD ALREADY PASSED through New York City. But apparently, Spain had been hard hit. All of Madrid was paralyzed, according to the article. Theatres and moving picture houses deserted, and the tramways crippled because of the illness of its employees.

Kitty's only small measure of comfort during these trying times was Samuel. They continued to see each other off the Bellevue campus, usually for dinner or lunch when Kitty was free. Their relationship had moved along quite quickly, but it felt right and natural to Kitty, as Mama had said she felt when she had met Papa.

Samuel called for Kitty unexpectedly at Osborn Hall a week after Moose's death. She received a message that he was waiting in the reception room. She hurried down to meet him. The tense worried look on his face brightened when he saw her.

"Kitty." He strode to meet her, taking her hands. "I must leave town for a few days. My father is ill."

"I'm so sorry. What is it?"

"He has a bad heart, and he was spading dirt in the garden when he shouldn't have been. I must go to him. But before I go, I want to ask you a question." He took her hand and led her to a sofa. "I hadn't meant to speak so soon—I haven't gotten a ring yet, but I confess I have developed an attachment to you, Kitty. My admiration of your quest to learn has translated into something else entirely."

Her heart beat fast as he looked into her eyes.

"We could get engaged now and arrange the marriage

later, but I don't want to leave without your answer. I hope to tell my parents the good news."

"Are you asking me to marry you?"

Samuel laughed. "My goodness, yes. I love you. Will you marry me? Be my wife and the mother of my children?"

The mention of children caught her up short. With all the discussions they had had on medicine, it occurred to her that she had never discussed her own plans.

She hadn't actually told anyone, even Mama, and now with a sinking heart, she realized she had to tell Samuel.

Samuel's brow furrowed at Kitty's hesitation. "What is it? What's wrong?"

"There's something I need to tell you." This was going to be hard. Would he understand?

"Is there an impediment to our being married?" He searched her face, his blue eyes worried. "Is there...someone else?"

"No, no. There's no one else."

"Then what is it? Tell me, please, and relieve my misery at your hesitation."

"It's just that I don't know how you'll feel about it, and I—"

Samuel groaned. "You're killing me."

"After I graduate from the nursing program..."

"Yes?"

"I want to go to medical school." There. She'd said it out loud.

Samuel blinked. "Medical school?" His voice went up an octave. "You want to be a *doctor*?"

Her shoulders tightened at his astonished reaction. "Why do you say it like that?"

"It's, it's unthinkable. A doctor!" Samuel sprang to his feet and paced the room.

Kitty winced, knowing she had spoiled the moment, but she wasn't surprised at his reaction.

"Impossible," he muttered under his breath.

Turning on his heel, he stalked back toward the fireplace. There, he stopped and glared at her. "I cannot even express my disapproval strongly enough, Kitty."

Her back stiffened. "You're doing a fine job of it, actually."

"Why medicine? It's no place for a woman."

"But being a nurse is? I wouldn't be the first. There are female physicians in this very hospital, Samuel."

"Yes, but they're—" He cut off his words.

"What? They're old? They're spinsters?"

"Yes." He sighed. "And some of the other physicians refuse to work with them."

"To their own detriment."

Samuel shrugged.

"You've said yourself I have a sharp mind. You know that I'm completely capable in character, determination, and intelligence to pursue and achieve my goal."

"I do know that." He shook his head and paced again. "But…if we were to marry…naturally I would expect you to give up nursing. To keep our home." He tried to smile. "And raise our children."

"I see no reason that I cannot do both."

Samuel changed tactics then, coming to where she sat rigid as an iron rod on the sofa.

He took her hands, and she started at the contact. "Kitty, it isn't feasible. I'd be a laughingstock." His brown eyes pleaded with her.

"Because your wife is capable, bright, and tenacious? I should think any man would be happy to have such a wife."

She disengaged her hands from his and stood. She

willed her face to remain calm. But inside, her guts roiled, and she needed to get out of the room before she became sick.

Samuel stood, too, and threw his hands in the air. "Do your parents know? I can't believe they would approve."

"To the contrary, my parents have always been supportive. When I do tell them, I know they will be thrilled for me."

She took a step toward the door and drew a deep breath. "So, this will end our...relationship then."

Samuel closed the space between them in three rapid strides and gripped her by the shoulders. "If you love me, Kitty, you won't do this. Please."

He stared down into her face and for a tiny moment she almost wavered.

But how could he ask her to give up the very thing that he had sought for himself?

Then she shook her head sadly and looked up into his eyes. "If you love me," she said, "you won't make me choose between the two."

She wrenched away and hurried out of the sitting room as quickly as she could. She managed to reach the lavatory on her floor before she was violently ill.

She laid her cheek against the cold porcelain as her future washed away like the toilet water.

TWENTY-TWO

A woman desiring to become a trained nurse should have exceptional qualifications. She must be strong morally, mentally, and physically; she must do thorough practical work; she must have infinite tact, which is another name for a cultured common sense.

Nursing Ethics, Isabel Hampton Robb, 1917

MAY 30, 1918

KITTY SLOWLY MOUNTED THE STAIRCASE, walked down the hall to the Superintendent's office, and paused outside the door with her hand on the knob. She straightened her shoulders and rapped on the door.

"Come," a pleasant voice said.

Kitty opened the door, and Miss Henrietta Hayes stood

to greet her, shoulders straight in her starched white uniform.

"Ah, Miss Winthrop, please take a seat."

Kitty did so.

"You wanted to see me?"

"Yes, Miss Hayes. I...I wish to withdraw from the nursing program."

Miss Hayes nodded. "Is that so? Why?" She picked up several papers on her desk. "When you made the appointment to see me, I asked your instructors for a progress report."

She leafed through the papers and smiled. "You're at the top of your class, Miss Winthrop, both in your studies and in your clinical rotations. Many students do well in one or the other, but you excel at both. I would surely hate to lose such an exemplary student."

Kitty didn't answer. How could she explain? All the joy in her studies had disappeared. Each day had become a struggle to get out of bed, dress, and give her patients the care they deserved.

And now, the sight of Samuel—her previous source of comfort—only added to her sadness.

Miss Hayes laid the papers down and fixed Kitty with a piercing look. "So, it can't be your studies. What is it then?"

"I'm not sure I'm cut out to be a nurse."

"But your instructors say otherwise."

"Must I have a reason?" Kitty drew a shaky breath. "I wish to withdraw."

"Miss Winthrop, I would be neglecting my duty if I didn't at least try to understand why a star pupil is suddenly ready to give up her vocation."

"Perhaps I never had a vocation. I'm..." Her throat thickened. She wasn't sure any longer about anything.

"You've had some losses in the last few months." Miss Hayes's tone turned gentle. "I know that."

Kitty twisted her handkerchief in her lap and didn't look up.

"It's difficult to lose a patient, especially when you have formed a bond with them."

She stood, came around the desk, and drew up a chair. She put her hand over Kitty's and stilled her nervous fingers. "And perhaps, it's still harder to lose a friend and classmate."

Tears welled up then and dripped off the end of Kitty's nose.

Miss Hayes gave her a kind smile. "As a nurse, you are privy to pain and suffering that other young people of your age know nothing about. And it changes you."

Kitty nodded and wiped her eyes. "I don't think I can do it anymore."

"Miss Winthrop, I will certainly release you, if that is what you want." Her voice softened. "But you will not be able to go back to who you were before you came to Bellevue."

Kitty raised her head.

Miss Hayes smiled. "Bellevue has changed you. But what's more important is, you have changed Bellevue. If you hadn't been here, Fayvel would have missed out on the comfort and friendship you showed to him and his parents. Maisie McCloud would not have had the help and encouragement that you gave her."

Miss Hayes patted her hand. "There are patients in your future that are going to need every bit of skill, knowledge, and comfort you can give them. So, are you quite sure this is what you want?"

Kitty didn't know what she wanted, except that she

couldn't stay at Bellevue any longer. Mama was going to be so disappointed.

With a little sigh, Miss Hayes stood, reached for a paper, and signed it.

Kitty rose, and Miss Hayes handed her the release.

"We'll be here when you're ready to come back, Miss Winthrop."

Miss Hayes was wrong.

Kitty left the office and closed the door behind her.

She was never coming back.

IN THE NURSE'S RESIDENCE, Kitty telephoned her grandmother at Seaside. "Oma? It's me, Katharine."

A pause, and then her grandmother's silvery laughter sounded in Kitty's ear. "My dear, how unexpected! But lovely to hear your voice."

"I...I wanted to apologize for...the last time we saw each other. The way I ran off so suddenly."

"Thank you for that, Katharine. I have missed you. How is school going?"

Kitty swallowed hard. "That's why I'm calling, Oma. I've just withdrawn from school."

"My goodness. Why?"

Kitty's throat thickened. "I...don't think I can speak of it right now."

"Of course. Of course. Well then, what are your plans, dear?"

"I don't have any. I thought, possibly...could I come and visit you for a while?"

"Darling, I'd like nothing better. But what about your mother?"

"I haven't told her yet. I don't think I can face telling her."

"Understandable." Oma's voice turned soothing. "Come and stay as long as you like. When should I expect you?"

"Today?"

"Marvelous." Oma's voice lifted. "I'll arrange a rail ticket for you. Can you get yourself to Grand Central?"

"Yes."

"I will have your room ready when you arrive. It will be our little secret for now."

"Thank you, Oma."

Kitty hung up the phone, picked up her suitcase and portmanteau, and headed out to find a cab, leaving Bellevue behind.

THE SHORT TRAIN ride to Newport on a sparkling sunny day brightened Kitty's mood. When she detrained, there was Barrett waiting with a white placard with her name on it.

"Good afternoon," Barrett said. "Nice to see you again, Miss Winthrop."

He stowed her luggage in the boot and opened the door for her.

Kitty sank into the deep leather cushions and sighed. The smell of polished wood and leather rose around her. She could go to bed and sleep for weeks. Maybe that's just what she would do.

Barrett drove through the huge wrought iron gates of Seaside and stopped before the marble staircase to the front door.

Oma came down the steps, her Japanese morning

kimono trailing behind her. She had a new wig, arranged in coils around her face. "Darling, you're here."

She enveloped Kitty in an embrace, then stood back and held her at arm's length. "My goodness, you're so thin. And pale."

"I'm tired, Oma. So very tired."

"Of course, you are, dear. I'm sure you've been working much too hard."

They walked up the steps together.

"While you were at school, I had a bedroom done over for you." Oma patted Kitty's hand. "I hoped you'd come and visit when you had time. Darling, you've absolutely made my summer."

Kitty followed her up the marble staircase and down one of the many halls.

"I hope you approve of the changes. I've had a bath drawn for you. After a nice bath and a good sleep, you'll feel better. And then we can talk."

Oma kissed her on the cheek and left, closing the door behind her.

Kitty sat down on the bed and lay back, torn between the idea of falling asleep right there or getting into the bath.

The bath won out, and a few minutes later, she was up to her chin in the steaming water perfumed with jasmine oil. She nearly fell asleep in it.

Half an hour later, with her fingers and toes wrinkled like prunes, she put on a nightgown, pulled back the covers, and fell asleep.

THREE DAYS LATER, Kitty sat with her grandmother at breakfast.

Sunlight streamed in through the French doors open to the veranda, bringing with it breezes scented with the tang of the ocean. Seagulls called overhead and the sound of the surf murmured on the shore below.

"You're looking so improved, Katharine," her grandmother said around a mouthful of toast. "Nothing like sea air to put the roses back in your cheeks."

"I do feel better, Oma." Amazing what a couple nights of deep, uninterrupted sleep could do. "And I can't remember when I last ate this well."

Having finished a second portion of Eggs Benedict, she rubbed her tummy and grinned. "I fear if I stay too long, I won't be able to fit into my clothes."

Oma smiled indulgently. "That will never happen. You've the same constitution as your mother. You'll always be slender."

She put down her fork. "And speaking of clothes, we'll have to get you some summer frocks if we're going to entertain. I've decided to have a costume ball next Friday evening, and I have just the thing for you to wear."

"That sounds delightful. I've never been to a costumed anything."

"Oh, it's ever so much fun, seeing what the guests decide to come as."

Kitty smiled at her grandmother, whose face had lit at the prospect of the ball. "I've heard about the famous ball, Oma. The one where you gained your entree into society?"

"Your mother told you about that?"

"No, actually, I'd heard the story somewhere."

"Did your mother ever mention me?"

Kitty hesitated. "No. She didn't. Until your letter came, I had always assumed you were—"

She cleared her throat uncomfortably and avoided her grandmother's gaze.

Oma smiled. "You thought I was dead?" She sniffed, her smile fading. "In a way, I was." The smile returned. "But that's over now, and we're a family again. Second chances are wonderful, aren't they, Katharine?"

She rose. "I'm going to find that costume now and bring it to your room for you to try on. It might need some minor alterations. And I can't wait to see it on you."

When Kitty went up to her bedroom a short while later, she found her grandmother waiting for her.

Oma clapped her hands like a little girl. "I'm so excited for you to see it." She pointed to the costume laid out on her bed.

"Oh, my." All other words failed Kitty. The glitter of gold in the bright morning sunshine almost blinded her.

"I had it made in Paris, especially for your mother. Years ago." Oma's lips thinned. "Although she never wore it."

"Really? Why not?"

"Oh, darling, I really can't remember. But it should fit you, I should think, you're like two peas in a pod."

There was a skirt, a separate bodice, a headdress, and matching jewelry.

"Is...is it Cleopatra?"

Oma clapped her hands again. "Smart girl! Exactly. Charles Worth made it." She picked up the skirt, black crepe-de-chine with embroidered gold scarabs on the train. "It's cloth-of-gold."

With Oma's help, Kitty doffed her day dress and slipped the skirt over her head. Gold and diamonds encrusted the bodice with straps of emeralds and diamonds. The jeweled girdle fit snugly over her hips and gave way to more cloth-of-gold panels to the hem.

"Dizzy me, Oma, this is heavy. It must weigh ten pounds."

Oma laughed. "I should think so with all the gold used to create it."

Her grandmother picked up the square Egyptian headdress made of cloth-of-gold with striped black and gold side panels studded with diamonds. An ibis with outstretched wings of diamonds and sapphires crowned the headdress and a jeweled ostrich fan completed the costume.

Oma picked up a jewel case that had been hidden by the skirt and pulled out a collar of diamonds and pearls for Kitty to wear around her neck.

"And this is the final touch." She held up a slim diamond bracelet with the head of an asp. She took Kitty's right arm and slid it to her upper arm.

Oma clasped her hands together. "You're brilliant, darling. Come and see."

She gestured to the cheval mirror standing in a corner of the bedroom.

Kitty walked over, the weight of the gold pulling at her shoulders. She barely recognized her reflection. The jeweled girdle emphasized her slim waist and hips, and the headdress certainly gave her an exotic flair.

She turned slowly, from one side to another, as the diamonds sparkled and the gold glittered.

"This must be worth a fortunc, Oma."

"It is." Her grandmother straightened one of the diamond-encrusted shoulder straps. "Way more than what I paid for it twenty years ago."

"I think I'd be afraid to wear it. Someone might kidnap me."

"Oh, don't you worry. I'll have detectives watching you all night."

Kitty laughed, then stopped when her grandmother didn't. "Are you serious?"

"Very." She glanced at Kitty's feet. "We'll have to get you some gold slippers. But you look perfect. How fun this will be."

She helped Kitty out of the costume. "There won't be anyone who looks like you, Katharine. I guarantee it."

———

KITTY HAD BEEN at Seaside for a week when invitations to the ball went out. For the last three days, she'd picked up the telephone to call Mama and, each time, laid it back down again.

Her grandmother had gone out this morning. The perfect time to call Mama. Not that Oma would eavesdrop but...

She picked up the receiver and dialed the number, her heart beating hard in her chest.

Two rings and she heard the telephone click. "Winthrop residence."

"Jenny? Is that you?"

"I dinna ken who else." Jenny's lilting Scottish words danced over the wire. "And how be it with ye, Kitty?"

Kitty swallowed. "Oh, fine, fine. Is Mama home?"

"I'll fetch her."

A moment later, her mother's soft voice answered. "Kitty?"

"Hello, Mama."

"Is everything all right?"

"Yes. Why?"

"You don't usually call me in the middle of the week."

"Oh." She hadn't thought of that.

"What's wrong, sweetheart?"

Kitty's chest tightened at the concern in her mother's voice.

"Mama, I...I withdrew from school."

Her mother gasped. "Why, Kitty? What happened?"

"Nothing. And everything."

"Where are you now?"

Kitty hesitated. "I'm at Oma's. At Seaside."

There was a long pause.

"I didn't know how to tell you." The words tumbling out in a rush. "I knew you'd be disappointed. And I didn't want to hurt you. I'm so sorry."

"Kitty, listen to me."

Kitty closed her eyes and clutched the receiver.

"I'm not disappointed. I'm sure you must have a good reason." Mama sighed. "I'm only sorry you didn't feel you could tell me."

"I know. I'm sorry. I should have."

"Can you tell me now?"

"I...I'll try." She wiped a tear away with the back of her hand. "So many things, Mama. I loved what we were learning in the classroom and applying it to the patients on the medical and surgical wards. But then, I...I got attached to some of my patients. And when they died, it was so hard. The suffering they went through."

The gruesome memory of poor Fayvel's face came back to her, and she broke down completely, sobbing.

"And then, Moose died of influenza." The words threatened to choke her. "And Samuel. Oh, I haven't even told you about him. And that was the last straw. All I wanted to do was get as far away from Bellevue as I could. So, I called Oma."

She tried to laugh but sobbed instead. "Newport is

about as far away from that world as the North Pole is from the South."

"It is. So, what is your plan then?"

"Stay for a while. And try to decide what to do next."

"All right, sweetheart. Please keep me informed."

"I will. But Mama, why don't you come down here? I know Oma would like that."

"This isn't a good time. I have a new group of wharf babies to place in homes, so I can't leave right now."

"All right. You're not angry with me? For not telling you right away?"

"No, sweetheart. But from now on, I want you to promise me you truly understand you can always tell me anything. And I mean that. No matter how terrible you think it is."

A small sigh came over the telephone. Kitty's heart skipped a beat.

"I was never able to discuss anything with my mother. And when I had you, I wanted it to be different. I wanted to be the kind of mother that you could come to for anything."

"I just didn't want to hurt you."

"I'm stronger than you think, dear. I did manage to stand up to your grandmother, didn't I?"

Kitty laughed. "Yes. Yes, you surely did."

"Kitty, a parent would rather know than not know. Even if it's painful. That's part of being a mother."

"I'll remember. Thank you."

"Goodbye, sweetheart. Call me soon."

"I will. Goodbye."

Oma breezed in followed by Barrett loaded down with packages. "I've got your slippers for the ball. Doesn't that sound lovely? Just like Cinderella."

She turned to the chauffeur. "Bring those upstairs. And don't drop any of them."

"Yes, ma'am." Barrett's muffled voice floated from behind the towering pile.

Oma unpinned her hat and set it on the hall table. "Who were you speaking with?"

"My mother."

"Oh?" Oma glanced into the mirror and pushed a curl back into place on her wig. "Did you tell her you were here?"

"Yes."

"And?"

"It's fine. I asked her to come down, but she can't at the moment. She's busy with her wharflings."

Oma pulled off her scarf and gloves and handed them to the waiting maid. "Why don't you invite one of your friends on Saturday for the weekend? Perhaps Miss Mulhaney?"

"That would be nice."

"She can have the bedroom next to yours. There's a connecting door for midnight conversations."

She gave Kitty a teasing smile. "Now I must be off. So much to do before the ball on Friday. I trust you can amuse yourself?"

"Of course," Kitty murmured.

When her grandmother left the room, Kitty picked up the phone and rang Annabelle to ask her to come out on Sunday and spend a few days.

FRIDAY EVENING, Kitty stood with her grandmother to receive the guests at the masquerade ball.

Some familiar faces and some new ones filed through

the receiving line. She met Howard Singer's new wife Trudy, a buxom brunette dressed as Marie Antoinette, and was introduced to Colin McConnell's fiancé, a Miss Cordelia Wannamaker from Chicago, costumed as Juliet to McConnell's Romeo.

Kitty's costume engendered many an envious and admiring glance, and so far, no other guest had come costumed as a Roman or an Egyptian.

But that changed when a man in Roman dress with silver armor, leather greaves on arms and legs, a white-plumed helmet, and not one but two swords, stepped forward to be received.

Kitty had to repress a smile as he kissed first Oma's hand, then hers.

"I thought you preferred to slip in unnoticed, Lord Eavenlea," Kitty murmured.

"Ah, yes, yes, that's usually true. But your grandmother persuaded me to make an entrance tonight."

He stepped back and admired her costume. "You make an amazing Cleopatra. And may I say how delightful it is to see you again?"

"Thank you." Kitty smiled. "And you are?"

"I'm disappointed. You can't guess?"

He stood back to give her a better look at his costume. Even his hair had been styled across his forehead in spit curls.

"I can't imagine that you are anyone but Mark Antony. Suggested by my grandmother?"

He bowed. "Yes. And now I see why." He eyed her costume.

"She does have a rather droll sense of humor."

Lord Eavenlea smiled. "May I hope to have a dance later, Miss Winthrop?" His pale green eyes sparkled at her.

"If I can move in this dress, then, yes. All this gold is incredibly heavy." She leaned closer, catching a drift of his sandalwood cologne. "Apparently this gown is so valuable it requires a Pinkerton detective to guard it."

She nodded sideways at the stocky man in formal dress who stood off to the side studying both of them. "He's been instructed by my grandmother not to take his eyes off me."

"Shouldn't be a difficult job." The earl's smile deepened. "I can barely keep my eyes off you myself." He bowed. "Until later, then."

Kitty greeted the next person in the receiving line. How easily she had slipped back into the role of a society girl.

As if Bellevue had never happened.

And she hadn't forgotten her dance lessons, or how lovely it was to waltz around a ballroom with an expert dancer like the earl.

Her dance card soon filled up as she once again assumed the role of a young lady accustomed to glamorous balls. Throughout the evening she made airy conversation, smiled prettily, and accepted compliments from handsome young men.

But if she were truthful with herself, as she did all these things without much thought, her heart was far away, thinking of an empty white bed on the Pediatric ward, and two new graves in the cemetery.

TWENTY-THREE

SOCIETY SEEKS THE GREEN FIELDS AND SEASHORE, SUMMER EXODUS NOT TO INTERFERE WITH WAR RELIEF WORK

The New York Times, Sunday, June 9, 1918

The day after the ball, Kitty sat on the terrace at Seaside enjoying a late breakfast with her grandmother, listening to the roar of the surf and feeling a sense of déjà vu.

Invitations addressed to her poured into Seaside. The Earl of Eavenlea had invited them onto his yacht today for a dinner cruise later this afternoon, and to Kitty's surprise, Oma had urged her to accept it.

"After nearly drowning last year, Oma, I'd have thought you'd want to stay as far away from yachts as you could." She chuckled at the memory of Oma's wig floating in the bay.

"Oh, I've quite gotten over that dunking, I assure you.

And the earl recently told me he'd had a new staircase installed. It unfolds itself somehow, so no more ladder. It's the latest thing, apparently."

"And why isn't he married or engaged yet, anyway?" Kitty took a bite of buttered toast. "Supposedly, he was the prime catch last season."

Oma took a sip of tea. "Oh, he still is. Just waiting for the right girl, I suppose." She raised a penciled eyebrow at Kitty.

Kitty shook her head. "Oh, no. Don't look at me like that, Oma. The last thing I need right now is to think about men."

Her grandmother laughed and patted her hand. "Of course, darling. Just have fun. That's all you need to be concerned with."

"We'll accept the invitation then."

"Wonderful. I'll go send him a note right away." Oma left the breakfast table and went inside.

Kitty took a deep breath of the salty air and sighed. It was so beautiful here. Most of her parents' brownstone would fit in her bedroom here alone.

Or Fayvel's family.

She winced at the memory of Fayvel's deep brown eyes looking up at her.

You're my favorite, miss.

Her poor little fish. But he was out of pain, and in heaven with the Lord, and she took great comfort from that. But how his family must be suffering still.

Sunshine reflected off the sterling silver tea service on the lace-covered table. Teapot, sugar bowl, and cream pitcher all elegantly monogrammed with *VKKL*, Oma's initials.

She picked up a heavy silver teaspoon, idly wondering

what it cost. Probably enough to support Fayvel's family for months.

She put the teaspoon down.

Fayvel.

His face haunted her dreams. She thought of him every day and lifted up a prayer for his parents when she did.

And Moose. And Samuel. That was even more difficult. She couldn't think of him without a visceral stab to the heart, so she pushed herself up and marched into the house to get ready for the outing with Oma and the earl.

———

IT WAS déjà vu again as she and Oma met the earl at the Newport Harbor dock and were taken out to the yacht moored in the harbor.

This time there were no other guests but Kitty and Oma, who ascended the new fold-out stairway and pronounced it 'excellent,' then took a comfortable seat on the aft deck and waved Kitty and the earl off.

"You two children run along and enjoy yourselves. I'm content to sit here and enjoy the sea air."

"I haven't thought of myself as a child for a very long time." The earl smiled as they walked the deck to the prow of the yacht. "And I doubt you have either."

"No indeed."

"I'm so delighted to have you on board today, Miss Winthrop. You disappeared so suddenly last summer I was completely devastated."

"Oh, I doubt that. I'm sure there were many young ladies clamoring for your attention."

"But none of them as exceptional as yourself."

Kitty frowned. She'd forgotten how trite some high society conversations could be.

"So where *did* you disappear to?"

Kitty leaned over the railing to watch the bubbles at the prow. "My father volunteered to serve as a chaplain in the Army, and suddenly all the social doings seemed ridiculous. So, I applied to nursing school and was accepted at Bellevue."

His eyebrows shot up to his hairline. "And that's where you've been all this time?"

"Yes." She studied him with an amused smile. "You're going to catch something if you don't close your mouth, Lord Eavenlea."

He snapped his mouth closed. "I'm sorry, I never expected such a thing. But it's really not something a lady does, is it?"

"Are you saying I'm not a lady?"

He shook his head, flustered. "No...no, not at all."

"I'm teasing you."

"Oh." Then he smiled. "That's a good thing then, because..." He shuffled his feet and stared down at her, his eyes a luminous green in the bright sunshine. "I hadn't meant to speak about my intentions so soon, but...I would like to court you, Miss Winthrop, but if you are set on this nursing course then..."

"I'm not going back." She turned away.

"And why is that?"

"I'd rather not discuss it if you don't mind."

"Of course," he hastened to reassure her. "I only wish to know if my attentions would be unwelcomed."

"I don't think I'm ready to be courted, Lord Eavenlea, although I do enjoy your company."

"Then that's all I will ask, for now, your companionship. I look forward to spending more time with you. And look..." He pointed ahead. "Egret Island. We've arrived at our destination."

A two-story white clapboard house with a mansard roof sat at the edge of the rocky island. A whitewashed tower rose from the house, crowned with a cupola of glass windows.

"The old lighthouse," Lord Eavenlea said. "No longer in use."

"It's aptly named," Kitty said. "Just look at all those egrets, and I believe there's a couple of glossy ibises, too."

Oma joined them as the yacht dropped anchor about half a mile from the island. The small dinghy ferried them the rest of the way.

The crew members helped them onto the rocky beach and then proceeded to unload bundles and boxes.

"I've arranged a table and umbrella for you, Mrs. Lindenmayer. I thought you'd be more comfortable that way. Set the table up first, Lennon," Lord Eavenlea said to one of the crew.

Lennon quickly unfolded a portable table and then set up the striped umbrella shade. He produced a lawn chair with a cushioned stool for Oma's feet as well.

Her grandmother sat down. "Quite nice." She propped her feet on the stool.

Kitty regarded all this with an amused smile. "And what have you got planned for me, Lord Eavenlea?"

He chuckled and plucked two wicker baskets and a short rake from the dinghy. "You're going to work for your dinner, Miss Winthrop." He handed her a basket. "Follow me."

Kitty sent a sidelong glance toward her grandmother.

Oma gave an indulgent wave of her hand. "Go on, dear, it's perfectly acceptable. I can keep my eye on you from here."

"Nice work," Kitty murmured as she followed Lord Eavenlea down the beach.

He laughed and colored pink. "I hope it wasn't that obvious I wanted you to myself."

"My grandmother is quite astute, Lord Eavenlea. I doubt you could pull the wool over her eyes."

"Exactly. I was fairly sure she wouldn't care to dig clams."

"Oh, is that what we're going to do?"

"And mussels." He stopped. "This looks good. It's the perfect time. Low tide."

Hopping on one foot, he pulled off a shoe and sock and then removed the other one. He rolled his pants legs up midway, revealing muscled calves.

"Am I going to do that?"

"It depends. Do you want to get your toes wet? If not, you can use the rake on the beach."

"Turn around," she said.

He obliged, and Kitty quickly undid her garters and shed her stockings and flats.

"I'm ready."

He turned and smiled at her bare feet. "Brilliant."

He hooked the basket over his shoulder, waded into the water, and she followed.

"You feel around with your toes on the bottom until you feel something. Here we go." He reached into the water and pulled up a small black clamshell. "Just like that." He popped it into the bag.

"That looks simple enough." She probed the bottom. "Ah." She leaned over and pulled out a rock. "Oh."

"You'll find some. We've got to fill up these bags if we hope to have a feast later." Quickly, he flipped two more clams into his bag.

Kitty waded off a bit. The water this close to shore was warm and waves lapped at her legs. The hem of her dress was already muddy, but she didn't care.

A moment later, she found her first mussel in a bed of reeds closer to the shoreline and let out a yell. "I've got one."

"Jolly good." He grinned at her. His hair had fallen over his forehead, giving him a rakish look.

Soon her basket was half full as the reedy shore bed turned out to be a regular Klondike of mussels.

The air grew warmer as the sun moved higher until Lord Eavenlea straightened and rubbed his back. "I'm about full. You?"

She held her bag out, full nearly to the top with wet black shells. "Yes."

"We've got enough," he said. "And I think we'd better get you out of the sun. Your nose is turning pink."

She touched her nose with a wet finger and sure enough, it was tender, despite the protection of her broad-brimmed straw hat.

"Time for tea," Lord Eavenlea said, "and a well-deserved rest."

He took her bag and slung it over his shoulder with his. They waded out of the water and walked back to their campsite.

He handed the mussels to Barrett, who took them over to a rudimentary kitchen with a camp stove set up. "They have to soak in water for an hour or so, to give up the grit and sand in them."

"My word," Oma said. "You look positively raffish."

Kitty plunked into a chair shaded by the umbrella and stretched her feet out to the sun to dry. "It was fun. I've never had to find my own dinner before."

Lennon returned with a tea tray and a steaming pot, which he placed on the folding table before Oma.

"Would you do the honors?" Lord Eavenlea asked her grandmother.

"I'd be delighted." She proceeded to pour, and soon they were munching on shortbreads, scones, and petite frosted cakes.

Lord Eavenlea lifted his cup. "After tea, we can look at the tide pools."

"I'll stay here, and you two can go." Oma took a bite of her cake. "I don't care to put my ankle into one of those holes and break a leg."

They made their way back to the beach, leaving Oma to her pastries and tea.

The tide had run out, and the tide pools were full of sea anemones, starfish, and waving seagrasses.

"So..." Lord Eavenlea stirred the water in the pool with a gentle finger, causing the anemones to close. "How is it that you're not engaged, Miss Winthrop?"

Kitty blinked at the abrupt statement, and she must have gasped because Lord Eavenlea colored red.

"Pardon me, I didn't mean to ask that quite so baldly." He ran a finger around his collar. "Oh, dear. I've said the wrong thing." He cleared his throat. "Let me rephrase that. Is there anyone else?"

At this, Kitty laughed out loud. "My, you've become so much more direct since last summer."

"After you disappeared last summer, I realized I needed to be." He smiled. "Is there? Anyone else?"

The smile faded from Kitty's lips. There had been. The thought of Samuel's blue eyes and handsome face sent a dart of pain through her heart.

Lord Eavenlea scrutinized her. "I've upset you again." He touched her hand briefly. "I don't mean to cause you pain."

"You haven't." She straightened her shoulders and sighed, gazing out over the blue-green waters of the sea. "There was someone. A physician. But it's over now."

She looked up to find Lord Eavenlea watching her closely. "And that's why I'm not ready to see anyone else."

He nodded. "I understand." Then he gave her a mischievous smile, his green eyes bright in the sunshine. "Be sure to let me know when that changes, will you, Miss Winthrop?"

She laughed, and her heart lightened. "You'll be the first to know."

BACK AT SEASIDE later that night, Kitty said goodnight to her grandmother and went up to her room.

At the back of the closet, she found her portmanteau, drew a packet of papers from the side of it, and sank onto the padded banquette beneath the casement window.

A gentle breeze rustled the filmy curtains, carrying the scent of the white tuberoses blooming in pots on the terrace.

She opened the packet of papers and leafed through the pencil sketches Fayvel had given her until she came to the likeness of Samuel.

It was finely done. Fayvel had deftly caught the firmness in Samuel's square chin, the determination and warm good humor in his eyes.

Her heart ached as she wondered what he might be doing at that moment. Surely, he would be asleep in order to be up early for rounds at Bellevue.

Bellevue. A world away from Seaside.

She missed it.

TWENTY-FOUR

There are some things that money can't buy, like manners, morals, and integrity.

Anonymous

JUNE 16, 1918

SUNDAY AFTERNOON, Kitty asked Oma for the carriage to pick up her friend at the railroad station.

"Of course, dear. I've also invited Lord Eavenlea for dinner since it was Miss Mulhaney who introduced you."

Kitty's mouth opened to correct her grandmother.

"What is it, dear?"

Kitty closed her mouth and swallowed. "Oh, nothing, Oma."

She should have told her grandmother sooner that Miss

Mulhaney wasn't coming. Too late now. This was going to be interesting, to say the least.

All her misgivings disappeared when the bright red head and slender figure of Annabelle Boyle stepped off the train. "Ahoy, T2." They hugged.

"Dizzy me, it's so good to see you. I'm so glad you were able to get a few days off."

Baxter came around to take Annabelle's bag. "Is this all, Miss?"

"Yes. All my worldly goods."

The girls linked arms as they walked toward the car, Annabelle looking about her with great interest. "I've never been to Newport."

"Well, you can rest and relax, and we'll sit on the beach, and eat some wonderful food. My grandmother's chef is Parisian." She rubbed her tummy. "I think I've gained five pounds since I've been here."

"You do look well, Kitty. But oh, how I've missed you. We all have."

Kitty smiled faintly. "And I've missed you."

"Are you going to come back?"

"Always so blunt, T1. No mincing words for you."

"That's why you love me," Annabelle said with assurance.

Kitty laughed. "I do." Kitty patted her hand. "Maybe we can speak of it later. Right now, I just want to enjoy you being here. And..."

"And?" Annabelle waited.

"My grandmother suggested I invite a friend. But she meant from her high society people. And I didn't."

"Give me strength! Ye wee maggot, you've gone and done it now, haven't you?"

Kitty smiled ruefully. "I have."

"I suppose she'll throw me right out with all my bits and bobs."

"Actually, I don't really know what she'll do. I guess we'll find out. But I'm not worried. You can hold your own against anyone, Annabelle Boyle. You're the feistiest girl I know."

"I am that," Annabelle said. She patted Kitty's arm. "Faith and begorrah, but I do love a good clishmaclaver."

The carriage turned off Bellevue Avenue, and Annabelle sat up straighter as Oma's "cottage" came into view. "I'd no idea it'd be so grand." She stared at the towering marble columns that fronted Seaside.

The car rounded the curve that led to the front door and stopped. Kitty swallowed. There at the top of the marble steps stood her grandmother, smiling. Barrett opened the doors for them.

"Straight into the lion's mouth," Kitty murmured under her breath.

"Don't worry, I've brought my whip," Annabelle whispered.

Kitty smiled at her grandmother, whose own smile had frozen on her face.

They reached the top of the stairs. "Annabelle Boyle, this is my grandmother, Mrs. Vera Katharine Lindenmayer."

"Grand to meet you." Annabelle held out her hand.

She had deliberately exaggerated her Irish accent, and Kitty hid a smile.

Oma stared at Annabelle's hand and took her offered fingers in a limp grip. "It's my pleasure." Her voice was frosty, and she gave a sideways glance at Kitty. "Please come in. I'll show you to your room."

Lennon followed them with Annabelle's battered portmanteau, and Kitty had to stifle another smile at the look on her grandmother's horrified face when she caught sight of it.

But Oma was all smiles and politeness as she led the way upstairs and opened the door to the blue brocaded guest bedroom next to Kitty's.

"I'm sure you'll want to freshen up. We'll have tea at four."

She ushered Annabelle into the room, shut the door firmly, and turned to Kitty. "A word in private, please." She turned and strode away.

Kitty followed her grandmother's stiff back downstairs, across the marble foyer, and into the small room she used for an office to meet with the house staff.

Dizzy me, I'm in for it now.

Oma sat down at the tiny French writing desk and glared at Kitty. "And just what is that...that thing you've brought into my home?"

Kitty smiled pleasantly. "She's no 'thing,' Oma, Annabelle is my best friend."

Oma huffed indignantly and wrung her hands. "How dare you bring a woman of such low class here?"

"You told me to invite a friend. I invited one. I'm sorry she doesn't meet your expectations."

Oma slapped her hand on the table, sending papers scattering to the floor. "You know whom I believed you would invite. And you didn't disabuse me of the notion."

"Miss Mulhaney isn't a real friend, Oma. I barely know her. She's more of an acquaintance."

Her grandmother heaved a gigantic sigh. "What am I going to do now? It's too late to cancel dinner. What will he think?"

"Lord Eavenlea?"

"Who else?"

Kitty squeezed her fingers tight and kept her voice perfectly neutral. "I think, as a gentleman, he will be perfectly polite and charming. As will Annabelle."

Her grandmother stood up. "You're a minx, Katharine. I never suspected you would do such a cruel thing to me, but then," her voice hardened, "you are your mother's daughter."

"I am." Pride filled Kitty's chest as she echoed Annabelle's earlier words. "And I've never been happier to say so."

She turned abruptly and stalked out of the office.

"Where do you think you're going, Katharine? Come back here! We've got to sort this out."

Kitty ignored her grandmother's shouts and ran up the staircase as fast as she could, hurried to her bedroom, and locked the door.

Then she knocked at the connecting door between the two bedrooms. When Annabelle answered, she pushed past her and locked Annabelle's door, then fell on the bed in a fit of laughter.

"What is it?" Annabelle came and sat on the bed. "Kitty. What happened?"

"Oh my, she is so angry." Kitty shook her head. "I thought her head was going to explode. She was purple with rage."

Annabelle giggled. "You've done it now, T2."

"She doesn't like anyone to thwart her plans. I feel a tiny bit guilty, but I really wanted to see you." Kitty jumped up.

"Come on." She went back to her own bedroom and straight to the closet, pushing the day dresses aside to get to the evening gowns. "No, no, no, maybe, aha!"

She pulled a gown off the rack, pulled Annabelle over

to the cheval mirror, and held the gown in front of her. "Perfect!"

It was shimmering aqua silk embroidered with silver spangles and an inset of silver lace at the bust. It was sleeveless with slim shoulder straps. Triple strings of silver bugle beads draped from the bodice to the waist and attached to embroidered silver rosettes.

"Try it on." Kitty pushed the dress into Annabelle's hands.

Annabelle obliged.

"It fits you like a dream. You're gorgeous, T1."

Annabelle stared at her reflection in the mirror and ran her hands over the silk that snugly sheathed her hips and flowed to the floor. "Is it really me?"

Kitty laughed. "It certainly is, and I'm sure Lord Eavenlea is going to fall in love when he sees you in this."

She went back into the closet. "I have the jewels to match, too."

Annabelle walked into the closet and examined the row of gowns. "Which one are you going to wear?"

Kitty plucked one off the rack. "This." She held it up in front of her. "What do you think?"

"It's lovely," Annabelle said reverently.

Pale iridescent green silk and champagne lace at the yoke. Sleeveless, too, with sheer lace straps.

Kitty put the dress back and sat down to rootle through the jewelry casket. She pulled out a shimmering opal and diamond necklace with matching earrings and handed them to Annabelle.

"This goes with yours. And this matches the green." An antique amethyst and green peridot necklace and earrings accented with diamonds dangled from her fingers.

Then Kitty frowned. "My feet are bigger than yours, though."

"Not to worry," Annabelle said, "I actually have a pair of evening slippers with me that will do."

Kitty giggled. "No one will be looking at our feet, anyway. Now, would you like a tour of the house, Annabelle?"

Annabelle wrinkled her nose. "Will we run into your grandmother?"

"No, she usually rests in the afternoon, especially before a social engagement, so I think we're safe."

Annabelle changed out of the gown and hung it up.

"Take your hat," Kitty said. "We'll go down to the beach after."

It took nearly an hour to show Annabelle all the formal and informal rooms of Seaside, and Kitty finished the tour with the gardens that faced the ocean and then took the stony path to the beach.

Kitty had brought a rug with her and after she spread it on the sand, they took off their shoes and stockings and waded in the surf, then sat to dry their feet.

"So..." Annabelle sat up. "What happened? Are you going to tell me why you left Bellevue? Was it Moose?"

"That was part of it." Kitty sighed. "...and Fayvel." Dear sweet, precious Fayvel.

"I know he was attached to you. And you to him."

"Yes." She sighed again and idly sifted sand through her fingers. "And I can never forget him."

"That's a good thing, isn't it? To be remembered after we pass from this earth?"

"Yes. But the way he died. So horribly. And to see his parent's suffering." A pang went through Kitty as she wondered how the Orenstein family was coping with their loss.

Annabelle squeezed her arm. "I know. But thankfully, he was unconscious at the end."

Kitty nodded. "I was in a fog for days after that. And then...Samuel."

Annabelle waited.

"The last time we met he expressed his desire to marry me."

"Oh!" Annabelle sat up straighter. "My goodness."

Kitty punched the sand. "Until I told him I wanted to go on to medical school."

"What? You never told me that."

"I hadn't told anyone yet." She stared at the water.

Annabelle gave her a sympathetic smile. "Let me guess, he was horrified?"

Kitty nodded. "Flummoxed, really, at first." She laughed grimly. "If you could have seen his face. Like a drowning fish."

She imitated Samuel dumbly opening and closing his mouth, and Annabelle laughed. "Then he recovered his powers of speech. And told me it was out of the question."

Annabelle shrugged. "It would be a rare man who could accept it."

"But why not? Women can vote now in New York. Surely, it's only a matter of time before we're allowed entrance into other masculine professions as well. It's not that odd. Female physicians do exist."

"It's going to take a lot longer for men to understand *why* you'd want to do it." Annabelle stared out over the sea. "I think it threatens them. Threatens their idea of how things have always been done."

Kitty nodded. "But it's happening everywhere. Women

working for the war effort in places where previously only men did. Out of necessity."

"Ah, but what happens when they all come back?" Annabelle dribbled a handful of sand. "Sure, and they'll want their old jobs back, too." She pushed a stray curl off her face. "My goodness, this sea air is making my hair wild."

"I'll help you put it up later."

Annabelle sat back. "And so...you haven't said how you left it with Samuel."

Kitty sifted a handful of sand through her fingers, isolating a sea shell. "He said I had to choose. Him or medical school."

Samuel had sat there, so sure and certain, his smooth handsome face imperturbable as he waited for her answer with a tiny smile on his face.

"Ouch," Annabelle said.

"Yes." Kitty threw the shell into the water.

"And you said...?"

Kitty sighed. "I told him if he loved me, he wouldn't force me to choose."

"T2, my goodness, that must have been difficult."

"It was. And then seeing him at the hospital so often, and the deaths of Moose and Fayvel, I don't know, something inside me shriveled up. I had to get away."

Annabelle glanced back at the mansion. "So, you came here?" She snorted. "Sure, and it's about as far away from Bellevue as a body could get."

She waved at the ocean. "And the view is far better than the East River, absolutely."

She turned to Kitty. "But are you sure that all this," she fluttered her hand at the house behind them, "the beautiful gowns, the balls, the parties are really going to make you happy?"

Kitty shrugged. "A year ago, I thought so, when I discovered that I had a very rich grandmother with a famous name. At that time, I thought there could be nothing more wonderful than making my debut and actually wearing the gorgeous gowns I designed on my sketch pad. And then it happened."

"You made your debut?"

Kitty nodded. "Yes. The ball was held at the Metropolitan Opera House, and it was very grand and expensive."

"What happened? Why on earth did you apply to Bellevue?"

"The war happened. My father enlisted as a chaplain. My mother and I saw him off. And the world, my world, changed."

"You wanted to be useful?"

"Exactly, T1."

"Well." Annabelle sat up and leaned toward Kitty. "I don't think you've changed, except for the better. It's all still in there."

She pointed to Kitty's heart. "Don't you think that it's the very sensitivity we have for our patients that makes us better nurses? Or doctors?"

She sat back and fixed Kitty with a piercing look. "Would you have wanted Fayvel to have been cared for by a nurse who didn't give a fig for him? Saw him as just another patient to take care of? Don't you think he was better off precisely because you did care so much?"

Kitty blinked. "I...I never thought of it like that. I thought I was too weak, too affected, ...too *something*...to be a successful nurse."

"Remember our pledge at the capping ceremony?" Annabelle gripped Kitty's hand. "The last part, 'and devote myself to the welfare of those committed to my care.'"

She squeezed Kitty's hand. "That's what you were doing. With every bit of your being, you devoted yourself to Fayvel's welfare. And even though he died, he was better off because you were there with him. Don't you see?"

Annabelle's words washed through Kitty like a cleansing stream of water, pushing away the dark thoughts and loosening the iron band around her heart.

She nodded slowly. "Maybe that's true." She touched Annabelle's dear face. "You've given me much to ponder, T₁."

"I certainly hope so," Annabelle said, "because I need you back at school."

Kitty smiled. "I promise to think long and hard on it. But now, we'd better get back and ready ourselves for this formal supper party. And show my grandmother a thing or two."

LORD EAVENLEA and Oma were on the terrace when Kitty and Annabelle came down.

And as Kitty had predicted, the earl was indeed the perfect gentleman. Conversation was pleasant, if not scintillating, and not even Oma could find anything to criticize in Annabelle's demure comportment.

But the biggest surprise came after dinner had ended and they left the formal dining room to have their post-dinner sherry and port.

The French doors to the terrace were all open to the sea breeze that fluttered the gauzy drapes and tinkled the crystals in the chandelier overhead.

"Oh, what a lovely instrument." Annabelle walked over to the grand piano sitting on its own raised dais at one end of the room and ran her finger over the polished lid. "A Bosendorfer Imperial Grand!"

"Do you play?" Oma arched an eyebrow and no one in the room could doubt the taunting quality in her voice.

"A little. I've only dreamed of ever playing on such a magnificent instrument such as this, though."

"Oh, please, do play for us, Miss Boyle." Oma motioned with a languid wave of her hand. "I'm sure you're *perfectly* charming. Something Irish perhaps?"

Kitty sucked in her breath and the earl's eyes widened.

But if Annabelle was insulted, she displayed no sign of it. She bowed slightly in Oma's direction. "I would be delighted to attempt a piece for you."

Oma rang for Percy and had him open the lid and set the prop. Then she settled herself in a lounge chair, with the earl next to her, while Kitty took a seat more forward.

Annabelle sat down on the piano bench and arranged her skirts. Her slender figure perched with an impeccably straight posture, and anyone would have thought she had been born to this life.

Then she raised her hands and haltingly played a set of scales.

A self-satisfied smirk stole over Oma's features.

Annabelle glanced sideways at Kitty. And winked.

In the next moment, her hands lifted and came down on the keys, and the music soared in the room as Annabelle played like one possessed, her fingers flying up and down the full length of the keyboard.

Oma's mouth opened in a perfectly round O as the music crashed and reverberated through the room in long, flowing passages that seemed to use every key on the board, slowed to a beautifully slow section in the middle, and ended with a variation of the opening bars.

When the piece finished, a stunned hush pervaded the room as the final notes died away.

Then the earl jumped to his feet and broke the spell, clapping his hands. "Brava! Brava, Miss Boyle! That was superb!"

"My goodness, T1, where did you learn to play like that?"

Kitty rose and hugged her friend. Percy and some of the maids had gathered near the door, nodding and smiling, and had obviously listened as Annabelle played.

Annabelle turned and addressed Oma, who remained frozen and speechless on the settee.

"I thought that the Chopin Scherzo number 2, opus 31 was the best piece I could play on an Imperial Grand, Mrs. Lindenmayer. The Imperial is the only piano with ninety-seven keys, as I'm sure you know? Eight full octaves." She smiled. "I hope I did the piece justice and pleased you?"

Oma rose a bit unsteadily from her seat. "You did indeed, my dear. It was beautiful. And now, I will say goodnight."

The earl bowed. "Good night, Mrs. Lindenmayer."

The girls said goodnight, and Oma hurried from the room, looking as if she had consumed one too many glasses of champagne.

Lord Eavenlea pulled out his pocket watch and glanced at the time. "Dear ladies, I must also bid you a good evening. I have an early appointment tomorrow morning."

He took Annabelle's hand and kissed it. "You were marvelous, Miss Boyle. Just marvelous."

"It was wonderful to meet you," Annabelle said.

"I'll walk you out." Kitty took his arm and they walked

through the mansion to the front entrance to wait while Percy had the earl's carriage brought around.

"Your friend is delightful, Miss Winthrop. I think it's fair to say your grandmother was a trifle shocked."

"That's the understatement of the year."

If Oma had sought to put Annabelle in her place, Annabelle had certainly turned the tables. Kitty knew her grandmother had no musical ability and certainly hadn't known that there were ninety-seven keys on her grand piano, let alone what a scherzo or an opus was. Kitty grinned, just thinking of it.

"Your carriage is here, sir." Percy stepped up with the earl's hat and cane.

"Very good." The earl turned to Kitty. "I will see you next Monday at the regatta?"

"Of course. I'll be there to cheer Fortitude on. I hope you win."

He smiled down at her, his green eyes soft. "I hope I do, too."

He held her gaze a little longer than necessary, giving Kitty a jolt. Double meaning there.

They'd had no further discussion of courting, and she was content to have Lord Eavenlea as a friend. He was fun and easy to be with, and she didn't think she had given him any encouragement that their situation had changed.

But something about the look he'd just given her told her otherwise.

***

KITTY WENT BACK to find Annabelle playing the piano softly.

"Ti, you continually surprise me. I never knew you could play like that."

Annabelle laughed. "Runs in my family. All my sisters and brothers play, and my father teaches music. And we've got one famous pianist in the family, George Alexander Osborne. He was a friend to Chopin, as a matter of fact. I suppose I ought to have told your grandmother that, aye? That might have impressed her."

Kitty chuckled. "If she even knows who Chopin is. I think you did enough to impress her tonight. It's good for her. Maybe it will make her think. But why didn't you continue on with your music then? You could have become a concert pianist yourself."

Annabelle shrugged. "Perhaps. But I'm not cut out for that life. You must practice hours and hours a day, every day without fail, and give your whole life to it. I'd rather be a nurse at Bellevue any day. It's much more interesting. And rewarding."

Annabelle stretched her shoulders. "And I don't know about you, but I'm ready to get out of this dress and take my hair down."

"Good idea. Let's change and go down to the beach."

Ten minutes later, they were sitting on the beach in their nightgowns and their hair in loose braids.

Annabelle lay back on the blanket and looked up at the sky. "Would ye look at that?"

Kitty lay back next to Annabelle. Stars studded the clear night sky overhead and a slim crescent moon hung low over the horizon. The surf whispered quietly on the sand, and it was peaceful after the lights and fussiness of the formal dinner.

"I saw Dr. Hayden this week." Annabelle's voice was matter of fact.

The peace Kitty felt evaporated like rain on hot pavement.

"He asked about you."

Kitty rolled over. "What did he say?"

"He wanted to know where you were. He looked anxious."

"Hmm. What did you tell him?"

"That you'd left school."

"That's it?"

"Aye. I didn't think you'd want me to say more than that. He looked unhappy. I think he misses you. He wanted your address."

"Really." Maybe he was really missing her and thinking about her. Heaven knows she thought about him continually.

"I didn't give it to him. Should I have? He's still got it bad for you, Kitty."

Kitty shrugged. "I don't know. We left it at an impasse. Nothing I can do about it."

"Well, you've left school, aye? So, what's to stop you now? You can marry him, all impediments removed." Annabelle nudged Kitty and gave her a sly smile. "Unless you're coming back?"

Kitty had told the earl that she was never going back. And she had meant it at the time. But now...what was there to stop her from going to Samuel and agreeing to be his wife?

Would it be enough?

Or did she want more than that?

TWENTY-FIVE

ALLIES FORGE AHEAD, BATTLE GROWS
FURIOUS, AS ENEMY BRINGS UP BIG GUNS AND
BEST MEN TO MAKE A STAND ON THE VESSEL.

The New York Times, July 23, 1918

Kitty sat in the small dining room, exchanging conversation with Viscount Tarnley, seated to her left.

Oma had asked several of Lord Eavenlea's friends to a quiet informal supper tonight, and the Viscount seemed eager to make conversation, but Kitty couldn't stop thinking about the newspaper headlines this morning.

She hadn't had a letter from Papa in a while, nor had Mama. He had written so regularly to both of them that this long lapse of time without one had caused Kitty to imagine all sorts of unpleasant reasons why. Reading headlines about furious battles didn't help.

A month had passed since Annabelle's visit. Four weeks

of parties and balls, luncheons, teas, and picnics on the beach.

And she was growing restless, although she would hardly admit why to herself. She would have to make a decision soon. The summer was nearly over.

Lord Eavenlea had been uncommonly quiet during dinner. Even as she chatted with the Viscount to her right and Lady Duff-Gordon to her left, Kitty noticed that his intent gaze continually searched for hers.

There was a certain pleased glint deep in his eyes. And he kept patting his breast pocket as if to reassure himself something was still there.

Then she caught her breath. Oh, no. He was going to propose tonight. Realizing this only solidified the quietly growing realization that she wanted to return to school.

After dinner, the gentlemen withdrew to the study for port and cigars, while the ladies retired to her grandmother's salon.

The secret smiles Oma had sent Kitty's way all evening now made sense. Kitty grimaced. Did she dare plead a headache and retire to her room? Then she smiled wryly at Annabelle's voice in her head.

Just get on with it, T2!

Lord Eavenlea held back as the guests departed.

Oma turned as the door closed after the last guest. "I'm off to bed now, but do stay a little longer, Lord Eavenlea." She gave both of them a beaming smile.

He bowed. "Thank you for a lovely evening, Mrs. Lindenmayer." He took her hand and kissed the back of it.

"I hope we have many more of them," she said sweetly. "Good night."

She swept up the stairs and paused on the landing to

bestow a last beatific smile on both of them. She looked like the proverbial cat that had swallowed the canary.

Lord Eavenlea turned to her. "Won't you come out to the terrace, Miss Winthrop? There's a full moon tonight."

"'Come into the garden, Maud,'" Kitty murmured.

"'For the black bat, night, has flown,'" Lord Eavenlea quoted. "Tennyson. Very good. But let us not take that elegiac poem for our own, Miss Winthrop. I would choose Lord Byron."

> She walks in beauty, like the night
> Of cloudless climes and starry skies,
> And all that's best of dark and bright
> Meets in her aspect and her eyes.

KITTY WINCED AT HIS RECITATION. *Dizzy me, this is going to be bad.*

He offered his arm, and they strolled through the marble halls as

Kitty tried madly to figure out how to let him down gently. Hadn't she made it clear to him that she wasn't interested in marriage?

They walked to the wrought iron railing at the edge of the terrace that overlooked the sea.

The rising moon cast a mellow ivory path across the waves. Lanterns had been lit here and there, and all about them glowed the cloudless starry skies of Lord Byron's poem. It was a spectacularly beautiful night.

Too bad she was going to ruin it.

Lord Eavenlea cleared his throat, turned toward her, and took her hands. His palms were damp.

"Miss Winthrop, I think you know that I have formed an attachment, of the sweetest and most precious sort, to you."

"Lord Eavenlea, I—"

"Let me finish, my dear." He smiled at her. "I've dreamed of a night like this all summer."

He fumbled in his breast pocket and pulled out a tiny box. Then he got down on one knee. "Dearest Kitty, will you mar—"

"Please get up," Kitty said.

Lord Eavenlea blinked rapidly and held up the box. "Does that mean yes? But...but you haven't even seen the ring."

"It's not the ring, Lord Eavenlea." She sighed, feeling like she was about to slaughter an innocent animal. "It's you. I can't marry you."

He gasped and struggled to his feet. "But why? I thought you enjoyed my company."

"I do. I have. It's not that." *Oh, dear, this was difficult.*

"Then, what is it?" He had flushed a dark red, his eyes nearly bursting from their sockets.

"Maybe we should sit down."

"Sit down? I can't sit down. I can't *think*, Miss Winthrop!" He paced back and forth, wringing his hands." Then he stopped in front of her. "Why? Why can't you marry me?"

Kitty hesitated. "Things have changed. I've changed." She took his hand, and he started at the contact. "Please, come and sit, and I will try to explain."

She dropped his hand and walked to one of the wicker chairs. He followed her silently and collapsed into another.

His shoulders were slumped, his expression downcast, and a pang went through Kitty for him.

"You're a wonderful man, Lord Eavenlea, and I think you'll make a fine husband."

He sniffed at this and shook his head. "For someone else, is that it?"

"Yes. I'm so sorry. I plan to go back to school, finish my nursing, and then go to medical school."

"You said you were done with that," he said accusingly. "I distinctly remember."

"I thought I was. But now, I know I'm not. Please forgive me."

He sat back and folded his arms across his chest. "Does your grandmother know your plans?"

"My grandmother? No, I haven't told anyone yet, except you."

He smiled faintly. "Be prepared for fireworks then."

Kitty frowned. "What do you mean?"

"It means I have to start all over."

Kitty shook her head, not understanding. "To find a wife?'

His lips twisted in an ugly grimace. "To find another heiress."

The words struck her like a hammer blow. "What? I'm not an heiress."

"You will be. At least according to your grandmother."

Kitty's thoughts reeled. "I know nothing about that."

A worse thought occurred to her, and she jumped up from the chair, knocking it backward. "Is that why you want me to marry you? You thought I had *money*?"

"It doesn't really matter now, does it?" He shook his head. "But no. I do care for you. I think we could have had a good marriage."

He stood and started to say something, then stopped. He took a step away and turned back, hesitating, pulled in two directions like the butterflied shrimp they'd had at dinner.

Then he straightened as if he'd made a decision. "I don't know whether I should tell you this or not." He searched her face, his brow furrowed. "Are you aware that your grandmother promised me a dowry? A very large dowry?"

Kitty's jaw fell open. "I had no idea." She sank back onto the wicker chair, her thoughts going in ten directions at once.

"I thought so." He sighed. "Then you'll be even more surprised to know the amount she promised me if we married."

Kitty clenched her jaw. She should have foreseen this. "How much?"

"Two million dollars. One million to be paid when our engagement is announced and another million on the day of our marriage."

He grimaced as she gasped again and put her hand to her mouth.

"I don't know if I should have told you or not." He sighed. "But I wish you luck when you tell her your plans. Now that she won't eventually have the Duchess of Eavenlea as her granddaughter."

He stood. "I'm sorry you won't marry me, Miss Winthrop. It wasn't just the money. I truly do care for you. But I can appreciate that your path in life is in a different direction from mine."

He took her hand and kissed it. "And now, goodbye."

She sat, frozen, as his footsteps retreated, and she was left alone.

So, her grandmother had bribed Lord Eavenlea. Her

mother's words in the carriage after Kitty had met her grandmother came back to her.

I detested the life my mother had planned for me. To fulfill her ambition for a royal title in the family, she tried to force me to marry a man I didn't love!

Was that what this was?

Had this been her grandmother's plan all along? No one could be that coldly strategic, could they?

She paced back and forth on the moonlit terrace, then stopped. Her grandmother's bedroom window was dark. It was too late to ask her now.

But first thing in the morning Kitty was going to find out.

SLEEP WOULDN'T COME. Kitty tossed and turned all night as those three words ran through her head.

Two. Million. Dollars.

Bright sunlight streamed into her bedroom the next morning. If the clock was correct, she'd overslept. It was almost noon.

Kitty jumped out of bed, washed, dressed, and quickly packed the few articles of clothing she had with her that hadn't been paid for by her grandmother.

She left her valise in the marble foyer and asked a surprised Percy to call her a carriage.

She ran up the marble staircase two steps at a time, down the long oriental-carpeted hall that led to her grandmother's suite of rooms and knocked loudly on the door. Without waiting for an answer, she opened the door and went in.

Dressed for guests, her grandmother sat at her dressing table as her maid Fleurette fixed her wig.

Now as Kitty stood in the center of the opulent chamber that reeked of gold and ostentation, all the frills, ruffles, and swagged silk draperies made her feel smothered.

"Good morning, Katharine." Then Oma frowned and her sharp gaze flicked over Kitty. "Why are you wearing that?"

It was one of her old dresses from home, a breezy summer seersucker.

"It doesn't matter. I'm here to have a chat with you."

Her grandmother waved her hand. "I haven't got time now. I'm already late for my luncheon party as it is."

Then she paused and her eyebrows lifted. "But do you have any happy news for me?"

"I'm afraid not." Kitty's chest tightened. "You bribed Lord Eavenlea to marry me? How could you do something like that?"

Her grandmother glanced at Fleurette, who put down the dress she had taken from the wardrobe and scurried off.

"Now what is all this about?" Oma gazed at herself in the mirror and applied a dusting of face powder. "I have no idea what you're referring to, Katharine."

Kitty scoffed. "Oh, don't lie. He's already told me the truth."

Her grandmother's eyes narrowed. "He shouldn't have done that. You need never have known."

Kitty blinked. "Are you serious? You must be mad."

Her grandmother bristled. "Don't you dare speak to me in such a tone."

Then her face softened. "I want you to have a good start in married life, Katharine, that's all," she said soothingly as one would speak to a child. "Something to put away."

"Is that what it was? Or was it to ensure that the Lindenmayers would have a duchess in the family to boast about? The final cap in your social career. Your grand-daughter, Duchess of Eavenlea?"

"Now, Katharine—"

Kitty held up her hand. "No. I don't want to hear any more lies."

Her breath came in gasps, and she could hardly see straight as blinding enmity rose in her chest.

"That's what you did to my mother, wasn't it? You wanted her to marry a duke, and you forced her, almost had her, until she found the courage to stand up to you and leave him at the altar. And then you cut her off. Not one word until the day you sent the letter."

"She was useless." Oma's voice dripped with contempt. "After all I had done, groomed her for years to make a magnificent match, on her wedding day she discovers she has a backbone."

Oma sprang to her feet, her face mottled. "In front of the cream of New York high society, she walked away from the altar. I was humiliated! Humiliated, I tell you. She caused a scandal which to this day has not been forgotten. You've no idea what your mother did to me."

Her voice softened. "But you're different, Katharine. You're nothing like your mother. You've understood and recognized the advantages I provided for you, so it will all be worth it in the end. Now have you something important to tell your Oma?"

Kitty froze, as a new and incredibly painful thought wormed its way into her heated thoughts. "Oh, my good-ness. That was it, wasn't it? After all that time—"

She shook her head in disbelief as all the pieces fell into place. "You found out somehow that she had an attractive daughter, didn't you? You reached out to her, knowing she wouldn't refuse your offer of reconciliation because she is such a loving and forgiving woman. All so you could get your claws on me."

"You're twice the woman she was." Oma smiled cruelly. "I told her she'd be sorry someday that she crossed me."

Kitty caught her breath. "It's even more than wanting a title in the family, isn't it?" Kitty shook her head. "You never wanted to get to really know me, did you? In the end, it was all for revenge."

Her voice shook as anger overtook her. "You wanted revenge on your own daughter. How despicable."

"Are you through?" Her grandmother's lips twisted. "Because the sooner we get this behind us, we can start to plan your wedding. We'll have it in New Y—"

Kitty laughed, incredulous. "There's not going to be a wedding, you scurrilous old hag."

"How dare you?" Her grandmother sputtered. Then she sat up straighter. "What?" she screeched. "No wedding?"

"No wedding. I refused Lord Eavenlea last night." Oh, it felt so good to say it.

"No-o-o!" Her grandmother wailed. "You can't do this to me."

Kitty shook her head, disgust overwhelming the anger. "It's all about you, isn't it? How dare you try to control other people's lives like they're pieces on a chessboard? You make me sick."

The rage dissipated, and a deadly calm flowed over Kitty. "You're right about one thing. In some ways, I am different from my mother. You won't find me as forgiving as she is."

She started to pull the diamond and aquamarine ring off

her finger and stopped. She could sell it and give the money to Fayvel's family. "You'll never see me again."

Oma's face flushed dark red and a vein in the middle of her forehead stood out. "I'll disinherit you, Katharine! You won't get a penny if you don't apologize to me immediately."

Kitty laughed. "I don't want you, and I certainly don't want your money.

She turned at the door. "Goodbye and good riddance."

She left and slammed the door hard, oblivious to the shrieks behind it, and turned to find half of the household staff anxiously hovering in the hall.

Percy stepped forward. "Is everything all right, Miss?"

"It is now," Kitty said.

"THE CARRIAGE IS HERE, MISS." Percy hesitated. "I'm sorry to see you go but I understand why you must."

Kitty smiled grimly. "I suppose all the staff knows by now. I hope she won't take her anger out on you and them, Percy."

He shrugged. "We are accustomed to it, Miss." Then he took her hand, bowed low, and kissed it. "It's been an unexpected delight to meet you, Miss Katharine." He straightened. "Please send your mother my regards."

"I will."

Percy picked up her valise and headed for the front door.

"Wait just a moment, Percy. I left some sea glass on the terrace, and I want to take it with me."

She hurried to the stone-flagged terrace at the back of the house and opened the French doors.

A round table had been set up there, shaded with a white lace umbrella, and place settings of china and silver for four.

A Chinese urn with purple buddleia and pink roses sat in the center of the white linen tablecloth, and the ladies sitting there were drinking champagne from crystal flutes.

They stopped talking when she stepped out onto the terrace. It was Mrs. Oehlrichs, Mrs. Vanderfelder, and Mrs. Belmont. All dressed and hatted to the nines for luncheon.

"Why, good afternoon, Miss Winthrop," Mrs. Oehlrichs said.

"Good afternoon, ladies. Don't let me interrupt you."

She walked to the edge of the terrace where she had laid the glass on the wrought iron railing. But they didn't resume their conversation as she pocketed the glass pieces, and she could feel their eyes on her.

The overheard conversation in the Ladies' lounge at the Met ball over a year ago came back to her as clear as if it happened yesterday.

"And what are you about today, Miss Winthrop?" Mrs. Oehlrichs asked in a silky voice.

She exchanged a knowing glance with the other two matrons as Kitty turned around. "Seeing the earl?"

Anger streaked like a red-hot coal from the pit of her stomach to the top of Kitty's head.

"Oh," Kitty said sweetly. "It's Miss Winthrop today, is it? But at the Met ball last year you called me the interloper, did you not?"

Mrs. Oehlrichs choked on her champagne. "W-what?"

The blue egret feathers on her hat quivered as she set her glass down and glared at Kitty.

"How impolite, Miss Winthrop." Mrs. Vanderfelder's heavily corseted bosom heaved. "I'm sure your grandmother would be outraged to hear you address your elders so rudely."

"Is that so, Mrs. Vanderfelder? As outraged to hear that you called her 'an overblown hostess?'"

Mrs. Vanderfelder sputtered. "I never said such a thing."

"Oh, but you did. I wonder what 'old lady Lindenmayer' would think about that?"

Mrs. Vanderfelder's plump face flushed crimson, and she snatched her stiffly starched napkin off the table to fan herself.

"That's enough." Mrs. Oehlrichs slapped her diamond-ringed hand on the table and the dishes rattled. "What impertinence."

"I'm only telling the truth. Repeating your exact words." She paused. "Oh, but maybe that's what you meant by me 'queening it' over everyone that night, Mrs. Oehlrichs."

Mrs. Oehlrichs rose, the turkey wattle under her chin shaking with fury. "I won't stay here to be insulted."

Kitty laughed. "I was in the ladies lounge the night of the Met ball. I heard your entire conversation."

She smiled sweetly. "And I have an excellent memory. So, tell me, how can you be insulted with the truth? But please don't leave. I'm off to return to my mother. Or, as you called her," she said, turning to Mrs. Belmont, "the famous Evangeline Lindenmayer."

She turned, enjoying the insulted huffs and the "Well, I nevers," behind her, when her grandmother walked through the French doors.

Her eyes widened, no doubt with the shock that Kitty was still here.

"Don't worry, I'm leaving," Kitty said to her astonished

grandmother. "Have a wonderful time with your..." She paused a beat and cast one backward glance at the outraged women. "Your *friends*."

She found Percy lingering in the drawing room as she exited the terrace, and she cocked an eyebrow at him. "Did you hear all that?"

The silver-haired butler tried to maintain his usual unflappable dignity but failed, and he smiled sheepishly. "I did." Then his smile stretched ear to ear. "And it was just glorious!"

AT THE TRAIN station in Newport, Kitty purchased a ticket to New York City, and from Grand Central Station on 42nd Street, she took a cab and stopped a few blocks away on East 67th Street to walk the rest of the way on the sun-dappled sidewalks.

Children played jacks on the stoops of the brownstones that lined the street while housewives visited with their neighbors. She had to dodge a row of small boys playing leapfrog on the sidewalk outside of East 70th Street.

Kitty stopped before her family's dear old brownstone and basked in the feeling of being home. Home! Where the person she loved more than anyone else in the world would be puttering about the kitchen or reading in the parlor or making plans for her wharflings.

She ran up the steps and burst through the front door. "Mama," she called, "I'm home!"

Her mother appeared at the top of the stairs, her spectacles on and a paper in her hand. "Oh, my goodness, Kitty!"

She dropped the paper and hurried down the stairs, holding her arms open wide.

Tears smarted in Kitty's eyes as she went into her mother's embrace. "You were right, Mama," she whispered into her mother's neck. "I should have listened to you."

Her mother pulled back to search Kitty's face and gently touched her cheek. "Oh, my darling girl, I'm so happy to have you home. Do you want to tell me about it?"

Kitty smiled ruefully. "Yes."

Mrs. Mac came from the kitchen with flour on her hands to greet Kitty, and then Jenny appeared with a basket of roses cut from the garden.

She dropped it flat on the floor at seeing Kitty. "It's my wee bairn come home." She hugged Kitty ferociously.

"Would you brew us a pot of coffee, Mrs. Mac?" Mama asked. "And bring us some of those lovely scones you baked this morning."

With their arms about each other, mother and daughter walked into the parlor to have a good long talk.

An hour later, exhausted with all her confessions, Kitty lay with her head in her mother's lap. "And the worst thing, Mama, is how I hurt you. I feel terrible about that." Kitty sat up. "Please forgive me."

"Darling, of course, I forgive you. I'll admit, it was difficult to see your grandmother showering you with all these gifts. After our initial visit, I began to suspect her real motive. But I knew you were a sensible girl. I believed you'd figure it out for yourself."

Mama laughed. "And I spent a lot of time on my knees. Praying for you and your father. But haven't you left one thing out? You haven't mentioned Samuel."

Kitty sighed. "It hurts to talk about it. We continued to see each other quietly. It felt right and so comfortable to be with him. And then, right at the end of the semester, he came unexpectedly one night to see me at Osborn Hall. His father was ill, so he had to leave and wouldn't be back for a while."

Kitty bit her lip. The memory of Samuel's disappointed face sent a pang of regret through her.

"And?"

"He asked me to marry him."

"Oh, my."

"But I had to tell him something first, something I hadn't told anyone yet. I want to go on after graduation to medical school."

"Darling, that's wonderful! I'm thrilled to hear it." Then she covered Kitty's hand with her own. "But Samuel wasn't in favor of it?"

Kitty shook her head. "No. Wouldn't even consider it. So, I told him no."

"That must have been so difficult."

"It was. Terrible. That was the final straw that broke the camel's back, I suppose. I withdrew from school a few days later."

"Oh, Kitty, I wish you had told me." Mama's blue eyes clouded.

"Don't worry. I'll never keep anything from you again. I've learned my lesson. So, here's the last thing. I want to go back to Bellevue."

"I'm so glad." Mama's face lit up with joy.

"I want to finish nursing school and then go on." Kitty wiped her eyes. "So, I must call Miss Hayes this afternoon and speak to her about it. The funny thing is she said I'd be back. I didn't think so at the time, but she was right, too."

AUGUST 1, 1918

. . .

MISS HAYES WAS DELIGHTED to hear from Kitty, and a week later she was back at Bellevue in her old room. She had missed a semester, so she would be behind Annabelle and the other girls and graduate at a later date.

But Kitty didn't care. She knew exactly where she belonged now, and she returned to her studies with clear eyes and fresh enthusiasm for her patients.

The nursing shortage at Bellevue had worsened as the war in Europe went on. Many nurses had joined the Red Cross to serve at hospitals in France, which in turn led to the student nurses being accorded more responsibility for patient care.

Kitty stood and surveyed the medical floor she was in charge of—thirty-six beds full of patients.

She had two students with her to care for all of them, girls in their first semester: Miss Floyd, a tiny scrap of a girl, and Miss Blake, a plain-faced country girl.

Only one patient was troublesome tonight. Mathias Eisenmenger, a feisty eighty-year-old German lawyer, had fallen in court while trying a case and fractured his leg in two places. Mr. Eisenmenger had spent the last four weeks on the ward encased in a cast from hip to ankle on his right leg.

Once he'd begun to feel better, the nurses couldn't keep him in bed, especially since he'd learned how to get around in a wheelchair, even though the cast had to weigh as much as a small elephant.

The night nurse had told her one of the orderlies had found Mr. Eisenmenger in the stairwell at four a.m., attempting to go down the stairs in his chair, and had barely rescued him in the nick of time.

Kitty was determined that no such incident would happen on her shift, and she had Mr. Eisenmenger's bed moved next to the nurse's desk, where she used a cloth restraint to tie him in his chair and then fastened his chair with a belt tied to the desk leg.

That worked moderately well until mid-morning when there was a terrific clatter and a screeching noise. Kitty looked up to see Mr. Eisenmenger dragging the desk behind him as he fought his way to the ward door.

It took all three nurses to pry his fingers off the door-frame and drag him back into the ward.

"Mr. Eisenmenger." Kitty wheeled his chair close to the nurse's desk, pulled a chair over, and sat down next to the patient. "Where is it you want to go?"

"*ZuHause*. Home."

He drummed his fingers on the arms of his chair and glared at her from under bushy gray eyebrows. "Out. Of. Here."

With each word, he poked his forefinger sternly at her.

"Well," Kitty said, keeping her tone matter-of-fact, "you're progressing very well. Just two more weeks and the cast will come off and you *will* be out of here. But meanwhile, if you fall down the stairs and break more bones, you could be here for months. You don't want that, do you?"

"*Nein*." Mr. Eisenmenger smiled at her, his blue eyes sparkling.

"So then." Kitty made her voice stern. "Can we agree there will be no more escape attempts?"

Mr. Eisenmenger pursed his lips as if he was considering it. Then he shook his head. "*Nein*."

Kitty sighed. Keeping one hand on his wheelchair, she reached for the telephone and put in a call to maintenance.

A few minutes later, Otis, a barrel-chested man who

serviced Bellevue's furnaces, came to the floor with the item she had requested.

"Here be what you wanted, Miss." He held up a padlock and a length of steel chain in his work-hardened hands. "What's it for?"

"I'll show you."

Although Mr. Eisenmenger put on the brakes with his feet, she managed to force his wheelchair over to the heavy-duty enameled-iron sink at the front of the ward. The sink was big enough to bathe an adult in, if needed, and weighed a ton.

"Please chain the wheelchair to the pipe, Otis."

Otis' eyes widened. "Yes, miss."

It took no more than a minute or two. Kitty and Otis stood back and watched as Mr. Eisenmenger pulled against the chain.

When his wheelchair didn't budge, he started yelling furiously at them.

Otis scratched his head. "What's he saying, miss?"

"I presume he's speaking German. And I don't think he's complimenting us on our plan, that's for sure."

"That orter keep him in place, I guess." Otis chuckled. "He sure is mad. Anything else you need, miss?"

"Thank you, no."

Otis left the ward, and Kitty returned to dispensing medication, glancing up to check on Mr. Eisenmenger every few minutes.

He continued to try experimental tugs on the chain, but after an hour he seemed to have resigned himself to staying in one place. One of the student nurses had given him a newspaper, and he seemed to be reading it.

Samuel came onto the ward mid-morning and, at the sight of him, Kitty's pulse shot into the stratosphere.

All her plans to remain cool and aloof when she encountered him for the first time since she had returned to Bellevue flew straight out the tall windows lining the ward.

She ignored him as he walked over to the desk and examined Mr. Eisenmenger's attachment to the sink. "Rather unorthodox way to restrain a patient."

His friendly voice overcame her better judgment and she turned to face him. His smile and the warmth in his blue eyes almost undid her.

Did he think he could act as if nothing had happened between them?

"If you have a better idea, please tell me, Dr. Hayden."

Her voice came out sharper than she intended. But she didn't need any criticism this morning, especially from him. "That patient is determined to get to the stairwell, and that's the only thing I could think of."

Dr. Hayden raised his hands in an amiable show of surrender. "It's unusual is all. Rather like you."

Because she wanted to go to medical school? Blood rushed to her face as she turned back to the doctor's orders on her desk. "Apparently, I am. Much too unusual for you, *Doctor*."

She saw him stiffen from the corner of her eye, then turn and walk away. His retreating figure left an ache in her heart. She didn't want to be mean, but she didn't want to encourage him either, especially since he had such a rigid idea of what a "proper" marriage should be.

She pushed him out of her head as best she could and went back to work.

She was at the end of the ward changing a dressing when there came a violent clanking of chains.

A moment later, a tremendous crash reverberated

through the room. Screams and a whooshing sound followed.

Kitty ran up the aisle and yelped as water streamed over her shoes. Like a madman, Mr. Eisenmenger furiously rolled his chair toward the ward door, dragging the screeching sink behind him and carving a deep furrow in the wooden floor. Water gushed from the broken pipe like a fountain, showering the closest patients, who were yelling and screaming.

At just that moment, Dr. Winkler arrived on the scene. "We have to find the water shutoff," he yelled.

Pandemonium broke loose. Other staff rushed in from outside.

Kitty picked up the phone and dialed the operator. "We have a water pipe break emergency on Ward C. Send help."

Then she ran to Mr. Eisenmenger, wheeled him to the far end of the ward, and assigned Miss Blake to stay with him.

A moment later, maintenance men and hospital workers rushed into the ward. She had the men move the patients away from the water as the plumbers wrestled with the pipe.

At the end of the shift, she surveyed her water-soaked domain. The patients had been removed to other wards.

The plumbers had finally managed to cap the pipe. Most of the water had been mopped up. Mr. Eisenmenger had been placed in a private room with a one-to-one orderly, hired at the hospital's expense.

Now people from administration had arrived to assess the damage.

At this inopportune moment, Samuel entered the ward and walked over to where she sat, wet and frazzled, at the nurse's desk, writing up her report.

He leaned against the side of the desk "I'm sorry to see your plan didn't work. For what it's worth, I thought it was a good one."

She didn't answer. She didn't need his sympathy or the way her heart jumped every time she caught sight of him.

"If you think it would help, I could speak to the administrators on your behalf."

Kitty stood. "I can defend myself quite well if need be. I'm independent, remember? I don't need your help."

They stared at each other, and then Dr. Hayden stepped back. "Very well, Miss Winthrop," he said, his voice resigned.

He turned and left her for the second time that day.

Kitty groaned. No one was happy with her tonight. Not Samuel, nor the patients, the plumbers, Administration, and certainly not Mr. Eisenmenger.

TWENTY-SIX

GENERAL PERSHING SENDS LIST OF CASUALTIES

The New York Times, August 14, 1918

Kitty stopped in the dining room early this morning.

She had awakened early and had time to sit and eat her breakfast instead of rushing off to the ward with a piece of toast in her hand.

She took her plate of bacon and eggs to a quiet table on which the previous occupant had left a New York Times.

She pulled it over to read the front page and one head-line immediately caught her attention.

Spanish Flu Here, Ship Men Say
Officers of Norwegian Liner Attribute Four Deaths During Voyage

to the Disease

KITTY PUSHED her plate aside and read the article. Apparently, the ship's officers insisted it was the Spanish flu. Upon arriving in port, ten more men and women showed serious signs of illness.

But the doctor who treated them insisted it wasn't the Spanish flu, for if it was, he said 'they would not have passed quarantine.'

The sickness had been brought on board by a third-class female passenger from Finland, who died four days out. An assistant cook, who had looked after the third-class passengers, also contracted the disease and died four days later.

The symptoms were unusual, high fever accompanied by lung pains and delirium. The victims who survived were so weak it took weeks to recover.

It didn't sound good.

Deep in thought, she approached Ward C. Dr. Hayden was there making his rounds earlier than usual.

The ward was almost full, and she was in charge, having the most experience of any of the other student nurses assigned to the unit.

Samuel looked up as she approached, and his face brightened, and then he immediately frowned. "Good morning, Miss Winthrop. I see all the damage from the affair of the ripped-off sink has been repaired."

Why did he have to remind her of that day? She nodded tightly. "Will you need my assistance this morning, Doctor?"

She kept her voice cool and professional. Charge nurses

usually accompanied doctors on their rounds if they so desired.

Samuel shook his head. "I think you'll be busy enough without me taking up your time." He glanced about the ward.

"Very well." She turned toward the nurse's desk to get report from the night nurse.

"Kitty..." His voice stopped her. "I miss you."

She missed him too. Having to see him every day was miserable.

But it was he who had separated them with his old-fashioned notions of what a wife should be. And apparently, she wasn't it.

She didn't reply and continued down the long line of beds, appraising each patient as she went, and noting two patients who would need immediate assistance.

She took stock of the two student nurses and two probationers assigned to her, along with an orderly who had been sent over from Ward B. She gave them their duties and went to personally assess the young sailor who had been brought in last night after emergency surgery for a ruptured appendix.

His dressings were bloody, and he tossed and turned in a feverish state. But his vitals were normal, except for a slightly elevated pulse rate. It was normal to run a slight temperature after surgery.

She recorded her findings in the patient's clipboard at the end of the bed and went to assemble what she needed to do a dressing change.

Much later, her twelve-hour shift almost over, Samuel returned to the ward. He was pale and drawn, walking slowly as he approached the desk.

"Kitty," he said, his voice broken.

She stood. "What is it?"

Samuel passed a trembling hand over his face.

"Are you unwell?" She came around the desk and led him to a chair.

He sank down on it while she poured him a glass of water from the pitcher on the desk.

"Doctor, what is it? Are you ill? Shall I call someone?"

"It's my brother." He fumbled in his suit jacket and withdrew a slip of paper.

She caught her breath. It was a Western Union telegram.

THE SECRETARY *of War desires me to express his deep regret that your brother,* Private FC James Hayden, was killed in action on the night of 7 August in France. Death was instantaneous and without any suffering due to bombardment of his foxhole. No body recoverable. Letter to follow.

"OH, SAMUEL." She pulled another chair up next to him, ignoring the surprised look of one of the student nurses, and gently touched his arm. "I am so deeply sorry."

Samuel covered his face with his hands. "How am I going to tell my parents? This will kill my father. He's barely recovered from his last illness."

He took the telegram from her and stared at it. "I can scarcely believe it to be true. But it says it right here." He groaned. "Jimmy, Jimmy."

"Everything all right here?" Dr. Winkler had approached the desk quietly, frowning.

"Dr. Hayden has just received word that his brother was killed in action in France."

"Oh, no." He looked at Dr. Hayden, then at Kitty.

"Would you kindly see to it that he gets home?" Kitty rose. "I cannot leave the ward."

"Of course. Come on, Samuel." Dr. Winkler stopped and put an arm around Samuel.

Samuel stood and allowed himself to be led away by Dr. Winkler. He cast one backward glance at her, his face haggard and broken, and Kitty's heart twisted inside.

She'd seen other people receive such telegrams. They never brought good news.

Shaken to the core, she finished her duties and reported off to the night nurse coming on at seven o'clock.

Once in the seclusion of her small bedroom at Osborn Hall, she sank to her knees next to the bed and prayed for Samuel and his parents, her father and mother, and all the brave soldiers fighting in France from all over the world.

Amid the sadness weighing down her heart, one tiny tinge of hope flared in her heart. In his grief and extreme sorrow, Samuel had sought her out.

AUGUST 28, 1918

THE CARILLON BELLS OF ST. George's a few blocks away rang out the old hymn *Holy God We Praise Thy Name* as Kitty pulled the sober black dress from her closet. The last time she'd worn it had been for Moose's funeral, and she hadn't expected to don it again so soon.

The Herald Tribune lay open on her bed, turned to the obituary page.

Kitty glanced again at the photo of James Hayden. How like Samuel he looked, with the same dark hair falling over his forehead, and eyes she suspected were the same deep blue as his brother's.

Barely a beard to shave and the contours of his face soft and not yet completely defined. She knew he was eighteen, but he looked heartbreakingly younger in this photo, staring dreamily into a future which he could not imagine held his death.

Annabelle peeked around her door. "Ready, T2?"

"Not quite."

Kitty pulled the dress over her head and fastened the jet-black buttons. She swept her hair up into a chignon and placed her hat over the mass of hair. Its high, pleated crown completely covered her hair and had a low brim that partially shielded her eyes.

Annabelle was dressed soberly as well, in black, with a velvet cloche hat.

It was a short streetcar ride to St. Patrick's Cathedral on 5th Avenue on a sunny summer afternoon. Many of the city's residents were out for a Sunday walk, leading dogs or pushing baby carriages.

Children played on the street corners, and automobiles filled the road, with an occasional horse and carriage among all the shiny black auto fenders.

Kitty and Annabelle walked up the steps of the cathedral toward the immense bronze double doors with carved likenesses of the saints.

Once inside, an usher greeted them and handed them a program. "Please proceed all the way down the main aisle and go around to the Lady Chapel."

It was cool and dim in the church after the heat and bright sun outside. Jeweled light slanted down through the tall blue and dark red stained-glass windows high in the nave.

They walked down the mosaic floor of the aisle toward the altar, passing towering white marble columns that joined Gothic arches and soared to a deeply vaulted ceiling hundreds of feet over their heads.

"I've never seen a church this large," Annabelle whispered.

"It's formidable, that's for sure."

The aisle curved around what Kitty assumed was the high altar, raised as it was on its own dais.

The Lady Chapel revealed itself as they continued walking. Chairs had been set up, and most of them were filled.

Kitty and Annabelle took seats in the rear and quietly listened as family and friends eulogized the life of young James Hayden.

Finally, Samuel stood.

Kitty gasped at the sight of his reddened eyes and worn, weary face. Annabelle pressed Kitty's hand.

"Thank you all for coming." His gaze moved over the small group of people in attendance and when he came to Kitty, his eyes brightened.

"My little brother Jimmy loved life, and he looked upon each day as another opportunity to see the beauty in this world and ponder the significance of the world to come. He loved ice cream and practical jokes, and if he were here today, he would doubtless try to prank us in some way. He loved his country and felt strongly about fighting in this war against the evil behind Germany's attempt to take over countries. And now, he has made the ultimate sacrifice with his life."

He stopped to clear his throat. "You have honored Jimmy with your presence here. The Hayden family sincerely thanks you and bids you a good afternoon."

Slowly, people rose and left the chapel. A few stopped to speak with the family. When most people had left, Kitty and Annabelle went forward.

Samuel took their hands. "So good of you to come. Let me introduce you to my parents."

He released their hands and turned to the elderly couple standing next to him. The senior Mr. Hayden was thin and wasted looking, his back bent, and he leaned heavily on a cane.

Mrs. Hayden wore her mourning attire with an elegant flair, but tears had furrowed tracks down her face and her eyelids were bruised and swollen.

"Mother, Father, these are two of the student nurses I work with at Bellevue. Annabelle Boyle and Kitty Winthrop."

Mrs. Hayden smiled and shook Annabelle's hand. Then she turned to Kitty, took both of her hands in hers, and looked deeply into Kitty's face. Then she nodded. "Bless you both for coming."

Samuel walked outside with them and stopped on the top step.

"I'll see you back at Osborn Hall?" Annabelle quirked an eyebrow at Kitty.

"Yes."

She and Samuel stood silently and watched Annabelle descend the flight of steps.

Kitty longed to comfort Samuel somehow, to take away

the pain in his eyes. But she didn't have the right. She was the one who had broken their relationship.

"Kitty," Samuel said. He looked down at her, his eyes sad. "I miss you."

Pain lanced through her. "I miss you, too."

She cringed at the hope in his eyes and shook her head. "I'm sorry, Samuel."

Her words came out choked. Then she turned and hurried down the steps.

TWENTY-SEVEN

Spanish influenza on ship reaching US. French vessel held at quarantine has several cases among its 471 passengers.

The New York Evening World, September 4, 1918

DR. WINKLER STOPPED by the nurse's desk on medical ward B where Kitty was in charge with two probies and one first-term student nurse assisting her.

The spindly physician had gaunt features and small stature with arms that appeared too long for his frame. And he was one of Bellevue's top surgeons. "How goes it, Miss Winthrop?"

"Quiet at the moment." She glanced down the line of beds that stretched along both sides of the aisle.

Most patients were resting quietly after their morning care, and the probationers were refilling water pitchers at the bedside. Brilliant September sunlight streamed across the ward beds through the tall windows.

"And how are you?" Kitty asked.

Normally an outgoing, extroverted man, the last few days on the ward Dr. Winkler had seemed preoccupied and not his usual jovial self.

"Oh, fine, fine." He expelled a heavy sigh. "I'm hearing some rumors, and I don't like the sound of them."

"About what?"

He grimaced. "Spanish influenza at Camp Devens in Massachusetts. Lots of cases."

"There isn't much of anything about it in the papers." Kitty glanced at the New York Times in the trash can.

"Exactly. And that's what worries me." He frowned. "That, and a letter I received from an old friend who lives in France. He says influenza is rampant there. But again, nothing much being reported."

He shook his head. "I've got a bad feeling about this. Wondering if it's coming our way."

"There *were* a couple lines about a few cases reported on a French ship that came into port last night."

Kitty retrieved the Times, turned to the last page of section three, and handed it to Dr. Winkler. "They're being quarantined at New York Presbyterian."

The doctor pursed his lips as he read the short blurb. "There's sure to be more then." He went off without saying goodbye, muttering to himself.

Nearly every one of the thirty-six beds on the ward had a patient. Appendectomies, gall bladder removals, laparotomies, hysterectomies.

Kitty made her rounds, checking incisions and dressings, taking temperatures, assisting with bed baths, and passing nourishment.

She stopped at the bedside of Mrs. Veino, a pretty

blonde woman of thirty-five who'd had abdominal surgery three days ago.

The patient had suffered at home for several days thinking the pain in her abdomen was from her menstrual cycle.

The pain had eased on the fifth day, and she felt better until she began to run a high fever and became delirious.

Her husband brought her to Bellevue, where emergency surgery revealed the ruptured appendix.

The pain had decreased temporarily after the rupture, which spewed the infectious matter into her abdomen. Iodoform dressings had been applied to absorb some of the secretions draining from the infected wound.

The first two days post-operatively she had done well. But today, the morning of the third post-op day, something had changed. The patient tossed and turned in the bed, and her face was flushed.

"I've a headache, nurse." Mrs. Veino rolled her head around on the pillow. "And please take that away." She pointed to the breakfast tray of mutton broth with bread crumbs. "I'm not hungry."

"I'm sorry to hear that." Kitty took the clipboard from the foot of the bed. Temperature and pulse had been normal during the night. But the patient hadn't slept much. "Are you having any pain?"

"Just a little." Mrs. Veino moved restlessly on the bed.

"Let me take your pulse and temperature, and then I'll try to make you more comfortable."

The temperature was now 100°, and the pulse a bit rapid at ninety beats per minute. Kitty wrote the numbers on the clipboard and removed the offending breakfast tray. She gave Mrs. Veino a bed bath and changed her damp bed linen.

"That's better." Mrs. Veino turned onto her side. "I believe I could sleep now."

"That's the best thing for you," Kitty said.

The patient appeared more relaxed, but something didn't seem right, although Kitty couldn't put her finger on it. She decided to keep an extra special eye on Mrs. Veino as she went down the long line of patients waiting for care.

At the end of her shift, Kitty checked on Mrs. Veino last. She had slept most of the day, but her temperature had risen to 100.6°.

Kitty reported her concerns about Mrs. Veino to the oncoming night nurse and left the ward, certain the patient was in good hands.

But the next morning, Kitty found that Mrs. Veino had deteriorated overnight.

She was plucking at the bedclothes with feeble fingers and muttering under her breath.

Kitty did a quick assessment. The temperature was now 101.8° and her pulse one hundred and ten. Her abdominal incision looked fine, her belly was flat, and secretions from the draining wound had decreased.

So, what was causing the elevated temp? The night nurse had put a call in for Dr. Johnston, the patient's surgeon, and Kitty made a second call to his office to express her concern, hoping he would arrive soon to make rounds.

Throughout the morning, Kitty worked to ease Mrs. Veino without success. By noontime, the patient had developed a bright red rash on her face, chest, and arms.

She was retaining urine and even worse, she'd become delirious, calling for her mother. The abdominal incision and drainage hadn't changed from the earlier assessment, so it didn't seem that the abdomen was the problem.

As Kitty studied the rash, a tiny bell went off in her head.

Two weeks ago, they had studied the solutions and types of dressings used on wounds with their accompanying side effects and contraindications.

Iodoform.

Iodoform dressings had been used because of the copious draining secretions. In some cases, the iodoform itself could be absorbed, causing poisoning, even death.

Should she remove the dressing? Or should she wait for the surgeon to arrive? But she had no way of knowing when he would come.

She called the hospital operator and asked her to page Miss Trent.

Miss Trent called a few moments later, and Kitty relayed her concerns to her nursing instructor.

"It could be the iodoform," Miss Trent said. "Some patients don't react well to it. When is Dr. Johnston coming?"

"I don't know. That's the problem."

"Well, I'm stuck here on Ward B. We've got a patient hemorrhaging, so I can't come right away." She paused. "You're a smart girl, Miss Winthrop. I encourage you to use your good judgment and go with your gut."

Kitty replaced the handle on the phone cradle.

Go with her gut?

Kitty moved to the bedside and considered the patient. Dr. Johnston was an imperious physician known for his short temper in the operating room and his tendency to throw instruments if he was handed an incorrect one.

He wasn't a man she wanted to upset.

But, if anything, Mrs. Veino's face was more inflamed

than before, and the rash had moved down to her lower legs and feet.

Her pulse was thready now and weaker. A dangerous sign.

Kitty ran to the clean utility room to grab some supplies and hurried back to the bedside. She uncovered Mrs. Veino, removed the iodoform dressing, and washed the incision and the surrounding skin with sterile water to remove any iodoform dust she could see. Then she covered the incision with plain sterile gauze.

Dr. Johnston arrived a short time later and went directly to the patient's bedside. Mrs. Veino had lapsed into a stupor. He took her blood pressure and pulse and examined the wound.

Then he shouted orders to increase her fluids and apply cold compresses to her head and body.

Kitty moved frantically to obey the doctor's orders, praying under her breath for the patient's recovery.

Maybe she shouldn't have removed the dressing? It wasn't her responsibility. Would she be sent home now for overstepping her bounds?

Four hours later, Mrs. Veino seemed to be improving. Her temperature was going down, and she had recovered consciousness, although she was very weak.

Dr. Johnston had remained on the ward, seeing his other surgical patients while keeping a watchful eye on Mrs. Veino.

Before the end of the shift, he asked Kitty to call Miss Trent to the floor, as he had something to say to her, Kitty, and the probationers.

Kitty had Miss Trent paged, and a few minutes later, her instructor hurried unto the ward.

Dr. Johnston scrutinized them with a stern eye. "Who removed Mrs. Veino's dressing?"

Kitty stepped forward, her heart thumping in her chest. "I did, Doctor."

Dr. Johnston studied her. "And why did you take that action, Miss Winthrop?"

"I...I thought it might be the iodoform, Doctor," she stammered. "Her symptoms seemed to fit what we learned about iodoform dressings in class a few weeks ago."

"Go on."

Kitty gulped. "The rash and the delirium appeared after her dressings were changed this morning and fresh iodoform dressings applied. So, I removed the dressing, washed off as much iodoform as I could, and called for you."

He nodded slowly.

Kitty's belly clenched as a pang of nausea rose in her throat. Would he redress her here in front of the probationers and all the patients within hearing?

Dr. Johnston gave her a long assessing look. "Remarkable power of discernment, Miss Winthrop. You've probably saved her life."

He turned to Miss Trent. "I commend you on your student. We need fifty more like her."

With that, he turned and left. Kitty stood stock still, paralyzed.

Miss Trent gave her a broad smile. "I also commend you. You used your nursing judgment and improved a patient's chance of recovery."

Kitty let out the breath she'd been holding. "Thank you."

"That's going with your gut." Miss Trent nodded. "Also known as nursing intuition. Listen to it, Miss Winthrop.

Make your own assessments of your patients and never let another nurse's opinions affect your judgment."

TWENTY-EIGHT

INFLUENZA EPIDEMIC HITS CAMP DEVENS

2,000 Soldiers Are Stricken and Washington is Asked to Send More Doctors and Nurses

The New York Times, September 15, 1918

ELEVEN DAYS LATER, the first influenza cases were admitted to Bellevue.

Kitty set up an isolation unit in Ward A for a young sailor home on leave from France and two workmen from the Port of New York.

All three men were in their early twenties, had high fevers, and complained that their lungs hurt.

Kitty worked to make them comfortable, sponging them, offering fluids, and administering aspirin powders.

All three were worse the following morning. The sailor

tossed and moaned on his bed and screamed when he was touched.

The high fevers continued and even morphine didn't seem to help much. Kitty noticed a blue tint creeping over their skin, starting with the face and moving down over the chest. Bloody mucus drained from their noses and the sailor had it running from his ears.

When Kitty walked into the isolation ward on the third day after their admission, the three beds were empty.

"Died about six a.m." Miss Simpson, a probationer for two weeks, scrubbed the bare mattress. "One right after the other. It was awful."

That seemed odd.

Influenza typically had a longer course, and fatalities were usually limited to the very young and the elderly. These three young men had been in the prime of their manhood, well-nourished, and strong.

Miss Simpson dropped the washrag into the bucket. "If this is what it's about, then I don't think nursing is for me."

She glanced about the ward of men filled with influenza patients—coughing, vomiting, moaning—and shuddered. "I'm going to withdraw today and go home."

"Better to find out early." Kitty gave her a sympathetic smile. "But this is unusual. You've had a difficult introduction. Baptism by fire, I think it's called."

"Maybe so. But it's too hot for me." Miss Simpson picked up the bucket. "Goodbye."

Nursing wasn't for everyone, which was certain. And this influenza was different from what Bellevue had seen in the spring.

It was alarming, but she didn't have much time to think about it because Admitting called. Five more men were being admitted for influenza, or as some laypeople called it, the grippe.

With the help of the probationers assigned to the ward today, Miss Field and Miss Blake, she got them settled in their beds.

Patrick Murphy, 26, a dock worker.

John Beckley, 33, a printer.

Mason Abraham, 36, a cook.

Aaron Mandel, 30, a piano salesman.

And Ashford Stuart-White, 35, a professor from Columbia University.

Five men from five different walks of life with the same illness.

The rest of the shift flew by as Kitty and the probies sponged the men down for their fevers, emptied their spit basins, and tried to administer fluids.

"Miss Blake." Kitty followed the probie into the dirty utility room. "Be careful when you're emptying the basins into the hopper. Keep your head back, or turn your face away, so you don't get splashed with the contents. And make sure you wash your hands well before you return to the patients."

"Yes, Miss Winthrop." Miss Blake was a sandy-haired, petite young woman with a no-nonsense attitude. "I'll be careful."

It was time to give aspirin again. Kitty went down the line, taking temperatures. There wasn't one under 103°.

Mr. Mandel's temp was 104.6°. "My joints hurt something awful, Miss." He groaned as he turned onto his side. "I've never been this sick in my life."

"Here." Kitty handed him aspirin and morphine tablets. "Drink the whole glass of water, please. You need the fluids."

Mandel took the meds and lay back down. "How long is this going to last? I've got to get back to work." He stopped and turned away to cough. "I—I have a family to support." He fought to draw in some air.

There was no way to know. Especially if it was the same illness that had struck down the first three men admitted to the isolation unit. "Rest as much as you can. Drink as much water as you can. That will help."

He moaned again and then grimaced. "I'm sorry...to make so much noise. I can't help it."

"It's all right. Try to sleep. The morphine will start to help soon."

At lunchtime, Mr. Murphy and Mr. Beckley seemed a bit better. They were able to take some soup and swallow the aspirin, although both complained of severely sore throats. She made a mental note to get some lozenges for them.

Mr. Abraham, a stocky fellow with ropy muscles, had lapsed into semi-consciousness and was difficult to arouse. The spit basin on the bedside table was half full of blood-streaked foamy mucus, and his respirations were wheezy and wet.

By the end of the shift, Mr. Beckley was worse, Mr. Mandel was unconscious, and Mr. Abraham was dead, his skin color so dark, he looked black.

Kitty performed post-mortem care for him. What was this deadly disease? What could end the lives of vigorous young men so rapidly?

How were their families even going to recognize them?

TWENTY-NINE

In proportion to our population, there are no alarming symptoms about the spread of influenza in NYC.

Dr. Royal Copeland
The New York Times, Friday, October 4, 1918

TEN MORE PATIENTS had been admitted with influenza during the night.

Partial screens had been placed between each pair of beds to contain the bloody secretions they were coughing up, and the nurses and doctors started wearing gauze masks tied over their faces.

Kitty answered the ward telephone. "Six more patients coming up now," the admitting nurse said. "And more coming in."

She readied the beds, set up water pitchers, and checked her supply of aspirin powder.

One by one, the patients arrived, one elderly man and

five young men, all feverish and coughing, several hawking up blood.

By noon, influenza patients had filled half of the beds in the second isolation ward, and she called the nursing supervisor to request more help.

Two probationers were sent to assist her: Miss Fields, a stocky girl with pink cheeks, and Miss Donohoe, a tall, slender brunette.

They had been in the program only a few weeks, as Miss Simpson had been, and they were standing close together near the nurse's desk, their arms tightly crossed, looking scared to death.

Kitty helped them tie on their cotton masks and set them to sponging the patients to bring their fevers down.

A shriek echoed through the ward and a washbasin clattered to the floor as the elderly patient lurched up and hemorrhaged blood over the bedclothes. The probationer screamed and backed up until she hit the next bed.

Kitty hurried over. "Miss Fields, please, control yourself."

The probie was as white as the sheets and shaking badly. Kitty took a firm hold of her arm.

Miss Fields gasped and tried to recover herself. "I-I'm sorry." She swallowed. "I've never seen so much blood."

"It's all right. You're doing fine. Take a minute to calm yourself and then go fetch me some clean linen and warm water."

The probationer left hastily, and Kitty turned to the patient, who had collapsed back onto the bed.

His entire body, a pale white on admission, had darkened, and his eyes had rolled up into his head. His breath became ragged and shallow.

With Miss Field's help, Kitty turned him over, washed him, and changed his linen.

At the end of the shift, Kitty's legs felt so heavy she could barely manage the walk back to Osborn Hall after her shift ended.

Annabelle was in the foyer when Kitty went in.

"T1. How goes it?"

Annabelle had charge of Ward C, the third isolation unit now. Her nurse's cap sat askew on her head, and she had lost a cuff. "I'm exhausted."

"Let's go get cleaned up and get some dinner."

"Good idea."

They trudged up the stairs to the fifth-floor bathroom, collected some clean clothes, and removed their uniforms to soak in the sink. Then they took a hot bath to wash away the blood and secretions.

"I just want to put my feet up." Annabelle groaned. "I don't think I've ever been this tired."

"Let's get dinner and bring it back upstairs."

Kitty chose roast beef and mashed potatoes and plucked a copy of the New York Times from the back table.

Once back in Kitty's room, Annabelle took the chair and propped her legs on the bed, while Kitty piled pillows at the other end to raise hers.

As she devoured her roast beef and read the paper, she could barely keep her eyes open.

They called it an early night.

THIRTY

2000 NEW CASES IN NEW YORK CITY

The Influenza Archive, October 10, 1918

THE ALARM BELL went off way too soon, and Kitty had difficulty waking up. She had slept like the dead and the alarm had rung a long time before she stumbled out of bed to turn it off.

She stopped for a cup of coffee in the dining room. Ruth and Florence were sitting together, and she took a seat at their table. "Morning, ladies."

"Morning," they said together.

"Is it really morning already?" Florence took a sip of coffee. "I feel like I just went to bed." She yawned and hastily covered her mouth. "Pardon me."

Ruth pushed eggs around her plate with her fork. "I'm tired, too. What a day yesterday. And I feel as if it's not going to be any better today."

"I know." Kitty noticed she had one of her cuffs on inside out and unbuttoned it. "It's been brutal."

More influenza patients had arrived during the night. By the end of the first week, another isolation ward had been set up in the surgical women's ward.

The probationers could barely keep up emptying spit basins and changing bloodied linen, while Kitty administered aspirin and morphine and beef broth to the men who could keep it down.

Many of the patients, once past the grueling fevers of influenza, went on to develop pneumonia.

She pinned a linen towel over her bloodstained uniform and kept going.

All afternoon, orderlies brought influenza patients to the ward until there were no beds left.

Miss Trent stopped by. Her normally calm and efficient persona had disappeared. Her face was haggard, and her normally impeccable uniform had blood on it.

Her voice, however, was as cool as ever. "Miss Winthrop, how is Ward A doing?"

Kitty glanced down the aisle. Men coughed and moaned and cried out in delirium. "As well as can be expected."

Miss Trent nodded. "How many cases of influenza have been admitted?"

"We're full. How many cases have been admitted to the hospital?"

"Over a hundred. We've had to put pallets on the floor in the women's ward. And—there's no sign of it easing."

THIRTY-ONE

3100 NEW CASES IN NEW YORK CITY

The Influenza Archive, October 11, 1918

KITTY WALKED into Ward C and sighed.

Her shift hadn't started yet, but she was already tired. The student nurses' days off had disappeared, and they were all working sixteen-hour shifts.

She hadn't been able to keep up with washing her uniforms and had donned a plain blouse and skirt this morning, covered from shoulder to ankles with a surgical gown.

She glanced down the double row of beds, each partially curtained by screens, and lifted a silent prayer for strength as she began her duties.

An hour later, she was at the bedside of a young man, Nino Maffeo, twenty-one years old, who had been on the ward for twenty-four hours.

At first, he responded to treatment and Kitty thought he would make it, but hours later, he began to cough up red blood clots and foamy mucus.

Dr. Winkler said that fluid was pooling in his lungs from the pneumonia that had set in.

She helped him sit up and drink some water. Nino put his hand over hers, holding the cup, and raised agonized eyes to her. "My wife, she is dead." He dropped back against the pillow and sobbed. "Who will take care of my *bambinos*? Who?" He rolled over and hid his face in the bedclothes.

Kitty offered up a silent prayer for him, touched him briefly, and passed to the next bed.

Hector Johnston, a railroad man, lay on his side and coughed into a handkerchief. "I can't breathe." He gasped, his breaths coming in shuddering wheezes. "I feel like my innards are comin' out—" He went into another spasm, and when that was over, fell back on the bed, exhausted.

Kitty sponged him and changed his bed linen, before moving on to the next patient, Adam Whittaker, a twenty-year-old farm laborer.

Even before she touched him, she knew he had expired. His face and limbs were a dusky blue. She pulled the sheet over his face and moved on.

The entire shift continued the same way. By the time it was over, eighteen men had expired, a few who had been admitted only that morning.

When she gave the day's report to the oncoming nurse, she stayed over to help perform post-mortem care. An orderly had come over from Ward B to help Kitty transport the bodies.

She followed him down to the hall to the freight elevator that would take them to the basement morgue.

After this, she could go home and take a bath and fall into bed, just like yesterday, the day before that, and the day before that. She was so tired she wasn't even sure what day of the week it was.

She lurched to a halt as the orderly stopped suddenly in front of her. "What is it?"

"We're here."

The air was noticeably fouler. The morgue door stood thirty feet further down the hall, but bodies in shrouds were piled up along both sides of the corridor leading to it, four and five to a stack. And over everything hung the sickly-sweet stench of decay.

"There's no room anymore, miss. Hasn't been for two days. That's why we have to ice them."

He pointed to the blocks of ice piled on top of and in between the corpses. "But they're coming today to take 'em all to Hart's Island, thankfully."

He grunted and heaved the final corpse onto the stack.

THIRTY-TWO

4300 NEW CASES IN NEW YORK CITY

The Influenza Archive October 12, 1918

BY THE END of the fourth week, all elective surgeries had been canceled.

The nurses and doctors wore cotton gauze masks tied over the lower half of their faces. After cleaning her cap several times of blood spots, Kitty left it off. When things returned to normal, she would wear it again.

She almost couldn't remember what normal was.

Each day was a hard slog of caring for patients, washing bloodied bodies and linen, and administering medicine to those who were conscious enough to take it.

There was no end to the work. The students were too tired to do anything after their shift but wash, eat, and sleep.

The patients admitted with influenza were dying more

quickly. Some admitted in the morning were dead by midnight.

There was barely time to strip and wash a vacated mattress when it was filled by a patient lying on the floor. And as soon as floor space became available, another patient filled it.

And if they lasted more than three days, sometimes their extremities became gangrenous, due to lack of oxygen. Ordinarily, that would mean immediate emergency surgery. But following the appearance of gangrene, certain death wasn't far off.

Kitty was on Ward B today, the women's medical ward. Every patient there had influenza. There were no other admissions.

Orderlies wheeled a new patient in, and they were having difficulty keeping her on the gurney.

Kitty went to help them and glanced at the clipboard. Miss Johanna Davis, twenty-two years old.

"We're going to get you into a bed, Miss Davis."

Miss Davis grabbed Kitty's hand. "I shouldn't be here. I can't have influenza." She stopped talking to cough. "I did everything the doctor said." She gasped when the spasm ended.

Kitty helped the orderlies transfer Miss Davis to a pallet on the floor.

"No, no," Miss Davis moaned. "I did everything...I was supposed to."

"What do you mean?" Kitty asked, while covering her thrashing limbs with a blanket.

She didn't need to take the woman's temperature. Her body radiated heat.

"Outside." Miss Davis gasped. "I stayed out in the cold

garage. I slept there on a cot. That's what the doctor said to—"

She broke off and turned aside as another violent coughing fit overtook her. She collapsed back onto the pallet. Blood flecked her lips. "I sat on the stoop in front of the house....and watched the carts go by...piled with the dead..." She closed her eyes and lapsed into a fever-induced sleep.

When Kitty left at midnight, Miss Davis was dead.

THIRTY-THREE

Miss Elizabeth Lloyd Key, a granddaughter of the author of "The Star-Spangled Banner," died on Sunday night of pneumonia, following Spanish Influenza. She was 18 years old.

The New York Times, Tuesday, October 15, 1918

THE NIGHTMARE SEEMED NEVER-ENDING.

Though Kitty and her assistants worked as hard and fast as they could, the stench of urine, feces, and blood hung over the ward.

The third-year medical students were on the wards now. All medical and nursing classes had been canceled. Each night they made many trips to the morgue.

Kitty sat by the bedside of one young man, unidentified, who had been brought in this morning. He was semiconscious and didn't speak except to mumble "*Madre.*"

Whereas the flu had originally taken several days to run its course, the time frame had shrunk as the disease became more lethal, and the now-familiar cyanotic color was creeping over his extremities. His lower legs and feet were already black.

On the bedside stand, the New York Times was open to the casualty list. The headline glared up at her.

654 NEW CASUALTIES ANNOUNCED BY PERSHING
TOTAL NOW IS 52,206

KITTY COULDN'T STOP herself from searching the list for her father's name, holding her breath as she did so and only letting it out after his name didn't appear. Further down another article caught her eye.

TEN MORE HEROES WIN WAR SERVICE CROSS

AS SHE READ THE ARTICLE, she almost dropped the paper when she found her father's name on the list.

CHAPLAIN MAJOR JOHN WINTHROP, assigned to the 2nd Battalion, 16th Infantry Regiment, has earned the Distinguished Service Cross in September 1918 at Meuse-Argonne.

He displayed exceptional bravery and devotion to duty by repeatedly leaving the first-aid station of his battalion to care for the wounded, and voluntarily exposed himself to terrific artillery and machine-gun fire to administer the last rites to the dying.

At imminent risk to his own. life, he worked to improve the conditions of the aid station and fearlessly conducted burial services under fire.

KITTY'S HEART swelled with pride. That sounded so like Papa with his gentle determination and courage. She would call Mama as soon as her shift ended to make sure she had seen the notice.

She rose and sighed. In the few minutes that she had taken to read the newspaper article, the young Italian man had expired. She checked his pulse and respiration, then asked Miss Blake to notify the doctor on call to come and pronounce him.

Her shift finished a few hours later. The oncoming nurse, a new graduate named Mary Ellen Danis, had dark smudges under her eyes and looked as tired as Kitty felt. No one was getting much rest these days.

"Good afternoon, Miss Winthrop." Miss Danis cast a practiced eye down the long aisle of the ward. "Still full."

Kitty nodded. "As soon as we have a bed empty, Admitting fills it." She looked down at her written report. "Not much to tell you. Mr. Eisenmenger is back."

"Your nemesis." Miss Danis smiled, and it lit up her weary face. "That sink incident was the funniest thing to happen around Bellevue in a long time."

"Maintenance didn't think it was funny." Kitty gave her a wry smile. "Nor did Administration."

She glanced at the bed closest to the nurse's desk, where the elderly lawyer slept fitfully. "I don't think we need to worry about him escaping. He's too weak to hold his head up."

Kitty left the ward and headed towards Osborn Hall. Her legs felt heavy from standing all shift, her feet were swollen, and she was bone-tired. She intended to go straight to bed, but first, she wanted to call Mama.

In the parlor of the dormitory, she pulled a chair over to the hall table where the telephone sat and dialed the number. It rang a long time before someone picked up.

"Hello?" a breathless voice said.

"Mama?"

"Darling, how are you?"

"You sound out of breath. Have you been running?"

"Yes. Mrs. Mac has the day off, and I've been out with some of my wharflings, getting them settled in new homes."

"You need to stay home as much as possible," Kitty said, more sharply than she meant to. "Influenza is everywhere now."

"I know. But I had an offer of two good homes, and I couldn't turn that down. You know me."

"I do." Mama would never turn down a request for help. "Please take care of yourself."

"I am, darling, please don't worry about me."

"Did you see the Times this morning?"

"I'm afraid not. Didn't have time. Why?"

"There's an article about Papa. He's received an award for bravery under fire."

Mama's gasp came over the wire. "Oh, that's wonderful."

"Go find the paper and read it. I've got to go to bed."

"I will. Take care of yourself. I love you."

"Love you *more*." Kitty hung up the receiver before her mother could reply. Ha. Got her that time.

The smell of pot roast drifted through the parlor from the dining room behind it, and Kitty's mouth watered. Maybe she'd eat first and then go to bed.

But she was almost too tired to eat. She climbed the four floors to her room, resting a moment on each landing.

It took the last bit of strength she had to wash her face and hands before she fell into bed.

THIRTY-FOUR

4875 NEW INFLUENZA CASES IN NEW YORK CITY

The Influenza Archive, October 19, 1918

KITTY SWISHED the mop back and forth across the long aisle between the double row of beds in Ward C.

The patients were coughing and hemorrhaging so much blood that the floors had become slippery and dangerous.

She leaned on the mop handle to catch her breath and glanced at the bloody water in the pail. Her surgical gown was covered in it, and she needed to change it again.

There was a tap on her shoulder, and Kitty turned to find Miss Trent.

Even her instructor's normally spotless white uniform hadn't survived the onslaught of patients admitted to Bellevue in the last week. "I have a note for you. It came in to the hospital operator."

Kitty put the mop down. The note had one cryptic sentence.

Kitty, call me as soon as you can. Mama.

"Oh, no." Kitty clutched her throat as the room whirled around her.

"What is it?" Miss Trent put a steadying hand on Kitty's arm, and the moment passed.

"Something's happened. But my mother hasn't said what."

Fear clamped around Kitty's heart. "It has to be my father."

Oh, please, dear God, not Papa.

"Go and call her now. I will watch the ward until you come back."

"Oh, thank you so much. Thank you."

Kitty tore off the surgical gown and disposed of it before leaving the ward. She washed her hands and face and then hurried through the maze of hallways and stairs that was Bellevue and ran across East 26th Street to the nurse's dormitory.

Thankfully, no one was using the one telephone. With shaking fingers, she dialed home.

A moment later she heard her mother's frantic voice. "Hello?"

"It's me, Mama."

"Oh, Kitty."

Her mother broke into sobs and Kitty's heart sank. "Is it Papa? Is he—dead?" She could hardly bring herself to say the word.

Mama recovered herself. "N-no, darling, he's not dead. But he's missing in action in France. I received the telegram an hour ago."

Kitty picked up the telephone base and sank onto the rug with it, her knees weak. "Oh, no."

Mama's ragged breath carried over the telephone line.

"He'll be all right, Mama. He has to be. We must stay strong."

"I know." Her voice broke. "But he might be a German prisoner. I've read something about their prisoner-of-war camps and—I don't think I can bear to think of him there."

Kitty gripped the telephone receiver tightly. "Then don't. He's probably not a prisoner. With everything that's happening over there, there are bound to be mix-ups. How can they keep track of every soldier?"

"Yes." Her mother sounded doubtful. "I know there isn't anything we can do. Except pray even harder." She sighed. "And how are you, darling? I feel calmer just hearing your voice."

"I'm fine. Nothing that twelve hours of sleep wouldn't fix. But this epidemic is bad. Are you still healthy? Anyone in the neighborhood have influenza?"

"Yes. Most of the homes on this street have one or more family members ill. I've been bringing them soup and helping as I can."

"Stay inside, Mama. Don't go out. Please." The thought of losing her mother to this horrific ravaging sickness made her ill.

"I can't do that. I must help them. It's pitiful. The Albertsons next door?"

"Yes." Joseph and Kathleen Albertson had moved into the neighborhood a year ago, with three young children and another on the way.

"Both dead."

"Joe and Kate?"

"Yes. Kate's mother is there, caring for the four children. It's so sad."

"Jenny? Mrs. Mac?"

"Fine. So far."

Kitty exhaled in relief. "If you must go out, Mama, wear a mask, please. Tie something over your mouth and nose. It might help."

"I will. One more thing. Your grandmother is ill. With influenza." There was a long pause. "And...and she's asked for you. She's at Seaside."

Shocked, Kitty didn't reply. That was the last thing she expected to hear.

"Kitty?"

"I'm here." She sighed. "Should I go to her?"

Her mother hesitated. "I don't know. Can the hospital spare you?"

"Not really. But they will release us if a family member needs care."

"It's your decision, sweetheart."

"I can't believe she'd ever want to see me again. Not after the way I left."

"Perhaps she wants to reconcile with you?"

Kitty snorted. "Yes, that's what we thought a year ago."

"I know." Her mother sighed. "I can't advise you."

"Mama, I've got to get back to the ward. I'll call you tomorrow."

"All right. I love you, Kitty."

Kitty smiled. "And I love you more."

"Not possible," her mother said and hung up.

Kitty got to her feet and put the telephone back on the table. Then she picked up the receiver again and dialed the telephone number for Oma's house at Seaside. It rang a long time before it was picked up.

"Lindenmayer residence." The raspy voice on the other end sounded stressed.

"Percy?"

"Yes. Miss Katharine? I'm so thankful it's you."

"How bad is it?"

"Terrible. And some of the maids are ill, too. And Barrett, oh, miss, he's close to death. His family came and took him home yesterday."

Barrett, the strong, silent chauffeur. She didn't know how old he was but judged him to be no more than thirty.

"How are you?"

"So far it hasn't touched me. Hale and hearty as ever."

"I'm glad to hear it. I can take the late train tonight. Can you have someone pick me up at the station?"

"It will have to be me. Most of the staff have left and gone home to their families."

"Can you drive, Percy?"

"Why, of course."

"All right then. And Percy, is there any aspirin powder in the house? And anything for pain?"

"Aspirin, we do have. I don't know about the other."

"I'll look when I get there. And have the cook make a pot of beef broth with some vegetables."

"Yes, miss, I'll see to it."

There was a click, and the connection broke.

KITTY SECURED PERMISSION TO leave Bellevue for a few days. She packed a bag and called for a cab.

The driver who picked her up had a mask over his nose and mouth, as did Kitty. The streets were deserted. The occasional pedestrian wore the same white mask.

Grand Central, usually a busy bustling hub of activity, was virtually empty. Her footsteps echoed in the cavernous space as she walked across the marble floor to purchase a ticket.

The train to Newport held a third of its normal passengers, and all but a few wore masks and sat apart. When a man began coughing a few seats ahead of Kitty, people near him got up and moved.

No one spoke. No happy chatter or buzz of conversation flowed through the train car. Passengers sat quietly, staring out the windows to the darkness outside.

Percy took her bag when she detrained. His wavy silver hair, always well-oiled into submission, was mussed and stuck out on one side and his mustache needed trimming.

"Thank you for coming, Miss Katharine." He took her bag.

"Please, Percy, will you call me Kitty?" His tired face tugged at her heart, and she gently touched his sleeve. "The time for formalities is past, I think."

He nodded. "I would be delighted, Kitty." A tiny smile crossed his lips. "But we mustn't let Madame hear. She would fire me on the spot."

They reached the Pierce-Arrow, and Percy put her bag in the trunk and opened the door for her.

"So, any change in their conditions?" Kitty asked when Percy got into the driver's seat.

Percy shook his head, making the one troublesome lock of hair bob. "Not really."

"Who has been nursing her?"

"Fleurette...until she fell ill herself yesterday."

He turned the key and started the engine. They drove the rest of the short distance in silence until the car rounded the curve on Ochre Point Avenue and Seaside loomed up before them. The splendid mansion had always been brilliantly lit at night when Kitty had been there.

Now most of Seaside's windows were dark and a gasp escaped Kitty's lips.

"I know. Looks different, doesn't it?" Percy shook his head. "I can't remember a time like this in all the years I've worked for your grandmother."

Percy drove around back to the servants' entrance and took Kitty's bag from the trunk.

Overhead a million stars blazed in the clear night air. She paused to take a deep breath of the salt-scented air and listen to the muted roar of the surf on the seashore not far away.

Dear Lord, give me strength.

"I will put your bag in your old room," Percy said.

They walked in together. "I need something from it first." She set the bag on a hall table and pulled two surgical gowns and masks out. "I'll go right up to my grandmother."

Only a few months ago, the mansion had been the scene of parties and glittering balls, its rooms and terraces filled with light, music, and the chatter of guests.

Now as she ascended the curving marble staircase, the house had a shuttered, closed feel and her footsteps were loud in the stillness.

Kitty walked down the carpeted hallway to her grandmother's suite of rooms in the east wing and knocked gently. When there was no answer, she opened the door. Oma's bed sat like a throne on a raised dais encircled by a carved wooden railing. Her agonized breathing echoed through the room.

Kitty removed her coat, put on the gown over her dress, and tied on the mask.

As she approached the bed, her grandmother cried out. "Who's there?"

"It's me, Oma. Katharine." She sat on the edge of the huge bed and took Oma's hand. She wasn't wearing a wig and had lost most of her hair.

There was something unutterably sad about her bald head, with only the few strands of hair clinging to it. Her eyes were sunken into her face, and the folds of flesh under her chin were wrinkled more than usual. Dehydration.

"Katharine? Am I dreaming? Are you really here?" Her frantic eyes searched Kitty's face.

"It's me, Oma." Kitty pulled down the mask and smiled, then replaced it. "How are you?"

"Terrible."

Oma's forehead was hot and dry, and her pulse bounding and irregular at one hundred and five beats a minute.

But there were no signs of the dreaded cyanosis creeping over her face and extremities, and she was lucid. All good omens.

"I'm here to care for you."

She stood and went to the dressing table to look at her grandmother's medications and found a bottle of opium tincture and another half-full bottle of laudanum.

Hopefully, she wouldn't have to use these, but she had them if needed. There was a nearly full tin of aspirin tablets, and Kitty had her grandmother take two of them with a full glass of water.

Oma moaned. "My back hurts."

Kitty took a couple of pillows. "Turn over, I'll try to make you more comfortable." She put a pillow between Oma's knees and wedged another behind her back, and her grandmother relaxed.

"I'll be back in a bit." Kitty pulled the covers up over her. "I want to check on the others and then get you some soup."

Kitty pulled the bell at the side of Oma's bed, and a few minutes later, Percy knocked on the door.

Kitty left the bedroom and closed the door behind her. "Where is Fleurette? I need to see her and anyone else who's ill in the house."

Percy nodded. "It's only Fleurette now. I put her in one of the guest bedrooms, to be closer to Madame, as I have been taking care of them both."

He stopped, and his face flushed red. "I hope that was permissible, Miss W—Kitty. I had no one here to ask."

"That was the right thing to do, Percy, no matter what my grandmother might say. She's lucky you stayed."

"I never thought of leaving her, even though, as you know, she can be difficult." He shrugged. "She's been my employer for forty years, and I have no family to speak of."

Kitty's heart sank when they entered Fleurette's room. Shaking chills and high fever racked the maid's delicate frame so badly the clicking of her teeth resonated through the room.

And she didn't respond to voice or touch.

Kitty looked over the medications at the bedside. Plenty of aspirin but no safe way to get it into her patient. "She might aspirate if I try to give aspirin orally. I need suppositories."

Percy frowned. "Nothing will be open at this time of night."

The Bellevue pharmacy compounded aspirin suppositories for patients unable to swallow. "I don't think they're available to the public. But I could try to make them if I can find something in the kitchen, cocoa butter or glycerin, perhaps. I have to try."

"I'll go start looking," Percy said.

In the bathroom, Kitty wet towels with cold water and packed them around Fleurette before tucking the aspirin tin into her pocket and going down to the basement kitchen.

It was a huge room with shining porcelain floors, marble countertops, and a wall of burners and ovens that could handle cooking a formal dinner for two hundred guests.

Gleaming copper pots dangled from an iron pot rack, and every imaginable kitchen utensil hung on a pegboard over the sink.

A square-faced woman with shingled hair, wrapped in a large white apron and stirring a pot on the stove, started when Kitty walked into the warm kitchen.

"Yes, miss?" She bobbed a little curtsy.

"So sorry. I didn't mean to startle you. I'm Kitty Winthrop, Mrs. Lindenmayer's granddaughter. You must be new?"

"Just temporary, Miss." She put the spoon down. "I've come to help out since my father is still ill at home. I'm the cook's daughter, Adele."

"Ah, you're Jacques DuMain's daughter. How is he?"

"Better." She brushed her sleeve against her perspiring forehead and sighed. "He seems to be over most of it, but so weak, like a baby."

"I hope he makes a full recovery. What we're seeing at Bellevue is that convalescence can be weeks or even months."

Adele appeared healthy, with a full figure and clear eyes. "Were you ill?"

"Yes, in early September, but I'm fine now. But how is Madame?"

"Stable at the moment. But Fleurette is very ill." Kitty glanced about the kitchen. "I need to find some cocoa butter or glycerin. Do we have any?"

"Go through there, miss." Adele pointed to an arched opening at the end of the kitchen. "You can look in the larder."

It was a wood-paneled room with cabinets from floor to ceiling, and Kitty started opening doors and drawers.

The sheer amount of dry and canned foods seemed enough to feed a small army. She found a mortar and pestle that would be useful. Aha!

She pulled out the tin of cocoa butter and returned to the kitchen, where the scent of basil and thyme hung sweetly in the air.

"Is that the beef soup?"

"Yes, miss. It's ready."

Adele ladled some into a bowl. The meaty broth was full of carrots and smelled delicious.

"I think we'd better mash some of these carrots to make it easier to digest."

Kitty got a fork from the drawer. "Could you keep this warm and send it up with a big pot of tea for Mrs. Lindenmayer in about thirty minutes?"

"Of course."

Kitty moved to the marble counter, took the aspirin tin from her pocket, and ground twelve tablets with the pestle. Then she added a dollop of cocoa butter and mixed it in well.

Now, how to shape the suppositories?

She eyed the utensils on the pegboard. Maybe a pastry press would work? "Adele, do you know where the pastry implements are?"

Adele nodded. "Right here." She walked to a cupboard

holding all manner of cake pans, fluted pudding molds, and pie plates.

"I need that thing you use to decorate a cake, what's it called?"

Adele's eyes widened. "A pastry bag?"

"That's it."

Adele pulled out a drawer. "Right here."

Kitty examined the contents. Cloth bags with a hole at one end and trays of metal cones, each with a different top. "How does it work? I need to form a certain shape."

Adele picked up one of the bags, dropped a tip into it, and tightened her fingers around the opposite end. "You fill the bag with icing, and you pipe out the shape you want."

"I need a bullet shape."

Adele chose a tip with a serrated circle. "This might work."

"What could we use to try it first?"

"I've got some leftover icing from last week. Would that do?"

"Perfect."

Adele retrieved the icing and loaded it into the bag. She pulled over a cutting board and piped the frosting onto it. 'When you're decorating a cake, you move the bag different ways."

Adele demonstrated a line of dots and long bars. "Like this. Other tips give different effects."

"I need to make a suppository of this." Kitty pointed to the yellowish mixture in the mortar. "And it needs to have a narrower end. Tapered."

"Ah." Adele replaced the tip with one that had a plain opening. "Like this?" She piped the frosting onto the board, making it swell in girth by applying pressure on the bag, and then snapping it off at the end.

"Yes! That's it."

Adele rinsed the tip off while Kitty got a clean bag. Adele put the bag together and held it open while Kitty carefully spooned in the mixture of aspirin and cocoa butter.

"Now, let's pipe it onto a plate so it can go into the refrigerator. I need to get six even ones out of this so each will equal two aspirin tablets."

Adele nodded and fetched a plate. Then, carefully, she piped six perfect oval plugs.

Kitty clapped her hands. "Brilliant." She carried the plate to the refrigerator and placed it on a shelf. "That will harden up the cocoa butter so I can administer them."

Adele wrinkled her nose. "Please do not ask for my assistance with that."

She raised her hands and backed away, a horrified look on her face. "That is not my area of expertise!"

Kitty laughed. "Don't worry, I won't. You've been a big help. Thank you."

She walked briskly through the quiet house and up the long marble staircase to Fleurette's room.

There wasn't much change that Kitty could see. She rewet the towels on Fleurette's body and went to check on her grandmother.

Oma slept, and Kitty found the fever had broken when she touched her grandmother's forehead, cool and damp with perspiration.

Oma stirred and broke into a coughing spasm. Kitty helped her sit up. Thankfully, there was no blood in the secretions.

Kitty settled Oma on her pillows and checked her temperature. A hundred degrees and the pulse regular at ninety beats. For the moment, she had improved.

Kitty got a basin of warm water and washed her grandmother. She had finished and changed the sheets on the bed when Percy knocked at the door with the tray from the kitchen.

Adele, bless her, had sent up two bowls of the hearty soup and two teacups, plus a warm loaf of bread and butter.

Kitty pulled the dressing table bench to the bedside and put Oma's bowl of soup on it.

Oma flapped her hand and waved it away. "I can't eat." She leaned back against the headboard with her eyes closed.

"Nonsense. You must. You need fluids and nutrition."

Oma opened her eyes and glared at Kitty. "I've told you. I can't eat!" The turkey wattle under her chin swung with the vehement shaking of her head.

Kitty shrugged. "Do you want to survive?"

Oma blinked. "Whatever do you mean? What a question, Katharine. Of course, I want to survive."

"Then eat this." Kitty used her best charge nurse voice that brooked no disagreement. "If you want me to stay and care for you, then you're going to have to follow my instructions."

She held a spoonful of soup to Oma's lips. "You must eat."

Oma opened her mouth and took it. As Kitty patiently fed her grandmother the bowl of soup, she reflected on the fact that someone as cantankerous as her grandmother would probably survive this particularly deadly influenza and anything else you could throw at her.

The soup finished, Kitty poured a cup of tea and sugared it well. "Sip this. Are you having any pain?"

"It hurts when I take a deep breath. And my bones ache."

Kitty checked her watch. "I'll give you some more

aspirin in a couple of hours. After you finish the tea, try to rest. I'm going to go check on Fleurette."

Perhaps she should move Fleurette into Oma's room. It would be easier to care for them, and she could keep an eye on them at the same time. Oma would have a fit at her maid being nursed in the same room, but it would make so much more sense.

But even before she opened the door to Fleurette's room, Kitty knew she wouldn't be moving the young maid anywhere. Her torturous respirations could be heard through the door.

Kitty hurried to the bedside. Fleurette tossed her head from side to side, and moaned, her pillow and sheets soaked with perspiration. Kitty checked her rectal temperature. One hundred and five. The suppositories might be hard enough by now to use.

Kitty removed the maid's nightgown and repacked her body with the cold towels. She returned to the kitchen and pulled out the tray of suppositories, gratified to find they were firm to the touch. This could work.

Back in the sickroom, she turned Fleurette on her side, administered the suppository, and placed pillows to keep her in position so the medicine could absorb and do its job.

Fleurette's body struggled so hard to breathe that the tendons in her neck stood out sharply and the skin between her ribs retracted with each tormented breath.

After she washed her hands, Kitty took the bottle of morphine tincture and dropped a dose into the side of Fleurette's mouth, where it would pool in her cheek and absorb.

There wasn't much else she could do for her. After a while, Fleurette's breathing eased a bit. The bluish tint of cyanosis appeared around her mouth. An hour later, Fleurette's face, neck, and shoulders were blue.

Kitty needed to check on Oma, and she rang the bell for Percy, who appeared a few minutes later, his hair mussed and his eyes heavy.

"Were you sleeping, Percy?"

"Yes." He straightened his collar. "I've made a pallet in the butler's pantry, so I can hear if I'm called."

It occurred to Kitty that she had no idea where Percy usually slept. "Where is your room?"

"In the carriage house. Madame fixed an apartment for me on the second floor a few years ago. But since she fell ill, I've been sleeping in the house."

Kitty nodded. "I can't leave Fleurette right now."

Percy glanced at the trembling figure in the bed and shook his head sadly.

"Could you check on my grandmother? If she's asleep, just leave her, and as soon as I can, I'll go to her. And then go back to bed." She tried to smile. "I can't have you getting sick. Are you eating?"

"Yes. Adele has kept after me."

"And you're still feeling well?"

He nodded. "Yes."

"Alright then. I won't ring for you again. Try to get some sleep."

"I will." With one last glance at Fleurette, he left.

Wearily, Kitty checked her watch. Three a.m. Soon it would be dawn.

She turned at a choking noise, as Fleurette's body convulsed, and foamy mucus and blood ran from her nose and mouth.

When the convulsion was over, Kitty cleaned her up as

well as she could and changed the bed linen once again, heaping the soiled sheets in the bathtub.

She washed her face and hands, and after returning to the bedroom, opened a window to freshen the room with the scent of autumn pine.

Then she pulled a chair to the bedside and sat down wearily to wait.

Two hours later, as fingers of pale golden light streaked the sky, Fleurette was dead.

THIRTY-FIVE

Copeland refuses to close schools. Sees no reason to put ban on public assemblages because of influenza.

4,930 *NEW CASES IN CITY*

The New York Times, October 19, 1918

IF KITTY HADN'T KNOWN that Fleurette was Caucasian, she wouldn't have been able to determine her nationality, as her body had turned almost black from oxygen deprivation.

Kitty washed Fleurette's wasted body, straightened her limbs, and put a fresh sheet over her.

On her way downstairs, she looked in on her grandmother. She slept and her breathing was normal.

No fever, so Kitty removed her bloody surgical gown and gauze mask and threw them into the tub in Oma's huge bathroom, then washed her face and hands thoroughly. There was going to be a lot of laundry to do.

She found Adele and Percy in the kitchen, drinking coffee. "Mmm, that smells so good."

Adele got up and poured a cup for her.

Kitty added cream and sugar and took a big sip. "That is heavenly." She set the cup down. "I'm sorry to tell you that Fleurette has passed away."

Percy made a strangled noise deep in his throat and his eyes filled with tears.

Kitty touched his sleeve. "I'm so sorry, Percy. I did all I could."

"I'm sure you did, M—Kitty. It's just—she was so young. She had all her life before her—" He broke off, unable to go on.

"We need to have someone come and get the body."

Percy pulled out a handkerchief and blew his nose. "I will make the arrangements. I took the liberty of ordering some coffins last week when the staff started to fall sick. I'd heard there was a shortage, so I wanted to be sure we had one for Madame if—" He broke off, his face ashen.

"That was wise, Percy." She took a sip of coffee. "How many do you have?"

"Three."

"I hope we only have to use the one. Did Fleurette have any family?"

"They're all in France. I will have to send a telegram."

Kitty winced. How awful to receive such a message. And how sad that Fleurette had to die so far from home, away from her loved ones.

"You must be hungry, miss," Adele said, glancing at Percy. "How about some bacon, eggs, and toast?"

"That would be lovely, Adele, thank you."

Half an hour later, after she'd had eaten and downed a second cup of coffee, she felt much revived. She got a clean gown and mask from her bag and returned to her grandmother's room.

Oma still slept, and there was no fever or coughing. Kitty sat on the sofa at the foot of the bed and put her feet up.

It looked as if Oma had turned the corner. Kitty ought to call her mother and let her know, but she could barely keep her eyes open. She put a pillow under her head and decided to rest for a few minutes before she made the call.

Sunshine slanted through the windows when she woke a few hours later to someone calling her name in a quavering voice.

"K-Katharine?"

"I'm here, Oma." Kitty sat up and rubbed her eyes, then got groggily to her feet and went to the bedside.

The sight of her grandmother's flushed face and hoarse breathing knocked the fatigue out of Kitty like a thunderclap.

Only a few hours earlier, she had been resting comfortably. Now her grandmother's forehead felt like fire. Rectal temperature 105°.

Kitty turned to go, intending to run down to the kitchen and get a suppository, when Oma reached out and grabbed her hand.

"Don't go," Oma said, her voice weak. "Stay...with me." Her eyes were wild and terrified, the white showing all around as she clung to Kitty's hand.

"I'm not leaving you, Oma. Do you think you can swallow some aspirin?"

"I don't know...I'll try." Her head fell back on the damp pillow.

Kitty gently disengaged her hand and poured a glass of water. She took two aspirin tablets from the tin and helped her grandmother swallow them.

"Drink all of it," Kitty urged. "You need the fluids."

"Hurts." Oma clutched her throat. "Ohhh, it hurts. Everything...hurts...so much."

She lurched upright in the bed and broke into a coughing spasm. Blood-streaked mucus dripped between her fingers, and Kitty's heart sank.

When the spasm passed, Oma dropped back onto the pillows, panting and spent.

Kitty washed Oma's face and hands and removed the blood-stained nightgown, then sponged her down with cool water and changed the top sheet and coverlet, all the while praying for her grandmother to live.

Kitty took the bottle of morphine tincture and measured out a dose. "This will help, Oma," she said.

"Sit...with me. Please?"

"Of course." Kitty pulled over a chair upholstered in Oma's favorite pink silk, sat down, and took her grandmother's hand.

Oma gazed up at her, her eyes sunken in their sockets. "I didn't dare to hope that you would come. Not after..."

"It's behind us now. Just think about getting well."

"Your mother...is...she...?"

"She's fine, Oma." Kitty squeezed her grandmother's fingers gently. "She's helping everyone in the neighborhood. Don't worry about her."

Tears oozed from the corners of Oma's eyes. "She had such a tender heart when she was a little girl."

"She still does," Kitty said, smiling.

"But I...I did...t-terrible things to her, Katharine." A sob escaped her. "I wasn't...I wasn't a very loving mother."

Kitty knew this was true. But what was the use of speaking about it now? It was too late to do anything about it.

How sad it was that Oma had missed out on knowing what an incredible woman her daughter had turned out to be. "Shh, rest. Try to sleep."

"I can't sleep." Oma picked at the coverlet with her other hand. "Every time...my eyes close...it all comes back to me."

She stared into the distance, her gaze unfocused. "She was the light of my life...until..." Her face crumpled. "My beautiful girl. I had such grand plans for her...until that Winthrop came along."

Even though her grandmother's voice was frail there was no mistaking the contempt in it. "It was all Otto's fault. Letting that boy into the library. I told Otto as much. How was I to know Evangeline would slip away there when her tutor fell asleep?" Her lips twisted. "I should have fired that old bag."

Kitty couldn't keep silent at this. "Did it never occur to you that my mother wasn't happy with your choices and plans for her?"

Oma turned her head and fixed her rheumy gaze on Kitty. "I always knew what was best for her."

Kitty shook her head and pressed back a retort. Thank God her mother had found the courage to refuse the duke at the altar.

And what her mother had endured afterward. Cut off from her family. Prevented from seeing her dying father.

"She wanted to marry him, but...I put an end to that." Oma smiled faintly. "I forced her to accept the duke's proposal of marriage."

Oma's hand slipped out of Kitty's. "And then, on her wedding day, she refused to go through...with it."

Her words slurred and her eyelids drooped. The morphine was taking effect, and soon she would sleep. "I was so...angry..." Her eyes closed.

Kitty gazed at the fragile blue veins on her grandmother's eyelids and the crooked fingers covered with diamond rings and tried to imagine having so much pride that she would cut off the daughter she supposedly loved for twenty years.

And Mama was the dearest, sweetest, most loving woman on earth, as far as Kitty was concerned. And her grandmother had missed out on watching her only granddaughter grow up.

It was Oma's terrible, tragic loss, only realized now on her deathbed.

How incredibly sad.

Kitty dozed off and on, waking frequently to check on Oma. By early afternoon, she began to hallucinate, plucking with feeble fingers at the coverlet and crying out.

"I'm here." Kitty captured her grandmother's flailing hands. "I'm here."

Oma turned and gazed at Kitty with bloodshot eyes. "Oh, Evangeline, I'm so glad." Her grip tightened on Kitty's fingers. "After all the awful things I did to you. Locking you in your room for weeks, threatening to shoot Jack. Forcing you to accept the duke's proposal of marriage."

Kitty's breath caught in her throat. Mama had said that her mother was cruel, but threatening to kill the man Mama loved?

"Can you ever forgive me, Evangeline? For everything I did?"

Oma pulled her hands away and turned her face into the pillow, weeping.

What would Mama have done? Even as this thought went through her mind, she knew.

Kitty touched her grandmother's shoulder gently, and Oma raised her tear-stained face.

"I forgive you," Kitty said gently. "I forgive you. For everything."

Oma released a shuddering breath. "T-thank you, Evangeline. Thank—"

She lurched upright into a coughing spasm, spewing blood-streaked mucus over the coverlet.

The spasm went on for several minutes, and when it finished, Oma collapsed onto the bed, semi-conscious, her breathing labored. The dreaded blue shadow encircled her mouth.

Should she call Mama? Would she want to be here?

Kitty pondered this as she washed her grandmother and changed the bedding. She positioned Oma on her side with pillows to support her and went downstairs to make the call.

Mrs. Mac answered. "Winthrop residence."

"It's Kitty, Mrs. Mac."

"Kitty, dear, how are you?"

"I'm well. And you?"

"We're all doing the best we can. It's terrible hard for your mother, though. She's missing Mr. Jack so much. And now, now that he's missing—"

Kitty cut in, not wanting to think about it. "I'm at my grandmother's house. Is my mother there? And why are you answering the phone?"

"Jenny's a bit under the weather. And your mother's just come in. Hold on."

A moment later Kitty heard her mother's soft voice. "Darling. How are you?"

"I'm all right. And you?"

"Tired. But well."

"Does Jenny have influenza?"

"I think so."

Kitty's heart sank.

"Don't worry," Mama said. "I'm wearing my mask. How is my mother?"

"Not well. That's why I'm calling. I didn't know if you wanted to be here...at the end."

There was a pause.

Kitty hesitated. "She thinks I'm you, Mama—and she asked for forgiveness."

Her mother's sigh came over the line. "I do forgive her."

"I thought you would. So, I told her that. It seemed to ease her."

"How much time does she have?"

"Not long."

"Would you think it terrible of me if I didn't come? I hate to leave Jenny."

"I would understand completely, Mama, if you didn't. She's told me some of what she did to you. And now, knowing what I know, I am amazed that you ever gave your consent for me to meet her."

Mama laughed softly. "It was difficult." Her voice sobered. "I tried to believe that she truly desired reconciliation."

"How was I ever so lucky to have you for my mother?" Kitty's throat thickened. "I love you, Mama. Please stay well."

"I will, darling. And I love you more." The line disconnected with a click.

Kitty smiled at the telephone receiver. Mama always seemed to get the last word on that.

She hung up the phone and went to the kitchen where Percy was having lunch with Adele, *coq au vin*, by the smell of it.

"I'm sorry to disturb you, but have you called the funeral parlor yet for Fleurette?"

"Not yet." Percy stilled and set down his spoon. "Why?"

Kitty sighed, hating to say it. "Wait, then."

"Madame?"

Kitty nodded. "I'm afraid so. Won't be long now." She examined the two of them. Eyes clear, color good, breathing normally. "You're both still feeling well?"

They nodded.

"All right then. I'm going back upstairs."

"Won't you have something to eat first?" Adele started to rise from the table.

"Not right now. Perhaps later."

After all the blood and secretions, the thought of eating turned her stomach.

The smell of blood filled the room when Kitty returned. Oma had endured another coughing fit and there was fresh blood in the bed and on the floor.

Kitty cleaned it as well as she could and opened another window for a cross breeze to freshen the air.

Blood drained from Oma's ears now, as well as her nose and mouth, and each breath was a gurgling, wrenching struggle.

Kitty tucked a towel under Oma's head and sat in the chair to wait as her grandmother's labored breaths grew further and further apart.

Was there anything lonelier than sitting at the bedside of a dying soul, knowing there wasn't anything to be done?

Just waiting. Listening to each agonized breath, wondering if it was the last, as the little French ormolu clock on the dressing table ticked away the seconds of a life.

And it all came down to this.

Vera Katharine Kohl Lindenmayer had a position at the pinnacle of high society, millions of dollars in the bank, diamonds and jewels, a designer wardrobe, and huge mansions with Italian marble floors and priceless art.

And for what? She was dying alone.

With one granddaughter in attendance, who had come more out of duty than love, and one elderly servant with no family of his own.

How unutterably sad.

Oma never regained consciousness and died an hour later, her body as dark blue-black as Fleurette's had been.

As she had done for Fleurette, Kitty washed her grandmother's body, changed the linen, and covered her with a clean sheet.

She went downstairs to console Percy and call her mother. Then she went to her bedroom and drew a hot bath. After soaking a while, she put on a nightgown and fell into bed.

IT TOOK a while for Kitty's tired brain to register that something was amiss as the rural towns and villages of Rhode Island passed by outside the train windows.

Her trip to Newport the night before last had taken place after dark. Now mid-morning, the usual weekday bustle was absent. No trucks or wagons moved in the streets.

Instead of children playing in the grassy yards, housewives hanging laundry on the clotheslines, farmers harvesting crops and cutting hay in the fields, the towns and villages were deserted.

She had to look hard to find any evidence of life. One man, old and bent, hurried along a sidewalk. A dog rooted through a garbage can.

But almost every house they passed had bundles lying on the porch or in the yard, wrapped with cords.

It should have penetrated sooner. She had done the same thing for Fleurette and her grandmother.

The bundles were bodies.

Corpses, some small, some large, wrapped in sheets for shrouds, tied with rope, and left on the porch or in the yard.

In some places, there were two, three, and four corpses on one property. Whole families?

Kitty wrenched her head away and closed her eyes.

Dear Lord, have mercy on us.

THIRTY-SIX

500,000 INFLUENZA CASES IN NYC
MORTALITY IS HIGH

Epidemic of Influenza Dwindling Rapidly in Military Camps, Civilians Suffer Worst.

The Brooklyn Daily Eagle
October 20, 1918

IT DIDN'T SEEM possible that things could be worse at Bellevue, but they were.

Every bed was filled, with more patients lying on pallets on the floor between the beds. As soon as one patient died and the bed was emptied, another patient took it.

Bellevue had a proud tradition of never turning away any patient who needed treatment, and as a result, cots had been set up in the hallways and the main floor foyer.

Even the outside verandas had patients bundled in

blankets on pallets, even though the weather had turned cold. The hospital had run out of mattresses, so pallets were being made out of straw, covered with sheets and blankets, and every available closet that could be emptied was in use.

Kitty plunged back into the maelstrom as soon as she arrived at the nurses' dormitory, donned her uniform, and reported to Miss Trent.

"Relieve Miss Emminger on Ward B, if you please, Miss Winthrop." She paused and searched Kitty's face. "Your grandmother?"

Kitty shook her head. "My grandmother's dead and her maid also."

"I'm so sorry. Are you well?" Miss Trent's piercing gaze gave Kitty the once-over.

"I am. I did get some sleep before I took the train back."

"Excellent."

Ward B was the women's surgical unit, although all elective surgeries had been canceled and every medical and surgical ward in the hospital was filled with influenza patients.

Kitty found Florence rinsing sheets in the dirty utility room. Her surgical gown was streaked with blood, and her freckles stood out starkly on her pale complexion, but her eyes lit up when she saw Kitty.

"Kitty! Oh, I'm so glad to see you." She glanced at her soiled gown and Kitty's clean uniform. "I'd hug you, but..."

"I know. How are you?"

"As well as can be expected, I suppose. Your family?"

"My grandmother's dead and her maid. What about yours?"

A shadow passed over Florence's face. "My little sister is ill, and my older brother Richard. But Mama told me not to come. She's handling it."

"Our maid, Jenny, is ill. My mother's taking care of her."

The thought of her mother contracting influenza sent fear down Kitty's spine. Best not to think about it. "Anyway, I'm here to relieve you."

"Bless you. I'm just about dead on my feet." She stripped off her surgical gown and threw it into the bin.

"Any report?"

Florence shook her head. "There isn't much we can do. Aspirin and morphine, or laudanum."

———

AT THE END of her shift, she reported off to the oncoming nurse, washed her face and hands, and walked through Bellevue toward the nurses' dormitory in a haze of fatigue.

"T2! Wait."

Kitty turned at her name. Annabelle ran toward her, her coat open and no hat on.

Kitty frowned at her friend. "It's freezing out here, Annabelle. Good grief, where's your hat? You know better."

"I'm too hot. It's so stuffy on the ward. What a relief to breathe some fresh air." She fell into step with Kitty. "How's it going on C?"

"I was on B today. It's bad. You?"

"Horrible. Some of the probationers are sick now, and they're on my ward." She sighed. "And Ruth Horton was admitted this afternoon."

"Oh, no." Pretty, petite Ruth from Far Rockaway? One of their original small group.

"She's stable at the moment. Fever isn't too high."

But that could change in an instant, and neither girl said it out loud as they crossed 26th Street toward Osborn Hall.

A small, bedraggled figure rose from the low stone wall that surrounded the dormitory as they approached the entrance.

"Oh, miss," the bundle of rags said, "we need help."

It was a little girl, about seven years old with dark braids wrapped around her head under a threadbare hood.

"Miriam?" Kitty said, astonished. She glanced around, but there was no sight of Mr. or Mrs. Orenstein. "Are you here alone?"

Miriam nodded. "E-everyone is sick. My tatti said to find you. C-can you come?" Her teeth chattered as she looked up at Kitty with pleading eyes. "Oh, p-please, w-will you?"

"Yes. Yes, I'll come. Let me think for a moment what to bring." She turned to Annabelle. "This is Fayvel's sister, Miriam."

"I'll come with you."

"No. You should rest. And sleep."

"And let you go traipsing alone about New York City on a dark night, ye wee eejit?"

Annabelle's blue eyes were steely. When she was set on something, there was no dissuading her. Kitty smiled. It would be a comfort to have her there.

"All right then. I won't argue with you." She turned to the little girl, who had no gloves. Her worn, broken boots were soaking wet. "We need to get you warmed up first."

They walked into the foyer of Osborn Hall, which was blessedly warm. "Sit here, and wait for us, Miriam. I'm going to get you something to eat first. And take off those boots so your feet can dry."

Miriam sat on the long wooden bench and pulled off her wet boots, revealing worn wool socks full of holes.

"Those socks, too."

Kitty's lips tightened as she pulled off her wool scarf and wrapped it around Miriam's lower legs and feet. The child's poor wet feet were covered with chilblains.

Annabelle touched Kitty's arm. "I've got some things I can pull together. I'll go collect them."

Kitty nodded and considered Miriam. The poor child was half frozen. "If anyone asks what you're doing here, tell them you're with me."

Miriam sank back onto the bench and put her feet up. Kitty took off her coat, draped it over the child, and then felt her forehead. It was cool to the touch. No fever.

Miriam closed her eyes and nestled closer into the warmth of Kitty's coat. She probably shouldn't be here. There was a strict quarantine on all houses and tenements that had influenza.

Kitty bit her lip, but she wasn't about to send the child back into the cold night alone.

The dining room was nearly empty. With everyone eating at such odd hours, large pots of soup had been left out, wrapped with towels to keep it warm, and trays of wrapped sandwiches that could be grabbed and eaten on the go, along with fruit and cookies.

She filled a bowl with beef barley soup and took half a loaf of bread back to Miriam.

The girl was asleep with her mouth open, and her pinched face tore at Kitty's heart.

"Wake up, sweetheart. I've got some supper for you."

Miriam opened her eyes and sat up, rubbing her eyes.

"Here you go," Kitty said. "Be careful, now. It's hot."

She left the girl to eat and went into a closet off the parlor where the Lost and Found Box was located.

Unbelievable the things people lost, but they would be put to good use now. There were several wool sweaters, and a scarlet coat that might fit Tirzah, the oldest sister. And gloves, a pair of sturdy leather shoes, and several scarves and hats.

Kitty took all of it, went upstairs, and found a laundry bag to put it in. Then she looked through her closet. She had several sets of long underwear which she never used, and she threw them into the bag.

The bottle of aspirin tablets from the dresser went into her pocket. She wouldn't be able to bring any morphine. It was doubtful she would find any pharmacies open at this hour either. On the way out the door, she stopped and pulled the wool blanket off her bed. She might need it.

In the hall, she stopped at Ruth Horton's room. Ruth was a tiny young woman, not even five feet tall. And Miriam, despite the lack of good nourishment in her diet, was almost the same size as Ruth.

Kitty touched the doorknob and then hesitated. Should she? She grimaced and opened the door.

Ruth's room was perfectly neat, the bed made, and her toilet articles laid out at the side of the sink. And there, in the bottom of her closet, were three pairs of leather boots.

Kitty took a pair with laces instead of buttons. In a dresser drawer, she found a pair of striped wool socks.

She would buy Ruth a new pair when she was discharged from the hospital. *If she was discharged*, a voice in her head said.

Kitty thrust the thought away and hurried back downstairs.

Annabelle waited with Miriam, who had finished off the soup and bread.

Annabelle had packed some items of clothing for the family, too. "I've got some sandwiches. Didn't see any way to take soup unless we lugged the whole pot. And I filled a pocket with cookies."

"I see that," Kitty said, a grin lifting her lips. Miriam was eating a peanut butter cookie as fast as she could.

Kitty knelt at Miriam's feet and pulled Ruth's socks over her bare toes. Miriam's eyes grew large when she saw the leather boots in Kitty's hand. "Are those for me?"

"They are." Kitty slipped them on and laced them. Then she wrapped the wool scarf around the lower part of Miriam's face and neck and pulled the hood up. "Now, do you have any coal at home, sweetheart?"

Miriam shook her head. "Not in such a long time, miss." She shivered. "It's been awful cold."

"Wait here." She looked at Annabelle. "I'll be right back."

She hurried down the hall to the back of the first floor, where a utility door led down to the basement.

She'd been down here once before when there had been a scavenger hunt during a Christmas party.

The basement was huge, as large as the entire footprint of Osborn Hall. There were offices and janitorial closets, but what Kitty was after was at the far end of the basement, where nine industrial coal stoves heated the entire building.

There were two maintenance men working the stoves, and Kitty recognized Otis, who had brought up the chain to fasten Mr. Eisenmenger to the sink.

Otis glanced up and nearly dropped his shovel. He was stripped to the waist and covered with soot. "Can I help you, miss? You oughtn't to be down here."

Kitty spied some burlap sacks off to one side. She picked one up and walked over to the coal bin. "I need some coal, Otis. Won't be but a minute."

"What you gonna do with that coal, miss?"

Kitty filled the sack as quickly as she could, hoping she could carry it. "I need it."

"For what?" Otis took a quick glance at the other operator. "Um, I don't think you should be taking that coal. It belongs to the school."

"We could get in trouble, Otis," the other man said.

He was a hulk of a man, with muscles bulging out of his sleeveless undershirt. Black streaks covered his face, chest, and arms.

"I know it, Joe."

"I can pay for it." Kitty tried lifting the sack experimentally. If she could sling it over her shoulder, she could manage it. "How much do you want?"

Otis shuffled his feet. "I wouldn't rightly know."

Kitty let the bag sag at her feet. "Otis, not far from here there is a very poor family, ill with influenza. And they haven't had any heat in their tenement apartment for some time. That's why I'm taking it. If you want to report me, go ahead. I understand your position, and I certainly don't want to get you in trouble."

"You're going to help them?" Joe pressed closer.

"I am."

Joe picked up the sack and slung it over his shoulder. "Let me carry that up the stairs for you."

"God bless you, miss," Otis said. "Come back if you need more."

Tears smarted at the corners of Kitty's eyes. "Thank you."

She turned and hurried up the stairs after Joe. He set the bag down on the top step and opened the door. "We're not allowed on the first floor, miss, otherwise I'd take it all the way for you."

"Thank you, Joe." Impulsively she leaned over and kissed his sweaty cheek.

His eyes widened, and he smiled, revealing a missing front tooth. "No, thank *you*, Miss," he said, before he shut the door.

Kitty lugged the sack down the hallway, passing a few students who looked at her with curiosity, and reached the foyer.

She dropped the sack of coal and handed the scarlet wool coat to Miriam. It was too big and hung nearly to her ankles, but it would keep her warm.

"Let's go." Kitty slung the coal sack over her shoulder and picked up the other bag of supplies, while Annabelle took Miriam's hand. Lugging their bundles, they went out into the freezing night.

It wasn't any warmer in the streetcar that took them to Delancey Street. The Board of Health had decreed that all streetcar windows had to be left wide open for ventilation during the epidemic.

The icy wind that whipped through the streetcar made Kitty's jaw tighten and her teeth ache. She glanced at the well-made leather boots on Miriam's feet, taking comfort knowing the girl's feet were warm.

There were two passengers on the streetcar with them. Both had masks over their faces and sat apart. Miriam took the lead when they left the streetcar. Rotting garbage littered the road, and Annabelle suddenly stopped short.

"Faith and begorrah." She pointed to a long bundle lying in a doorway. "Is that what I think it is?"

"Yes." Kitty glanced at Miriam. "I'm afraid so. I saw the same thing on the way back from Rhode Island."

More bodies appeared in the front yards and porches of

the ramshackle tenement buildings as they went down Pitt Street.

Most were wrapped in sheets and tied with rope, but one unfortunate man lay face down on a stoop. Kitty hurried Miriam past it.

They arrived at 197 Pitt Street. More wrapped corpses in vestibules and landings greeted them as they trudged up the stairs to the fifth floor. Annabelle choked and held her scarf over her mouth and nose. The stench of decay worsened, and the dread inside Kitty spiraled higher with each step they took. What would they find when they arrived at the Orenstein apartment?

Miriam touched the mezuzah on the doorpost and brought her fingers to her lips. Then she opened the door. Kitty could see her breath when they entered.

It was warmer on the landing than in the apartment. The smell of vomit and blood hit them like a tidal wave.

"Oh, no," Annabelle whispered.

One small kerosene lantern burned in the kitchen. Kitty dropped the sack of coal and hurried to the small bed under the apartment's single window where Tirzah lay, unconscious and shivering.

Kitty took off her coat to cover Tirzah and turned to Miriam. "Can you light the stove?"

Miriam nodded.

"Fast as you can. Okay?"

Annabelle followed Kitty into the tiny kitchen where Fayvel's parents lay on a single bed under a pile of ragged quilts. Kitty dropped to her knees next to them.

Dried blood crusted the bedclothes. Mrs. Orenstein's face had the same dark dusky blue color that had become so horribly familiar. Her face still had a vestige of warmth. She had probably died while Miriam was trying to get help.

Mr. Orenstein had labored and wheezy respirations. Fresh blood flecked his lips. Fluid in the lungs. And he was burning with fever.

The coal stove lit with a hiss in the other room.

"We should bring him into the other room, closer to the fire," Annabelle said, exchanging glances with Kitty.

She nodded. Closer to the fire and away from the dead body of his wife. "I brought a blanket."

Miriam was sitting close to the stove, holding out her hands to the heat, when Kitty retrieved the blanket from her bundle.

Back in the kitchen, she folded it into a long rectangle, and together she and Annabelle lifted Mr. Orenstein onto it. Then they folded the soiled bedclothes over Mrs. Orenstein. She would have to remain where she was for the time being.

They carried Mr. Orenstein into the next room and put him on the floor close to the stove. Then they took hold of the bedstead and pushed Tirzah closer, too.

Miriam looked up from the stove. "What about muter?"

Kitty put her hand on Miriam's shoulder. "She's gone to heaven, little one. I am so sorry."

Miriam's dark eyes filled with tears. She looked down at her father lying on his pallet. "Tatti?"

"He's resting, sweetheart. Let him sleep. I've brought some medicine. We'll see what we can do for your father and Tirzah, too."

Miriam's gaze went to Tirzah, who was moving restlessly in the bed, moaning.

"I'll see if there's anything to cook for soup," Annabelle said, her face grim and tight. "Will you help me, Miriam?"

Miriam sniffled and wiped tears away. "Yes." She pushed herself to her feet and went to join Annabelle.

A moment later there was the rattling of pans as Miriam showed Annabelle where the necessary things were.

Kitty turned to Tirzah, who had stopped shivering. But she had a high fever. Her dark hair had come undone from its braids and lay in tangled knots on her shoulders.

Kitty pushed the hair off the girl's hot forehead. "Tirzah? Can you hear me? Tirzah?"

The young woman opened her eyes and gazed at Kitty. "You came," she said. "My muter...tatti?"

"Your father is right here. I've come with a friend to help take care of you."

"...good of you..." Tirzah whispered. Her eyes were sunk deep in her head. "Muter?"

Kitty bit her lip. "I'm sorry." She shook her head. "So very sorry."

Tirzah nodded and closed her eyes.

The room warmed slowly. Mr. Orenstein's eyes fluttered open. He caught sight of Kitty. "M-miss..."

"Save your strength, Mr. Orenstein." She patted his arm.

"M-Miri? *Zeezinkah?*"

"Miriam? She's here."

Mr. Orenstein tried to say something, and Kitty leaned closer to hear. "My...baby."

"Miriam?"

He nodded and tried to speak again, but Kitty couldn't make it out. He tried again, with great effort. "Miri...after... she will be...alone..." A tear escaped and rolled down his face.

Kitty flinched and took his hand. "I will take care of Miriam," she whispered. "I promise."

He sighed deeply and closed his eyes.

Annabelle came to the kitchen doorway as the scent

of frying onions filled the small room. "I found some onions, potatoes, and carrots. And some chicken fat to make a broth." Annabelle smiled. "Miriam calls it *schmaltz*."

Kitty winced, remembering Fayvel explaining *kishke* to her. She was almost glad he wasn't here to see what was happening to his family.

Neither Tirzah nor Mr. Orenstein would be able to take any soup, but it was keeping Miriam busy. Kitty got the aspirin tin, some water from the kitchen, and tried to rouse Tirzah again.

But she didn't respond, and in the flickering light of the kerosene lantern, the terrible dark shadow crept over her face.

Kitty sighed. *Dear Lord, have mercy on us, Amen.*

Miriam came back into the room. "The soup is almost done." She yawned and curled up next to her father and fell asleep, still in her coat and new boots.

Annabelle came in, drying her hands on her skirts.

Kitty shrugged helplessly. "I can't get any aspirin down either of them."

Annabelle studied their patients and shook her head. "I think it's too late for aspirin, Kitty. I'm sorry."

Kitty reached over and felt Miriam's forehead. No fever. She'd been exposed to influenza for at least the last few days, but so far didn't evidence any sign of it.

Kitty leaned against the side of Tirzah's bedstead. "I brought some sandwiches. Want one?"

"I'm too tired to eat. I just want to close my eyes for a moment."

"I know. Me, too."

The coals in the stove had died down when Kitty awoke later and fumbled for the watch pinned to her blouse. Five a.m. She didn't know how she would make it through her shift today at Bellevue.

A choking sound rose from Tirzah.

Kitty jumped up and moved aside as Tirzah coughed up big clots of blood. She turned the girl onto her side and wiped her mouth. After the coughing fit passed, Tirzah sank back into unconsciousness.

When Kitty turned to check on Mr. Orenstein, he was dead. She covered his blue face with the blanket. Annabelle had sprawled onto the floor and still slept, as did Miriam.

Kitty checked Miriam again, relieved to find no sign of fever. It looked as if the little girl would be the sole survivor of the Orenstein family. She wanted to pray, to cry out to God and ask why, but she was too exhausted to formulate the words.

At that moment, Tirzah began to convulse, her breath wheezing between gritted teeth. Kitty held her as her body fought desperately to live, bucking with the effort to draw a breath. A few moments later, she, too, had breathed her last.

Kitty released Tirzah's body and buried her face in her hands. When would this long dark nightmare end?

There was a gentle touch on her head, and she looked up to find Annabelle.

"They're both gone," Kitty said. Anger welled up inside her from some deep dark place. "Why? How could God take her entire family?"

"I don't know, Kitty."

"How will we tell Miriam?"

Annabelle shrugged. "I don't know." Her face crumpled. "I don't know," she choked out. She covered her mouth with her hand to hold back the tears.

"I'm sorry." Kitty stood and put her arms around

Annabelle's heaving shoulders. "I didn't mean to sound so angry. We'll get through this."

Kitty held Annabelle until the sobs subsided. "I'll call my mother when we get back to Osborn Hall. I'm sure she'll take Miriam in."

Annabelle took a deep breath and wiped her eyes. "I'm all right now. We'd better get going." She stooped and shook Miriam gently. "Wake up, dear. It's time to go."

Miriam sat up and rubbed her eyes. "Is it morning already?"

Her wide-eyed gaze went to the covered body of her father, and then to Tirzah, whose face was also covered. Annabelle must have done that.

Miriam's lips trembled. "Is my tatti dead?"

"I'm afraid so." Kitty took the girl's hand. "And Tirzah, too. I'm so sorry."

Miriam's brown eyes filled with tears.

"Miriam," Kitty said gently, "I'm going to take you with me, and bring you to my mother's home. She'll take care of you."

Miriam nodded mutely.

"Is there anything you'd like to bring with you?"

"Yes. The samovar." She pointed to the shining copper urn. "We empty water first."

Annabelle tried to lift it. "Oof. Wow, it's heavy."

Kitty helped her lug the samovar into the kitchen and empty the tank into the sink. Even with the water gone, it weighed at least fifteen pounds.

"Anything else, Miriam?"

The child nodded, went back into the kitchen, and returned with a pair of shears. Quietly, she knelt next to her father, uncovered his face, and cut a lock of his curly gray hair. She moved to Tirzah and cut a long brown ringlet. Then Miriam hesitated and looked at Kitty.

"I'll do it." Kitty held out her hand.

Miriam handed her the scissors, and Kitty went into the kitchen to clip a lock of Mrs. Orenstein's hair.

Miriam pulled some thread from her mother's sewing basket to wrap the locks of hair. She tucked the hair into the pocket of her coat. "I have to use the privy," she said, her voice small.

She went into the kitchen and took the key off the hook. Without another word, she opened the door and went out.

"The poor child." Annabelle sighed. "Her whole family."

"I know. It's awful. We'll have to notify someone about the bodies."

They buttoned their coats as they waited for Miriam. The little girl returned and hung the key on the hook. "Could we give the soup to the Liebermans?"

"Of course," Kitty said. "I should have thought of it."

"And the rest of the coal?" Miriam picked up the heavy sack.

"Let me carry that," Annabelle said. "We'll give them everything we brought."

The three of them left the apartment. Kitty set the samovar down by the front door and took one of the bags from Annabelle. Miriam carried the soup and knocked on the door for 181 Pitt Street at the end of the dim hall. There was no answer. Miriam knocked again. After a few moments, heavy footsteps could be heard, and the door opened a crack.

A gangly man of perhaps forty peered out. "Yes?" Then he saw Miriam holding the pot. "Miri, is that you?" He opened the door wide.

"I brought you some soup." She held up the pot. "And some coal."

Mr. Lieberman took the pot. "Thank you, thank you. Are you well? Your family?"

Miri shook her head, her lower lip trembling. "All gone."

He staggered back as if struck. "Oh, no."

"Your family, Mr. Lieberman?" Kitty asked, hoping it wasn't as bad as the Orensteins.

"My wife is sick. The children are well, so far." He tried to smile at Miri. "She will be happy for the soup. Thank you." He put the pot down inside the door, then turned back and stooped down before Miri. "I will say Kaddish for your family."

"Thank you." Miri kissed his cheek. "I'm ready to go now," she said to Kitty.

Annabelle handed the sack of coal, along with the sandwiches and the bags of clothing, to Mr. Lieberman. "For the children."

She emptied her pocket of cookies into his hands. Silently, the three of them walked down the dark staircases to the deserted street. It was a cold, quiet ride back to East 26th Street.

When they arrived at Osborn Hall, Kitty telephoned her mother. "Mama, I've got my own wharfling now."

THIRTY-SEVEN

2,000 OPERATORS ARE ILL
Telephone Company Explains the Need of Curtailing
Service.

The New York Times, October 22, 1918

"What do you mean, darling?" Mama's puzzled voice came over the wire. "What's happened? Are you all right?"

"Yes. Yes, I'm fine. I've had a very long night." Kitty's knees felt weak. *Lack of sleep,* one corner of her mind said. *And possibly hypoglycemia,* as she hadn't eaten for a while.

She glanced at Miri, fast asleep, curled up in one of the upholstered armchairs in the parlor. The poor child. She had to be exhausted, mentally and physically.

"What's this about a wharfling?"

Kitty sighed. "I spent last night at the Orensteins' tenement. Fayvel's family?"

"Yes."

"The entire family, with the exception of one little girl, died of influenza."

"Oh, Kitty, I'm so sorry."

"I know. Here's the thing. Miri, the survivor, is about eight. And she has no one now."

"I'll take her. Is that what you're asking?"

"Yes." Relief flooded through Kitty at her mother's always willing generosity. "Yes. I can't keep her here with me. And I promised—"

She broke off, her throat thickening as she remembered the desperation in Mr. Orenstein's eyes. "I promised her father as he lay dying that I would take care of her." Then she remembered. "And Jenny? How is she?"

Mama laughed softly. "Much improved. I can hardly keep her in bed. She's afraid I'm going to make a jumble of her laundry cabinets."

"I'm so glad. Watch her closely, Mama. Usually, once the fever is over, the patient is very weak. Don't let her get up too soon."

"I'll try, darling. Now shall I come and—"

"Miss Winthrop! What is the meaning of this?"

Startled, Kitty dropped the telephone receiver and turned to find Miss Trent, freshly powdered and uniformed for the day, glaring at her.

"And what is that child doing in the nurses' residence?"

Kitty retrieved the telephone receiver. "Mama, I will call you right back."

She hung up the receiver and faced Miss Trent. The nursing instructor tapped her foot, her arms across her chest, and studied Kitty.

"I apologize for my appearance, Miss Trent. I've been up all night. When I came off my shift and arrived home yesterday, that little girl was waiting for me. She's Fayvel

Orenstein's sister. She'd been waiting for hours in the cold. She said her whole family was ill with influenza and asked me if I would come."

Miss Trent's face softened. "I see. So, you went?"

"I couldn't say no. Annabelle Boyle came with me. She's gone up to her room to sleep for an hour before her shift starts this morning."

"And the family?"

"All dead." Kitty swallowed. "Except for Miri. That's why she's here. I couldn't leave her."

"Of course, you couldn't."

"My mother is going to take her into our home. She has a ministry to homeless children who live on the wharves."

"Ah." Miss Trent studied Kitty. "I don't think you'll be in any shape to work your shift today. You or Miss Boyle. I will arrange replacements for both of you."

A rush of gratitude went through Kitty. "My goodness, thank you so much. Then may I have permission to take Miri to my mother's this morning?"

"Yes. And let me think. Why don't you take tomorrow off as well? Stay with your mother at home tonight and come back tomorrow evening."

Kitty gasped. "That would be wonderful, Miss Trent. How can I ever thank you?"

"No need," Miss Trent said crisply. "You're a good nurse, Miss Winthrop, and you've been working very hard. Some rest will ensure you are able to continue doing so. I must be going now, to get those arrangements in place."

Kitty ran upstairs, knocked on Annabelle's door, and peeked in. Annabelle lay on her back, staring at the ceiling.

"Hey," Annabelle said. "I can't sleep. One of the girls told me Ruth Horton died early this morning."

"Oh, no." Kitty winced, thinking of Ruth's borrowed boots, now on Miri's feet. "That is so sad. Poor Ruth."

She came into the room and sat on the edge of Annabelle's bed. "When is this epidemic going to end?"

"What if we get it, Kitty?" Annabelle's lips tightened. "I'm scared."

"I know." Kitty took a deep breath. "I am, too. But Miss Hayes said anyone who wants to go home can."

Annabelle nodded. "And no one did."

Kitty tried to smile. "I guess we're more dedicated to Bellevue than we thought."

"Or to our patients."

Kitty patted Annabelle's hand. "I haven't forgotten what you said to me last summer. About 'devoting ourselves to the care of our patients' as it says in the Nightingale Pledge. That's what we're doing now, I guess."

"And scared to death doing it." Annabelle smiled faintly. "It helps to know you feel the same way."

"I do. If you feel like you're going under, tell me. We've got to support each other. And before I forget, I came up because I ran into Miss Trent in the parlor. She was shocked at how I look and shocked to find Miri sleeping in a chair. I explained where we'd both been. She's giving both of us the day off. So go to sleep, T_1."

"Faith and begorrah, it's a miracle." Annabelle turned onto her side and pulled the blankets up over her shoulders. "Maybe I can sleep now, knowing I don't have to get up in less than an hour. Turn off my alarm, would you?"

Kitty obliged. "I'm taking Miri to my mother's now. I won't be back until tomorrow. I'll see you then. Sleep well."

A FEW HOURS LATER, Kitty lay on the sofa in the brownstone with her feet up.

Both Miri and Kitty had eaten a big breakfast of eggs and French toast after long soaks in the tub, and for the first time in days, Kitty felt relaxed and comfortable. And safe.

Now, freshly washed and shampooed, and wrapped in an old pink bathrobe of Kitty's, Miri sat on the rug in front of Mama, who was combing her curly brown hair.

Mama looked up at Kitty, who was almost asleep. "Darling, why don't you go up to your bedroom and have a nice long sleep? And later, we can all have supper together and have a good visit. I'm going to put Miri to sleep in the spare bedroom."

"All right, Mama." Kitty rose, walked to her mother, and dropped a kiss on the top of her head. "Love you."

"Love you more." Mama smiled.

Kitty went upstairs and fell into her bed, the sheets sweetly scented with her mother's lavender, and was almost instantly asleep.

THIRTY-EIGHT

"I had a little bird,
Its name was Enza.
I opened the window,
And in-flu-enza."

Children's jump rope rhyme, 1918

October 24, 1918

The short rest and time spent in her mother's company revived Kitty.

Amazing what a good night's sleep could do. And to see her mother healthy had done a great deal to relieve Kitty's anxiety.

Now she was back on Ward C, with Miss Fields, a probationer, and a first-term student nurse, Miss Stenson, from Far Rockaway.

Samuel was down at the far end of the ward, making

rounds. He'd said good morning to her and gone about his work.

He hadn't smiled, and he was pale with dark circles under his eyes. Kitty wondered if she had them, too.

It occurred to her that she hadn't actually looked at herself in the mirror for days, instead moving through her tasks like an automaton. She probably looked a fright, but it didn't matter.

Kitty straightened at a patient's bedside, the basket in her arms piled high with bloody linen. She blotted her perspiring forehead on her sleeve and turned in time to see Samuel suddenly slump to the floor with a horrific thud.

Kitty dropped the basket and ran down the aisle. He had hit the floor so hard he'd cut his forehead and blood streamed from the laceration.

"Samuel!" She managed to roll him onto his back. His body was hot, his face flushed. His lips were moving but no sound came. She touched his forehead and jerked her hand back with a cry of dismay. He was burning up.

Oh, no, no, not Samuel.

"Miss Fields." She heard the terror in her own voice. "Call for an orderly, please. And notify Dr. Winkler that Dr. Hayden has fallen ill."

She used his handkerchief to put pressure on the forehead laceration, loosened his collar, and pulled off his suit jacket and vest. His pulse thundered along at well over one hundred and twenty beats per minute.

"Samuel, please." She bent over his limp body and stroked the damp hair off his forehead. "Please, please, don't die on me," she whispered.

The orderly arrived with a stretcher, and with Miss Field's help, they lifted Samuel onto it. He moaned as they moved him, cutting Kitty to the quick.

A bed near the nurse's desk had been emptied a quarter of an hour before, and they moved him to it.

Kitty pulled the screens around the bed and quickly stripped off his clothes. She covered him with a sheet and went to fetch water to sponge him.

Dr. Winkler arrived, his kind face grim and tight. Samuel had begun to toss restlessly in the bed. He examined Samuel and sighed. "It's the influenza."

He uttered a curse and looked at Kitty. "You know the protocol. I'll write the orders. Aspirin, fluids, supportive care. Morphine for pain."

"Yes, doctor."

"Get me a suture kit, and I'll sew up his forehead."

Kitty assisted Dr. Winkler suture the laceration. When the last suture had been placed and Dr. Winkler had left, Kitty sponged Samuel down one more time, lingering over his broad forehead, his strong chin, and the whip-like scar that traced his jawline.

He couldn't die. He couldn't. She lurched to her feet. She had to be strong. For Samuel and every other patient on the ward.

She dissolved the aspirin powder into water and tried to force some of it through Samuel's lips. She sponged him repeatedly, trying to bring down the fever consuming him.

And when he began to cough foamy, bloody mucus, she sank to her knees at the side of the bed, buried her face in the covers, and prayed to God to spare him.

The next twenty-four hours were an amalgam of fatigue, fear, and the refusal to give up on the man she now realized was the love of her life.

But she couldn't stay with him. The rest of the sixty patients on the ward had to be cared for, and she was the nurse in charge.

When her shift was over and she had been relieved of her duties, she went to his bedside and took his hand. She laid her head down on the bedclothes and prayed.

THIRTY-NINE

EPIDEMIC DECLINING

A decrease of 2,085 new cases of influenza yesterday justifies confidence in the belief that the epidemic is declining in this city, as it is throughout the country.

The Brooklyn Daily Eagle, October 20, 1918

THE NEXT THREE days were a blur of work and sleep. And Samuel.

Every moment she could spare, she sponged him. The third day was the worst. He was delirious with the fever, calling out hoarsely for his mother.

She sat at his bedside for a while when her shift ended. She wanted to stay at his side, but she had to be back in only a few hours, and she had to eat and sleep.

Florence Emminger was in Ward B now, ill with influenza, and several nurses, nursing students, the probationer Miss Fields, and doctors, including Dr. Johnston, had fallen ill.

"Dear God, please, make it stop," she whispered. "Make it stop. Have mercy on us."

Suddenly Samuel shouted her name hoarsely. "Kitty! Kitty!"

She captured his flying hands and squeezed them tight. "I'm here. I'm here, Samuel."

At the sound of her voice, he opened his bloodshot eyes. "I'm so glad," he croaked.

His limbs relaxed, and he fell asleep. When she touched his forehead, it was cool and damp with perspiration.

Praise the Lord almighty! The fever had broken.

She sponged him and changed his linen. When she was finished, she leaned over to kiss his forehead. "I love you, Samuel. Please get well now."

She left him sleeping comfortably. He had turned the corner.

"Thank you, Lord," she said. "Thank you. Thank you."

Now, God willing, he would make a recovery, although it might be weeks before he could return to his duties.

Maybe the epidemic would be over by then.

FORTY

INFLUENZA REACHES A NEW LOW MARK

Drop of nearly 2,000 under previous day's report of new cases in city. Care of orphaned children Copeland's chief concern now.

The New York Times, November 1, 1918

ON THE FIFTH day since influenza had struck him down, Samuel had fully regained consciousness.

Still too weak to sit up, he lay propped on pillows while a probationer fed him beef broth when Kitty arrived a few minutes before seven a.m.

"How's the invalid?"

She put on a bright smile for him, but it wasn't easy. Florence Emminger had died last night. Six more nurses and Dr. Winkler were ill with influenza and the pneumonia that followed it. She tried not to think about it.

Samuel made a face. "Never liked broth."

"How are you feeling?" Kitty felt his forehead. Still cool.

He shrugged. "Weak."

"That's to be expected," she said in her best clinical nurse voice. "You must rest. I just dashed in to check on you. I'm on duty in—" She checked her watch. "One minute. I'll look in on you later."

Samuel tried to say something, but she left. Now that he was on the road to recovery there wasn't anything left to say.

FORTY-ONE

21,000 Children Orphaned By influenza

The New York Times, November 9, 1918

A headache awakened Kitty in the early morning darkness before her alarm went off.

She sat up groggily and waited for the room to stop moving. None of the girls had had enough rest in the last two months, and the temptation to lie down again was strong.

In the last two weeks, wards that were meant to hold thirty-six patients now had twice that and then some. No wonder her head hurt.

She got to her feet and grabbed hold of the doorframe as a thread of nausea curled around the pit of her stomach.

Breakfast could wait. Perhaps at dinner she'd have more appetite. She dressed in her uniform, tied on her apron, and went to report for duty.

Annabelle found her not too much later. "No breakfast this morning? You missed the mutton broth."

Kitty gagged at the mention of it, and Annabelle frowned. "You don't look well, T2. Don't you be getting sick on me."

"I'm fine. I've got a headache, that's all."

Annabelle touched her forehead. "You feel warm. Let's get your temperature."

Kitty shook her head. "I'm fine, just tired. Aren't we all? I'll see you at supper tonight."

Even though the epidemic was thought to have reached its peak, patients still lay on the floors, between the beds, and any place a few square feet of space existed.

The nurses worked steadily to ease the suffering and assist the dying. As soon as a patient died, the bed filled again.

She helped an orderly bring a body to the morgue, which had filled to capacity yet again. As before, shrouded corpses in stacks lined the hallway.

Kitty finished cleaning a young woman and had gathered the bloody linen into a basket when the floor suddenly tilted up.

Dizzy, she sank to her knees as the room spun around her. She tried to get to her feet, but her lifeless limbs wouldn't respond, and she slid sideways onto the floor instead. The coolness of the tile against her cheek felt like heaven.

"Miss Winthrop?"

Miss Trent's urgent voice boomed into her consciousness, and Kitty squinted her eyes against the pain.

"Miss Winthrop!"

Kitty managed to open her eyes, but Miss Trent's face

blurred. Kitty shook her head and peered upwards again, but her vision didn't improve.

"Can you get up if I help you?"

Her head spun, but Kitty nodded and rolled over, managing to get her palms against the floor and push herself to a kneeling position.

Miss Trent put an arm around her and used her other hand to feel Kitty's forehead.

"You're burning up," she said.

Kitty's knees gave out once more.

"Orderly!" Miss Trent shouted. "I need an orderly here at once!"

Kitty had a foggy memory of being bundled off to a bed, stripped, and washed with cool water.

"I'm sorry," she tried to say.

The pain in her head worsened with movement and her throat hurt too much.

She awoke at dusk to find Annabelle sitting next to her bed.

"I told you," she said accusingly. "Now you've got the flu." Her blue eyes were worried.

"We're all working so—" Kitty's voice croaked and stopped. Her throat hurt so badly she could barely swallow. "Everything hurts, T1."

Annabelle stood. "I'll get you some aspirin." She stood and grabbed the back of a chair. "I don't feel so good myself."

She went off, holding onto the wall.

Kitty tossed restlessly in the bed, unable to find a position that would ease the hot pain that rippled through her joints and stabbed her lungs.

She could feel her heart thumping against her ribs and pounding in her ears as sweat rolled off her body.

Had Annabelle come back? She couldn't remember.

She propped herself on one elbow to drink water, knowing she was already dehydrated.

But the glass dropped out of her shaking fingers and shattered on the floor. The crash reverberated through her feverish brain like a bullet, and she moaned and fell back on her pillow.

The pain in her head, *dear Lord, take it away*. Her fever mounted, engulfing her, and melting her arms and legs into jelly until darkness rose and closed over her.

She writhed, searching for the light, but even with her eyes wide open, she couldn't see.

Then she was falling, falling, falling into a dark abyss. She hit bottom and seemed to be lying down.

Far above her, two specks of golden light shone out of the gloom. She waved her arms and somehow swam upward as the specks turned into ovals.

She floated higher and reached the two windows to look out.

She screamed.

She was looking through her own eyes, and for a tiny moment the world reappeared, and she was in her hospital bed, looking at Samuel's frightened face.

Then her grip loosened, and she fell again, down, down, down to the bottom and lay there.

The flashing electric lights of Coney Island appeared in circles and stars and the loop-de-loops of the roller coaster.

The rumbling of the wooden tracks burst into her ears and over her brain like a wild wave as the vivid, pulsing lights, green and blue and red and yellow, crashed together and rose to circle round her brain again, harder and faster each time until the lights fell away, and there was only darkness.

SOMEWHERE IN THE MURKY GLOOM, the faintest whisper of a cool breeze drifted across her consciousness.

Gentle fingers touched her forehead, soothing fingers. A cold cloth wiped her face, and she groaned, not wanting it to stop.

For a mere moment, the pain in her head lessened, and then the surging waves of fire cascaded over her, and the darkness returned. A roaring static filled her ears until she thought her head would burst.

Spiders began to crawl down the walls toward her. She screamed and wrenched away as the floor dissolved underneath her bed, and she was floating in the darkness.

A faint whisper, then more whispers, coming from the hall outside. Coming to get her. She had to escape, but she was paralyzed, her limbs like lead, and the ceiling descended toward her, to crush her to a pulp.

The bag of viscera taken from the autopsied body materialized in front of her, dripping blood, and soon that would be all that was left of her.

From far away, she heard someone scream, a long agonizing wail, and her body seized great, long, tonic contractions, and she could hear her bones cracking, the marrow within falling into the fire with a hiss.

The shattering of her bones drained away, and she was floating once more, but the pain ebbed.

The darkness lightened until a dreamy golden haze enveloped her. Musical notes descended from above, drops of liquid gold from heaven, an unearthly angelic song that pierced her with its sweetness—

"Kitty," a voice called from far away, "Kitty..."

Something inside her turned toward the voice, softly insistent and distantly familiar.

"Kitty...wake up, sweetheart...wake up now, it's time." Cool fingers caressed her cheek.

She took a great heaving breath and opened her eyes.

Mama's beautiful face gazed back at her. "Oh, dearest, you're awake. God has blessed us with His mercy."

Even as Mama spoke, weariness crept over Kitty's limbs, and she couldn't keep her eyes open. But this time, as sleep took her, there was no pain.

WHEN SHE WOKE LATER, she lay on her side, facing the tall windows that lined the ward.

Darkness pressed against the glass, but inside, the lamps glowed softly golden, and she felt safe and protected.

"Kitty. You're awake."

She turned at the deep voice. Samuel sat at her bedside. His face was pale, and there were dark circles under his eyes.

He had a bathrobe over the hospital gown, and he needed a haircut. Her heart turned over in her chest at the glorious sight of him.

He took her hand and kissed the back of it. "I was so worried. I thought I'd lost you."

She squeezed his fingers weakly. "W-we thought...we'd lost you for a time, too." Her voice was hoarse and raspy from disuse.

"You nursed me."

She nodded.

"You barely left my side. The nurses told me." His

fingers tightened on hers. "You've been so ill, I was afraid...
Kitty, I've been such a fool."

He leaned closer, his face tense. "Seeing you on your
deathbed forced me to see things from a completely
different perspective."

He kissed her fingers and her pulse jumped at the feel
of his lips on her skin.

"I don't care anymore if you become a physician. I don't
care if you want to run for president! You can be anything
you want, as long as it's with me."

Tears glistened in his eyes. "Will you marry me, Kitty?"
He choked. "That is, if you still love me?"

Joy flooded through her. "I never stopped loving you,
Samuel."

"So, you'll marry me, dear heart?"

"Yes."

"Thank you!"

"What are we celebrating?" Mama came around the
corner of the screen carrying a tray.

Samuel stood. "Mrs. Winthrop, your daughter has just
consented to marry me."

"How wonderful!" She patted her pocket. "And I have
more good news." She pulled out a Western Union
telegram.

"Your father has been found. He's alive in a hospital in
France."

Mama sat on the edge of the bed and showed her the
telegram. "He was wounded in a firefight. Badly injured."
Her face clouded.

"What, Mama?" Kitty's breath caught. "How badly?"

"He's lost his left arm and eye."

Kitty gasped. "Oh, no." Her handsome, dashing father,

disfigured. How terrible. But so many had lost more. So much more.

Mama touched Kitty's hand. "No matter. It will still be him. He'll be coming home in a few weeks." She clasped her hands together. "I am so thankful. For you, for Samuel, and for Jack."

"We have much to be thankful for." Samuel bowed his head. "Thank you, Father. For our lives and your provision and your eternal grace."

"Amen," Kitty said. "Has Annabelle been here? How long was I ill?"

Samuel and Mama exchanged a glance.

"What? What is it?"

Mama covered Kitty's hand with her own. "Dearest," she said, "Annabelle fell ill right after you."

"Where is she? I need to see her."

"She's gone, darling. I'm so sorry. Three days ago."

Pain ripped through her heart. It couldn't be. Not Annabelle. Not T1, that irrepressible stubborn Irish girl with the mop of fiery hair.

Sorrow rolled over Kitty, and she wept. She wept all the tears she'd held back for two months as the epidemic did its worst.

She wept for Jimmy Hayden and Ruth Horton. For Florence Emminger, for the Orensteins, and the multitudes who had perished in the epidemic. She wept for her father, and she wept for Annabelle.

When she had no tears left, she prayed and thanked God for her life, as a determination to understand this terrible disease rose from within her.

She would devote the rest of her life to science and studying this lethal influenza.

EPILOGUE

June 7, 1919

All of Mama's roses in the backyard bloomed for Kitty's wedding day.

She leaned on the sill of her bedroom window and breathed in the rose-scented air.

The dark days of death and loss last autumn seemed far behind her now. She had graduated from Bellevue with high honors two weeks ago.

And she was already enrolled to start medical school at Columbia University in September.

No one had been more surprised than Kitty to find out that Oma had left the entire Lindenmayer estate—cars, jewels, real estate, art, and stock portfolio—to her.

She had lost no time in arranging an annuity for Percy and setting up a college trust fund for Miri.

And one idea had been percolating for months now.

Funding and establishing an epidemiology department and lab at Bellevue, dedicated to the study of the deadly pandemic that had killed millions throughout the world.

Oma's money would finally be put to good use.

"Are you ready, dearest?" Mama hurried into the bedroom, dressed for the wedding in a blue silk dress that made her eyes bluer than forget-me-nots.

She stopped and clasped her hands as Kitty turned to face her. "Oh! You're such a beautiful bride." Tears rose in her eyes.

"Now, Mama," Kitty said, her throat thickening. "No tears. You promised."

Mama smiled and dabbed at her eyes. "I know." She put her arms around Kitty. "I hope you'll be as happy with Samuel as I've been with your father. That's my wish for you."

Kitty returned the embrace. "Thank you, Mama." She drew back. "For everything." Then she drew a shaky breath. "Dizzy me! Now you're going to make me cry."

"No more tears. This is a happy day."

Mama picked up Kitty's veil, sheer Alençon lace attached to a band of orange blossoms, and placed it on top of Kitty's hair. Gently, she pulled the veil over Kitty's face.

Mama smiled at her. "One minute, dearest." She opened the bedroom door and went out.

Kitty smoothed the white satin of her wedding gown. She'd designed it herself, a slightly beaded bodice with a soft swirl of a skirt, simple and unfussy.

She took one last look at her childhood bedroom and closed the door.

Papa waited, smiling, in full military dress uniform at the foot of the staircase. A jaunty black patch covered his left eye, and the empty left arm of his jacket had been neatly pinned up.

His smile grew wider as she descended the stairs toward him.

He offered his good right arm when she reached the

bottom. "My beautiful girl. You take my breath away, Kitty."

Together, they walked through the house to the garden where Samuel and the guests waited. Mrs. Mac and Jenny. Percy, dressed in an immaculate black tux with a top hat. Samuel's parents. Friends and family joined together to witness their wedding.

Samuel looked more handsome than Kitty had ever seen him, and her heart skipped a beat.

He took her hands and leaned in close, his brown eyes warm and intent. "Are you ready for the rest of our life together, my love?"

She squeezed his fingers back. "I am."

The End

AUTHOR'S NOTE

I finished writing my story, More Precious Than Gold, in 2017.

I had spent the previous two years researching WWI and the Pandemic Flu of 1918 before I started to write the story of Kitty Winthrop and her family.

I never expected to experience a similar pandemic flu in my lifetime.

Now, as then, the pandemic flu affected whole families, although the Pandemic flu of 1918 disproportionately affected people in the prime of their lives, in the 20 to 40 years of age group.

Over 100,000 children in New York City alone were left orphans due to the flu.

Epidemiology is the study of the patterns, causes, and effects of disease conditions. Hippocrates has been called the father of medicine.

The first known person to examine the relationship between disease and the environment, Hippocrates developed the idea that sickness was related to the four "humors" of the body: air, fire, water, and earth.

He believed that the cure to disease was to remove or add the humor in question to balance the body. One result of this led to the practice of bloodletting.

In the middle of the 16th century, a Veronese physician named Girolamo Fracastoro proposed a theory that invisible particles causing disease were alive.

In 1675, when Anton van Leeuwenhoek developed a microscope powerful enough to visualize these living organisms, modern germ theory of disease was born.

Dr. John Snow is known as the father of modern epidemiology for his investigations into the cholera epidemics of the 19th century in London.

He noticed that certain areas of London had significantly higher death rates and linked that to particular water pumps.

His identification of the Broad Street pump as the cause of the Soho epidemic is considered the classic example of modern epidemiology. He employed chlorine to disinfect the water and removed the pump handle, which ended the outbreak.

It is estimated the Pandemic flu of 1918 affected 500 million people, or about one third of the world's population. Total deaths are estimated at 50 million with some estimates at 100 million or more.

It still stands as the single most deadly event in recorded history.